LIGHTNING
AND
FLAMES

REFORGED II

V. S. HOLMES

AMPHIBIAN PRESS

This is a work of fiction. All of the characters, organizations, and events portrayed in this novel are either products of the author's imagination or are used fictitiously.

None of the material within was created, in whole or in part, using AI technology.

LIGHTNING AND FLAMES

Amphibian Press
www.amphibianpressbooks.com
www.vsholmes.com

Cover by Ben R. Donahue
www.bendonahueart.com
Printed in the United States of America
ISBN : 978-0-9961330-2-9

Incredible praise for the world of
BLOOD OF TITANS

Smoke and Rain

International bestselling fantasy and winner of NewApple Literary's 2015 Excellence in Independent Publishing Award

"Holmes weaves a tapestry of the forthcoming events with the skill of a thaumaturge...In [the] seductive opening few lines so much of the nidus of this fantasy tale is hinted...Wade deeply into these waters for a fine curtain raiser for REFORGED. V.S. Holmes quite simply demonstrates that she is an artist of significance"

- The San Francisco Review of Books

"A well developed and subtly-layered world...filled with compelling characters and dangerous magic"

- Aurealis Magazine

"The very first page hooked me with the simple yet elegant narrative...The characters' dilemmas were revealed in perfect timing yet kept me wanting more, and Holmes didn't disappoint with dropping tidbits of emotion, character growth, and internal struggle among all the the action and war-time maneuvers."

- Kathrin Hutson, author of *Gyenona's Children*
and The Unclaimed Trilogy

"I couldn't put it down to save my life and I couldn't turn the pages fast enough. The plot line was incredibly unique ... Holmes gave me a lot of the things I look for in a wonderful story and so much more."

- Cassandra Carpio, *The Bookish Crypt*

Lightning and Flames

"The atmosphere surrounding this saga is intoxicatingly real...Very highly recommended... This REFORGED volume elevates the reader even more, adding to the obvious stature of V.S. Holmes' literary presence. Very Highly recommended."

- The San Francisco Review of Books

"Holmes' prose perfectly illustrates the incredible, world-shaking horror unleashed when Alea and Arman's magic clashes with that of the gods."

- Aurealis Magazine

Madness and Gods

"...This tale focuses on the political struggles of its characters with few traditional trappings of the fantasy genre...it takes fantasy's ability to explore complex issues such as gender, mental health and human rights through allegory, and refocuses back on the issues themselves...while new and secondary characters now take centre stage. The new protagonists are interesting and richly drawn..."

- Aurealis Magazine

Books by V. S. Holmes

BLOOD OF TITANS

REFORGED
Smoke and Rain
Lightning and Flames

RESTORED
Madness and Gods
Blood and Mercy

REBEL
*Treason's Tears**

STARSEDGE: NEL BENTLY

Travelers
Drifters
Strangers
Heretics
Fugitives
*Emissaries**

SHORT FICTION
"Nowhere Fast" (*We Came to Dance*)
"Starfall" (*Vitality Magazine*)
"The Tempest" (*Out of the Darkness*)
"Disciples" (*Beamed Up*)
"Familiar Waters" (*Love and Bubbles*)
"Mere Primordium" (poem, *Mystic Blue Review*)

*forthcoming

*To those who have known the failing of strength
and still found the will to endure.*

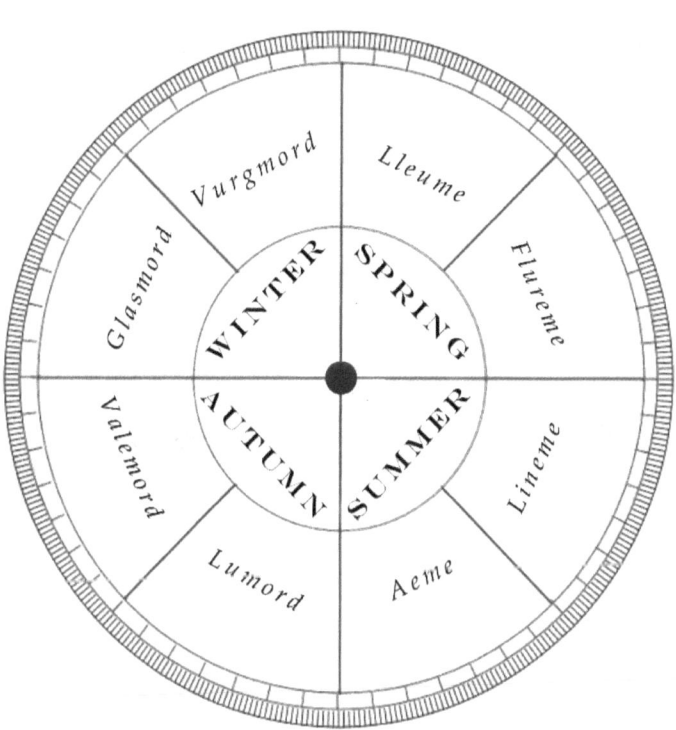

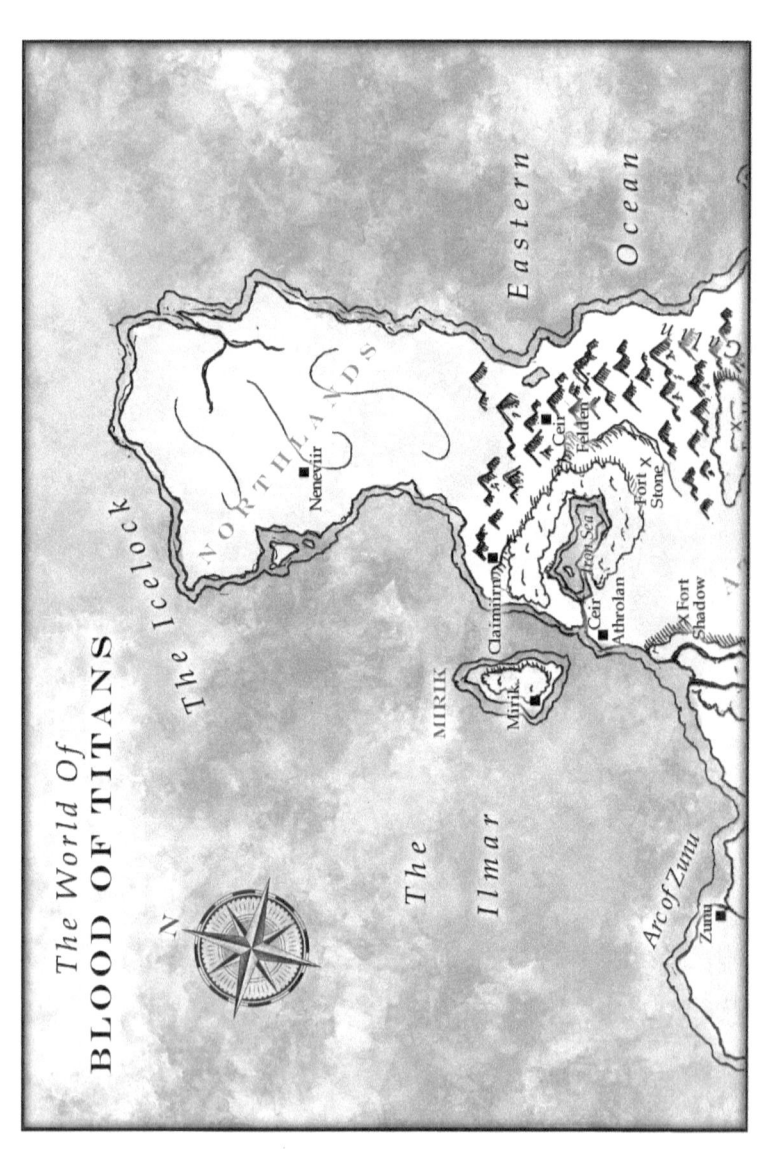

The World Of
BLOOD OF TITANS

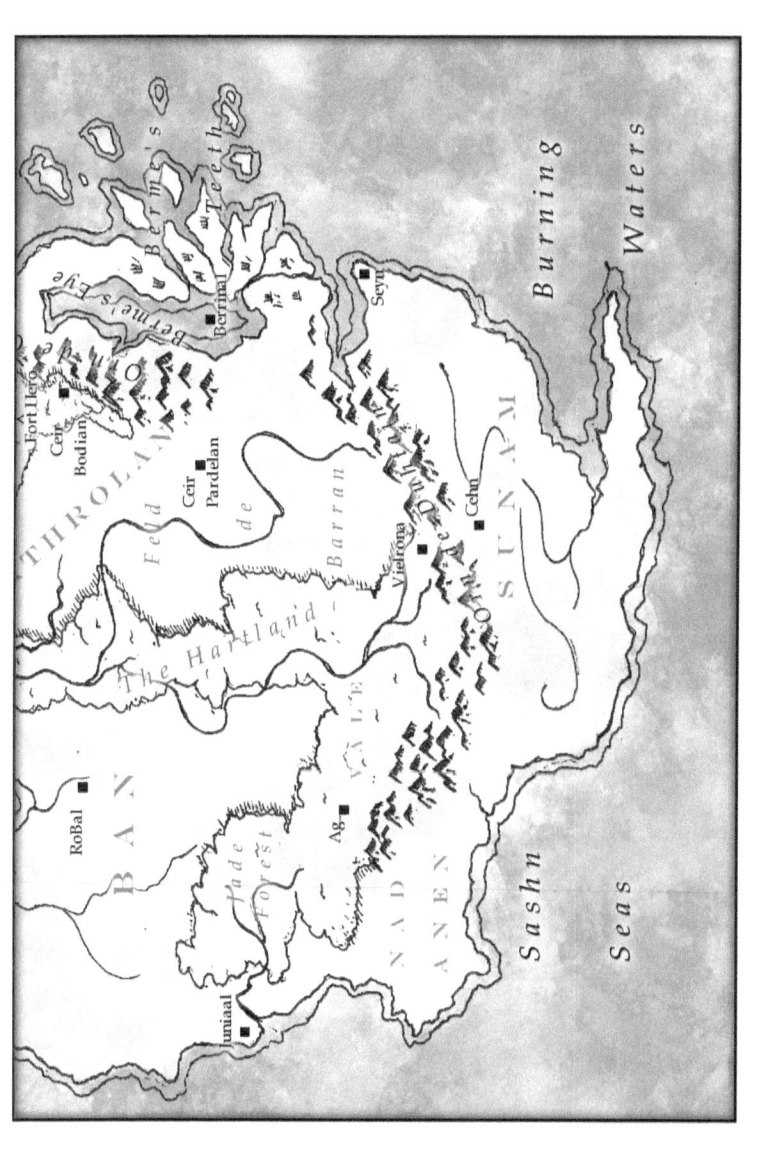

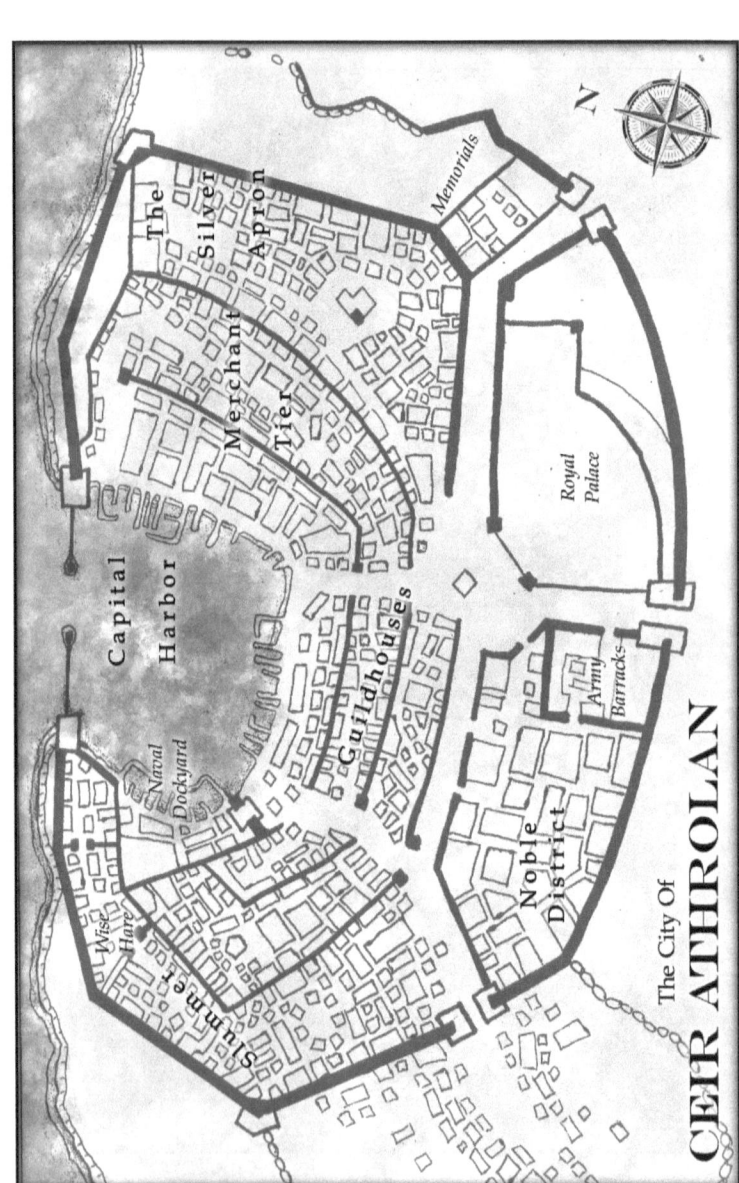

N

The City Of

CEIR ATHROLAN

Capital Harbor

The Silver Apron

Merchant Tier

Memorials

Royal Palace

Guildhouses

Naval Dockyard

Army Barracks

Noble District

Wise Hare

Slummer

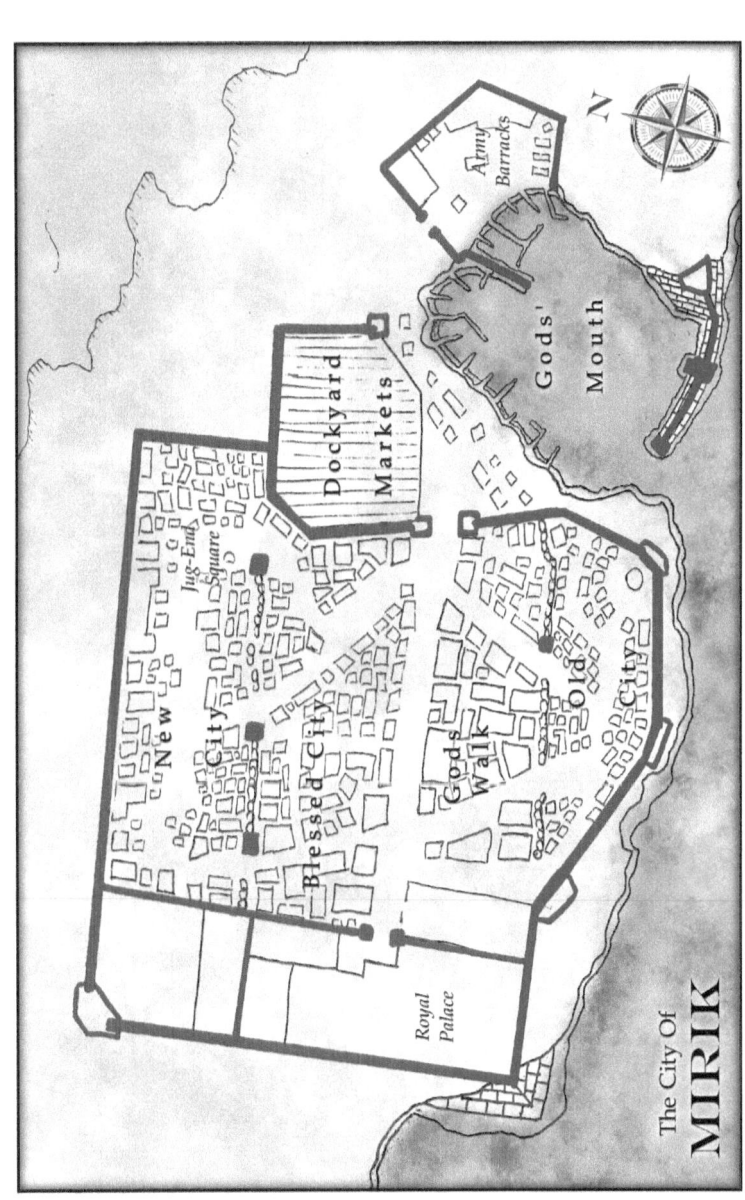

The City Of
MIRIK

A DARKNESS IN
THE MIND

CHAPTER ONE

The 36th Day of Lleume, 1252
The City of Ceir Athrolan

THE WIND OFF THE OCEAN bit at Alea's cheeks with salty teeth. She smiled, not minding the cold. It was a lover's bite, nothing more. She preferred the hour just before dawn. The city below barely stirred. It was as if she were the only woman in the world. It should not have been a comforting thought. She leaned on the palace parapet. Below, a runner was bringing her letter to the queen and to Arman. She hated goodbye, hated explaining herself. *The Dhoah' Laen shouldn't have to explain herself so often.*

"You thought you could sneak away without me knowing?" Arman's voice was low, the hint of a smile blunting the accusation.

"Not really. I thought I might try, though." She brushed a strand of black hair away from her face. "I leave today. In an hour."

"So you said." The blond man leaned on the wall beside her. "Are you nervous?"

Nervous was such a simple word. Emotions were not simple things. Yes, she was nervous. She was terrified. The shadow crouching in the back of her mind was excited. "A bit. I'm not certain how to feel. Elle's my mother, but I have no memory of her. I'm excited, too. Learning to control this thing will be good. Hopefully I'll learn more about myself as well."

"And what then? Will you be full Laen? Cold? Austere? Proud?"

She looked over incredulously. It did not matter that she knew he was afraid, that she could see the tremble in his hands. "You're scared I'll be different? What if I want to be?"

"You act as if you're alone in this battle. All the Laen do. You never share your plans. You're not alone. You never will be." He dug his fingers into the rough, weathered stone. "Fates forbid you actually tell me anything."

"You've been a part of this journey since the beginning."

"But have I known any detail until I absolutely had to? Did I know you were going to battle before you announced it to the queen? Did I know you were hurting before you got drunk?" He shook his head. "Damn, I didn't know you would draw my daggers in Fort Shadow until it was too late."

She closed her eyes. She was tired. Sleep could not banish the deep, aching fatigue that weighed on her mind. She was too exhausted to deal with one of Arman's tempers. "Perhaps if you assumed I was a person, those decisions wouldn't have surprised you."

"How can I protect you when I'm ignorant? Your refusal to explain anything cost me my life!"

She drew back as if he'd slapped her. This was why she hated good-byes. Everything left unsaid bubbled to the surface, jumbled and painful. "What?"

"You disarmed me in the middle of battle."

"And you have no idea what I paid to bring you back. You may have been there, you may remember it, but you will never understand the cost." Her words were low, almost a curse, almost a sob. She shoved away from the parapet. "I don't know how long I'll be gone—a week, a month, a year. However long it is, I hope to fate I do change. And I hope when I come back I'm everything they need me to be." She hunched her shoulders as she trotted down the staircase. The wind howled through the series of open windows. It was still a lover's touch, but this time it stung with anger.

Φ

The 39th Day of Lleume, 1252
The City of Mirik

Bren tilted his chair back on two legs. His feet ached. He had worked the entirety of the day and was glad for the rest. *I'm getting old if a day's work tires me.* Athrolan's navy had set up a makeshift headquarters in Mirik's old army barracks. Though the flags were now Athrolani turquoise and white, it still felt as if he was in the wrong room.

A stack of books sat on his desk, mostly ones he had found in a chest tossed on a rubbish heap. A washed spittoon held three rolled maps. He opened a tattered copy of *Raulde's Tales for an Officer.* The pages smelled of dirt and wet soot.

He winced as someone pounded on his door, but called for them to enter. Seeing the thin man leaning on the doorframe, he scrambled to his feet. "Commodore Veren, good evening."

The man waved Bren's formality away. "The patrol exploring the southeast quad of the city sent word back from the slums a few minutes ago. Said they found something unexpected and need extra hands. I'm sending you and Parlin with the reinforcements."

"I'll be down in a moment, sir." When Veren had gone, Bren gathered his scout-pack with a frown. *Parlin's a speakwell. Why would they need negotiations in an abandoned city?* A thrill of foreboding crawled up his spine. The city folk who worked for the army during Azirik's time were rough. He had never known where they lived—they were like animals, appearing and disappearing at will. After a moment he strapped on his sword and joined the group gathering in the courtyard.

"Patrol said they were in the slums. We'll start there. Keep your weapons ready, eyes sharp." The shipman shouldered his own gear and headed off at a steady jog. The men fell into a line behind him. Bren took up the tail. They'd been scouting for days now, and the men knew the city well. After a dozen minutes they arrived at the broad wall that separated what had been upscale residences and inns from the grime of the slums. The broken gates hung at an angle, allowing them to pass through two-abreast.

"Jug-end Square." The shipman glanced about them. "This place is a warren."

"The east wall, down that way." Bren pointed right. "In all the books it's the worst area." He ignored the muttered insult of "Parchment-nose." *If they had been in Mirik's army, where the predominant order usually involved "later" or "wait," they'd understand.* The city was quiet and the spring rains—heavier than usual for Mirik, but far lighter than those in Athrolan—turned many of the streets into marshlands. The gutters were more formality than functional.

Over the squelch of their boots, Bren heard voices, most in Athrolani. Their path rounded a bend and they entered a small square bordered by haphazardly built and repaired houses. The patrol ranged about, hands on their weapons. Their expressions were annoyed. Surprised, perhaps, but not frightened. Most stared at the largest of the houses. It was an old thing, originally built in the over-hung style of old Miriken architecture. Now it was derelict. Torchlight burnt in the windows.

Bren edge around the men to the shipman who led the original scouting group. "Guilie, what happened?"

"Damned urchin-clan jumped us as we crossed the wall. Stole half our packs before we could blink. We chased them here where they holed up. They're like rats, jabbering in a tongue I've never heard."

Parlin stepped forward, the thin man straightening as he prepared to speak with the thieves. "Men of Mirik, I speak to your natures. We come not to roust you from your homes. We come instead to ask your help."

Bren groaned and glanced at Guilie as Parlin continued. "They don't give one Toar's hair for helping us. All he'll do is make them laugh if we're lucky, drive them away if we're not."

"Parlin's good at speaking to stubborn nobles. Common-folk with heads as hard as cobbles are another thing entirely. Appeasing to their morals will be hard when to a one they look as starved as a man can be and still walk." He glanced at Bren. "You deal with these folk at all?"

Bren's mouth was a grim line. "They've been here since before the city closed. We hired them, traded with them sometimes. They speak Common, but with a Miriken accent so thick it sounds foreign." He absently fingered the amulet around his neck. "There were several dozen then, I think, but those were the only ones we saw."

"Close to a score were the ones that jumped us."

"Azirik said for every one you see there are four more in the woodworking." Bren turned his attention back to Parlin's futile efforts. After another exasperating minute, Bren nudged the speak-well's shoulder. "I dealt with these folk before. Might I try?"

Bren saw the relief in the man's eyes and moved towards the house. The boards creaked as men shifted inside. *Sighting their bows, no doubt.* He grimaced and edged a few paces closer before looking up to the higher windows. "Kit of Jug-end?" He used their word for people. "We mean no harm to you or the city. In that, Parlin spoke true. We come to repair and strengthen her for the war. We thought you'd all have left."

The square was quiet, save for the guttering of torches and the patter of feet behind the walls. Finally a shutter in the door cracked open. Eyes glinted in the darkness beyond. "That ye, King Azirik?" The dialect of the gruff voice left half the consonants from the words. "Kit dealt with ye. Afore ye left the city."

Bren raised a hand against the torch glare to see the speaker. *Perhaps the resemblance is greater than we knew. Who else suspected my blood?*

The door opened and a man stepped out. A stubby, scavenged arrow was nocked to his recurved bow. The weapon was drawn, but lowered. He stared a second longer, then the bow came up quickly, sighted on Bren's chest. "Yer not Azirik."

The Athrolani shifted, raising their own weapons. Bren raised an empty hand. "No, but I'm his blood. I served as a lieutenant in Azirik's army."

"No longer?"

"Mirik was a great city and could be again. My allies, the Athrolani, promise to help make it so. Time was we traded with them." Bren offered what he hoped was a friendly smile. "What are you called?"

"Arik Oland of Mirik." The man did not lower his bow, but his gaze appraised the men before him. "And ye?"

"Former Lieutenant Brentemir Barrackborn of Mirik."

"Yer his son."

Bren had never considered himself Azirik's son in the way most men were sons. *Owning your blood is the first step to surpassing it.* "I was raised by the army, truly, but yes. I'm his."

Arik approached then, curiosity replacing wariness in his gaze. Deep shadows hung under his eyes and hollowed his cheeks. His clothes bagged around thin limbs.

"The years have not been kind to you, have they?" Bren asked.

Arik shrugged. "The city's dead. The army was our only livelihood."

"You're welcome to come across the harbor with us." When the man made no move, Bren prodded. "We've food and we could talk. And it's simply conversation, nothing sworn, nothing promised. Just talk."

Arik shifted his meager weight once, twice, then raised his voice. "'Ken that? King's son wishes us to dine with his ally-men." Dust and mold filtered down as the houses' occupants moved towards the street. Bren could have sworn the men and women suddenly vastly outnumbering the Athrolani had appeared magically in the street. His brows raised, but he extended a hand to Arik. "Thank you, Master Oland."

Arik shook the hand, a grudging respect growing on his features. "Where this sup you offer?"

Bren laughed and did a rough count of the three-score Kit. "I hope we have enough!" The trip back through the city was shorter and the mood lighter. The Athrolani laughed ruefully as they tried to decipher the bright, quick talk of the Miriken. Bewilderment and incredulous stares welcomed the crowd back into the barracks.

The rafters of the dining hall rang with Miriken chatter. Bren wedged himself next to Arik with a smile, sliding a second plate over to the man. "Try these. I'm not much one for gravy, but they're good." He watched Arik shovel the food into his mouth for a minute. "Are you their leader?"

Arik shrugged. "Someone had to take them up. We stayed in the back alleys of the city. There was nowhere to go, no money to buy passage on a boat south. The army was our lifeline."

Bren looked away. "No one should have to eat garbage to live."

"We damn near starved o'er the winter." Arik's thick lips curled. "But now ye come in to take Mirik's crown and shine 'er up bright."

Bren choked on his ale. When he finished sputtering, he waved away the pounding on his back. "I beg pardon?"

"Ye've come to be the new king, yes?"

"I was bred a fighting man. Queen Tzatia will take over Mirik's ruling. Perhaps Mirik might rise on her own again, but it would be years from now. She'll be fostered under Athrolan's guidance." He tried to keep the guilt from his voice, but the expression on the Miriken faces made him turn away.

Φ

The 40th Day of Lleume, 1252

Alea eyed the woman at the bow. Elle was unremarkable for a Laen woman. Her black hair was laced with silver, her bright eyes nested in crows' feet. Years among humans had not treated her well. "How old are you?"

Elle glanced over, brows raised. "Fifty-seven."

"Laen age differently?"

"Slower, usually. It appears you grew like a human girl, though."

"Not entirely." Alea looked out at Mirik's harbor, her gaze distant. She still was uncertain how to treat her mother. "What are we looking for?"

Elle leaned beside her daughter with a sigh. "Simply a place in the woods. Mirik was once a larger island. It broke into three during the Division. One piece belongs to the gods, another to the Laen. The Rakos left their third to the humans as shelter. Because they were here, long ago, this is the place where the barriers are thinnest." She glanced sidelong at Alea. "I don't suppose you wish to spend the night in the capital."

"You want to see Bren." Alea ran a hand through the tangled hair the wind pulled from her braid. She was not sure whether Bren wanted to see their mother yet. He had seemed indifferent. The ship creaked as the sails were furled and she glided up to the dock. "You think he wants to see you?"

Elle's eyes sharpened on her daughter. "You think he doesn't?"

"I think we're at war and every moment counts." Her surrender came as a sigh. "I've letters I want to send before we go, however, and I didn't manage a proper good-bye." She shouldered her pack, not waiting to see if her mother followed. The dock seemed to sway under her feet and she stumbled. *No sooner have I learned my sea legs then I'm back on land.* She laughed softly at herself and took the stairs from the dock two at a time. Mirik may have once been beautiful. The stone was a rich brown and the steep hills beyond thickly forested. Alea made for the barracks, her steps unconsciously quickening as she approached. She heard Elle's murmured apologies as the older woman wove through the sailors mooring the ship.

The barracks themselves were clean and tidy, though Alea suspected it might not have been so two weeks before. Alea waved over a young deck-boy by the flagpole in the courtyard's center. "Might you tell me if Lieutenant Barrackborn is here?"

The boy's eyes were huge as he stared up at her. When Elle appeared behind her, he swallowed once, then nodded quickly. "Right this way, ma'am."

The officer's rooms were more spacious than those of Athrolan's forts, and lined against the outside wall. Bren's door was propped open with one large boot and the sound of turning pages drifted from within. Alea hesitated at the door, glancing back to where Elle waited at the top of the stairs. Finally, she knocked. "Bren, it's Alea."

The sound of scrambling preceded her brother jerking the door open with a broad grin. "Alea! I was starting to wonder if you'd changed your mind. Want to come in?"

"We're only staying for a few hours."

"We? Did Arman come with you?"

Alea glanced over her shoulder. "No. It's someone you've not seen in a long time." She stepped aside and gestured Elle forward. Bren's face sobered. He blinked, then stepped back and slammed his door.

Φ

Bren leaned his forehead against the door. It was rude and pathetic, but he did not care. He had expected to never see her again. Even after hearing Alea and Arman's story, he had convinced himself she was not real. *At least to me.* He wished Alea had warned him, wished that their mother had written beforehand. *I can't hide forever.* He drew a breath and straightened. He finger-combed his hair, certain that he only made it worse. Finally, he opened the door.

Alea leaned against the far wall. Elle's face was downcast. When the door opened, slower this time, they both glanced up.

He could not look away now. "I'm sorry. I was surprised." He shifted then stepped back. "Would you like to come in?" Alea sat on his bed, their mother taking the seat at his desk. He could not sit. His nerves hummed from a dozen unnamed emotions. "I thought I didn't remember you. I thought I'd never recognize your face."

"But you do?" Her voice was low and warm and more familiar than anything he'd ever known.

"I know you." He blinked hard a few times then fell to his knees. His arms wrapped around her waist and his head buried in her lap. "Ma, I'd know you anywhere."

Φ

Alea looked away from the exchange. She was not jealous, exactly. She had just as much claim to Elle as Bren. Her chest was tight and she felt displaced. It was a strange sensation akin to nostalgia, but more hopeless than homesickness. She wondered what it would have been like to mother a child. She had acted nursemaid to many children in the ihal's household, but that was worlds away from motherhood.

When Bren finally drew back, his eyes were bright and his smile delicate. "I hadn't thought you'd come here together." He looked at Alea and the warmth in his eyes dulled her unease. "You have to leave?"

She nodded. "I know you want to talk, but we've little time. None of us are sure how long this quiet period will last. Is it strange to be in Mirik again?"

His expression slid back into that of the soldier. "Real talk can wait. It's a bit uncomfortable being here. This is Selmar's room. He was one of our.... He was one of Azirik's knights. This is home. I learned to fight downstairs and seeing it dismantled is painful. How was the sail?"

"Good enough," Elle answered. "I enjoy ships and sailing—I lived in Marl Mere for a time."

Bren grimaced. "The farther from water I am, the happier I'll be." He glanced over at Elle. "Is Le'yne far? Is it different?"

It was odd that he spoke questions that should have occurred to Alea. She was focused on other things; greater, darker thoughts plagued her mind. They did not allow for trivial concerns. Elle explained the island as she had to Alea, the younger woman only half-listening. Their speech continued to be punctuated by comments echoing greater, pending conversation. Alea thought it was decidedly awkward.

It was during a short period of silence, Bren staring at his boots, Alea at her hands, that the watch called for noon time. Alea's eyes flicked up to Elle.

Bren followed the gaze. "You're leaving?"

Alea nodded. "Can I ask a favor?"

Bren sat forward. "Of course."

She handed him a thin envelope. "Send this to Arman for me, once I've gone." When Bren frowned, she sighed. "We argued."

He laid it on his desk, looked at Elle, then back to his sister. "Very well." He rose. "Will you go alone? Do you want me to ride with you?"

Alea interrupted Elle's impending invitation. "Alone is fine. We'll not take you from your reading." She rose with a brief smile and waited by the door.

Elle touched Bren's face gently. "I know we said talk would come later. Seeing you stand before me, tall and strong and intelligent, fighting for what you love—it makes all the difference. I have made dozens of poor choices. In many ways I wronged you both, but you're flourishing in spite of that." Her smile pulled taut from everything unsaid and she squeezed his hand. "Stay safe."

They stepped from the room, but Bren grabbed Alea's hand as she made to leave. "You may not have been the mother I yearned for, but I'd still like a goodbye."

Alea laughed at that and embraced him. "I suppose when I next see you, it will be war." Her throat was tight. She had wept enough in the past months to not be ashamed, but tears would not come. She glanced down the hall, seeing that Elle stood at the top of the stairs. She waited a pointed moment until their mother descended out of earshot. "I'm scared. What if I can't learn enough? Or in time?"

"You will. Arman will learn his power. I'll build a fort here. We'll all be ready. When the gods come for us, we'll be ready."

"The siege was horrible, Bren. I kept thinking it wouldn't get worse, but it did. I know it still will. I fear I'll lose you both." There was a darker fear that flexed its claws into the edges of her mind, but she would not, could not speak it. "I fear I'll get you killed."

"Alea, you can refuse to give a soldier orders, but when battle comes he still goes to war. You owe that soldier orders and arms and armor to win."

"Arman's not a soldier."

"Horse-shite. He became a soldier the moment he swore his oath."

"I meant he's more than just a soldier." The words sounded petulant.

"Then what of the general and the men of Athrolan? What of Narier?" Alea shot him a scowl and he heaved an exasperated sigh. "Arman might have his head up his arse, but I don't. I know where you spent your nights. It certainly wasn't in the infirmary tents with that orange-haired giant." His tone softened and he took her shoulders. "What of me? We will fight whether you order us or not. The least you could do is accept that and give us what we need for victory."

"This was rather what I argued about with Arman. A bit more heated and personal, but this was certainly a piece." She sighed. She was tired and had no idea what to expect from the next part of her journey. "I hope in Le'yne I learn about myself, not just my power."

Bren hugged her again. "I hope you learn there is no difference between the two."

Φ

The 40th Day of Lleume, 1252
The Island of Mirik

The heavy scent of wet loam drifted between the trunks. It was not yet the wooly green coat that Mirik would boast through summer, but the forest was edged in the glow of spring. Alea followed the narrow path, her strides out distancing her mother's. If it was a conscious gesture, Alea did not indicate. The wood was etched in game and walking trails, the only road well overgrown. Alea was not sure which of those their path was, but it was well worn and deserted. They did not speak other than to remark on wildlife or warn of low-hanging branches.

After two hours of walking, the path curled left, following the base of a steep hill. Elle ignored the turn, pushing on up the slope. The loose leaves from past autumns pattered from under their boots as the two women climbed. The sky above was the clear, bright gray of an overcast day.

Elle paused as they crested the hill. Her head was up, her silver hair whipping back in the wind that swept through the clearing ahead. "There are not many of us left." Her eyes fixed on the center of the glade. A granite slab rested there.

Alea could not tell if Elle's abrupt words were a warning or a plea. Perhaps it was a confession. "Are they all in Le'yne?"

"All I know of. We're the last to join them." Elle entered the clearing, her steps reluctant. "There are just over a score of us now. We were all born from Laen alone. Our power is faint. We have little left."

Alea stopped beside her, looking down at the slab. It was unremarkable save for the lack of leaves dusting its surface. It was dark, reflecting no light, though its surface was smooth. Alea realized her mother's comment had been an excuse. A year ago Alea would have looked around, memorizing the world around her. Now darkness writhed in her mind, pushing her forward, shoving her from the precipice of fate. Her eyes hardened and she stepped onto the stone. "You're wrong. You have me."

CHAPTER TWO

The 47th Day of Lleume, 1252
The City of Ceir Athrolan

ARMAN GLARED AT THE SHEETS of rain sliding down his window. The year's first month lived up to its name's meaning of "Time of Rain." Arman was tired of the weather. He and Alea had ridden for so long that the indoors held no interest anymore. His body itched to be in the open air. *Vielronan farmers planted weeks ago. Wes and I would use the time away from the markets to catch up on work.*

The rain made the wavy glass functionally opaque. He traced designs across it, smiling as the condensation evaporated with a hiss at his fingertip's heat. A knock interrupted his momentary entertainment.

The page in the hall bowed clumsily when the door jerked open. "Master Arrowlash. For you from Mirik." He held out a thick envelope.

Arman thanked him absently as he closed the door and turned the letter over. The handwriting designating the sender was rough, though the writer had clearly strived for neatness: *Brentemir Barrackborn.*

Arman scowled. He dreaded the letter's contents. *He'll tell me she's gone to Le'yne. She's gone to the one place I can't follow.* He broke the seal and unfolded the first piece of parchment.

> *Arman,*
>
> *Alea left tonight. Our mother was with her. It's strange to think the entrance to their world was right here in Mirik. Before she left she asked if I'd send the enclosed to you.*
>
> *I hope she returns soon, even if it heralds approaching battle. What of Athrolan? Are you learning about the Rakos or is it all battle-talk? Being in Mirik is strange. We'll be called back in a month's time for a progress report to Her Majesty and I hope to go along.*
>
> *Bren*

Arman read the note quickly, his hand tightening on the envelope as he read the word "enclosed." He and Bren were far from comrades, but they had made strides. In Alea's absence there seemed to be nothing left but to correspond. He made himself write a response detailing the events in Athrolan and any other small talk he could summon. He rang for the page and sent the letter out before turning to Alea's. He almost did not want to read it. *If I don't read her goodbye, perhaps she'll not have actually left.*

He stared at the seal for several moments. It was one of the plain designs of the wax-stamps in the Athrolani guest chambers. She had written it before leaving. The silence in his room was somehow not solitary enough, and so he climbed the southeast tower, where they had last spoken. The rain had slowed to misting.

Arman,

I hope this finds you well. I'm sorry for our argument. I was angry. I've been angry a long time now. I can't even remember why, most of the time. Bringing you back changed me. I suppose it changed you too. Difference is, I did not change for the better.

Seeing you and Bren on the battlefield and on our ride north, I realized how little I knew of the world. My refusal to share with you and the consequences of that are evidence enough of my naiveté. That is changing. I am afraid of what will come. War, certainly, but deeper. I'm afraid what I will become and if I've deceived you all.

It's time I learn to be without your protection. Perhaps when I return I will be able to stand alone. Perhaps I'll be the leader I'm assumed to be. Perhaps I'll be what you need. Perhaps I'll finally be strong.

Luck, Rakos.

Lyne'alea

Arman re-read the letter before tucking it away. He was not certain what to make of it. Her tone was distant, but naked. It was almost an invitation, a prelude to something new. He leaned on the wall, watching the fog writhe around his arms. She was already stronger, wiser. *What will become of her guard when she no longer needs him? What does she think I need from her?* He shook the thoughts away and mentally reached out, feeling the heavy clouds part before his mind. The moisture was a stinging distraction, an icy counterpoint to the burning of his skin.

Φ

The 49th Day of Lleume, 1252

The City of Ceir Athrolan

Eras had felt truly humble twice in her many years. She remembered the inertia that filled her upon reading Alea's words. Eras was reserved, though perhaps not as obviously as Raven, and withheld her opinion until the woman claiming to be the Dhoah' Laen rode into Fort Stone. She was insignificant in the shadow of Alea's might. The Dhoah' Laen had a long road yet to travel, but the sheer potential that filled the girl's veins astounded Eras.

The general leaned back in her chair, watching the firelight lance through the goblet in her hand. Despite her multifold duties, life had been dull in the spring of last year. Sure, Athrolan had warred with the Berrin and Azirik slid farther down the slope of madness. Those were constant things. *Everything changed when Her Majesty received that letter.* Her eyes rested on her own stack of unopened envelopes.

She leaned forward to finger the rough edge of a plain, dirty envelope. Letters from An'thoriend always looked as if they had traveled the world with him.

> *Eras,*
> *I would have liked to help during the siege, but I am glad I did not see the end. She is terrifying. Magnificent, surely, but terrifying. I've heard rumors enough about what happened to her guard, about what she did, but nothing from you. It is not like you to avoid such news.*
> *Unless it horrifies you.*
> *I am moving north, despite my brother still ruling the Northlands. Perhaps I won't be able to avoid him any longer. I intend to visit Azirik one last time, determine*

where his camp lies, and perhaps see his son before I cross
into the tundra. You say he does not want to rule?
   Have you spoken to Tzatia for me, yet?
   Love and luck, fetali,
   An'thor

Eras traced the Ageless endearment for "sister" with one scarred finger. An'thor had been the only other creature to make her feel as small as Alea had. He took everything with humor, if not with grace. Eras had never had a friend so close. He was right about her reasons for ignoring what Alea had done. She had expected the Dhoah' Laen to be powerful. She had expected her to crumble mountains and flood seas.

She had not expected her to defy the world's greatest laws.

She was glad Alea had left the city. Perhaps when she returned, the horror left in the wake of her actions would be lessened. Now Eras could focus on the Rakos pacing through the palace. *He needs a mentor. He needs what An'thor was to me.* She turned to the small shelf of tomes and journals behind her desk. Many were old, though most were younger than she. Her rough hand brushed the spine of a thin, tattered book.

Her eyes flicked to the letter in her hand. Alea barely had control and she had turned the world on its head. The Rakos were known for their violence. What would Arman do if given the power? Before she changed her mind, she penned a reply, her quill scratching across the paper in swift, fluid script.

The letter was pointed and sent out before the last bell of the night. If anyone knew what to expect from a Rakos brimming with power, it would be An'thor. This war would force them to call on alliances long since turned to enemies.

Apprehension grew in her chest. She knew where they would ask her to ride. She was comfortable being Athrolan's rather exotic general. Going home would mean facing a past she would rather ignore.

A frown creased Eras's brow. Arman's unflagging devotion woke a wistfulness that she had long since forgotten. *Raven and I would never have such legend-worthy romance.* They were both too practical for frivolity and too dedicated to the crown for marriage, children or even regular trysts. Her mouth twitched. *But company never hurt.* She made her way across the castle quietly. Raven answered after one knock.

"What is it?" His face was tired, but the lamps said he had not gone to bed. "Another attack?"

"No, nothing so serious. I'm just thinking too much."

He took in her relaxed clothes and the steadiness in her eyes. "Then we'll talk until your mind is eased." He stepped aside to let her in, and closed the door softly behind.

Φ

The 1st Day of Fluerme, 1252
The Isle of Le'yne

Dizziness swept through Alea's body, churning in her throat. The shapeless blur surrounding her cleared, the world solidifying abruptly. Her stomach heaved. She stumbled off the slate slab, blinking in the suddenly bright light. Steep, dark mountains formed the horizon behind her. Cliffs dropped away below her, topped with a cluster of buildings. Blue-green grasses blanketed the fields rolling from the village to the mountains' foothills. She shuddered, shaking tendrils of black and gray fogs from her shoulders. She stepped from the slab, stumbling when her boots met soft earth.

She had expected a mighty city. "This is Le'yne?" Her voice rasped, as if from disuse. Alea was perversely happy to see that Elle looked as ill as Alea felt.

Her mother nodded. "Like us, it has diminished." She pressed a thin hand to her brow. "Shall we get you settled?"

Alea frowned as they descended the hill. "Do they know we're coming? Do they know what I am?" If Elle had not spoken to her own daughter, could she have reached across worlds to communicate with her sisters?

Elle's prolonged silence was far from comforting. "Lyne'alea, your existence is a complicated thing. We thought we knew who was the Dhoah' Laen. When I bore you, I realized we had been wrong. I also realized that living as Laen, fleeing Azirik, would only get us killed. I had almost lost faith in what you were. I never got the chance to tell them about you."

Alea sighed. *Another battle. Another struggle against people who need me, disbelieve me, and don't understand.* Her fatigue and dark mindedness was turning her usual worries into angst. "What did you tell them?"

"I told them I found another of our kind, hidden like I was."

"Are they so far removed from the world that they don't see what happens?" Alea frowned, navigating the steep hill with stumbling steps. She pictured Le'yne like a floating island, omniscient over all the world, watching, directing.

"We feel the world's energy, feel the rising and falling in the balance. Mostly falling now. That is interpreted. When there were more of us we would communicate with our sisters between the worlds. There is not enough power for that now." She stopped at a low wall.

It and the houses were made of stucco, but of a kind that Alea had never seen. It was rough and dark, dotted with glittering black mica. It matched the sand below the cliffs. *Perhaps now is not the time to mention that.* The houses were all of a single level, the roofs tiled in gray slate. Nothing was grand or austere, save for the open hall perched on the highest point of the cliff top. Silent lightning flitted across the dark clouds bruising the sky.

"So will I meet the others now, or will you explain the situation first?" Alea fiddled with her skirts. The houses were lit, and the small sounds of people preparing for supper drifted through the village. Somehow even that managed to sound unwelcoming.

"I'll explain. I'm sure you want to rest and gather your thoughts beforehand anyways." Elle led her through a narrow opening in the wall and onto a gravel path.

The stones crunching under their boots grated on Alea's raw nerves. It felt like being introduced to the Athrolani court again. *Except this time they can't be fooled.* Her lips tightened as Elle paused at a dark cottage nestled against the rise of the hill. Her mother fumbled with the latch then swung the door open. The smell of dampness hung in the still air. Alea followed Elle up the stairs and into the small kitchen. It was cold, and dust lay thick across the countertop.

"Is this where you lived?"

"A long time ago when I was very young." Elle looked about, breathing softly, as if disturbing the dust would break some tentative composure. She shook herself and briskly pulled a flint from a drawer and lit the lamp on the table. She dug a cloth from a stack on a shelf and began to dust. "There are two rooms down the hall. The second one is yours. Make yourself at home."

Alea retrieved the flint from the kitchen and lit the lamp that hung from the hall's ceiling. The light was dim and only served to make the white walls look bleaker. She pushed open the door at the end of the hall, half expecting a barren room with a cot.

Though the kitchen had been left to the mercy of dust, thin sheets covered the furniture here. Another lamp hung from the ceiling and she had to clamber on top of a chair to light it. She dropped her pack by the door and began to pull the sheets away. Her brows rose. The bed was large, the heavy frame carved from the same dark wood as the door. Blocks of slate decorated each of the four posts.

She revealed a desk next, and a large chest at the end of the bed. The pieces were all blocky and simple, lacking elegance or any beauty without function. The sound of cleaning in the kitchen was replaced with low voices. Alea winced. She was not ready to face that challenge. Instead, she unpacked her things, tucking her few clothes into the chest beside a stack of folded blankets. She turned down the bed, but her nerves sang too loudly for sleep.

She leaned her brow against the cool wood of the bedpost and stared out the window. It had neither muntins nor glass, the air eddying through the hole in the wall. *Even the breeze smells strange.* It was balmy, just cold enough to warrant long sleeves. The undulating voices in the other room grew louder. She had spent nights wishing she was not the

Dhoah' Laen. Now her anger at potentially being denied surprised her. *What if they refuse to train me?*

She undid her tangled braid and raked her fingers through her hair. She was tired of the debate—she was all powerful, she was coddled, she was terrifying, but an abomination. *And now I'm shut in my room, again waiting for others to decide my fate.* She sighed angrily and threw the leather tie across the room. Sloughing off her cloak and shawl, she strode down the hall and into the kitchen.

Though the village was not what Alea expected, the Laen themselves were. There were only six crowded into the kitchen. Their sharp words stuttered out when she entered. She had stored a smile for this first encounter, but at the stern frowns, she realized it should wait for another day. "There is some dispute?"

"We appreciate your hope and duty to us, miss, but you must realize you cannot be the Dhoah' Laen. Elle is sorely mistaken. It is understandable, given the hopeless times and war. We all grasp at straws sometimes."

Alea frowned, letting the expression line her brow more deeply than usual. She would use everything she had. "Why haven't you told them?" Her eyes scanned the faces of the women before her, but her words pierced straight to Elle. "They wouldn't argue if you had, so don't lie to me. I'm tired of lies." Her tone was quiet, but not calm. Under its surface trembled cold, bitter anger. She had lost so much, given so much for this—her family, her home, her peace. *My humanity.* They would not make it in vain.

"Tell us what, Elle?" It was not the eldest woman who spoke, but she was the tallest. "There is something we've missed?"

"I thought you read the energy. Surely you felt something." Alea's gaze flicked to the woman who appeared to be their leader.

"She refers to the battle at the Athrolani fort." Elle looked over at a woman seated at the table. "Mera, you mentioned a small surge of power. I believe to that is what she refers. She did a noble thing and destroyed a small piece of our enemies."

Mera frowned. "I did see such a thing, but it was shadowed by something else. Something stranger. I fear the gods are attacking us here. I can't say how they would, but our dead were wounded."

The words sunk into Alea's mind, churning, dredging darkness from the corners like footsteps in the silt of a stream. "Actually, that is to what I refer." Anger made her mimic sound mocking, but she did not care. "Your dead, you say. You mean their souls? The great silver shell that holds the souls of all the beings that have ever died?"

The tall woman turned, her silver eyes narrowing to blade-thin slits. "How can you know that?"

"Because I am the one that tore them open. I am the one that made them bleed. You think I have tainted, pathetic, unnatural power. I tell you, you are wrong! I can kill with Destruction and so, too, can I give life with Creation. You say you've not seen the like of my power — it's because you've not seen the Dhoah' Laen. Elle knew from the start what I would become, so she hid me, far better than you ever hid or protected the poor women you thought would save you."

The tall woman stared at her, lips thinned to a hard line. Her silver hair was so thin and light it was almost transparent, and drifted in the wind skirting the edges of the room. "You are a foolish child." She spat the words, but the brightness in her eyes betrayed her fear.

Alea felt darkness roil through her, but she could not be certain if it was her mind's shadow or the blackness of power. It was a heady feeling, cold and electric. She fixed the Laen with a pointed stare. "Then don't you think you ought to teach me?"

CHAPTER THREE

The 3rd Day of Fluerme, 1252
The Isle of Le'yne

DAWN LOOKED MUCH LIKE dusk, which looked much like a dark, overcast day. Alea rose early. She told herself her body was still used to the early mornings on the road and during the siege, but the humming in her limbs told her otherwise. *It's this place. The air, the earth here, it's different.* She was supposed to be learning, filling her days with study and exciting new tasks. She felt useless already. The dress she pulled on felt odd after months wearing breeches underneath and she laughed at how much her life had changed.

Elle sat at the table in the kitchen, staring out the window.

Alea felt as if she had interrupted a private moment and paused, one hand on the door frame.

Elle blinked, as if dragging herself back from a distant, unseen shore. "How did you sleep?"

Alea lifted one shoulder in a shrug she had learned from Bren. "Well enough. It was quiet, and I am used to business surrounding tents or the sounds of the forest." She edged over to the cast iron stove and felt the side of the kettle resting on its surface. It was hot, and she glanced sidelong at her mother. The woman had been up for far longer than a single cup of tea, it seemed. She poured herself a mug, leaning against the counter as she drank. It tasted of earth and stone, but cleared her head. "I would like to meet the others this morning."

"I think you made enough of an impression for a few days, don't you?"

"I meant those that weren't there last night. Your people aren't so few as to number just a dozen."

"They're your people too, you know."

Alea's gaze flicked to Elle. "Then perhaps they should make an effort to treat me as such. I'm beginning to wonder if you're the only one who wants me here."

"You're not making it easy to like you." Elle leaned back. "I wanted to spend the day showing you about the village, making introductions as we go."

"And my teaching?"

"Are you in such a hurry to return?"

"I'm eager to end this war." It was poorly spoken diplomacy. She finished her tea in one deep sip, forcing the liquid down with a wince before turning to rinse her mug in the wash basin. She had schooled her features into neutrality by the time she turned to leave. Alea shielded her eyes against the sky as they stepped into the yard. Lightning glinted still, ceaseless and silent above the clouds that bruised the sky. The house's kitchen garden had overgrown its bounds and the smell of herbs underfoot was welcoming.

Elle held open the gate for Alea. Under the strange, uniform brightness of an overcast day, Alea was afforded a clear view of the village around her. The hill behind them was crisscrossed with decorative gardens and stone sculptures, each section walled in stone. The houses radiated from the hill like a threadbare petticoat. Elle's steps were too calculated to be casual, and Alea's nerves hummed louder. *This is another battle, another hurdle for me to test my power against.* She thought of the other hurdles she had faced and the destruction that seemed to result. *Are they ready for me?*

"There is Ielya, one of our herbalists." Elle nodded to the woman crouched in an elaborate tangled garden. "Much of our time is spent trying to preserve whatever is left of our people — our knowledge and our crafts."

They wove towards the hall and despite the promise of introductions, Alea found the conversation closer to a lecture that included no one but themselves. The walk through the walled areas along the hillside proved more interesting. Most of the sculptures were either abstract feats of balance, the deeper meaning of which was lost on Alea, or memorials. Single Laen sat in meditation or quiet thought before some of the figures.

Alea paused to watch one of the women, brow furrowed. "You said you don't have the power to create another Laen. How is that? Can't you just pull up more?"

Elle fixed Alea with a wary gaze. "What we have in our bodies is finite. It is all each may ever have. When we die, the power passes into another place. If we are killed in certain fashions, then that power is gone forever. Either way, the others cannot access it."

Alea only hummed in response. Her own power was bounded only by the limits of her mind and body. Something told her it was unwise to explain that now. Though the grass had been maintained, the space just under the hall was disused. A line of stones stretched along one wall. They were all roughly the shape of a duck's egg, but varied in size from twice Alea's height on the right to smaller than her spread hand on the left. Alea frowned at the smallest stone nestled in the grass. It was no larger than her smallest finger. "This is a training court."

"From many years ago, yes. New Laen learned to control their power here." She looked at Alea pointedly. "And so will you."

"I understand learning control, but we should focus on a larger scale. My power moves oceans, not puddles and playing with pebbles will not help me win the war."

"Your training is non-existent and I cannot build without a good foundation, which is something you seriously lack. Worse, I must knock down the shoddy one you've haphazardly built without guidance." Elle moved towards the gate to the rest of the village. "There is more for you to see."

The discussion was clearly over, but Alea's mind whirled. She disliked the layered metaphors and the assumption that they knew her power better than she. *They've admitted to never seeing the like. How can they know what will work?*

The other side of the village was much the same. Alea wanted to scream at the monotony. She shook the thought away and tried to quicken her pace. There was only one building large enough for Alea to consider it sprawling. The single door was wide enough to be two, and stood propped open with a smooth stone. Alea realized she had stopped listening to Elle and, instead, stood on the steps. The depths of the room were dim, but the air was fresh. Shelves of books and scrolls lined the walls and stacks of wax tablets stood in one corner.

An older woman paused in wiping down the spines with a dry rag. She pushed her mass of silver hair away from her brow when Alea entered.

"I wondered when you would come. Where would you like to start?" She was not one of the women who had visited the night before.

"The beginning would be best." Elle stepped in beside Alea, her thin lips pursed. "It's a shame she was not raised with knowledge of us."

"If she had been she'd be dead. Now go on." She made a shooing motion with a blocky hand. "I'm sure your house needs attention after all this time."

Elle wavered in the doorway, eyes flicking between Alea and the older woman. When she left, it was wordlessly.

"I'm honored to meet you, my lady." The woman offered Alea a gnarled hand and a bright smile. "I'm Mera. I tend the books here."

Alea glanced around at the books rather than meet the woman's clear gaze. "You're a librarian?"

"Historian, actually."

"This is the history of the Laen?" Alea brushed a finger down the spine of a thin book. "There's so little."

Mera's bright eyes inched over Alea. "Much was lost. This is what was saved and what I've been able to remember. Soon I'll write about you."

"I'm to read all this? Before the battle?" Years of reading surrounded her.

"We have had our entire lives to study and the deepest truths are ingrained in our blood. But you? You're half Laen, truly, yet more powerful than any of us." She drew a breath. "I can't say what you need to know." She pointed to the stack of tablets and returned to her dusting. "Begin there."

Φ

The 15th Day of Fluerme, 1252
The City of Ceir Athrolan

Melt water thundered through the aqueducts, echoing across the city. Spring had set in with a will. It was not the water, nor the wind that woke Arman, but the clanging bells above the barracks. He shoved aside his blankets and peered out the window. The torches on the towers glowed warmly, but were not the massive blazes heralding an attack. He shoved his boots on and made for the door.

He crossed the main entrance hall of the palace and caught a glimpse of lightning through the thick glass of the aviary. The drum of rain grew louder as he crossed from the palace to the stables. Inside the barracks beyond, the buzz of purposeful conversation warred with the sounds of the storm. The men rushed about, many of whom Arman recognized from the outguard. He grabbed the arm of a passing captain. "What is it?"

"Aqueduct burst. We're to help the masons before the warehouses flood." He waved Arman away. "Back to bed with you."

"I can help." The man was gone and other soldiers jostled past, more than a few shooting foul glances towards him. Arman stared after them, incredulous. These were the men he fought alongside just a month before. They had eaten and bled beside one another.

"Rakos, you'll not make enough of a difference to warrant being up." Indred clapped Arman on the back. "Thank you, but we'll do just fine." He turned back to the men, barking orders and ushering them out towards the streets. "Up and out lads! The water will not wait for your boots to be laced!"

Arman watched the men leave. He had attempted to spar with the soldiers a few times since the siege, but to no avail. As soon as he approached, the men disappeared, spitting retorts or ignoring him completely. He sighed angrily. He wanted to say it was the Rakos blood, that it was his proximity to Alea. He knew it was neither. *They look at me and see a man who should be dead. Who was dead.* Looking in the mirror unnerved him too, but he could not walk away from his own skin. *Time was, I might have shunned a man brought back from death.*

He peered down at the warehouse district, half swallowed by mist. He was angry at the men, surely, but more angry at himself. When had he started letting others get the best of his spirit?

Φ

Indred's men milled about the mess of the warehouse district. They hesitated at the water churning between the buildings and the massive arches of the aqueduct. Frost wore at the stone each year, and the cracks finally burst at the pressure of snowmelt behind them. The masons had already arrived, their laden carts parked a tier above.

"Thank fates our kings carved the city in steps, eh?" The officer clambered onto one of the great struts. The broken stone was cleared away to allow metal troughs to reroute the flow. The work was tedious and the icy water sent several soldiers into racking coughs. It was past midnight before masons' mud could be laid. A file of soldiers formed to pass stone along to the jagged gap. One of the men fumbled the slab in his hands as he brushed the eerily hot palm of the next man in line.

Arman glared back at him, his curls dark and plastered to his brow. "No one needs to like me for me to help." He spat the words before tugging the stone from the soldier's grip and passing it alone. He worked tirelessly, ignoring the looks. The stones were held in place by great buckled leather straps until the cement set. The gap was nearly closed when the entire structure shuddered. A deep groan became a scream as stone and metal bowed. Arman watched the straps stretch a second before they snapped. *They'll never make it in time.* He dragged himself hand-over-hand up the iron ladder in the stone support, wincing as shards of stone rained onto his head. He locked his legs around the upper rungs of the ladder and pushed. Heat rushed through him. The stone groaned again, a strap whipping past and biting a deep line over his cheek. The stone held for a breath, then another. His arms screamed at the effort and he closed his eyes, letting the heat fill him. His legs hardened, his arms stiffened and he pressed his full weight against the incredible pull of water.

"I cannot hold this forever!" He pitched his voice over the roar of the water.

Shock only lasted a moment before the soldiers exploded back into action. Another layer of stones was added, more metal bands hammered into place. Arman was dimly aware of the sky growing lighter. Half an hour from dawn, they gingerly released the troughs and knocked away what was left of the broken dam. Arman's body was stiff and he had long grown numb to the icy water still spraying lightly from the cracks. His mind had sunk so deep that it took a moment to realize someone was shaking his shoulder

"Arrowlash!"

His own breath chuffed hotly against his bare shoulder as he peered down at the man. Pain began to creep through his concentration.

"You can let go."

Arman turned slowly back to the stone before him, tugging his hands free. They refused to move for a moment, then wrenched away. He slid down several rungs of the ladder before he remembered how his legs were supposed to move.

At the bottom there were tired grins and a cloak. His back was clapped and hands were offered in greeting and introduction. He found it all very distant and strange.

"Leave him be until he gets food and ale! Man needs to warm up!" The man who had helped him down waved a hand to disperse the men. He glanced at Arman and offered his own hand, despite his words. "I'm Witt, lieutenant under Indred."

Arman flexed his hand into feeling before taking the man's arm. The vague sensation of skin brought his mind crashing back into his body. "Arman." He followed the mass of men moving towards the barracks. Their steps grew lighter at the smell of food wafting from the mess hall. Arman turned towards the door to the palace, but Witt's voice broke through his damp thoughts.

"Rakos!" Witt's shout arched from the door to the baths. "We're headed into the city for drinks after we get dry — care to join?"

Arman blinked. *Melt water must wash all transgressions clean.* "It's morning."

The man shrugged. "We were up all night. We can sleep in the afternoon."

For a moment Witt was another friend, another dark-haired, drinking man. Arman found a grin creeping onto his face and he threw his hands up in mock surrender. "Very well, I'll change and meet you back here." He waited until out of sight of the men before breaking into a run. He may have been an inhuman creature, but he sorely missed having friends. It took him only a moment to change. The numbness that stiffened his skin was replaced by burning, and he absently checked his hands and feet for frostbite before tugging on a cloak and boots.

The inn was a tall, broad building that took up an entire block of houses between two small streets. It was in the residential area two tiers above where the aqueduct burst. Arman followed the soldiers to one of the four common areas and sat down on a stool with a grateful sigh. The group numbered close to a dozen, and more trickled in as the morning wore on.

"Drink up, you earned it right enough." A large man pushed a mug of ale to Arman. "I'm Sousa."

Arman grinned and took a long sip of the drink, watching a few others gather around.

"I never thought that stone would set proper! Every winter this happens!" A dark-haired man made a rude noise two seats down.

The Rakos leaned forward. "Every winter?"

"Not so badly," the man amended, "but often enough." He offered his hand across Sousa. "Kal Smytheson."

Arman took it. "Arman Arrowlash."

Kal laughed at that. "I know." He gestured to the mug in front of Arman. "Be careful with Ma Hexion's fire ale. It'll get you tossed before you taste the second sip!"

Arman grinned. "It burns like the tar-whiskey we brewed in winter back home, though it tastes far better."

Kal made a face and Sousa frowned. "Tar-whiskey?"

"Made from whatever was too rotted to be saved from harvest." The men groaned and Arman grinned.

"Did it at least get you laughing before it killed you?"

Arman took another deep draw. The alcohol must have burnt, he supposed, but it felt only distantly warm. "My friend, Kam-Rit—a true bantam when it comes to women— wanted to bed up with this butcher's daughter two lanes down. We were all out one evening, drinking tar-whiskey, and we told him that we'd brought a love-luck potion from the market. We convinced him that in order for it to work, he had to dance under her window pretending to be a tom-turkey, chortling like the birds do. Poor fool was so tossed he did it. Never heard from the lass, you can believe, but surely got the attention of her father!"

Sousa laughed. "Where's home, Arman?"

"Vielrona's Lows. My Ma owns an inn there."

The Athrolani frowned. "I thought you came with the Dhoah' Laen?"

"We met there this autumn." Arman finished off his drink and gestured for another. "I've guarded her since." He glanced at Kal. "What about you two? Do you hail from Ceir Athrolan or one of her other cities?"

Sousa thumped his chest. "Born and bred in this very district!"

Kal waved the other man's pride away. "I'm from Marl Orna, just over the hills to the south. It's a small town, but nice. I've settled here, though. My wife's family owns an old inn in the slums. Her grandfather built it and I hope to tend it to pass on to our children."

Heat flashed through Arman's mind at the thought. He wondered if he would ever have that kind of peace. "You have many?"

"Only the one, a girl of two, but we expect our second within three months."

Arman raised his mug in congratulations. "May they be strong and wise."

Sousa shook his head. "I cannot imagine a one-woman life, myself." He proved the words by looking over their barmaid as she delivered more ale.

A man across the table interrupted. "That's simple because no woman can stand you long enough, Sousa." He turned to Arman, his grin broadening. "What of you, Rakos, do you take women besides the Dhoah' Laen?"

Burning filled Arman's skin. "Excuse me?"

"Is she more powerful in bed than in battle?"

Arman's nerves bristled and he turned his gaze fully on the man, raising his lip enough that his fangs were obvious. He wondered at the shadow crossing the man's features. "Walk away. Now."

The man fell silent, wary, but still contemptuous. He grabbed his drink angrily, swearing as it sloshed.

Arman looked down at his mug. The sounds of the common room were distant, and his ears buzzed. A hand on his shoulder jolted him back into the room.

"Hasian makes almost anyone angry," Kal promised. "He only joined up for the coin and when battle arose it proved him a coward. He hates us for it, and your lady who sparked the war." He sat back. "So the tales of you and she are true, then?"

Arman frowned. "What tales?"

"That you love her, not just guard her. Love only her."

Arman looked at the swirling brown of his ale. "I'm her guard." He pulled a grin onto his face as he changed the subject. "So tell me of the wonders of Ceir Athrolan."

Φ

The 17th Day of Fluerme, 1252
The City of Mirik

The overcast skies gave way to the pale, cloudless blue of proper spring weather. Winter's chill was all but gone and in the sunshine it was almost hot. Bren leaned back against the Great Wall surrounding the city, legs dangling off the scaffolding as he unlaced his shirt. "We're close to halfway, Lanav."

The soldier laying stone above him patted the sun-warmed rock. "Aye, we should have the entire west wall finished by the time we report to the queen."

The view had improved with the weather. The still, green harbor water lapped over the crumbled breakwater jutting from the tongue of land at the city's southwest corner. The land rose from there in tall, natural bluffs along which ran the wall they now repaired. The dark, blue-gray of the open ocean far below sparkled at the wave's crests. This was not the Mirik Bren remembered.

Lanav followed Bren's gaze. "Looks near warm enough for a swim, eh?"

"I'd give you two gold pieces if you didn't come out singing like a eunuch. The water may look like spring, but it'll not feel like it until well into Aeme."

Lanav climbed down the ladder to stand beside Bren. He peered up at the sun. Their timing was informal as none of the city's bells were re-hung. "What say we take our midday now, Barrackborn? Bring back that frayed rope."

Bren heaved himself up. "I'll be glad when this work is done." He was a man of movement. Construction was not his interest or his talent. Several other teams from stations along the wall joined their path back to the barracks. Seeing the single ship bobbing in the harbor, Bren wondered absently if any books he had requested from Athrolan's library would be among the supplies. Mirik's library had suffered under Azirik's rule. Most of the valuable texts were sold to fund the war. *There is something wise to be noted about giving up knowledge in trade for violence.*

A squire appeared at Bren's elbow when they entered the courtyard.

"Lieutenant, Mariner Helonin wants to see you, sir."

Bren excused himself and crossed to the officer's quarters. The planning room door was ajar, and he knocked at the jamb.

"Come in, Barrackborn." The mariner and several of his officers sat around the small table. A map of the city stretched before them.

Bren took the seat Helonin indicated. "You asked for me?"

"We breached the palace a week ago, as you know. We're opening the treasury tomorrow. Her Majesty the Queen noted you might wish to be there."

"I've no more claim to be present than another." Bren shrugged, but his body hummed. *This is my country!* "Did she mention why?"

"If you take the throne, the treasury, and all that it contains, is technically yours." Helonin fixed him with an intent stare. "Have you thought on that at all?"

Bren ran a hand through his hair. He felt chastised, as if he'd forgotten to practice his stance before training. "Not enough to make a decision." He had made a decision, but it was not one he was prepared to announce to a room of men who expected him to choose differently.

"If you still wish to come with us tomorrow, we leave at dawn." Helonin turned back to the map and began discussing the entrance to the warren of underground tunnels that held the treasury. Bren excused himself and went to find food. It was the same meal he had loved the day before, but now it was soot on his tongue.

"I heard from Dettan they're opening the treasury tomorrow." Lanav thumped down beside Bren. "That why Helonin wanted to see you?"

"He said I could go. Thought I'd want to see what could be mine, I guess."

"They're hoping you'll take her off their hands. Mirik's expensive to maintain. I don't blame you a bit for not wanting it—give up a life like ours for pomp and papers?" He made an exaggerated pantomime of spitting.

Bren laughed and cleaned his bowl with a slice of bread. "Come on, that wall will not build itself."

Φ

The 18th Day of Fluerme, 1252

Bren was certain the Kit flanked them, an unseen shadow among the broken buildings of his childhood. He wondered if they were as hopeful as Helonin. *Do they think I'll have a change of heart when I see the inheritance?* His heart was heavy. His tattered tunic and dented armor said enough about how drained the coffers had been. He had barely looked at the palace since arriving, though he did not admit to avoiding the place.

Now, with boots thumping the faded tiles, he did not recognize it. The halls were dusty and most of the valuables were long since stripped. The main hall was broad and bore a curved double staircase. His eyes lingered there, knowing that in the warren of corridors beyond his father had grown up. Somewhere, up there, something had made Azirik a madman. He tore his gaze away and instead examined the stones under his feet. He ignored the eyes of the other men as they gauged his reactions.

The palace sat on a twisting network of tunnels dug into the cliff-rock. The higher caverns held servants' quarters and the kitchen storerooms. The lower ones stored anything from old arms and armor to forgotten documents. Those to the east were used as crypts. A large, well-lit tunnel led down beneath the throne room to a metal door. It had once been closed with several padlocks and bolts, all but one having been cut through by Athrolan's smiths.

The last took only a few minutes to break through. The doors were pushed open and a collective breath was drawn. In all, Bren thought it rather anticlimactic. He grabbed a torch with the others and stepped through the doorway. Before him, glimmering in the light of the patrol's lanterns and torches, was what could have been his. It was more gold, silver and jewels than he had ever seen in his life. Each alcove of the circular, pillared room held decorative armor, crowns, jewelry and actual coin. Chests, upended, open or locked, were stacked around the pillars and a large cabinet in the back held thick, ornate tomes. Bren drew a shuddering breath. It may have been a greater worth than any lieutenant had a right to see, but it was a poor fortune for a kingdom. He slid his torch into a bracket on the wall and lowered himself onto an intricately carved chair.

Helonin handed each man a tablet. "Pair up and take an alcove. Write all you find and if you can estimate a worth, do so. Captain Quarier and I are watching, so pocketing anything will be unwise." There was scattered laughter as the men began to work. After a moment Helonin went to Bren. "Are you going to help?"

Bren nodded, not looking up.

"Regretting your decision, lieutenant?"

Bren shot the man a glare, though he knew there was no cruelty in the mariner's words. "You and I both know this is a sorry sum to run a land." He took the tablet from the man.

"I'm just ashamed to see how far Azirik drained his kingdom trying to kill his daughter."

Φ

The 20th Day of Fluerme, 1252
The Isle of Le'yne

Alea drew the anoher bundle of tablets from the shelf, laying them out on one of the small tables. Her days were spent reading, punctuated by awkward silences over tea and meals. Though history was one of her least favorites, reading was her only respite from guarded stares and blatant gossip. These tablets began a few weeks before the gods overthrew the Laen and were written by one of the gods themselves. He was a god of the ocean, and called himself Berm. *The same Burme that the Berrin worship?* She filed that away for later consideration. The first few tablets described the god's family, the palace and his love for the sea. Alea skimmed the words, though they were beautiful. Before the war she would have enjoyed the man's descriptions. Now she had darker interests. Now she had a war to fight.

She paused when the tone of the writing changed abruptly.

> *This morning the sea was in turmoil and the waves gray. I went to private counsel with King Numon. I expected him to ease my unrest about his speech yesterday. He did the opposite. He told me many of the godlords were tired of paying homage to the Laen. They were tired of them allowing us an understanding of only facets of the world.*

He told me he intended to overthrow them. I left, unsure if it was possible. Numon called a counsel this afternoon. There, in the center of our hall was Milady Queen Lynelle. She had arrived out of good will, to settle a dispute. Those who follow Numon forced her to think this was the way of balance, the overthrowing of the Laen. And then they attacked.

I cannot — I will not — recount the horror or the betrayal that followed. She split the world in three and Numon's guards drove those of us who protested from the palace. The Rakos attacked, but they were too late. The palace burnt as we fled before the walls between the worlds solidified. My son was with me, but his mother and my daughter fell.

Now it is evening. We stand on the shores of the Rakos's land. The Isle of the Gods is gone from the horizon, and Le'yne, too. I do not know what we will do, for our brothers and sisters are either dead or traitors. This morning the sea was in turmoil and the waves gray. I should have listened.

Gooseflesh marched along Alea's arms. She glanced up from the tablet. "Mera?"

The older woman looked over, brows raised. "Yes?"

"The gods, the ones who upheld the Laen laws, the ones loyal to the Laen, what happened to them?"

"I cannot say. They disappeared into the piece set aside for the Rakos, hidden among humans. Eventually I imagine their blood faded, as did the Rakos themselves."

Alea ran a hand down the engraved wax, thinking of Arman. *But the Rakos did not die out. Not completely.* She glanced out the window at the ocean, brows furrowed. Below, the waves were gray.

CHAPTER FOUR

The 21st Day of Fluerme, 1252
The City of Ceir Athrolan

THE EMPTY TABLE BEFORE the library's bank of windows served as a pointed rebuke, as opposed to inspiration. Arman glared at it before nosing about the shelves. There were plenty of books that mentioned the Rakos, if he cared to read children's tales. He opened older histories at random, flipping through the pages as gently as his impatience allowed. "'Greatest bond known to man,' 'Powers of heat and fire,'" he quipped, scanning for anything useful.

His broad fingers paused on a history of Vielrona. Though it was dry and held little new information, the card tucked in the back detailed other comparable books. Most tomes had similar cards, and it spoke to the organization of the Athrolani historians and scribes. He backed up a pace, peering down the shelf for the war log the card suggested. It was a slim tome, and battered enough to have been the original, though the penmanship suggested it was a copy. He navigated his way back to the table and opened the cover. He was greeted by an ink rendition of the portrait from his own book of tales.

The man must have only sat for the one. Arman grinned and began to read.

> *The Rakos garrisons scattered across the continent guard the largest Laen cities. It has been suggested that they are forts, like our own, but from what I have seen, that is not strictly correct. Garrison is simply the only word I have. Anyone who wishes to enter the Laen city must pass the gates, and if the sight alone does not scare one off, then the inhabitants of the gatehouse well might.*
>
> *It's been said that the Rakos keep monsters, or make them the way the Laen made the gods. If that is true, then I question the Rakos's sanity. These creatures are not made of flesh and soul. They are earth and fire and burning anger.*

Arman ran his fingers over the sketch on the opposite page. It was a monster, by human standards. The flesh looked like stone. Some sort of fluid oozed free where the skin cracked at the joints. Great plates curled up at the edges. Any echo of a human shape was overshadowed by the horns branching from the head and shoulders. Lumps on the back could have been wings or armor. It hunched, as if uncomfortable standing on only two legs.

Arman imagined it was a fearsome sight in person, but all he felt was pity. Still, a grin grew on his face. He reached over and tugged the bell pull. *My power may be an enigma and fairly useless thus far, but intimidating armor can never go wrong.*

Arman turned to the serving man who appeared at the bell's ring. "Could you bring me the sketching materials from my room, and deliver this to General Aneral?" He scribbled a few lines on a scrap of parchment and handed it over. When the man had gone, Arman turned back to the book, flipping through to the sections that described actual battle. His ability to transform his arms into smoke was fascinating, but he had yet to read that any Rakos had such an ability. Full-blooded Rakos controlled fire, from what he read, and the explosion of the campfire on the road hinted he might as well.

He spent the rest of the morning designing armor that echoed the monster. He was not a man who leaned towards armor, nor had he ever designed any. *General, please don't tear all of this apart.* In the back of his thoughts was another, the idea that the Rakos had created these monsters. What if he could do the same?

He was almost through the third sketch when he heard the general clear her throat from a few chairs away.

"That serving man told me a dead man wanted to see me. Took a moment to realize what he meant. You look well, for a dead man."

Arman grinned. "Death becomes me, what can I say?"

"Quite. What did you need?"

He handed her the papers, watching for any reaction as she perused them.

After a moment she sat, looking closer. "This is armor."

"Yes. I found a drawing of one of the creatures the Rakos created—Earth Shakers they were called it seems. Though I'm still uncertain what my actual purpose is, I thought looking like a gods' nightmare would be a good start."

"Have you been finding any information on your actual powers? Armor is a good start, and this is a fine design, but it's only armor. Armor protects you, and you are a weapon."

Arman sighed. "There are few mentions of the Rakos in this library—foolish humans too afraid to even mention us in books." Contempt burnt in his words, though it was unconscious.

Eras glanced up from the design, her hazel eyes narrowing on him. "Watch that pride. It can lead to bigotry." The warning was softened by her smile, but only just.

He rose and went to the window, looking out on the overcast day as she continued to examine his drawings. "My temper is getting worse. I have slight abilities, but they are more parlor tricks than anything else. That was the first light in days." He shrugged. "I don't rightly feel Rakos most of the time. I feel things I know are because of the power, but nothing that feels different from myself. Just new."

"I imagine you were always a Rakos in some fashion."

Arman snorted. "For someone who wields fire and earth I did a terrible job in the forge."

"You were a smith?"

"Not really. My father was, as was my grandfather. My friend, Wes, took over the clients when my father died. I did the jewel work and the designs."

"Breaking the earth's natural form would have been hard for someone whose soul was made of earth and metal. I'd bet your designs leaned towards natural shapes and rough surfaces. Organic things."

Arman stared at her. He wanted to make a rude comment about her having knowledge beyond what was rightly appropriate. It irked him that she was right. It irked him that the blood had controlled him for so long. *Have I ever been my own person?* Had he ever been simply Arman? "It doesn't make sense, general. I'm a diluted mess of old, forgotten power."

"That is no excuse for procrastination. We both know you could try harder."

Arman snarled. "I do what I can! Unlike milady I have no race of mentors eager to help me learn, to answer my questions! They're dead! Whatever is in my blood is an echo, nothing more!" Every sentence grew in volume, his words grinding on the stony rumble of his power.

"You have me, but I'll be damned if I feed you knowledge. I don't know what will resonate with your abilities."

"I'm human! I'm no Rakos guard, able to call forth monsters to shake the ground." He stormed down the stairs. He knew the anger simmering under his skin would prevent any more studying. He rubbed his temples as he walked. His words to Eras about his temper had been an understatement, and a large one at that. As a boy he had been quiet, slow to anger. Now the smallest things made him fume. He was not even certain why he was so angry with the general. *Is it because she thinks I'm a Rakos, or because I'm not one?* He had read that the Rakos had fearful tempers, but there was little else about what he could expect as he delved deeper into that side of his ancestry. With a snarl he shoved his hands into the pockets of his light jerkin and made for the barracks.

Φ

Arman tripped over the package on his floor when he returned from the bars. It was closer to dawn than dusk and he bet that his veins contained more alcohol than blood. *And more of either than any Rakos power.* His blurring vision swung back to the package he had kicked under his bed upon entering. He fished it out and tore open the plain wrapping.

It was a thin book, bound like a journal, but in leather rather than the usual, cheap canvas. There was no title or embossing. A short letter was tucked into the front.

> *This was written by a dear friend, one whose voice you may recognize. He was one of the last to ever see the Rakos. Among other things, he tells of their powers and what their offspring were capable of.*
>
> *Should you want more advice or clarity, I am here. Though I'd appreciate if you try to leave your bitterness at the door.*
>
> *-General Aneral*

He knew he had been rude, but was grateful the general had enough sense to realize his actions said far more about his thoughts on himself than about her. He undressed and crawled into bed, belatedly lighting a lamp before opening the book. He liked the author immediately.

> *I would like to say this tale began in a time of peace and happiness, but I would be lying. ...*

Φ

The 38th Day of Fluerme, 1252
The City of Mirik

Bren straightened with a groan. "Damned if I'm going to survive this without becoming as twisted as a crone." Crouching for the better part of an hour that day had done little to help his back. He winced with pain and relief as his backbone popped. He trudged up the stairs towards his room with a sigh. His thoughts had darkened in the bowels of the palace and he could not shake the nagging feeling that he had forgotten something.

Helonin waited by the lieutenant's door. "We sail for Athrolan in a week's time."

Bren was used to the characteristic lack of preamble. "The city is coming along well, sir."

Helonin leveled an appraising stare at the younger man. "Will you return here once we are through at the capital?"

Bren frowned at his boots. He understood the respect behind delivering the question in person, rather than by squire, but he wished he were alone to think.

"You've been an asset, at least in dealing with the city-folk and helping the men learn the streets. If you wish to stay in Athrolan, however, you've given us enough."

"One pair of hands can make a difference, and the Kit are still uneasy." Bren glanced at the man. "Thank you, though."

Helonin clapped him on the shoulder. "We'll be glad of the help. There was another reason I came to find you." He drew out a plain iron box the size of his palm. "This is from the treasury. It might mean something to you. If not, then its missing won't matter."

Bren nodded and thanked the mariner again. When he had gone, Bren ducked into his room. He had thought returning to Mirik was the only option. Realizing he could train with the soldiers and Arman in Athrolan made him question his hasty choice. Mirik was home, and he had missed her sorely, but his heart felt every broken stone. He shook the indecision away and sat on his bed. The box was heavy in his hand and he flicked the lid open, curious. A heavy ring was tucked into a bed of forest green velvet. The band was wide and simple, sized for a large hand. The translucent diopside was native to the iron rich rocks of the island. Bronze shaped into a snake wound over the flat face of the olive gem. Bren's mouth fell open. It was the signet ring of Mirik's king.

Helonin had made a bold statement and Bren suddenly made sense of the mariner's words. *If this means nothing to me, it will not matter that it's no longer among Mirik's treasures.* Bren's continued denial of the throne was judged by many. *When the castle is made into an Athrolani fort my choice will have been made.* He tucked the box into the back of his desk's drawer and drew out a blank parchment to write Arman. His letter would be sent on the schooner leaving that night.

Φ

The 48th Day of Fluerme, 1252
The City of Ceir Athrolan

Helonin hid his amusement at Bren's seasickness, but his men were less kind. The lieutenant found himself the butt of most jests during the three-day sail to Athrolan. The boat docked late in the afternoon and he could not rush down the gangway quick enough. Most of the sailors disembarked to the navy barracks lining the western edge of the harbor. Bren shouldered his pack. The queen was putting him in the palace for the week.

"Barrackborn!" Arman leaned against a piling near the street.

Whatever surprise Bren felt at the man coming to greet him was erased by the man's changed appearance. As he wove through the crowd he noted Arman was now nearly as broad as him. They grasped arms, Bren frowning inwardly at the unnatural dry heat of Arman's skin. "How have you been?"

"Well enough, though rather bored. You?" Arman fell into step beside him as they headed towards the palace.

"Much the same. Rebuilding a city is tedious work." He drew a breath. "It's good to have a change of scene — Athrolan's streets are a bit livelier than Mirik's."

"You mentioned city-people. Are they really as wild as the soldier's paint them?"

Bren shrugged. "They're odd, certainly. Mostly, they are desperate. Hopefully Athrolan will bring enough business to Mirik to give them food and money of their own again. Though who knows if they remember how to live in society." They continued, swapping stories of the days since they had last spoken.

Bren's room was the same as his last visit. Arman leaned against the doorframe while Bren unpacked. "Her Majesty plans on holding the report in the morning tomorrow and the day after. The rest of the week will be to decide what to do from here. Did you have any plans for the evening?"

"Food and drink, in that order. Why?"

Arman grinned. "I have a bar you should see. I can come by your room when we're headed into the city."

"I'll see you then." Bren put away his few belongings, including a thin journal he had used to record the meetings with the Kit. He rang for bath water and spent what was surely an embarrassing length of time soaking. He was dressed when Arman knocked on his door.

"We're meeting the others in the street." Sure enough half a dozen soldiers waited on the corner of Palace Way.

Bren was curious to see the lively greetings they afforded the Rakos, and more so when Arman exchanged laughing barbs with them. He had never seen the man so relaxed and he wondered how much of Arman's grim exterior had been due to Alea.

"This is Lieutenant Brentemir Barrackborn," Arman introduced. "Bren this is Sousa, Kal and Witt. Over there is Joen, Cennen and Hexion. Hex's sister owns the tavern." Bren was warmly welcomed as they started down the street.

"So Barrackborn, did ye hear about the Rakos here saving the Warehouse District?"

Bren glanced at Arman. The sailors in Mirik had brought word of the floods and Arman had mentioned them briefly, but this was news. "No, actually."

Sousa crowed excitedly and began the tale. Somewhere along the line Bren discovered the man's love of story-telling included exaggeration. He repeatedly glanced over at Arman to determine what was fact and fancy. Even without the license Sousa had taken, it was an interesting story.

"And then he put Hasian in his place — nearly beat the man to Toar and back!"

"Enough, Sou," Arman interrupted. "Save some stories for when he's drunk enough to believe them." The excuse was a thin one, but the men accepted it and Sousa quickly picked up another tale.

Bren's interest was piqued. *Exactly how much has changed?* He watched the changed mannerisms of Alea's guard, eyes narrowed. He wondered what she would find when she returned.

Φ

The 1st Day of Lineme, 1252

Buzzing conversation filled the meeting hall when Bren arrived with Arman. The day before had been serious and quiet, but its topics fueled the discussions now. The colonels and general were already there, along with the commander. The noise ceased abruptly when the queen arrived. She smiled as she took her seat, her gaze resting on each of the gathered officers. Bren watched her, curious. *This is what they want me to become – minus the headdress, perhaps.* She looked as benevolent as ever, but there were lines across her brow that had not been there a few months before.

"Welcome, all." She glanced at the scribes perched behind her velvet elbow. "Shall we begin?" The conversation began with new maps of Mirik and reports on the amount of stone used and gained from the city. The treasury reports would take a day unto themselves, but the rough sum put a frown on Queen Tzatia's face. Bren relayed his dealings with the Kit and their way of life. Hearing his home touted like a prize, to be divvied as the spoils of war made him sick. He mentally cursed his involvement in the meetings. He hid a clenching fist under the table.

"Lieutenant?"

Bren glanced up, blood flushing his neck in embarrassment. "Forgive me, your majesty, I was deep in thought."

Tzatia hid frustration well, but her eyes were tired. "Sir Helonin said you had thoughts on the city, the plans?"

Bren leaned forward to orient himself with the maps facing the queen. "I know your majesty intended her for a fort, but I was looking over the plans from King Brenterik's reign and had a thought." He pointed to the swath of cobbles stretching between the city walls and the harbor. Helonin had been unreadable when Bren brought his thoughts forward a week before and the lieutenant was eager to share. "A market here would be perfect for trade—Toar knows the island has enough timber. Trade routes could be re-established. The temple and noble districts, where most of the stone is, could be rebuilt as residences. Fields could replace the old slums and graze royal flocks."

Tzatia's soft cough interrupted him. "Lieutenant, these ideas would certainly raise the city. I think it would be wise to note, however, while there is enough money in Mirik's treasury for such endeavors, we would be fools to spend it thusly. There is a war on, one her king started."

The anger at seeing his home torn apart, bankwasted, and pillaged rose, and determination took the reins of his mouth. "What of afterward, your majesty? I have enough faith in my sister to believe there will be an after. To let Mirik fall when its port could open up the northern ocean, would be madness."

The queen's face hardened. "The northern ocean has nothing but Ageless iron and ice to offer. You speak as if you rule Mirik, when you have expressed distaste for such a title. I remind you that you cannot have the glory and power of a king with the responsibility of a soldier. Choose your course and hold fast to it, otherwise you are simply wasting our time."

Bren's mouth snapped shut and he looked down. He wanted to storm from the room, but it would only serve to drive the queen's point home. "Forgive me, your majesty. Of course you are right." His words were polite, but he spat them from his mouth with venom. He did not hear the remainder of the meeting and was the first to leave when they were dismissed, ignoring Arman's offer to go to the tavern again.

A knock interrupted him as he forgot his rebuked pride in a book. He glowered, tempted to pretend to be out. A second knock came and he jerked the door open. "What, Arman?"

Instead of the expected visitor, Reka leaned against his door frame. "I thought Arman was lying when he said you had holed up here. I heard the queen showed you your station."

Bren made a face. "I'm sure everyone has heard. Did he send you to drag me out to drink?"

"No, but I'm headed for a mug-full, if you wanted to join me." She grinned. "Last I saw you, we were stumbling into the infirmary at Shadow."

Bren tugged on his jerkin and locked his door. "I didn't expect to see you." He tucked his hands into his pockets as they walked. "I thought the Bordermen were scouting with Athrolani patrols."

"We are. My patrol rode in this morning. You'll be going back to Mirik and I thought I'd visit while I could." She turned down another set of side streets, different from those Arman had taken. The road wound along the upper tier of the city, curling around the western edge of the harbor. It was a seedy area above the navy barracks and shipyards. The farther they walked from Palace Way, the darker the alleyways became.

"You don't go to the same tavern as Arman's friends?"

"There are a few I enjoy. Which is theirs?"

"It's called the Lily and Ahonsa, based on some lewd Athrolani myth, if I remember." Bren laughed. "Bars and sex seem to be firm bedfellows."

Reka snorted a soft laugh. She had clearly adjusted to the Athrolani humor. "No, that's not one I visit. I prefer a storytelling to a brawl. Does Mirik have alehouses? Arman mentioned you were eager to be...." She frowned. "You call it tousled?"

He threw a friendly arm around her shoulder. "Tossed. Mirik had only the alcohol that we shipped over, and we drank over the barracks' fires. I'm tired of the company of bone weary men."

Her eyes crinkled in a Border grin. "That the only reason you wished to drink with me?"

"You make me sound like a boor. It could have been for good conversation."

"You are a boor," she joked as they ducked into the loud warmth of the alehouse. "Now, what will our first pints be? Whisky or spice-mead?"

Bren called for the second and they wove through the tables to a set of chairs by the musicians. The tavern was well built for the district. Each of the pillars had been carved into a well-dressed hare standing erect. Some had headdresses and skirts, others tunics and monocles. Bren snorted, despite the obvious quality of the craftsmanship. "Reka, what is this place?"

"The Wise Hare. It might be odd, but they have good music and mead."

As if summoned by her words, the serving woman arrived. A small tray balanced on her pregnant belly. She grinned at them, plunking the drinks down along with a plate of seasoned meat. Reka's feet tapped in time to the quick music after their first two drinks. After the fourth, Bren convinced her to join in the dancing. Her leathers were better suited to the forest, but she moved easily, hands above her head. She twisted in a choppy, yet rhythmic, dance that must have been Border. The firelight highlighted her body and Bren wondered absently how the male warriors could ignore the fact that their companions were female. After a few turns Reka taught him the complex steps to another one.

"What is it?" He pitched his voice so she could hear him over the lively music.

"A dance for luck in battle."

At her words Bren noticed how some motions were parries or strikes. One even looked like the launching of an arrow. He tried the steps again. It was close to midnight when they returned to the palace, their route far more wavering than before. Bren wordlessly opened his door and stepped aside in an invitation. She tugged off his jerkin and shirt, her own already on the floor. As her hands moved to the laces of his breeches he wondered if there was a dance that would make him a good king. Her lips drove the thought from his mind and he fell back onto the bed. Reka landed on top of him with a rare, low, laugh.

Φ

The 3rd Day of Lineme, 1252
The Isle of Le'yne

Gray fog burst on Alea's chest with cold splinters. "Do not close your eyes. You cannot see if someone attacks!" Elle raised her hands to throw another ball of mist.

Alea reached down again, eyes open now, but it was difficult to visualize her power while distracted by the training court around her. She pulled a tendril into her hands and sent it towards the largest stone. It dissipated before it hit. "I don't feel the way I normally do. I don't have those emotions."

She had not had them since the siege. The darkness crouching on the edge of her thoughts kept anything more than the trivial from her heart. She was scared to call it apathy, scared to think she might never *feel* again.

"You have never used your power without fear?" Elle pressed a hand against her brow. "Breathe deeply. Remember the sensation of your power filling you. Follow that." Elle gestured to the smallest stone. "Now, pick it up and turn it over. Gently."

Alea glared at the accidental insult, but turned to the rock. She pushed power through her fingers and shoved. The stone disintegrated into sand. She heaved a sigh. "If the Berrin and Azirik are so powerful, why must I learn the small things? Whatever I must do to them needs to be massive."

"Control, Lyne'alea. Your power is not just a force, not just an extension of your hand, but a weapon. You will need to have control, lest you hurt your allies."

"I am the Destroyer and you have not let me forget the only time I used Creation. Those are not things done at a whim." She turned back to the rocks and focused. By noon, she was no closer to completing the task.

Elle straightened her dress. "Perhaps we ought to start even smaller. As children we would sit for hours, just feeling our power. Unlearning poor habits is harder than learning good ones."

"You act as if we have all the time in the world, Elle." Alea rubbed her face, hoping to scrub frustration from her body. "I understand this is my blood and I have no choice in that, but I've taken up the mantel of a war I had no interest in, even after it robbed me of the only life I knew."

"We are not weak humans like Athrolan's queen. We cannot be dazzled by the first sign of black fog." The voice behind Alea was deep and hoarse. "Learn your ignorance – there were many women we thought might be the Dhoah' Laen."

Alea turned to see the tall, elder Laen from her first evening.

"Lyne'alea, this is Elai." Elle's gaze was fixed on the older Laen's sandals.

Alea met the woman's eyes. "They are dead and I am here. Destruction is not a simple thing to master. It may be easy to forget, hiding in this monotonous world, but war does not wait. I need knowledge now, not in a year."

"You showed incredible stupidity bringing that boy back. You damaged our power irreparably."

"Boy?" Alea turned to Elle, incredulous. "The same boy you asked to bind himself to me? The same boy who is taking up a duty you thought was dead? We took whatever boyhood he still had." She glanced at Elai. This was not a conversation to have when angry, but her only method of communication with the Laen seemed to be argument. "If you wish to teach me, you might bother to understand me first." She stalked out of the yard, realizing she sounded like the child she insisted she was not. "This lesson is done. Perhaps tomorrow one of you will have come to your senses."

She was relieved to find the library deserted. She took up her place at the table and opened a tome. It detailed the spread of the different races and the waning of the Laen's power. *The Rakos died out, the Laen died out, the only gods who were our allies died out.* She disliked the theme.

"We know you deserve respect." Mera's voice was soft and kind.

Alea looked up. The anger was draining from her. "Then why do I feel as if it's the opposite?"

"We're scared of what you can do. You're supposed to save our race. You are mighty and sweeping and terrifying."

"I do not want reverence either. I want to be seen as an equal, a woman, a daughter. I've given up so much for this war. There is very little left inside of me to give." Her voice broke and she looked down, ashamed at her tears. "I know what I did was dangerous and terrible. I know what it made me. Yet, none of you have thought to ask me why."

"I'm sorry, Lyne'alea. Most of us never knew a life other than this. You have. Finish your reading. Perhaps Elle will talk to you tomorrow." She pressed a hand to Alea's arm. "She's never been a master of words, your mother."

"We share that, then, if nothing else." When she had gone, Alea sat back. Bren had told her how frustrating his armor-cleaning had been as a boy. She had thought the siege was her armor-cleaning. Now she was not so certain. *Elle reached me from across a continent. Faint, but Arman saw her.* She touched her power and reached her mind out across the ocean. It was a familiar path. *I swam through this with Arman's soul.* The thought caught in her throat and she shook her head to clear it. She focused her mind and pressed through the electrified barrier between the worlds. Her mind raced over the water. Mirik glowed, a tiny constellation of copper-red stars. She followed the brown-laced ball of light that was her brother's. Curiosity flitted across her thoughts. Though he shared her blood, his soul looked the same as any man's. He sat at a desk, reading.

She nudged his consciousness. *Brothermine?*

He jumped, surprised. "Alea?"

Yes! How are you? I miss you.

"Toar, how are you doing this? Or have I been up too late and am hearing things?"

No, it's really me. How is Mirik?

"We're working through the city, clearing rubble, searching for anything that will help. It's slow. The queen wants to make it into a fort. And you, how are you? Are you learning a lot?" He tilted his chair back on two legs.

I'm learning a lot, though not what I expected. More about myself, which is useful.

"I've been doing heart-searching, too. Everyone seems to want me to be king. We just returned from Athrolan today, actually. During our report the queen told me I needed to choose what role to have. Her exact words were 'you cannot have the glory and power of a king with the responsibility of a soldier.'"

Well then. If you wait too long the decision will be made for you. She laughed at the face he made. *Have you decided?*

"I think a picture is fast forming." He sighed. "Enough of my problems. What have you learned?"

That I am nothing like the Laen want me to be.

His eyes widened. "That sounds unpleasant."

Rather. They argue over how to teach me, what to teach me, and the nature of my power. I read a lot. Some of it is quite interesting. What remains unwritten by the historians is even more interesting.

"I think most history is interesting."

You and Arman both. I prefer fables and poetry, though this is changing my opinion somewhat. I still feel useless. I think we were wrong – this is my armor cleaning. She felt her power shudder and she sighed. *I think I ought to go. I'm tiring. I miss you.*

"I miss you, too. Visit me again, if you can."

I will. Her mind raveled back to her body quickly, leaving her feeling cold and alone. The book would not read itself, however, and talking with Bren had centered her thoughts for the moment. She turned back to the page before her with a frown. She was ashamed of so much, yet none of it was what the Laen told her she should regret.

CHAPTER FIVE

The 8th Day of Lineme, 1252
The City of Ceir Athrolan

ARMAN WANTED ANSWERS. THE last time he wanted information he burnt a man from within to read his thoughts. Arman tipped his head back onto the cool plaster of the dome. Dawn was one of the few times the early summer heat-haze dissipated long enough for the faint shadow of Mirik to appear on the horizon. In the stillness, his heartbeat was thunder. He had yet to sleep, and now it was dawn. The journal Eras had lent him sat on the stone beside him, a silent and patient companion.

He closed his eyes against the blooming light of dawn. *Surely I could ask the other parts of myself.* He sunk into his own thoughts, following the curls of white-gold power that knotted the surface of his mind. The air was a caress on his over-heated skin. There was a history tucked away in his thoughts, a litany of everything the Rakos had ever been. He had not formed a question when he discovered the storm that waited ahead of their ship. It had been a burning, angry concept at the forefront of his thoughts as he punched through the other man's mind.

He gathered the few things he already knew about the Rakos, about his own abilities. He tied them about his thoughts like a cocoon. In his head, it sounded like a riddle. *I am fire. I am smoke. I am thought. I am earth.* The air felt colder as his body began to burn from within. His mind itched. A great tangle of information glowed in the center of his soulblood. It stung his mental touch. He traced the individual lines that snarled together, finally finding a free end. Ignoring the strange sensation, he grabbed at it and tugged. A thousand burning images bombarded him.

A Rakos stood on a mountain's peak, staring down at a statue of a regal woman beside a lake. The city still stood, not yet in ruins. The image flashed to that of a battle at the edge of the lake. Men swarmed the area, and the Rakos attacked. Monsters screamed from above, their tattered wings raining feathers. Flames burst from the Rakos's hands and mouths, smoke spiraling into the sky.

Who am I? Arman plunged down, under the surface of the pulsing knot. A blond man stood in a room, dark and windowless, a tomb without the coffin. He had dragged a body into the darkness and crouched over the monster's head. The man drew his knife and cut around the creature's brow, parting the scales and skin. A glimmer of gold and white shone through the layers of muscle. He parted the flesh further until his fingers could gain purchase on the metal ringing the creature's skull. Bone cracked as he finally wrenched it free. Arman winced.

A pair of yellow eyes blotted out every thought, glaring into his mind and soul with burning fervor. Its voice was manic and keening. It took Arman a moment to decipher the words. Rather, it was a single word, repeated with the ferocity of a madman. "Fear. Fear. Fear"

Φ

The 11th Day of Lineme, 1252

Arman began to wonder if the journal's author was quite sane. The humor and the wry biting words were familiar to Arman. He had spoken to men jaded by life. Sometimes he felt his own voice twisting into cynicism. The author certainly knew enough about the world, and it was the type of knowledge not learned in books, but from walking the road. He spoke of the Northlands wistfully, and of Athrolan tenderly. Arman was fairly certain the man that penned the pages before him had also left legends in his wake.

Arman flipped to a passage he had marked with a bit of string. The Rakos were mentioned often, and with curiosity, not fear.

> *I did not understand the true nature of the bond between Rakos and Laen. Nuirene brought back pieces of black rock-metal he called magnetite. They came from a star-fall. The rocks were heavy, and if brought near each other, would fly together. A large piece would collect thousands of tiny particles, but two pieces of the same size would collide with force enough to break a man's finger. Thus it is with power.*

Arman frowned. The man was not sane. Nevertheless, he wandered into the section at the back of the library holding books and maps regarding metals and rocks. It was mostly used by those seeking to build within the city, or to plan where the next mine would be dug. It was deserted and the shelves dusty. He ran a calloused finger through the dust by the tablets labeled "Ma-" and found a small wooden box. Across the top was a blocky stamp titling the contents as starstone. Arman opened the box to find a small velvet pouch holding two black spheres. At first they looked like polished metal, but the grain and swirls indicated they were, in fact, rocks. With effort he pulled them apart, letting them snap back together with a surprising crack. He repeated the action several times, amused. Finally, he replaced them in the box and returned to the journal.

> *The Laen power acts in one fashion, and the Rakos's in another. Though they are opposite, they are equal and in the equal opposition there is an attraction that cannot be defied and will break all in its path. Sometimes even those who wield it.*

Arman had agreed with everything written, but now, when called an equal to the Laen, he scoffed. At the time he wrote it, the author had never felt the power Alea radiated. Their powers were two pieces of a whole, but not equal ones.

Though better than the isolation before, Arman's life still felt dualistic. He spent the days as Arrowlash, studying, learning about Rakos power. At night he was Arman, drinking and carousing. It was an extension of who he had been in Vielrona. The disconnect allowed him to relax, but he knew eventually there would be no divide. One would bleed into the other and Arman would be lost forever in Rakos flames.

He glared at the ale in his glass, trying to determine whether he minded. The drink was a rich golden brown. Summer gold. It was a comforting color, familiar and warm. *Veredy's hair.*

"Eh, we lost Arman to his thoughts again."

Arman grinned and flicked his gaze to Kal. He let enough of his power into his body to make his voice rumble. It was a fun trick and rarely made them actually remember what he was. "Just deciding how long I should wait before I whip all your arses." He threw down another card, absently wondering which game they were playing. Would a Rakos enjoy drinking and card games? He did not know.

Φ

The 13th Day of Lineme, 1252
The City of Mirik

Bren tossed onto his side, staring out the window. It was dark and the view was poor. He was glad to be out of the tedious meetings, but Mirik did not feel like home. It only gave him more to think about. The queen's pointed words stung more than he admitted. *I am betwixt two roles and I try to act in both with the responsibility of neither.* He briefly wished he could talk to Alea. When he had been Azirik's man and thoughts kept him from sleep, Bren had walked out by the harbor to think, away from the boisterous chaos of the other men.

His boots were on in moments. He crossed the courtyard and slipped through the gates easily, calling a greeting to the guards. His usual course took him around the harbor, but he paused, looking up at the city gates. Changing direction, he chose the abandoned streets of the city. He was certain the Kit tailed him, but that only served to make the night feel more desolate. He turned west at the palace walls, following them to what had once been gardens. They were dense and overgrown now, but made a good ladder up the city walls.

He scrambled up quickly, perching at the top to look out over the waves. The walls were complete, ready to encompass the fort and town that would serve as Athrolan's northern-most outpost.

He leaned back against the tree stretching over the stone. "Come out, Oland. I know you're there."

There was silence for a moment, then a rustle as the Miriken climbed up to sit beside him. He was quiet, running his worn hand over the newly-lain stone. "Ye cleaned her up nice."

"Makes me wish I could remember what she was like at her might, before Azirik."

"When yer grandpap ruled."

Bren shrugged.

"What'll her fate be?" Arik fixed Bren with an unreadable gaze.

"Athrolan will make her a fort. She'll be an outpost for the kingdom, for trade and the like."

"And the Kit?"

Bren was quiet for a long minute. "I suspect you can stay here, work for the soldiers."

"And you think that will be different than Azirik? Better somehow? Ye should take her. Ye know her."

Bren put his head in his hands. "I'm not a king, Arik, I'm a soldier."

"Well, we're not a kingdom either. We're a rabble-band of starved thieves and opportunists."

Bren raised his brows. "You have any room open for a new member? If the queen doesn't give up this quest for my future I might run away with you."

"Do you fear the crown?"

"No. I don't deserve it, though."

"That alone would make you a better king than Azirik."

"He thought he deserved the crown?" Bren shifted to get a better look at his companion's features.

"Azirik wept when his pa died. Not in grief, but 'cause he feared the crown." Arik scrubbed his face with a rough hand. "You would really give up a crown for freedom?"

Bren rolled his eyes. "Honestly I'd settle for a hermitage." His face sobered. "What would you do were you in my place?"

Arik's expression grew thoughtful. "I don't know, truly. However I'll tell you this—I could have left the Kit here. I could have run to my cousin on the mainland and never looked back. Many did. I'd not be hungry. I'd not be poor. I'd feel a damn sight younger. But I don't know if I'd be happier." He shrugged. "This is home. She's not a great land, she's not a rich one, but she's pretty and she's mine." He sighed and heaved himself to his feet. "Pity you won't take her. You'd have the Kit's voice."

Bren stared at the dark water below and listened to the man climb down the wall. "How many are you, Oland?"

A long pause prefaced the words that finally drifted up from below. "Three score in the city. Twice that in the green." He used the old Miriken term for the forest. Bren turned back to the ocean. The conversation left him with fewer answers than before. It would be hours before he could sleep and dawn waited for no one. *Did you really expect to escape fate when your sister is the Dhoah' Laen?* He promised himself he would make a decision before be returned to the barracks that night. He sat on the wall for a long time.

Φ

The 17th Day of Lineme, 1252
The Isle of Le'yne

Frustration and embarrassment were familiar to Alea. Learning a new culture in Vielrona had been hard. Acknowledging naiveté while demanding respect had been worse. Neither were comparable to navigating the icy social waters of Le'yne. The day was crisp and the air rejuvenated Alea's wounded spirit as she walked up to the training court. Despite the outburst, Elle continued to teach her, but with little progress. If anything, Alea felt her hold on her power diminishing in the face of stress and distain.

This morning, however, Elle's faint smile was almost vulnerable. The kindness gave Alea pause. She nodded. "Good morning. Are we picking up where we left off yesterday?"

"We both know it's the wrong way to go about things, at least for now." Elle patted the ground beside her. "Instead of starting small with what you do with your power, let us start small with *how* you use it."

Alea sat cross-legged and rested her hands in her lap. "Taking a small piece, you mean?"

"I want you to bring it up, but do not push it out of yourself. Just feel it. Let it simply be around you."

It was difficult. Alea's power bucked like a horse trying to free itself from a tether, seeking any way out.

"Do not force it down. Spread calmness across, like a layer, holding yourself just in check."

Alea floated on a sea of black, icy fog. She glanced down, looking at the roiling ocean beneath her mental self. Lightning rumbled through the churning blackness. It looked like the clouds above Le'yne. Startled excitement broke her will and power flooded into her skin. Her eyes flew open and she gasped, clenching her fists as cold rocketed down her limbs.

"You held it. It was a moment, but you did it." Elle smiled. "Now, try again."

Φ

Alea frowned as she tossed herbs haphazardly into her mug. "I thought we were proceeding with order and precision." She almost succeeded in keeping vitriol from her voice.

"Yes, and in order to do so, I must understand you better." At Alea's accusing glace, Elle sighed. "Yes, Mera spoke with me. It does not change the fact that I'm curious about what you have learned to do on your own. Perhaps I can teach you better if I know what it is you're wielding."

"I don't suppose the other Laen are curious, too."

"If they are, their curiosity will not be satisfied today. It'll just be the two of us."

The pale sunlight lit the training court well and Alea propped her still-steaming mug on the ground beside Elle. She took a few steps away and tried to hide the shaking in her arms as they hung at her sides. She fell into herself, closing her eyes and pulling the swirling black clouds from her center.

Unbidden, thoughts of the past weeks unfurled in the wake of her power. *The Laen are disappointed. I am worthy of their respect.* Her jaw tightened. Another thought bloomed, this time from the darkest shadows in her mind. *I am worthy of their fear.* She stumbled over its bitterness. She gripped her power tighter, pushing the distractions aside and let it pour into her limbs. It filled her fingers then pushed out, towards the mountains, away from the village and Elle. The ground trembled under her physical feet, but her power was too tight for her to hear. She pushed it further, then let it retreat, curling back into her body and mind. The normal sounds of the village and hillside were replaced with terrible silence.

She blinked, eyes opening as blackness faded from them. The walls of the training court had been reduced to rubble. All but the largest stone was a pile of gravel. A ragged handprint had been carved into it, the edges of the fingers and palm coated in curls of hoar frost.

Alea did not have to look to know the Laen below stared from the streets and doorways of the village. Elle had taken several steps back. Alea turned her eyes slowly to her mother. "I rarely tell it what to do. Often I let it behave on its own. I'm lucky I can control it this much."

"You had less control before?" Elle's voice had lost its calm exterior. Fear and remorse rubbed the edges of her words raw.

"I used to sink into my power instead of drawing it through myself. We were on the road between Fort Hero and Fort Stone. I was practicing and my power got away from me. I destroyed the camp, broke trees, and killed one of the horses." She could feel the hard mask on her face cracking.

"How did you stop yourself?"

"I didn't. Arman spoke to me through his own power. When I relaxed, when my fear had lessened, I could control it again. Afterward, he told me to pull the power up instead of surrounding myself with it. Lest I drown, so to speak."

Elle smoothed her skirt with shaking hands. "One of us has studied the way we each use our power. Would you talk to her? She might have insight. I'm afraid I do not."

"It can't hurt." Alea knew she should be ashamed of scaring them, but a small part of her rejoiced. Perhaps they would finally listen.

Φ

Lelil was the oldest woman Alea had ever seen among human or Laen. Her silver eyes were set deeply into nets of folded skin. Her expression was the familiar calm facade. She ushered them wordlessly into her small house and gestured for Alea to sit at the table. Elle, she ignored.

Alea sat, staring at her uncertainly. *Should I explain myself? Surely what I just did was demonstration enough.* When Lelil held out her hand, Alea took it. The loose skin was soft and cool. She kept her eyes open and drew her power up. It was easier each time, as if the path would be broken in like a pair of boots. Lelil followed along the veins of Alea's soulblood. The additional presence was nagging. She withdrew and Alea let her power fade.

Lelil sat back, regarding Alea thoughtfully. After a moment she stood and went to stand at the counter. Her brows furrowed as if something out the kitchen window was distressing. "Are you tired?"

Alea looked up. She had wondered if the woman was mute. "I've been traveling and essentially rootless for months. Of course I'm tired."

"When you use your power, Lyne'alea, are you tired afterward?"

"Yes. Though often there is stress for other reasons as well. War does that."

Lelil ignored the barb. "And when you have used the most, what has happened?"

"It burnt my hands and I bled soulblood through the wounds. I was unconscious for days."

Lelil's expression tightened and she turned to look at her. "Our power is a ball in our wombs. Yours is rooted there, certainly, but it has branches wrapped around every vein of your being. There is little definition where one ends and the other begins. Your emotions trigger your power this way. Each time you pull your power through yourself, some soulblood is burnt away. With time it returns, but if you use too much at once it will kill you."

Elle rubbed her face. "How did you live through bringing that boy back?"

Alea looked down at the veins of power and soulblood still shining through her skin. "I almost didn't. I sank in the ocean, without enough strength to swim. I pushed his soul back to his body, but remember nothing more. Later he said he carried me."

The two women exchanged looks. "He is a strong man, to carry a creature so powerful and not be consumed by it," Lelil noted. She brushed her hands free of invisible dust. "I will discuss with the others what should be done. In the meantime, keep to your reading and mind your emotions."

Alea fell into step beside Elle after their abrupt dismissal. "You are not meeting with them?"

"My opinion is negated by my apparent affection for you. I fear what they will decide."

"Why?"

"I barely understand your power, but I know it cannot be treated the same as ours. Few of them understand that. They think your tiger should behave as our housecats, not realizing the two are different animals."

Φ

The 18th Day of Lineme, 1252

The view of the ocean made Alea think of Athrolan. She had not been there long enough to call it home, but nostalgia tinted every thought of the tiered city. *It is not Athrolan's cliffs I miss, but the person with me.* She shut her bedroom door carefully and sat on her bedspread. She had avoided thinking about Arman or their argument, but now she missed his steadiness. She connected to her power quickly and shot across the waves in minutes. Athrolan was a sea of crimson shimmering with all the souls.

A spot of white-gold pulsed brilliantly through them. She pushed herself closer until she could see him. He sat in the library, several books open before him. A deep frown creased his forehead and tension lined his shoulders. She moved closer to peer at what he read. It was a plain journal, written in simple, spiky writing. She reached out her mind and nudged against him, like she had with Bren.

Arman? The sensation was strange, like sliding off a glass window. He did not seem to notice her. She grabbed at more power. *Arman, can you hear me?*

He looked up, his frown deepening.

Arman!

He rubbed his eyes roughly. "I'm going mad, thinking I can feel her here." He gathered his tunic, folded haphazardly over the back of the chair and headed towards the door. He extinguished the candles and paused. "I miss you, you know. More than anything." He shook his head and left.

Energy drained from Alea and her mind followed her power back to her body. She flopped onto the pillows. *Why couldn't he hear me? Bren could.* She ran a hand through her hair. She felt more isolated than ever. She rolled over and wrapped her arms around her pillow. Elle called for her to come have lunch, but Alea stared unseeing out the window at the rolling waves for several minutes before finally going into the kitchen.

Elle was silent as she prepared their lunch. She set a pot on to simmer and turned to lean against the counter. "Talk to me?"

Alea jumped, surprised at the vulnerability in the words. "About what?"

"Your journey north, your childhood, your first love. There is so much I don't know." Elle's silver eyes were lit with a bittersweet glow. For the first time Alea felt as if she gazed on a mother. The emotion was uncomfortable to see on her normally stoic features and she looked down at her hands. Without eye contact she could be speaking to anyone, or to no one. "You did well, choosing the ihal to raise me. He was a kind man and intelligent. He must have understood more of the truth than I realized. He had many children, the younger of which I helped raise. His second-eldest son, Ahren, agreed to marry me. The attack came a week before we were to be wed. The Laen were there, six of them, and the one they thought was the Dhoah' Laen. I was so angry at them afterward. They abandoned me, abandoned my family after we had sheltered them."

Her voice faltered for a moment and she drew a breath. "You are right that I know little about your people – I was not raised by you, or even in an ally city. I do know about this war and about my power." She paused, forcing her words to be gentle. It was harder than she expected. "After years of inaction, I think action scares you. Last you saw me I was a child, and now you turn about and I'm grown. Treating me like a child now will not make up for those years." She finally looked up. "But you don't have to. I had a family, one you picked just for me."

"It is not anger behind my reprimands and reserve. It is fear."

"I know what I did was monstrous and dangerous, but did you ever think to ask me why?"

Elle looked down and shook her head. "That is not why I am afraid. I spent two decades pretending you were never born, because if I didn't, they might find you. Two decades of only loving you in my mind and dreams, Lyne'alea. Now you are real and breathing and angry and I'm still terrified to love you." She reached out to touch Alea's hand, but paused. She swallowed hard, her hand falling back into her lap. Neither moved to take the pot from the fire and the silence was broken only by the hiss as it boiled over.

CHAPTER SIX

The 21st Day of Lineme, 1252
The City of Mirik

SALT MADE THE COBBLES sticky under Bren's boots. There was an irony to Mirik being surrounded by ocean and attacking the woman who wielded its power. He followed the path from his first encounter with the Kit. They were odd, he admitted, and questionably sane, but he preferred their company to the Athrolani. Some deep part of him was sickened by the garish turquoise of their uniforms and pennants where vermilion once hung.

He broke into a jog and turned into the slums. The houses were tall, leaning over the street. Jug-end Square was the center of their domain, it seemed, and since the Athrolani's arrival, the place was tidier. If some nicer materials suddenly appeared in the Kit houses, no one seemed to notice. Bren rapped on the central door, eyes scanning the windows around him. Relations with the Kit were certainly civil, but Bren would not go as far to describe them as friendly.

"Ho, Oland." They may have accepted him more readily than they did the Athrolani, but he was still a vague other to the majority. Doors opened and shut and he heard a muttered order for patience. It was better than finding a bolt in his sternum.

The door jerked open. "Barrackborn." Even under the harsh lighting of the lanterns, it was clear Arik's face had fleshed out.

Bren raised a hand in greeting. "I have something to discuss with you." He shot a glance at the hall behind the Miriken. "Might I come in?"

Arik did not move from the doorway. His eyes narrowed on the soldier, head tilting to one side.

Bren did not rush the man, and forced his feet into stillness. The Kit kept to themselves. Often the only visitors allowed were unconscious or dead. He watched thoughts flicker over the older man's features for a moment. "One Miriken visiting another, Oland, that's all."

Arik sighed. The weight of the past decade wiped all fight from his face and he nodded. "Get in, then." He moved down the hall, not waiting to see if Bren followed. The houses shared walls, and the Kit had opened doorways between them. It created a warren of connected dwellings and meeting halls. While the endlessness may have been an illusion, Bren was willing to bet the buildings covered more ground than the actual palace.

Four minutes of walking brought them to a door at the end of a hall. Arik unlocked it and ushered Bren into a small two-room apartment. Dismantled crates formed a table, chairs and the platform for a cot mattress. Without offering tea or ale, he sat at the makeshift table and fixed Bren with an expectant look. "Well?"

Bren sat and drew a book from his jerkin. "Are you familiar with *Rauld's Tales for an Officer*?"

"Somewhat. It was controversial when scribed, if I recall."

"For good reason. Would you do me a favor and read the third piece? 'Treatise for a Common Man's King.'" He slid the book across the table.

Arik regarded Bren, one rough hand on the book's cover. "I'm not in the habit of reading for pleasure."

"Then consider this research." Bren shifted. He needed the man's opinion before he would admit his real reasons for the suggestion.

"Might this have to do with our discussion last week?"

"It might. Humor me though. Mirik is in shambles. She has no government. The only thing that could make her worse could be if Azirik himself returned."

Arik laughed. "You sound more like Brenterik every day." He glanced up, the nests of wrinkles about his eyes deep with mirth. "As kings went, he was a good man." He looked down at the book before them, a heartbreaking mixture of hope and dread on his features. "Is this something you wish to keep between us?"

"For now." Bren rose. "Mind showing me out? I doubt I could find my own way without getting lost. I've only just got my thoughts straightened out and it'd be a pity to starve to death in this maze."

Arik laughed, tucking the book inside his shirt before rising. "I doubt the Kit would let you starve."

Φ

Bren had gambled on having time to plan, to organize the Kit. He had yet to even formulate what he was actually doing. The letter sitting on his desk when he returned from the city crushed those hopes for more time. The parchment probably cost more than the clothes he wore. If the formal hand of a scribe was not enough, the bright ribbons and seals told him it was from the queen and it was no missive. The address stilled his breath.

> Addressing His Highness Crown Prince Brentemir, Heir Apparent of Mirik

Bren groaned. Every carefully thought-over piece of his plan fell through with an almost audible clatter.

> We wish to express congratulations of Ceir Athrolan and her cities on the reclamation of the harbor capitol of Mirik. Athrolan received word that the city has indeed been abandoned by Lord King Azirik of Mirik and his Gods' Army, and offers her own Naval Commander and a ship of her navy to continue its aide to raise Mirik's capital to its former strength.
> Ceir Athrolan and her cities hope that as acting king of Mirik, you will accept our extended hand of alliance against King Azirik and his Berrin allies in this war for Dhoah' Lyne'alea and her people. We look forward to your response within a fortnight.
> Respectfully and in peace,
> Her Majesty Tzatia, Queen of Athrolan, on behalf of Athrolan and her people

If Bren was unsure of the calculating intelligence behind the queen's benevolent smile before, now he was certain. "Damn, I'm a soldier not a king!" He tossed the letter into his drawer beside the ring and drew a clean sheet of parchment over.

> *Oland,*
>
> *Her Majesty called me out. She addressed me as Heir Apparent and all sorts of things and requested an alliance. I hoped we would have more time. Might I meet with you, and all the Kit and our allies? Your earliest convenience would be best.*

He sealed it and sent the letter off with a squire. His officer's log lay on the desk. He had not written since leaving Azirik's army. Now he opened it and stared at the blank page before him. *Rauld says that the best way to govern a people is to be that people. Azirik ruined Mirik with her own crown, and wounded the earth with another. Perhaps it is time we ruled without one.* He dipped his pen and began to write.

Φ

The 24th Day of Lineme, 1252
The City of Ceir Athrolan

Arman decided he and Wes should have taken up armor smithing years ago. The sprawling buildings of the royal armory were bustling, yet well kept, giving the illusion of chaos without the actual danger. He had handed over his designs for his armor, albeit with Eras's changes. Now he stared at the rough sketch and estimated price. He could buy his own forge with that sum. Perhaps two. He could retire and not work another day.

The money Wes had given him before they left Vielrona still weighed heavily in his purse, but it was nothing compared to the price of armor. He had not needed money in months and it was a strange feeling to worry about it again. He, Alea and Bren rested in a strange place of indecision. They did not need money, but nor did they work for a wage. Their expenses were covered by Athrolan, but Arman knew it was not an indefinite arrangement. Anxiety raced through Arman's veins. The smoke and metal scent of the forge was a heady concoction. He needed to be outside. He needed air. Armor would have to wait.

He ducked through the smaller south gate between the palace and the barracks and strode down the road. It led up through the wooded hills before forking to the west and south. The air was cool and within a few minutes the sounds of the city had faded. He walked until the trees swallowed him and all but the highest towers disappeared. The forest was full of animal noises and the wind, but nothing menacing. It had been a long time since he had been able to consider the woods safe.

He shook away the thoughts and broke into a lope. A mountain stream gurgled nearby, and he ran upstream, boots tapping as he jumped from rock to rock. His breath was barely gasping. He pushed himself harder, falling into his power, willing his skin and muscle to disappear into smoke. The resistance of air and gravity fell away as his body dissolved. His eyes fluttered open, mind still gripping his power. His limbs were twisting white smoke, nothing more substantial than dust motes in the sunlight lancing through the trees. Only his torso remained, and even that seemed closer to a ghost than a man.

Arman crowed at the success, and his voice was a keening shriek, too guttural to be a bird's, too grating to be human. "What do you think of this?" He had taken to conversing with the golden eyes that floated in the back of his mind. It warped his thought patterns enough to develop new ideas. Sometimes, even, he thought they answered him.

Smoke is only an echo of flame. Where is the fire?

Arman scowled. "I am no Rakos, burning the air with a single thought. I am just an echo of something mighty." He pulled up more power, coating himself with it and urged his legs faster. Except, it was not his legs that propelled him now, but sheer will. His body faded, skin and muscle writhing away to expose transparent organs, insubstantial bones. "If someone struck me with a sword, would it pass through me, leaving me unharmed?"

Fire is stronger than steel. Fire molds the earth as it wishes.

He topped the hill, a broad rocky outcrop with sparse tree cover. He willed his body to move faster, towards the cliff on the hill's southern face. With a final push, he dove over the edge. *Smoke is lighter than most air, floating on the currents like an equal.* Arman did not fall. He drifted, supported by the sun-warmed air that rose from the rock. His grin blossomed into a delighted laugh. The eyes seared through his thoughts, a thousand times more insistent. A wicked scar scored one, turning the edges of the iris a sickly white.

When will you stop playing and come find us?

Who are you? Arman pushed away, peering at the figure. It was a Rakos, all yellow hair and golden skin. *Where are you?*

I'm Eana. I thought I was the last. The grin was wicked and not playful in the least. *You'd find us if you bothered to look.* The familiar litany of a single word began. *Fear. Fear.* The man lunged and Arman gasped, dragging himself out of the tangle of someone else's thoughts. The distraction broke his hold and his body became abruptly solid. With a startled shout nothing like the war cry from a moment ago, he crashed to the ground.

He groaned, rolling over onto his hands and knees. His body was bruised, but nothing felt broken. His skin itched uncontrollably, as it often did after he used his power, but nothing could dampen his excitement. Even his pride was too astounded to be wounded. The Rakos ruled the skies, and now he knew how.

Φ

The 29th Day of Lineme, 1252

"Deal you in?" Sousa's invitation arched across the bar's common room upon Arman's arrival.

Arman snorted. "I'm rubbish at cards, I think we've discovered." He jerked his head toward the bar. "I still owe you." He ordered a round of whatever his friends had already begun to drink and meandered back to their table. Kal shimmied over on the bench to make room as Arman plopped down beside him.

Arman crossed his boots on the table and leaned back with a sigh. His spirits were high and his heart still raced from his earlier discovery.

"Arman, you got dirt and stone all over your boots." Sousa complained, making a shooing motion at the offending attire. "What did you do, wrestle a bear? Witt said you were out in the woods today."

Arman grinned. "I was practicing, testing some things I read about the Rakos." He rarely spoke about the less-than-human side of his blood, and hated the way it made his friends eye him sideways. Still, his mood was too good to be spoiled by a wary look.

Sousa's expression faltered and the grin he hastily pulled onto his face looked forced. The moment was broken by the delivery of their drinks. Arman gulped down most of his first mug, his mind scrambling for a change in subject.

Before Arman could pick a new topic, Kal glanced over with tempered curiosity. "Did you always know what you were?"

"No, I learned it several weeks after meeting milady." He shrugged. "I'll tell you true, though, it explained some things."

Sousa grinned, his change in mood indicating he had imbibed a fair amount already. "Why you had fangs, like?"

Arman whacked the man on the shoulder. "Idiot, I didn't have those my whole childhood."

"So you bound yourself to this all-powerful creature without knowing what you were? Not knowing if you stood a chance in the war?"

Arman stared into the swirling of his drink, absently telling himself that the drink was in fact swirling, not just his head. "I knew my blood when I bound myself to her. I didn't understand all the consequences though. If you saw her like I see her you'd not question it though."

"I think the same about my woman." Kal's eyes were distant and suddenly sage-like. "So the Rakos blood goes back in your family?"

Arman's response was interrupted by a bitter voice.

"Nah, his Ma bedded one damned ugly stranger when his Pa looked the other way. It's how the thieves of his city are—rut with anyone who looks twice."

Arman's gaze narrowed on the broad shape of Hasian standing over them. He straightened himself on the bench and extracted his arm from Sousa's grip before rising.

"Going to shoo me off again? Words do not scare me, little man. Yer just a corpse forgot he was dead." The smell of stale ale rolled off Hasian 's tongue on the tail of his words.

A month ago Arman would have noted it and backed down from a foolish fight. A month ago he would have laughed the stupidity away. Instead, his blood roiled through his veins. Heat raced through his body, rising faster than ever. His retort bubbled into a growl.

"Forget it, Arman. It's like talking to a wall." Kal tugged at Arman's arm. "We'll just leave."

"You can't fight when your lady's away? What's she doing, anyways? Bedding her way across the country? How else would she get any of us to fight for her? Narier said she's not much in the way of looks, but she's a warm place to stick it."

Sousa groaned, hiding his head in his hands. Heat flamed across Arman's face, turning his eyes yellow. He dropped his shoulder and tackled the larger soldier with a roar. A table crashed against the wall, ale slicking the floor. The two men grappled, no one willing to attempt to pull them apart. Arman's head came up for a moment, blood staining his face.

"Damn, he'll kill him!" Sousa shouted, finally reaching for his friend.

Kal shook his head and held Sousa back. "He'll kill you, too."

Arman heard nothing but the pounding of blood in his ears and the screaming of fire in his veins. His vision blurred, everything tinged gold. His hands glowed like white beacons to his eyes. The yield of flesh and bone under his fists was satisfying, and the resulting blood warm between his burning fingers. It tasted salty and sweet. Abruptly he no longer felt any blows. The roar of a landslide in his mind faded as the common room fell silent. He drew back, breath coming in heaving gasps. Blinking rapidly, he cleared his vision.

Hasian lay unconscious at his feet, bruises already coloring his face. A ragged wound marred his shoulder, bone stark against the dark blood and ale staining the floor. Arman shook the remaining haze from his eyes and turned to find Sousa and Kal. Their expressions were horrified. Sousa swallowed hard before pointing to the door.

Arman shouldered his way through the silent bar. No one tried to stop him. His friends followed him out. Once they were all in the street and the door shut behind them, he turned. "Why didn't you pull us apart?"

"You looked like a mad man, Arman."

Arman ordered his thoughts, each one scorching his mind. Adrenaline and rage were a seething ocean threatening to drown him. "Did I draw a knife? Take his? There was a wound on his shoulder."

Kal pointedly wiped his mouth, obviously meaning for Arman to do the same.

Arman reached up to feel his face. It was covered in blood and pieces of flesh. It was not his own. "Toar!" He turned his back, spitting repeatedly into the gutter. "Damned disgusting!"

Sousa looked down, making no argument. "Do you want us to walk you back? Hasian has few friends, but after that, people will come looking."

Arman backed away. "Don't think I can handle myself? Dead man in there says otherwise." His sentences were fragmented, stumbling over the disgust and rage thickening his throat. He would regret the angry dismissal, and the bloody fight, but that would be later. Now his skin itched and company was the last thing he wanted. He hunched his shoulders and strode down a darkened alley. He took a meandering route back to the palace, keeping to deserted streets. Heat radiated from his body, burning the blood from his skin with a sickly sweet smell. He was sane enough to be concerned, sane enough to be terrified. The lantern light in the general's window caught his eye as he approached the palace. He recalled her offer: *Should you want any more advice or clarity, I am here.*

A pregnant pause followed his loud knocking, then a chair scraped along the floor. Eras jerked the door open and peered into the hall. Her gaze inched over the blood-drenched man, but her expression remained unreadable. "What happened?"

"I don't know. May I come in?"

She stepped aside and pointed to a chair in front of her desk. She disappeared into the room beyond, returning with a wash basin and towel. "It's cold, but I suspect you won't mind."

Neither spoke while Arman cleaned the worst of the blood from his face and hands. He sat back when he had finished.

"That's not yours, is it?" Her tone was hard enough for the words to not actually be asking.

"I attacked a man tonight. He was drunk. So was I, until the fight sobered me."

She sat on the edge of the desk before him, arms crossed. "Why?"

"He slandered my mother and milady."

"Then I suspect he deserved it. You've been in brawls before, I assume. But you are not here because you fought your first fight. You were at Shadow, so you're not here because you killed your first man." She paused, her eyes narrowing. "Did you kill him?"

"Yes. I don't know. He wasn't moving." He looked down at his hands. They should have been shaking. "I beat him senseless, tore into him with my hands and teeth."

"Your vision blurred. You neither heard your comrades telling you to lay off, nor felt the blows inflicted upon you."

He was too tired to be embarrassed by the relief on his face. "This is normal?"

"It happens to soldiers to a lesser degree. It's a form of battle shock. What happened to you, though, is not normal. Not for a human man. Not for someone with a little bit of different blood in their veins, like me." She tilted her head at him, as if examining a curiosity. "You're not just a Rakos, are you?"

Arman ran a hand through his hair, wincing as it caught in snarls of matted blood. "I've read about the Rakos, general. There is mention of a change, something that makes regular guards more powerful, able to create the monsters I showed you. I am nothing like either. I'm a shadow of what the Rakos used to be." His elation at turning himself to floating smoke was gone, erased by dread and shame. "That book you gave me, it sounds like it was penned by An'thoriend. I was raised on his tales, and we met him twice. If he wrote this, he could have seen what I was. That proves that I'm nothing but a freak."

Eras shrugged. "An'thor is a dear friend, but not always present." She fixed Arman with her level stare. "There are some Rakos that were older, stronger, and they had a name. They were called Earth Shakers."

"Those are the monsters, the things the Rakos created."

Eras's expression softened. "No, Arman, they didn't create them. They became them."

Arman stared out the window thoughtfully. "General, could the Earth Shakers fly?"

Her brows twitched upward. "Why, can you?" When he did not answer, she sighed. "Lady Lyne'alea is unlike anything this world has seen. I wouldn't be surprised if she woke far more than the Rakos in your blood." She offered him a faint, sad smile. "One more thing for you to study."

Arman barked a laugh, the sound foreign in a throat raw from snarling. "If I didn't know better, I'd think you enjoyed tormenting me."

"Someone has to. You need guidance, Arman, and tonight only proves that. Everyone is too worried of what Lyne'alea's power would do if unchecked. I worry just as much about yours."

"Well, with a name like Earth Shaker, it's a small wonder." He looked down at his boots. "If I killed him, what will happen? There were enough people in that bar to know it was me. There's no running."

"I think given the circumstances, it will be all right, but be ready. I'll ask around and let you know in the morning."

He nodded and finished his drink. After a moment he looked up. "Do you think I'll ever go back to being simply Arman?"

"I can't say, but I'd imagine it would be difficult." She poured him a glass of water from a pitcher. "The road back home is often long and harder than we remember. Why do you ask?"

"After this, how would I go back to being a smith? An innkeeper's son? To being Veredy's husband? I'm not sure I want to, and that terrifies me."

Eras coughed on her own drink. "You were married? I must have seriously misread your relationship with Lady Lyne'alea."

"Not exactly. I was ready to ask my girl to wed. I was mid-speech when Alea discovered she was the Dhoah' Laen and started screaming in my mind. Awkward, that. I think Veredy misread things, same as you."

Eras leaned back. "Would I be prying to ask if things have changed?"

Arman laughed. "Perhaps, but I know as little as you. I thought we were friends for a long time. Now I'm not sure. Milady is complicated on the best of days." He finished his drink and rose. "Thank you, for talking."

Eras did not look up and her voice was soft. "If you care for my advice, I'll say that war changes people in unexpected ways. Times like these, even the hardest hearts break. Comfort never hurts."

Arman paused in the doorframe. "What about your hardened heart?" It was something he had not considered before. "Do you have comfort?"

"Now Earth Shaker, that is prying."

He answered her grin with one of his own and ducked out of her room. Her words had calmed his racing thoughts somewhat, but his body still stormed with confusion and adrenaline. The heat marched up his skin, leaving annoying prickles in its wake. He locked his bedroom door and rang for water to be pumped into his bath. He stripped down, grateful that a network of pipes averted the need for servants to bring water personally. The solitude suited his thoughts, and it would further damage his reputation to be seen covered in someone else's blood.

He scratched absently as he waited for the tub to fill. The skin of his shoulders flaked away, coating his fingers with metallic gold-white flakes. He frowned and backed up to the privy mirror to get a better look. His skin peeled back from the hard plates emerging from his shoulders. His heart pounded in his ears. *Scales.*

Φ

The 30th Day of Lineme, 1252
The Isle of Le'yne

The music was no tune she recognized. Athrolan's ball room was decorated for a celebration, though the room itself was deserted. It was spring. Her black dress was Athrolani, but the layers were Sunamen. A circlet of leaves held back her hair. Warmth blossomed on her back and she turned. Arman's boots were silent on the stone. He was dressed in white, his tunic stitched with gold. He smiled broadly and he offered her his hand.

"I thought you didn't dance."

"You've heard the tales – everyone dances at the end."

She whirled about with him, the music sounding like laughter in her ears. A breeze lifted her hair. The ballroom was gone and they were surrounding by ancient trees. Their clothes were simple now and their feet bare. What she could see of her hair was laced in silver.

Lines surrounded Arman's eyes — lines from years of laughing. "What do you want?"

The ballroom reformed and he was the youthful man she remembered again. "Is it this?"

She shook her head, heart pounding. "I want peace."

His expression melted into one of sorrow, his cheeks hollowing as his body aged, died, decomposed before her eyes. Still, he spoke, through broken teeth and desiccated lips. "Alea, people like you can't have peace."

She burst awake, the room cloying is its stillness. She needed air. She scrambled from her sheets and across her room, leaning out the window. Deep breaths of the cold air calmed her nerves and her heart steadied. She palmed her eyes against tears. *What was that?*

She pushed herself through her soulblood, using her confusion as an amplifier for her power. She reached out to Athrolan, raging in desperation. She found Arman easily. His soul's colors were brighter, almost blinding. He was in the slums and she moved closer until her mind walked beside him. A few soldiers were with him, joking with one another.

"Come on, Sousa – I doubt that tailor will appreciate you watering his storefront." Arman turned to the straggler standing at the corner of a building.

Alea gasped. His face was inches from hers. Heat rolled from his skin.

He frowned, reaching out. His hand hovered by her cheek and she leaned her head into his touch. His palm passed through her and her heart ached.

I'm here, Arman. I'm right here. Fates, look at me! Hear me!

Arman shook himself and turned back to his friends.

Dammit, Arman! I need you! She fell to her knees as he walked away, a new frown wiping the mirth from his face. She faded back into her body in Le'yne. Her tears returned. It was not practice that she lacked. Something about him was different.

She frowned. She used her power each time she reached out to Bren or Arman. Despite the command to not practice her power, she had, and done so with complete control. She had brought Arman back and it had not destroyed the Athrolani camp. Her eyes were wide in the dark. *When it stays in my body, I am in control.* Her heart hammered with excitement.

She jerked the door open to find Elle in the hall, hand raised to knock.

Elle blinked, startled. "Yes?"

"I realized something. Why were you knocking?"

Elle shook her head at the offered seat. "Elai decided." Her voice tightened. "They plan to bind you."

Alea frowned. She did not know the term, but foreboding crept up her spine. "Tell them not to – I found a way to control my power, just now, that's what I wanted to see you about."

"They won't believe you."

"What's a binding?"

"A mental cauterization. A permanent separation of your power from your soulblood."

Nausea rolled in Alea's stomach. She began to pace. "They want to cripple me. They cripple me and the gods will win." The whirling and planning and panic were familiar.

Comfort dissolved into danger, into the drive to fight or flee. This was the road all over again. *Except, now it's not the Miriken who want you destroyed, it's the Laen.* "I may be a monster, but only monsters kill gods, right?" She glanced up at Elle, her eyes burning.

Elle nodded an answer to the unasked question. "Ready yourself. Read as much as you can, center your mind. They will do it at sundown. I'll help you run before then." Her hands trembled and she grabbed Alea's hand, the first contact they had ever made.

Alea looked down at their hands. "How do you know they're wrong?"

"You destroyed our wall and carved your symbol into the largest stone. That is an obvious statement. I think you were wrong that your power does what it wants. It is your will at its purest state. The connection between your will, your mind, and your power is where your greatness lies."

Alea turned and began to pack. "What time is it?"

"Not yet midnight."

"Go, before they figure this out. I'll see you in the morning." When Elle had gone, Alea sat, eyes vacant. An hour passed. When every light in the village was dark, she rose and crept out of the house. Her bare feet burnt with cold as she padded across the gravel and down to the library. The door opened with a soft creak. *Whatever I'm looking for will be old, older than writing, older than thought.* She walked along the shelves until she found the wax and clay tablets. Her eyes scanned the frames fruitlessly.

"You'll not find it, my lady." Mera stood in the rear doorway, her robe loose over her nightdress.

"I don't even know what I'm looking for."

"You want to discover what you are – beyond Creation and Destruction."

"Is there an answer?"

Mera shrugged. "There is always an answer. You are asking whether it lies here or not." She turned and stepped into the small room at the back. "Come here."

Alea followed. The room was tidy. A long desk looked out over the ocean and flashing sky. A stack of blank tomes sat on one side, full ones on the other. "You record?"

"And re-write, if the scrolls are crumbling. There is so much knowledge to be saved." She drew the full tomes towards her. "The first Laen were good about recording. They had a strong connection to the balance that our power stems from. Granted, they all used a single, combined source, as opposed to the finite spring within each of us now. They were like you, in that way. The energy of the world was represented by the three races – the Laen of balance, the gods of knowledge and the Rakos of chaos."

"Where did they all come from?"

"I couldn't say. Many think it was lightning – it is still the only thing that can destroy our power along with our bodies."

Alea winced. "That is how they killed Lynelle."

"They channeled the power of all the gods through the god of lightning, Lord of Storms." She waved the thoughts away. "Enough." She patted the cover of a heavy tome. "The Laen predicted events based on shifts in the world's energy, like a sailor predicting the sea. The world had its own balance, one with greater dips and crests than our power. A huge dip predicted the Division, though they did not know what it would actually be until too late. A swell and an instability predicted you." She handed Alea the tome. "In here there is the war, its outcome and what comes afterward. There are no interpretations, for that is not what we do. That is for you to decide."

Alea regarded the book. "They don't want me to see this?"

"They do not know it exists." Mera rose and stretched. "I leave my study unlocked and goodness knows you must have trouble sleeping."

Alea laughed softly at the fabricated story. She glanced down at the book in her lap, running a hand over its cover.

Mera paused at the door. "Once you know something, you cannot un-know it. I give this to you because you need to know, but I am sorry."

Alea was left alone with her thoughts and a book that grew heavier on her lap. With determined fingers she opened it on the desk before her. At first she did not know what she was looking at. There was a horizontal line across the page with peaks and dips, some more severe than others and some barely a twitch of a scribe's hand. It looked like the charts her ihal's accountant made of profits over years. She peered closer, realizing it was similar, but it mapped power. She had expected something more convoluted, dry paragraphs perhaps. She traced the line with her finger, reading the captions beneath significant changes that had already occurred.

Towards the end she found a ragged dip that continued on for pages. The sight made her heart ache. *The Division of the world.* The corresponding crest on the opposite page made her pause for a moment. It was not as great as the Division, but it was larger than she expected. She had known her power was great, but seeing it stark and obvious was uncomfortable. A rough, ceaselessly changing line followed and Alea's stomach clenched. *Chaos. The war ends in chaos. We lose.* Heart in her throat, she turned the last page. There was another crest, three times the size of her own, larger even than the Division's fall. It trailed off into the binding of the book.

Energy flooded her body and she stared, unseeing at the ocean beyond the window. It was almost dawn. *Whatever happens in the war, there is an after. I might lose to the gods, I might win, but what comes after is more powerful than I could ever hope to be.* Her lips curled in a feral grin and she closed the book.

CHAPTER SEVEN

The 30th Day of Lineme, 1252
The City of Mirik

TWO DOZEN PAIRS OF EYES stared at Bren. It was something he would have to grow accustomed to, he supposed. The older and more influential of the Kit crowded into what looked like a common room. The smell of ale and dead rats confirmed Bren's suspicion that it was once a tavern. The faces before him were ruddy and worn, but fire burnt behind their eyes. He grinned. It was as if he looked into a broken mirror to see a hundred reflections of himself.

"I suppose you're curious. Arik said you were willing to hear me out, and I hope he's right. I gave him a passage to read, from this book." He held up *Rauld*. "It talks of an oligarchy—a government of a few men, rather than one king. They answer to many ministers who represent factions of the people. I imagine it's much how you rule yourselves now."

He had their attention, but he needed more than passing interest. "For a monarchy, it's dangerous stuff. For me, it's the brick for a foundation. For you, I hope it's an answer. Arik tells me I'd have your support should I wish to claim the crown. I'm asking you to join me in governing ourselves. I am a soldier, a military officer. I understand times of war. I would accept the role of acting king as head of the Miriken military. After the war I would step down to rule alongside others. Rauld calls these men Premiers, but that sounds daft to me."

"And why is this better than being ruled by Athrolan?"

Bren peered into the crowd. The lanterns at his feet blinded him to the farthest rows. "Tzatia is not Miriken. She is full of rolling fields and white stone. She does not have the green at her back. She has never stood on the red cliffs and looked out over the open ocean. Call me poetic, but we need someone who knows what we are."

"Why won't you take her up?" This time it was Arik who asked.

Bren met his eyes. Whether the question was curiosity or accusation, he could not say. "Azirik killed this city with the crown on his head. He burnt the soul out of the world with another. Perhaps it's time that we go without one." He glanced from face to face. He did not see smiles, but he saw relief. He had their hearts. "Arik, how many are in Talic, across the island?"

"Three score, ruled by the governor's nephew."

"Send word to them, and to those in the green, call our people home."

A young woman leaned forward. She dressed like a hunter. "Who should we say calls them, then?"

"Say their Military Commissioner is acting king, and he needs them." He knew his hands shook, knew his voice was low, and there were no rafters from which it could ring. A king might need steady hands, a booming speech. He smiled. He was not a king. He was Miriken, and he was home.

Φ

The Isle of Le'yne

Alea stood on the steps of Le'yne's deserted hall. An hour separated her from the dim light that passed for dawn. Alea brushed a hand over the wood of the door. *Elle said we would not enter here until after the war.* Nightly wanderings in places she was not allowed was a childish habit, but persistent. *War is already here, even if they cannot hear the clashing.*

She pushed the door open, surprised when it was not locked. The Laen did not need to hide things from one another, only from her. The air within the hall was still, but not stale. The exterior was plain. *What were you expecting – they dress in gray.* The single elaborate piece was the black wooden door at the opposite end of the hall. Silver and iron spirals inlaid the wood. Some had been treated to look iridescently blue, like a beetle's wings. The design was too regular to be decorative, but too asymmetrical to be artwork. *A language, then.* What it said was lost on Alea, but she recognized the emblem in the center. It was a silver handprint. It was not inlaid metal, rather it had been burnt into the wood. Her fingers shook as she laid her own hand over the mark.

Nothing happened. She let out a wry laugh. She shook away the thought of saying the words around the door. That was too theatrical for the Laen. They focused on directness and a single path. A grin blossomed on her face and her power curled from her hand. It did not sweep across the door's surface. Instead she forced each piece to follow the metal symbols. Sweat beaded across her brow and shoulders.

The click of the lock was soft and the door swung open. The stairwell beyond was dark, but the steps were smooth and broad. Alea's bare soles whispered on the stone as she descended. Something tugged her memory, but she could not place it. Was it the smell of the air? She stumbled when the stairs ended abruptly. It had taken many minutes, long enough that Alea guessed she was at the base of the cliffs. A gust of wind hit her as she stepped through the doorway into blinding light. It smelled of salt and burnt skin.

The pulsing sphere of souls looked different than before. To her physical eyes, without her power, they were blinding, the colors lost in brightness. The black wound across the surface was knit with blue, bruise-colored lines radiating outward like gangrene. She did not regret her choice to bring Arman back. There was guilt there, surely, but it was not for what she had done to the bleeding souls hanging before her now. For them, she only had disdain.

"Why?" Behind her Elle's voice was low, tinged with as much morbid curiosity as fear.

"Why did I do this?" Alea did not look away, merely turned her head to speak over her shoulder.

"Why did you do it for him? Protection?"

"Bren could have protected me. I can protect myself. I thought it was to repay my part in Arman's death. That's true, in part, but not my reason." Her eyes narrowed on the black, oozing wound. Selfishness marred the heroism and further darkened the terror of her actions. "I brought him back because I cannot fight this battle without him." It was not the full truth, but it was as close as she dared.

"But why did you leave them like this?"

"What is this place?"

Elle paused, but seemed to see that Alea was only taking a meandering route to her answer, not avoiding the question. "Before the Division this is where we created the Laen. A birthing chamber, if you will. Lynelle trapped the power of the gods' souls here so they might not access it."

"She trapped your power, too. As long as the gods' souls are bound here, the power of the Laen is trapped. Each of you dies and adds to the cage, but that power is gone, caught here." Alea paused. "I ripped them open because you'll need that power."

"The gods will gain power as well."

Alea shrugged. *Whether I win or lose, there will be an after.* "Then I'll handle them."

Elle shuddered. "You said you found a way to control yourself?"

"Every time I lost control it was because my power left my body. When I was attacked in Vielrona it came on its own, killing those men. In the tower when I was captured, it destroyed enemy and ally alike. It ripped all of Arman's knives away from him."

"All his knives? He has many?"

"He has a bandolier of them." Alea frowned at the tangent. "But I took them from him and the distraction caused his death. When I work through it, as if it is a glove over my mind, within my body, then I am in control." Her voice grew soft. "I was going to show you, today." She sighed and rose from her kneeling. "It is almost dawn."

Elle followed her back up the stairs in silence, their footsteps comfort enough. The white light of dawn streamed through the hall's open door. It was just warm enough to burn mist from the dew-drenched steps. Alea stopped at the top, looking down at the crowd of Laen who had gathered there. "Good morning." Alea met Elai's eyes. In the back of her mind, the shadow rose. It built, creeping through her thoughts.

"Lyne'alea, what are you doing here?" Elai's face was calm, her eyes almost compassionate. It made it difficult to hate her, and Alea realized she should not, actually, hate the woman.

"I was curious." The road between hate and respect, however, was a long one. "You've come to bind me?"

Behind her, Elle sucked in a sharp breath. "Lyne'alea."

She ignored her mother, eyes narrowing on Elai. *She believes violating my soul is what's best.* "Well?"

"You are dangerous, Lyne'alea. The sooner we mend you, the sooner you can recover and begin to learn properly."

Alea scoffed. "You want to know why I am here, standing on these stairs, unsurprised by this misunderstanding, this betrayal? Beneath our feet is a ball of battered, bleeding souls. Souls Lynelle trapped there in her desperate attempt to save you. She had little time so she panicked. I'm here to remedy what she has done. Beneath our feet there lies an answer, a fact, a task that only I can complete. And yet you wish to cripple me."

"You must not use your emotions as a conduit. They are unpredictable. Your mother only felt the barest emotions for your father, and look at the mess it created."

Alea felt the tense grimace on her face melt into a manic smile. "Exactly! Look at the mess! She bore a powerful son who defied Azirik himself and a daughter that can defeat gods and bind the world together. That's a damn foul mess! I can control my power and I'll die before I let one more person play gods with my life. I am Creation and Destruction." The shadow stalked forward, blotting out every last bit of serenity from the past few hours.

She stepped down from the hall, her grin broadening as the Laen back away. Hands raised, her icy power hit the sky.

"I am the Dhoah' Laen. You cannot separate one from the other." She ripped the lightning from the sky, pulling it into herself until she glowed through the black tendrils that writhed across her skin. The energy tingled, sizzled along her nerves. The lightning radiated from her, sparking off stones and buildings and scorching the grass beneath her. "You will not bind me. I am the Dhoah' Laen. *This is not a piece of me!*"

With the final sentence, she let the lightning crackle back through her body and into the clouds. The black curls retreated from her skin and the glow faded from her eyes. Power retreated until she once more looked like herself. She would never be simply Alea again. She read raw terror on the faces before her. Underneath the fear, however, was respect, and utter faith. "If you plan on fighting the gods, ready yourselves, because I am going to war."

Without another word she climbed towards the hills, the Laen parting like waves before the prow of a ship. Elle caught up with her at the slate slab. Alea looked over. "I'm sorry for what I did, but there was no choice."

Elle reached out, tucking a loose strand of hair behind Alea's ear. "They will thank you one day."

Alea laughed humorlessly. "Then you and I have different ideas of how this will end."

"They will need time to prepare."

"They have it. There are a few things I'll need to do before I confront the gods. Thankfully there is only their Crown left." Her battered fingers rubbed one temple absently.

Elle winced. "I'm afraid not. We had ours decades ago — centuries even — but it wound up in Claimiirn. The story of how that happened changes with each telling I'm afraid."

"Claimiirn?" Alea frowned. *Where have I heard that name before?* She remembered a different voice, gravelly with fatigue and lilting over the double "i" like a brook over stones in spring. "That's the old Athrolani capital, correct? I thought it fell before the House of Xain rose to power."

"It did. An'thoriend's brother sacked the place. Said it did no good having men so close to their lands. Not a pleasant man, Edrodene."

"You're telling me no one has bothered to find the damn thing before now?" She shook her head. "When I'm done, I'll find it myself."

Elle's eyes sparkled. "Seems the only way to get anything done with us, eh?"

Alea paused, looking up at her mother a moment. There was a tone there that she had not heard before. There was a fire, a rebellious edge that she recognized from her own rants to the Laen. She grinned abruptly, a real grin that would have fit better on her face a year ago. "Thank you."

"Stay safe—you and Brentemir."

Alea looked down. "Remember this day. Remember the faith you have right now." She stepped back on the stone slab and met Elle's eyes. "Soon it will be sorely tested." The air crackled as it swallowed her whole.

THE COLD AND QUIET
ACHE OF DUTY

CHAPTER EIGHT

The 31st Day of Lineme, 1252
The City of Mirik

ODDLY, MEETING WITH HELONIN seemed less important to Bren. He rapped on the mariner's doorframe, peering into the room. Helonin regarded his tea dispassionately. "Enter."

Bren stepped in and gestured to the chair across the desk. "Good morning, sir. Might I sit?"

"Ah, Barrackborn. Of course." He sat back, fixing Bren with a frown. "I thought you were going with the men to work on the temple district."

"That is why I came to talk to you, actually. No further work is to be done on the palace. I will need access to the treasury documents as well as its funds."

"Excuse me?" The frown turned into anger and impatience.

Bren knew Helonin had little opinion of him. To the mariner, Bren was only a hard worker and occasionally insubordinate. The latter scarcely applied when Bren's true superiors were the enemy.

"What grounds do you have to halt building? This is Her Majesty's outpost. Barring her word —"

"With all due respect, sir, Mirik is my home, not an outpost." He rested a hand on the desk, allowing the signet ring to knock against the wood. "The word of her acting king should suffice." It was barely an admittance, but when he met the mariner's eyes, he saw it was enough.

Helonin's expression softened. Puzzlement furrowed his brow now. "You said 'acting' king. Care to explain?"

"I am Mirik's Military Commissioner. Given this is a time of war, I am acting king until the threat passes, at which time I will rule with equal power as the other Lord Commissioners."

"And they are?"

"When we've determined that, I'll be sure to let you know." Bren grinned wearily.

Helonin laughed, shaking his head. "I do not envy you. What more do you need of me, my lord?"

"I'll take passage on a ship to Athrolan next week. I think Her Majesty will want an explanation in person."

"Wise man. Perhaps this little land is not doomed after all. I'll have the treasury documents sent to your room, and I'll draw up the orders to cease work." He tossed a heavy bag onto the desk from a drawer. "This is what we've been using for the work, and comes from your funds." After a moment he met Bren's eyes and held out his arm. "I wish you luck, my lord. You will need it."

Bren ducked out of the man's office, lightheaded as the knots in his stomach unraveled. He was halfway to the bell tower when the squire burst from the woods. The boy almost tripped in his haste as he dashed into the courtyard. Bren's eyes narrowed. He watched the boy pant out his message to Helonin, who pointed to the tower.

Bren turned back, reaching the open area by the harbor at the same time as the boy and raised a hand. "What is it?"

"She's back, sir."

Bren's eyes widened and he glanced at the woods. He did not need to ask which woman was in question. "When?" His heart pounded.

"She'll be here in an hour. Kit from the green sent word."

By the time the words were out of the boy's mouth, Bren was already running. He called a hasty thanks over his shoulder as he bolted toward the trees. *She's home. She's back.* How much his world had changed in just a year would always amaze him. He reached the hill after half an hour of steady jogging. The old muscles that knew how to march for days were slow to wake, but they remembered their task well.

He finally caught sight of her as he crested the hill. He had thought he would embrace her, laugh his relief for her return, babble about the change of his role and Mirik's future. Instead he stopped. The damp loam was quiet under his heavy boots. She was not the person who left a few months ago. She had been a girl, excited and impatient and angry. He barely recognized that girl's features in this woman's face. "Alea?"

She glanced up, a smile lighting her tired eyes. "Bren."

"You're home." He did not even dare to shift weight from one foot to another.

"I'm home." The ache and darkness in her eyes was fathomless. She swallowed slowly, as if past the lump of everything she had yet to do. "I missed you."

"I missed you too. Somewhere along the path we became siblings, it seems."

She broke into a run and collided with him. Her arms wrapped tightly around his body. "I missed a lot."

He held her for several minutes, chin resting on the top of her head. Cold control radiated from her, drawing gooseflesh from his skin. *She's done it.* "War, then?"

"War."

"Come on. Let's get you settled." He pulled away and moved down the path toward Mirik.

She laughed. "I'm certainly not attacking the gods on an empty stomach." She fell into step beside him. "How fairs Mirik? Last I heard you were upset with the queen's treatment of her."

Bren grinned. "A lot has changed, sistermine. I couldn't face Mirik falling any further, but neither could I really accept the role of king. I'm a fair reader, and one of the more interesting tomes I encountered is called *Rauld's Tales for an Officer.* He had a great mind for strategy, and after retiring from the army, became a philosopher. Do you know of him?"

Alea nodded. "He wrote *To Give the Poor Man a Crown.* It was an essay my foster-father loved."

"I don't know of that one, but I'll have to find a copy. He developed a proposal for a government without a king, ruled by a few men."

"An oligarchy."

He glanced at her curiously. "You are better versed in government than I expected."

She shrugged. "I enjoyed it more than history." She grinned suddenly, and he saw more of Azirik in her than before. "Shall I guess? You've made Mirik's government into one."

"I did." The initial numbness had faded into both terror and excitement. He turned them onto the worn cobbled road that led down to the city and barracks. "For now, I am acting king. This is a time of war, and I am the current Military Commissioner. Perhaps, when things have settled, I will step down."

"No you won't."

He glanced at her sharply. "What do you mean?"

"They love you. You may not be king, but doing away with the crown does not erase the feeling that you are their monarch." She squeezed his hand as they approached the barracks' gate. "But what you have done, I think, will be greater than any harm Azirik caused."

Bren snorted. "Your optimism is frustrating."

"Why, because you think we'll all die?"

"No, because you have faith in people, and I can't see why. Yet, half the time, you're right." He paused at the gate, catching sight of Helonin waiting. "Alea, this is —"

Alea brushed aside the introduction and stepped forward. "I am Dhoah' Lyne'alea."

The mariner bowed over her hand. "Welcome. I am Mariner Helonin. I can prepare a room for you. Will you be staying long?"

"I'm afraid not. A room would be lovely, but please excuse me, there are things I must discuss." She offered him a fleeting nod and moved past. Stunned silence filled her wake.

Bren's incredulous laugh bubbled free when they entered the hall to his room. "You just dismissed a mariner of Athrolan's navy. Without a thought. What, by Toar, did they teach you in Le'yne?" He unlocked his room quickly, letting her in before closing the door.

A smile flickered over her mouth. "Little, other than history, and exactly how impatient I can be. Their choices forced me to learn much, even if it was not the intention." She sank onto his bed with a sigh. "I've rested little, but I'm too full of adrenaline to sleep."

Bren leaned back in his chair, frowning. "Did you argue? I didn't expect you back yet."

"Our opinions differed." She picked at the skin around her fingers, luminous eyes narrowed. "They thought my power should be split from my soulblood."

Bren scoffed. "See, I knew I disliked them for a reason." He adopted a high-pitched voice. "There is a chance we could win. Let's make a mess of it!"

Alea smiled at the mimic. "They're single-visioned, that's all. I had to resort to fear to make them listen, which was unpleasant." She glanced out the window. "Have you gone to Athrolan to talk to Her Majesty about your new government?"

"No. I have yet to even write her."

Alea's brows rose. "You've dismantled her control and reformed Mirik's government without even notifying her? Surely Helonin said something."

"He didn't know until today." He drew the letter Tzatia had sent and tossed it to his sister. "This is what forced my hand. She called me out."

Alea scanned the letter. "Perhaps when I go to Athrolan you could join me, do some of your reforming there."

Bren nodded. "I was thinking of it, but I want to meet her from a point of strength, and I'm not sure I have it yet."

"Will you ever think you do?" Alea smiled at him. "For one so capable, brothermine, you have little confidence." She masked a yawn and rose. "As much as I said I couldn't sleep, I've had quite the few days and ought to at least try. Who knows when our next respite will come?"

He led her further down the hall to the finer rooms. Sure enough, one of the doors was propped open, the bed inside neatly made and a pitcher of fresh water waiting on the nightstand. Alea turned back to him. "I'm glad to be home."

He embraced her again, the tingle of power crawling up his arms from where they touched. "I'm glad you're back. Rest well. I might be working or in the mess when you wake, but the men will know where to find me."

Once she bid him a quick goodnight and closed the door, he returned to his room. A new letter waited on his desk. There was no sender's name on the envelope, only his new title and full name. He unfolded it curiously.

> *Barrackborn,*
> *Much has changed since I last spoke with you — for us both, it seems. I heard you speak the other day, in the Kit's hall. Quite the pair you've got, reforming Azirik's government while he still wears the crown. You're a better man than I expected.*
> *I hoped that sometime this evening we might speak. Send a response via Oland. He knows where to find me.*
> *Until then,*
> *An'thoriend Domariigo*

Bren stared at the letter for a moment then burst out laughing. *Alea's home, I'm acting king, Arman is developing power, and now the legend himself crawls from hiding.* He shook his head and rose to find some ale. Writing a response needed drink as much as their cause needed legends. *It's only fitting heroes emerge before battle. Toar knows we'll need them before the end.*

Φ

The 31st Day of Lineme, 1252
The City of Ceir Athrolan

Arman had yet to leave his room during normal hours. Late in the evening he escaped to the library, when he was certain Kal and Sousa were safely in a bar. Hasian had lived, though it was a week before the man could return to his soldier's duties. He could only see shadows through his left eye and his shoulder was too greatly injurred for him to lift his arm higher than his chest. Arman had yet to hear from the queen or the general about any consequences, but he was smart enough to know he was far from safe.

Most assumed it was shame that kept him closeted in his room. He let them assume. His anger had not subsided. For a week it raged, his skin slowly peeling back to expose the marble-like plates. He paced his room now, eyes flicking from the window to his desk, to the door. A small stack of papers sat on the desk, but he was in little mood to read missives. Spotting a stained envelope, he tugged it free. Bren's greeting was as carefree as ever.

> *Arman,*
> *I miss the taverns already, though my head does not miss the morning ale-sick. I hope your studies are going well. I feel like we've been holding our breath and are about to dive. Maybe I'm just tired of waiting. I'm a soldier, not a mason.*

> *It's good that Alea's learning more, even if she feels*
> *it's not what she should be studying.*

Arman frowned at that, and peered closer to the letter.

> *This waiting business is certainly helped by hearing*
> *from her every so often, even if her mind connections are*
> *faint and the conversations short. I suppose she talks to*
> *you more than me. Has she said anything about coming*
> *home?*
> *Until then,*
> *Bren*

Arman's fist clenched until the paper crumpled. He did not notice the edges smoldering in his hand until the black ashes drifted to the ground. *She goes to him and not me?* It was not that she spoke to Bren. The prejudice toward one another was all but gone. It was the fact that she confided in someone else. *Who protected her?* Anger welled in him. *Who died for her?* His breath shuddered. He had never been this angry. He grabbed his cloak and strode out of the palace before he destroyed something. *You think you can run off and leave me, without a word, and expect me to forget you?*

His steps were certain on the cobbled street leading to the loudest bar the soldiers frequented. Kal and Sousa were among the crowd at the back. He averted his eyes and found a secluded seat. He did not want conversation. He wanted to forget. A distant voice reminded him that it was not really Alea that angered him, but his own cowardice. He hated that he had yet to be honest with her, hated that he had treated her like a child. *And apparently, too little, too late.* He finished his first mug of fire ale.

Kal perched on a stool across from Arman after a few moments. "Wasn't sure it was you, at first. Glad to see you out." He frowned. "You look ticked."

Arman sneered at the man. "Just need a bit of drink."

"I thought the general told you not to drink, said it was part of your warning from the queen." Sousa sat on the edge of the table.

"You're a pecking hen, Smytheson. Everyone needs a drink and a tup."

Kal shot Sousa a look at the unusual vulgarity. "Have you taken lessons from Hasian ?"

Arman voice rumbled. "Leave me be. I'm no company tonight."

Kal shrugged finally, and returned to his table. After a few failed attempts at conversation, Sousa followed.

Arman was nursing his third mug when a hand touched his knee. It was a barmaid who often worked there, but her dark curls were loose and her dress nicer.

"I don't often see ye apart from yer friends."

He gave her a fleeting smile and turned back to his mug.

"Yer lonely."

He shrugged, taking another sip.

"You have been here awhile yet." She gestured to the stool beside him. "May I join you?"

He shoved his own seat down to make room for her, more out of politeness than interest.

She smiled nonetheless. "Ye didn't come around before a month ago. Did ye just join up? They respect you an awful lot."

"I joined the war last year." He wondered absently how she did not know the story.

She leaned back against the bar. "Has anyone told ye that ye look like the Rakos guard?"

He laughed, then realized she was serious. *No wonder she treats me like a man. She knows no better. Nor was she here when I fought Hasian.* "I've heard that a few times. Most say he's taller though." It was not strictly a lie. The thought that he was normal again, even just for a moment, made his heart light. "You're not working tonight?"

"No, it's Mara's night." She grinned. "Care to buy me a honey ale?"

Arman motioned the girl who must have been Mara over and ordered before returning his attention to his companion. "Were you raised here?"

"Just to the west, in the city's villages. I'm one of five daughters, so we each make our own way." Her mug arrived and she took a sip. "Did you come from a large family?"

"No. I helped my Ma run her inn and took over my father's blade-smithy after he passed."

Her eyes widened. "I cannot imagine losing my Ma or Pa." she tilted her head. "Ye crafted blades? Fighting must come naturally."

He shrugged. "I have a hand for knife-throwing and foot combat." He turned toward her a bit more. She was lively and curious, kind if not very bright. "I'm not a killing man, though. I prefer a good celebration—my city loved her festivals."

"Ye had many?"

"One for every forgotten season and some just because we felt like it and others out of habit." His smile was slight, but it felt good. "Does Ceir Athrolan have many?"

"Just the first of the seasons and midwinter and midsummer. We celebrate the first planting and the harvest. Mostly they are for the common folk, thought the palace needs little reason for a ball or feast. Tell me about yers?"

He thought for a moment then leaned closer. His hands waved, as if painting an image of Vielrona with his gestures. "The city is small, tucked into the hills, but every festival the streets are awash with lights. During midwinter we light a lantern for every person we loved and lost. The entire city glows and there is singing and dancing." He explained his favorite details. She bought him his next drink, and he hers until she laughed at each extravagant story. He could almost forget why he had decided to drink.

"Care to catch some fresh air?" Her offer was sudden.

He helped her into her cloak, though the air was warm. They moved further into the city, walking aimlessly. The moon was high in the sky and shed bright light across the quiet streets. It could not have been much past midnight, but the streets were deserted. "You should go south sometime, see the midwinter festival yourself."

She shivered and he absently put an arm around her shoulders, rubbing her arm.

At a street corner she paused, turning to face him. "Ye have a woman to go home to?"

He froze, suddenly realizing where he was and what he was about to do. *You'll never have Alea. This girl is here and willing.* "I've not had a woman in a long while."

"Ye can tonight, if you want."

You're just a man tonight. You have no future with Alea. He tightened his grip on her hand and lowered his mouth to hers. She kissed him once, twice, then lead him up the stairs of the building on the corner. It was a boarding house and her room was small. A single window overlooked the rear alley. Her bed was against the left wall and neatly made.

She stirred the small stove and lit a candle by the bed before stepping into his arms. She was modestly curved and her hands were knowing as they moved up his back and over his shoulders.

He returned her smile and wrapped his arms around her waist, trailing his lips down her neck. She smelled of hazelnuts and her warmth comforted and wounded him all at once. He pulled back and kissed her softly. She backed towards the bed and tugged off his jerkin. The familiar jolt of heat and attraction did not shoot through him. He felt no flush on his cheeks. *It's been too long – almost a year! I need to remember the steps.*

He pulled off his shirt and lay down atop her, propping himself on his elbows to kiss her again. He pulled back to look at her and she smiled. He distantly noticed her eyes were gray green. *Almost silver.* He pushed the thought away and moved to touch her again, but stopped. His body refused to respond. *She's beautiful, and yet my body is as moved as if I'm learning arithmetic.* He nuzzled her neck, willing himself to react, but to no avail. He sighed roughly.

"Are ye all right?"

He closed his eyes, his jaw working. "I don't think I can do this."

"What is it?"

He rolled off her and sat on the edge of her bed.

"Someone is in yer heart?"

He nodded, holding his head in his hands. "I'm sorry. You're a beauty and I would have been glad to be with you." Her hand froze on his shoulder and he glanced back at her.

Her eyes inched over the scars on his chest and the handprint over his heart. She brushed the hair from his eyes. "When we kissed, yer teeth.... Ye don't just look like him, ye are the Rakos." When he nodded she drew back. "The Dhoah' Laen. You thought you could get her out of your blood because we look alike, dark hair and pale eyes."

"Dammit, it's not like that, at least, not on purpose." Arman sighed. *It's not like any human woman could compare.* He knew the words would sound cruel and held his tongue. His eyes flashed yellow and his fist clenched her sheets. Wisps of smoke curled from between his fingers.

Her gaze hardened. "I think you should leave."

He dressed quickly, without looking at her or arguing.

She waited silently until he was at the door. "I'm sorry. Ye seem like ye would make a good lover. I hope she returns your feelings."

He did not answer and let himself out. He bolted to the palace, his mind anywhere but on his steps. He stumbled twice before he forced himself to slow. *This is ridiculous. Who heard of only being able to bed the person you care for?* He shoved his way through his door and fell onto his bed. His eyes stared at the bare ceiling. One hand drew Alea's letter from his desk. It was tattered from myriad readings. Each time the tone seemed different, as if the words conveyed her changing emotions. *Or mine.* He read it again, his fingers clutching the parchment. When the paper singed, he put it away, unwilling to burn it just yet. He had been happy to spend his life beside her as a friend, a guard. Now he wondered if he could stand that. *Who knows what she wants from this life, if she will be able to get it even. Who knows if I will?*

Heat built. The thought of Alea, both plain and with black fog in her silver eyes made his body ache. He closed his eyes tight and drew a shuddering breath. *Fates help me.*

Φ

The 31st Day of Lineme, 1252
The City of Mirik

Alea found better rest in the rumble of Mirik's barracks than in the peace of Le'yne. Her dreams were meaningless and forgotten when she finally woke. She rolled over, peering out the window beside her bed. It was dark and the moon was high. The air smelled of pine and freshly turned earth. She was still tired, but fatigue and hunger were pushed aside by something more pressing. She settled herself on the coverlet and closed her eyes. Her mind reached out to Athrolan.

The mental journey took moments, not minutes. Burning yellow-green blossomed in the depths of the city when she focused. Arman was in a common district boarding house. She arrived in the hall and stepped into the room, passed through the door as if it was nothing.

The room was dimly lit and it took her eyes a second to adjust. When they did, her breath stopped. Arman was in bed, bare-chested, his legs entangled with those of the young woman beneath him. Her dark curls were loose and her bodice partly unlaced. The floor bucked beneath Alea's feet and her chest clenched.

She did not remember returning to her body, only that she was back in her own room. Ice filled her skin. She was not certain what she felt. It was not as simple as jealousy, but she recognized the acrid taste of it in her mouth. Arman accepted her as the Dhoah' Laen before she even did herself. When she retreated behind the high, cold walls of her mind, he stepped casually inside of them. He did not force his way in, with loud words and narrowed eyes. *He's the only one who can step inside my defenses and not be destroyed.* When the world was a mass of confusing, distant muted tones, Arman was a point of brilliant color as real as her thoughts. Her stomach was too tight to eat, but she could not stand to be alone. Her hands fumbled with the breeches and jerkin left for her.

The mess hall was loud and the smell of food and ale strong. The chatter nearest the doorway died as she entered. Her eyes found Bren's, willing him to recognize the plea on her face.

She was grateful he saved his questions until they were shut once again in his room. She curled her feet under her as he lit the lantern on his desk. He sat beside her, frowning. "Are you all right? Do you want food? There's stew and bread. I think the fish is gone, though."

Her fingers knotted in her lap. The strange space between her mind and the world seemed suddenly greater, and even her own voice was muffled by the distance. "Did Arman speak of me at all?"

Bren frowned. "Not to me, not after our first letters. I sent yours, which I assume he received, since he replied to mine. I heard he bruised up a soldier in a bar for insulting you, but the tale did not come from him." He peered at her. "What is it?"

"Defending me is his duty. He said nothing?"

"Alea, he's a quiet man, and private, at least in regards to you. What is this about? Didn't you talk to him like you did to me?"

"I tried, but it's as if there's a wall between us. I could see him, hear him, goodness I could even feel the heat from his skin. Even when I shouted, it was like he barely sensed me. I was like a ghost. I thought I needed practice, then I thought it was because of the distance."

"Sistermine." He took her shaking hands in his own, but her voice stopped his words.

"I tried again, just now. I wanted to tell him I was home. I thought now that I was back, it might work. It didn't, though I didn't wait long enough to say anything. He was with a woman. In bed."

Bren's eyes widened. "What? No, Alea, you must have been wrong. It must have been someone other than Arman."

Her gaze pinned him, blazing angrily. "Bren, our souls are bonded. I can feel him breathing when he's in the next room. I know him." She turned away, anger bitter on her tongue. "Besides, I could see enough skin to recognize his scars." She pressed a hand to her stomach. "I feel ill, but my body is too tense to be sick. I don't know why this hurts. I can't even say if I'm angry."

Anger was fleeting and hot. They had made no promises, and so she knew his actions did not justify anger. She sighed, placing her head in her hands. Her words were direct and calculated. Behind the wall of eloquence she was safe. *Safe from what? Betrayal?* The Laen had betrayed her, she supposed, but neither had she ever truly trusted them. They had never promised not to hurt her. Had he promised to love her? Love only her? "He promised to keep me safe, keep my heart safe. And here, he's the one breaking it."

Bren's brows rose. "Alea, do you love him?"

She shrugged. "Our bond wasn't marriage vows and I know it. When someone is with you each step, helping you as you help them, facing each hardship and joy together, it's easy to forget."

Bren rested his forehead on her shoulder. "I don't know what to say. I didn't expect this. In my last letter I mentioned that it was a relief to hear from you while you were in Le'yne. Perhaps he thought your silence meant you didn't want to speak with him."

She drew a shuddering breath. She was too empty to weep. If she began, it would drain her until nothing remained, but a husk. "I can't be distracted. I will give all I have to the war. Everything else will come afterward."

Bren opened his mouth as if to speak, but a sharp knock sounded at his door. His eyes lingered worriedly on her for a moment, but he rose and opened the door. A squire stood outside, shifting from foot to foot. "Yes?"

"Lieutenant, I mean, Lord Commissioner, sir. There's a man here for you. Says he traveled a long way and you're expecting him."

"Commissioner is fine, Gecken." Bren glanced back at Alea. "Do you mind?

She shook her head absently. Her grief was deep, but contained behind the mighty walls of her calm and power. A simple visitor would not disturb her. "I can go, if you wish."

He waved her words away. "It's about the war, you should hear it anyways." He jerked a nod at the boy still hovering in the doorway, trying to glimpse the Dhoah' Laen.

"Show him up, then, and could you bring tea and mugs?" He sat once the boy was gone and looked back at his sister. "I received a letter from someone claiming to be An'thoriend Domariigo. You said you met him before?"

"Twice. The second time he told me about you, actually. I'm uncertain whether he is obnoxious or impressive."

Bren snorted. "I still don't believe my father's informant is the hero of the stories. The letter asked for a meeting tonight. It's either the legend or a madman."

"There is a statement in there about the lack of difference between the two." Alea offered him a distant smile. Further dark thoughts were interrupted when the squire returned with tea and a cloaked figure in tow. The boy set the tray down on Bren's desk and bowed himself out.

Alea's gaze narrowed on the man in the doorway. The wide cowl of his cloak allowed the lantern to light his pale face, and she noted the wrap around his head was the same as before, albeit further bleached by sun and stained from rain.

Bren rose and introduced himself. "You asked for a meeting?"

"Greetings, Commissioner." The Ageless man's words were rougher than before, as if his voice had walked the road along with his boots. His black eyes flicked to Alea's. Bracing himself against the doorframe with one hand, he slowly took a knee. "Last I saw you, my lady, you were but a promise. Now I look on the realization of every hope we've ever had. How can they think to stand against you?" He hauled himself back up and gestured to the room. "May I, sir?" His words indicated Bren, but his eyes never left Alea's face.

"Certainly." Bren pulled a chair out and began pouring tea.

An'thor unclasped his cloak and folded it and his head wrap over the back of the chair before sitting with a quiet sigh. He took the proffered cup with a nod of thanks and sat back.

Bren's wide gray eyes were fixed on the chipped, stained ivory horns sprouting from the pale man's temples. They were short and curved, like a bull's, barely reaching the crown of his head, but they easily marked him. The open curiosity told Alea her brother had never seen the man without a cowl or wrap before.

His gaze flicked to Bren. "I'm glad to see you were as clever as I hoped. It's not every man I can convince to desert Azirik's army."

Bren pulled a flask from his desk and added a healthy splash of alcohol to their tea. "Azirik did a fair share of convincing me himself, what with the blows and the anger and the threats." Bren waved the memories away and replaced the flask. "We're not here to discuss that, I assume."

An'thor took a deep draught then peered into the cup. "Is this wraith?"

"It is and older than Toar, but good enough for my purposes." Bren fixed the man with a pointed look. "You came here for a purpose, which I assume is better than drinking my liquor. My sister claims you're the An'thoriend of legend, and I know you only as a double-crossing maniac."

An'thor lips quirked. "Both can't be true?"

Bren choked into his drink. "You waltz in here, assuming I'm going to trust my enemy's informant?"

"He's not lying." Alea tilted her head. "This is the man who spoke to us in Vielrona, who told me about you in that wayhouse. He went by An'thor then, too. The Sunamen were not terribly familiar with your tales, but Arman heard a few." His gaze met hers as if over miles, not meters, and she realized his mind was shielded by as many walls as hers. "He bears enough marks of grief for a lifetime as long as An'thoriend's."

An'thor's eyes softened. "As do you, Dhoah'' Lyne'alea." He looked to Bren, one brow quirked. "May I continue, or is her word enough."

Though there was no contempt in the man's words, Bren scowled. "Very well, what did you wish to discuss, Sir Domariigo?"

"An'thor is just fine. I am no lover of honorifics. They make lesser men great. I came north to see what Athrolan was doing with Mirik. I arrived in time to hear you address the Kit. I thought I could ally myself with you. It would benefit us both. Will you hear my proposition?" When Bren nodded, An'thor handed him a parchment from his breast pocket.

Bren scanned it quickly before handing it to Alea. It was a letter with a reply written on the reverse side. The front was from An'thor, asking the addressee's opinions on the war. The reply was abrupt.

> An'thoriend
>
> *I agree it is shrewd for the Ageless to join the war. As king of Neneviir I have already rallied our warriors, though we are fewer than we once were. As always, I weigh the strength of the sides, and the benefits each offers. The choice is clear. You have my approval to approach the new Miriken lord and offer aide.*
>
> *Until battle,*
> *Edrodene*

She looked up. "What do you want from us?"

An'thor ran a scarred finger around the edge of his mug. "I want the Nenev to use their might for something useful, finally." He glanced up. "Honestly, I just want you to win. I'm tired of war."

Alea saw the ache of homesickness in the lines around his eyes. "You want to go back to Athrolan. I remember that tale, how you were banished from the capital."

"Tzatia is a fine queen, but she is scared. The only way I will find my way back into Athrolan is by your side, and I need to return to her. I know that kingdom's voice and she is crying loud and long."

Alea glanced at Bren. "You really aren't certain? Look at him — he protected the Laen for years, chased them across the continent several times at least."

Bren's mouth hardened. "He also informed for Azirik. Forgive me if I can't quite forget that." Bren regarded the Ageless man for a minute. "All right. I'll speak to the Kit."

"They were the first to accept me in Mirik. They brought me to your father." An'thor grinned, the expression making his face a bittersweet mixture of youthful energy and exhausted age.

Alea wondered abruptly how many of them would have the same features before the war was through. "I can entertain him, if you wish to go to the Kit now."

Bren rose. "I hope to leave within the week. Best to iron everything out that we can." He glanced between his two guests. "I won't be gone long."

Alea smiled inwardly. He had not threatened An'thor, or told her it was not safe to sit alone with a man she barely knew. It was a welcome change.

An'thor reached out, placing his hand on the desk beside hers.

It was a gesture so akin to Arman's it made her heart twist. *Will Arman turn into this? A sad shadow of a legend?* She frowned. "What is it?"

"I'm sorry." He looked down. "For my part in where your life has led. Not sorry for my actions, because we need you, but sorry for the pain they caused."

"You did not make me what I am. You may have told me, helped me, but you did not take my family." She leaned forward. "There is something more, An'thor, that you could do for us."

His brows quirked. "Something your brother can't know?"

Alea shrugged. "He has enough to worry after. Besides, it will not be easy, but must be done." She pulled a scrap of parchment from her brother's desk and hastily sketched a ring of metal and stone. She pushed it across the desk's top. "I'm afraid I have no skill at art, that is Arman's expertise."

"Aye, they say those with fire in their minds burn with creativity." His eyes fell to the image.

"It's old, the stones are dark blue sodalite and the metal is iron. It was in Claimiirn. Perhaps it's still there, perhaps it was looted. I need to know if you've seen it."

"I thought the Laen had their Crown."

"Obviously not. It was last seen in Claimiirn before she fell."

"Claimiirn has quite the treasury. It's been ransacked, surely, but if your Crown was found I imagine we'd know. You will search for it?"

"I'll go before the battle. I need to study more, understand the gods."

"When the time comes I will arrange passage for you, if you need it. And I'll keep my words to myself. I passed through the city on my way here. You know Azirik's made it his base camp?"

"It's a risk I must take. Azirik does not scare me."

"I wonder what does."

"I see a sadness in your eyes," Alea's gaze met his, a tenuous connection through the shadow surrounding her thoughts. "A sadness that used to be in mine, before a deeper darkness overtook it. I think you know what scares me."

CHAPTER NINE

The 35th Day of Lineme, 1252
The City of Ceir Athrolan

ARMAN GRINNED AS HE PRESSED back against the wall. His hold on his power was firm. Eras would arrive within a few minutes. She had enquired about his progress and he wanted to show her first-hand his new skills. Sure enough, her knock came. He called for her to enter and glanced down at his body. It was gone. Tucked in the shadow behind his window's curtains, he was invisible.

Eras glanced through the room with a frown. "Arrowlash?"

"Morning, general." He could not keep the impish grin from his voice.

Her eyes narrowed and began to trace each corner and shadow. They barely paused on him. "Are you washing up?" Her hearing was good. His voice had emanated from several paces to the left of his privy door.

"I'm right here, general." He stepped into the shaft of sunlight from the window. He glanced down at his body again. It was nothing more than a dust mote turned golden in the sun's ray. *This power could go to my head*. After a moment he slowly let his power fade from his body. Eras's eyes caught the change and widened as first his bones, then organs materialized. His skin crawled back into view and he met her gaze.

Her years of training and the Asai stoicism held her feet in place, but Arman caught the sudden bittersweet scent of fear. "You become invisible?"

"The eye does not see smoke, not really. I am but smoke drifting on the wind." Fully corporeal again, he spread his arms in a classic player's flourish. "What do you think?"

"I think you're horrifying. I think we can use you." Her eyes flicked to the exposed skin of his forearms. "I think you have something more than smoke up your sleeve."

He followed her gaze to the scales beginning to erupt from his tanned lower arms. "Ah, yes." He rolled his sleeves down.

"You need someone to take a look at that?"

"No. There is nothing a human doctor could do." He looked down. "There is something else I want to show you, but I think it'd be best displayed outside of the city limits."

"I've heard that before, and from men far prettier than you." Her mouth quirked and she jerked a nod at the door. "Shall we?"

Arman's spirits darkened at her jest and he shrugged on his jerkin with more force than strictly necessary. "Apparently my tastes are very narrow, and I regret to inform you that you do not fall within them." He strode down the hall and to the small gate beside the barracks.

Eras shot him a curious glance, but seemed to know better than to prod the testy Rakos. "So what are you showing me? Have you tested the limits of your power?"

Arman shook his head. "Not really, but I did discover something more useful, even than invisibility. You ever watch smoke after you blow out a candle?"

"No wonder you came to Athrolan, if that was your sole entertainment in Vielrona. But I suppose I know what you mean."

"It drifts, it floats. When I'm smoke, I can do the same."

"You can fly?"

He shrugged and ducked under a branch, holding it aside for her as she followed him further up the hill. "I guess." He had been avoiding testing the limits of his power, and was uncertain why. *Milady's power is known — it's beyond true understanding, but it is known to be Creation and Destruction. I, however, am a wild unknown..* He laughed humorlessly to himself. *Fangs and all.* He topped the hill and stepped into the center of the clearing. He noted with sick pride that Eras stayed back along the tree line. The familiar burn and exhilaration of his power filled him with itching and twitching. His body dissolved again, his form rising in white, whirling smoke. He climbed higher and higher, dozens of paces above the hilltop, before calling down. "General!"

She backed up, face tilted to the sky. "Where are you?"

He allowed just his face to reappear, partially fleshed and macabre, but more obvious against the bright blue sky. He grinned. "Up here."

Eras laughed. "You're amazing, truly." Her expression grew stern, the frown a shadow from his high vantage. "But come back down. There is more, more I've read, and more you have not tested."

He sank back to the ground, his anger itching. *Doesn't she know how hard I work?* When he was firmly back on the ground, he crossed his arms. "What do you mean?"

"Arman, you've been avoiding going deeper. Your abilities are phenomenal, surely, but you are Rakos. More than that, you're bonded to the Dhoah Laen. Don't tell me this is all you can do. What are you afraid of?"

"I'm not afraid! I can't do anything more. Not in comparison to her. I know it's nothing, but this is all I am."

She pursed her lips. "No, this is all Arman can do. What about Arrowlash? What about the blood inside you? You think Alea was never afraid of losing control—damn, she did more than once. She still tried."

"I'm not afraid of losing control!" His anger was already roiling. Heat rumbled up his limbs and his nose singed with the smell of forging metal. Coppery fluid filled his mouth as he bit down on the insides of his cheek. *She's trying to help.* The air around his skin rippled with heat and the glade flicked as if under a desert sun. "What's this going to do, general? Make Azirik sweat a bit? Gods won't like a soldier who reeks? Is that it?" The leaves of the closest trees wilted.

"What are you afraid of?"

"I'm afraid of what I'll become. I'm afraid there is no place for what I'll be, in this world, or in hers."

"What have you lost that makes you afraid of that?" Eras backed up further, her eyes wary, but not fearful, not yet. Each word was calculated, and it occurred to him than Eras had trained more soldiers than he could imagine. His powers were different, but the methods were the same.

His eyes squeezed shut. "Her." He felt the sharpness in the air as she tilted her head in a question. "She was able to talk to us, from Le'yne. She spoke to Bren, and never once to me. She left me here with a duty I never once questioned, and didn't even bother to speak to me."

"Arman, she's a complicated creature. She'd be even if she were only human. You know you wouldn't have it any other way. You're afraid of becoming something else — well you have no idea what creature will step off the boat when she returns. You need to be prepared for whatever she has become. You want her to see you as her equal? Become it."

He did not answer. Instead, eyes still closed, he raised his hands. He did what he had warned Alea against and fell into his power. Everything Alea was to him filled his thoughts. *Faith.* He died for her. She had almost done the same to bring him back. *Faith. Complete surrender.* The image of Eana's scarred golden eyes appeared in his thoughts again. *Fear. Find us. Fear.* Arman's power thundered through him, eating through his skin with searing heat. He opened his eyes.

The hilltop was in flames. The trees were black skeletons, his hands white flames. It should have been excruciating, but it was only pleasantly warm. His skin was a network of white-gold scales. He stumbled back. Eras was several paces further into the forest, her forearm raised against the heat and the glow.

His power faded back into his body and the fire around him died to a dull smolder. He crouched and placed his hands on the ground, drawing the blaze into them until it was extinguished. With the threat of forest-wide destruction gone, he glanced down at Eras. "Well?"

She stared at the blackened trees. "What changed?"

"Each step of the way she reminds me what I am, who I always have been, but have forgotten. In Vielrona she was vulnerable. I remembered I was a protector. In her absence, I remembered my anger."

"And now?"

"Faith. I need to surrender myself." He fell back onto the scorched ground, head in his hands.

Φ

The 36th Day of Lineme, 1252

Swelling around Arman's left eye had replaced the stinging of open flesh. The bruises were still obvious, and the green uglier than the initial purple. He was dressing for the training courts when a squire delivered the mail. Atop a letter from Bren was a summons.

> *Regarding your recent behavior, Her Majesty Tzatia requests your presence within the hour.*

Arman's stomach plummeted as he changed haphazardly into a finer set of clothes. Pomp and politics were more Alea's area, but he recognized the importance of this meeting. *The general said I wouldn't be exiled or anything half so dramatic. She said nothing about other consequences.* He raked a hand through his hair and tied it back. It had grown past his shoulders, more an Athrolani style than Vielronan.

The general was leaving when he arrived at the queen's chamber door. Her face was unreadable, but she nodded to him. "It won't take long, I promise."

He watched her go before gesturing for the steward Valadai to announce him. Tzatia was seated on a couch by a bay of windows. Tea sat, half-drunk before her. It was obvious the refreshments had not been brought for his benefit. Her nephew, Daymir, leaned on the broad window-sill, arms and legs crossed. Patience was clearly a familial trait. Arman suddenly wished he had Alea's hand on his elbow, guiding his actions. She'd murmur a soft joke to calm his racing mind and rising temper.

"Arrowlash, thank you for coming." Tzatia leaned forward. "I hope this will go quickly. I already spoke to General Aneral about the events of last week. Quite the advocate you've got yourself there." She sipped her tea, gray eyes flicking to his green ones. "Might I have your own account?"

"Where would you like me to begin, your majesty?"

"The beginning, perhaps?" Daymir's low voice was tinged with humor, but the hard look in his eyes showed it was no joke.

"The soldier crowd was going to the bars, and I accompanied them, as usual. I had a few drinks. It was close to midnight when Hasian spoke out against my Ma and Milady Lyne'alea — "

"Spoke out how?" Daymir asked, "I believe even I have spoken out against Dhoah' Lyne'alea at times."

"Better not have been like this." Arman's voice was steady, but low enough not to be a serious threat. "He said I was a bastard of my mom's paid union and that milady was bedding her way across the kingdom to get allies."

"I don't suppose you could have ignored it?" Daymir heaved a sigh, lips thinned in distaste.

"You ever been drunk, Lord Daymir? Ignoring is not really an option. Besides, I ignored him the last time and he needed a setting-right."

"I don't doubt he needed to be taken down a peg, only your methods for doing so." Tzatia pinched the bridge of her nose with a narrow hand. "You are our ally, and the general explained the situation with your temper. There will still be consequences. Commander Dorcal has a fleet sailing along the Northlands' coastline. There are rumors that the Berrin navy plans to attack us, and that is the way they will come. The general tells me you have some skills that will be helpful in battle, and seems to think you would benefit a sea voyage."

Arman's expression remained aloof, but his mind was scrambling. He felt betrayal at the general's suggestion. *She thinks I can fly alongside the ships? Ignite the enemies' vessels? I've barely discovered these abilities and she wants me to use them in war?* Instead of voicing his anger, he nodded curtly. "Certainly. When do they leave?"

"Less than a month. I will inform Admiral Fess that you will accompany him. He will meet with you separately to discuss details." Tzatia fixed him with a pointed stare. "If you have business here, I suggest you conduct it with discretion from now on."

Arman nodded and bowed himself out. His hands shook as he hurried down the corridor to the general's room.

Φ

Eras rubbed her face wearily. "The trouble is, Raven, I don't think he realizes they're equals. He's too wrapped up in how inadequate he is and he'll hurt anyone who says otherwise."

"I think both of them are insane. No wonder the Rakos died out and the Laen are hunted. They're mad, the lot of them."

Eras rolled her eyes and poured herself two fingers of a dark alcohol. "He won't be happy with me, either, telling the queen and all that."

"Why do you care so much?" His dark eyes narrowed on her. "I'll never understand your softhearted tendencies."

"If you consider me softhearted, Raven, you're the one who is mad. They may not be Athrolani or human or whatever other criteria of yours they don't meet, but they are magnificent. Besides, I needed a mentor when I was lost. Certainly he does, too."

A fist suddenly pounded against the door. "General!"

She shot Raven a pointed look and leaned forward in her chair. "Let him in, will you?"

"If you like ordering people about, get a squire, Eras. I'm a commander not a lackey." Despite his bitter words, he rose and jerked the door open. "What do you want?"

Eras hid a smile at Arman's confusion. The Rakos's face was flushed and she was not in the mood to agitate him further. "Let him in and for fate's sake be civil."

Arman had to step around the commander's bulk to enter, glaring at the man with open distain. His longer hair and beard only punctuated the feral expression.

"Arrowlash, have a seat."

"Have a seat? Do I look like a court dandy, general? You had my confidence." Instead he leaned on her desk, shoulders hunched and head low. It was not a posture of submission, but threat.

It did not work on her. "Arman, this is a monarchy. There is a very long list of people and places I have a duty to and you are certainly in the middle of that list. Her Majesty and Athrolan, however, are much higher." She absently wondered if he would point out that she did not say they were at the top.

He scowled. "Dammit! I've barely mastered my powers and you send me gallivanting out into the north sea."

"I did not send you, Arman, Her Majesty Tzatia did. Would you rather she put you to work elsewhere?"

"I don't take issue with the order, but now?" He shoved himself away from the table with a snarl. His eyes burnt, but it was not anger she saw there. It was fear. "Milady is home, finally, and you send me away?"

Eras's brows rose. *She's back?* The soldier in her sang at the approaching battle, but she had seen enough of this war to face it with dread in her stomach. "She's home? First I've heard of it."

"I can feel that she's here again. She arrived sometime a few nights ago. I was drunk at the time, I didn't realize it until the morning."

"Drunk? Again?" She waved away the excuse perched on his lips. "Never mind." She glanced at Raven. "Do you really think it's wise if you see her in this state? You're ready to dangle me from the window and all I did was inform the queen of a diplomatic solution to your attempt at murder. What will you do when she's not exactly the woman you remember? When she hasn't changed in the way you expect?"

"What the fuck would you know of that?"

She stepped around to the other side of her desk and folded her arms. He was unpredictable and she would rather face him on her feet then seated. *Besides, if Raven draws arms, I'll never hear the end of it.* "It is my job to know the state of affairs in my city, especially in times of war and when there are key players within our walls. You were seen leaving a bar with a young woman. You left her residence a little while later, angry. Well, angrier than usual. I suppose any man would be angry after so quick a dalliance, but regardless, I was under the impression that you had feelings for Dhoah' Lyne'alea."

Arman's breath rumbled in his chest and his eyes darkened. "I never said that."

"You never had to, Arman. This trip to the north might help cool your head. I don't know what Dhoah' Lyne'alea needs for this war, but I'm betting silver it's not a love-drunk school-boy." She had won the argument, if there had ever been one. *All that is left is for him to storm out angrily. I'll get a letter in the next week apologizing.*

He stalked towards the door. "Perhaps the next time you mentor someone, general, draw up a contract." He slammed his way out.

Eras shook her head in the wake of the outburst and poured herself another drink. "This war is making madmen of us all."

"You don't actually think he'd blame her for not being what he wants, do you? That would just be cruel."

She pressed her brow against the cool stone of her window frame. "That never stopped you from blaming me." The sunset was bloody and bruised. The spring storms had passed, but the skies were darker than ever.

Φ

The 37th Day of Lineme, 1252
The City of Mirik

Bren's gray eyes narrowed on the calm harbor. "I'll need two Kit to accompany me. And when I return I'd like whomever stays to organize themselves. We'll appoint other commissioners then."

"Not after the war?" Like Bren, Arik's arms were crossed.

The new commissioner glanced over and grinned. Flanking the main dock with identical stances, they could have been statues. It was not a bad image, two Miriken protecting what was left of their people. "No. If I die, we need organization. I've not come so far on so many sleepless nights to have it fall to shite. Who should I take with me? I'd like one to be you, but I think you would better serve here."

Arik nodded. "Agreed. When proper battle begins I'll come, with the rest of the soldiers." At Bren's surprised glance, he grinned. "You expect the queen to let you prance into battle with three men and a pale freak from the north? I think not. Anyway, take Kemmer A'hane and Aldac Missan. Aldac's a swordsman and knows our common ways. Kemmer's sister to the man governing Talic. She's young, but bright."

Bren nodded. "I'll send them letters this afternoon." He rolled his shoulders, watching as sailors prepared the ship before them for the sea. "I've left instructions for Helonin. He's to work with you as he readies to pull out. Will you see us off this afternoon?"

"Indeed."

"I'll send word from Athrolan about the war. How many you think will come?"

"For you? As many as can be spared. We'll have a few score. Outfitting them will be difficult."

"I'll take care of that. Make them ready before the end of the month."

Arik bowed himself away. "As ye tell, milord." The wry quirk of his mouth lent humor to the formal words.

Bren laughed as he returned to the barracks, the sound fitting for the clear day.

Φ

The 40th Day of Lineme, 1252
The Ilmar Ocean

Bren pressed his brow against the warm wood of the ship's rail. "Fates, not even the journey is easy!" His face was pale, his lips tinged gray.

"Just think, every time you need to come to Athrolan as a diplomat, you'll be at sea." Alea grinned over at him. The same wind that whipped her loose hair kicked the waves higher.

He groaned. With each lurch, her brother leaned over the rail with a hideous wretch. His stomach was long since empty. "Serves me proper, I suppose. Showing up in court and taking over the city they rightly conquered. 'Thanks for doing all the hard work, I'll take it from here!'"

Alea snorted. "Perhaps, though I doubt the hard work is over. Will you return to Mirik before the war?"

"If this is how I have to travel, I'll never go back." His next words were interrupted as Kemmer approached.

"Milord Commissioner, the captain agreed to stay moored for a bit before disembarking. I thought you might like to tidy yourself before entering the city." Her dark eyes flitted from his boots to Alea's and back.

Bren sighed. "You're godsent, Kemmer, thank you. It wouldn't do for our new allies to see me felled by a few days on the ocean." The woman jumped at the informal address and bowed awkwardly. She was closer to Alea's age than his and Bren had tried to break the formal front during the voyage, but Kemmer seemed as stubborn as he. "How long 'til we dock? Did you find that trunk of mine?"

The woman's silence made Bren glance up, despite his roiling gut. The white cliffs of Athrolan rose before them, half an hour's sail away. The noon sun turned the city into a beacon and made burnished gold of the summer-baked grass. Kemmer stared, open-mouthed, at the sight. Bren grinned. "Bit larger than Mirik, eh?"

She nodded stiffly. "Yessir. And your trunk is by your bunk, below. Aldac is dressing as we speak." Her eyes were still wide when she finally turned to look at him, meeting his gaze for the first time. "Thank you, sir, for picking me." She bowed and hurried down to the bunks to prepare for their arrival.

The sound of bells drifted from across the waves. Bren's brows rose. "I guess they've seen the ship's flag. They must know you're with us."

Alea nodded once and went to stand by the bow. She still wore plain clothes, but it did not matter. The chill of the sea flowed from her skin and Bren found even he was wary of meeting her eyes. He paused by her on his way down to the bunks. "You asked if I'd go back to Mirik. How much time are you giving us before battle?"

"I'll know when I determine how far Athrolan is from battle. I don't want to fight a war on my own."

Bren noticed she did not say she could not have done so, if necessary. A shudder went through him that had nothing to do with the pitching waves.

CHAPTER TEN

The 41st Day of Lineme, 1252
The City of Ceir Athrolan

DESPITE TZATIA'S ATTEMPT to see him before his official audience, Bren stayed holed up in his room with Aldac, Kemmer, and An'thor, carefully writing the details of his hastily planned government reform. There were issues that only time and hundreds of discussions would solve, but it was a start. He sighed as he finally he shoved the papers into an envelope and sealed it.

"This is only the beginning, I suppose. She'll have a dozen questions that I'll never be able to answer."

He glanced at An'thor. "When the page came to ask our titles, what did you say?"

"About myself or you?"

Bren shrugged. "Either one might make her scream."

"I politely told him to stick with 'Lieutenant Brentemir Barrackborn and companions.'"

"Toar, you make me sound like a sell-sex."

Kemer tried to disguise her snort as a cough, but dissolved into laughter after a moment. "Mirik's king, a sell-sex?"

He glared at her with mock anger. "I'm not her king."

"You are for now, sir." The hours working together had done wonders for her formal words, though Aldac still seemed to only communicate with single words.

Bren grimaced. "Regardless, we've just over one hundred seventy-six thousand Miriken Crown, which is about a hundred forty-five thousand Athrolani. It's dismal to run a country on such. I will order my own armor and both of yours. I'm asking for reports on Mirik's armory and requesting half the able-bodied men and women to sail over within the week. They're to train with the Athrolani soldiers until the battle. I'll save money by hiring a seamstress and smithy in Talic to make uniforms and repair what armor we have." He sighed. "I simply do not know how I'm going to do this."

Kemer leaned forward, pushing a loose lock of her hair away. "Begging your pardon. What if you paid the people in titles and land and housing instead of money?" Her voice was quiet, but certain.

Bren frowned and glanced at Aric. "I think the Kit might listen to that." He made a few notes. "Good thought, Kemmer."

An'thor's eyes were fixed out the window. "Will you tax them?"

"That'll be discussed I'm sure. I'll need to build her coffers some how, but our people are already impoverished." Bren gathered his papers, only to dig through them again as a thought struck him. "Kemer, could you send these across to Mirik please? I'll meet with you tomorrow to go over more."

Kemer tidied the pile carefully. "Sir, I was also told to remind you that the war address is in a month."

He frowned. He had forgotten completely about the address. "I have little idea what to expect."

"I'd imagine it's much like the ceremony of alliance, but with more war. It's a gathering of allies. You're to stand beside Her Majesty and your sister."

Bren sighed. "I'm not looking forward to being compared to Daymir." Above, the bells marked midafternoon. He groaned. "The audience with the queen is in half an hour. Go finish tidying yourselves, I'll meet you here when it's time." He glanced at An'thor when they had left. "Why does this feel worse than battle?"

"Because battle only kills you. This will embarrass you, disgrace your name, and ruin your future." His deadpan broke into a wicked smile. "I'll see you in a few minutes."

Bren rested his head in his hands. It was far too late to change his mind. *Would I, if it wasn't?* He heaved a sigh and shoved himself out of his chair. He stepped into the bath, scrubbing himself quickly for the second time that day. *If I'm going to embarrass myself, it damned well won't be because I stink of sea-sick.*

He jerked the wardrobe open with a frown. It held the fine clothes he had worn during his last visit. He was peering into it, still naked, when a light knock sounded on his door. He gathered a towel about his waist before opening it.

Alea was already dressed in the clothes she had worn for their first audience. Something was different, but Bren could not place his finger on it. She glanced at his appearance as she stepped inside. "Having trouble?"

He shut the door behind her and brought his own outfit into the privy. "No, we just had to write an outline of our new government for the queen." He fumbled with the ties of his breeches. "Are you as nervous as I am?"

She shrugged. "Not as nervous as I should be, perhaps. Is Reka in town?"

Bren's face sobered. "I asked after her when we first arrived. Her patrol was among two that never returned last month."

"Fates, Bren, I'm sorry."

"Me too."

He heard her walk over to the window. "Bren, the entire city turned out to watch us ride up from the docks."

"Fame does not sit well with you?"

"I don't care about fame. The entire city was here, and yet no sign of Arman. Do you think he'll be at the address?"

Bren drew a slow breath in silently as he finished combing his hair with his fingers. It was hopeless. "Alea, are you even sure he's in the city?"

"He's here. His room is next to mine. Right now he's somewhere on the roof of the palace. He's pacing and angry."

Bren stepped out. "I don't know what to tell you, sistermine."

She looked over, smiling at his finery. Her eyes threatened to overflow and flood the expression from her features. "Tell me you still love me. Tell me that even though I'm a monster, even though I'm waging war against the gods you worship, you'll still love me."

He wrapped her in his arms, but his words were interrupted by the quarter-hour bells. He pulled away to look at her. Her tears still had not fallen. Her words chilled him and he was even more uncertain than before. He took her hand and stepped into the hall. "Come on, we have a queen to impress." The others waited for him outside the door. Aldac and Kemmer had managed to find vermilion tunics and An'thor had not changed from his usual black leather and fur.

Bren led them to the throne room in silence, his broad fingers still wrapped around Alea's. When the squire stepped in to announce them, he glanced over. "I'll love you until the end of the world, sistermine."

The queen looked as calm as ever, but her bright eyes were wide with curiosity. "Dhoah' Lyne'alea, we are honored to host you again, despite our shared dark future. I trust your journey from Le'yne was uneventful."

All sadness had gone from Alea's face and she smiled graciously. "Indeed. I am honored to be here again. Your city is as beautiful and welcoming as ever." She stepped aside, allowing Bren to come forward.

Tzatia's eyes flicked to him. "Greetings, Lieutenant. Care to explain your cryptic arrival? Last we corresponded you were in Mirik. Not even my own officers will shed light on Mirik's situation."

He approached, giving her the bow of an equal. The rebellious part of him grinned gleefully as her brows furrowed at the apparent lack of respect. "Forgive my lack of communication, your majesty. It has been a tumultuous few weeks. I have come to accept your offer."

Her furrow brows rose. "What are you telling me?"

He clenched his hands around the envelope to hide their shaking. "On behalf of the Commissioners of the Miriken government, I, Lord Commissioner of the Military and acting king during this time of war, accept Athrolan's offer of alliance." He handed the envelope to a squire. "This document details the preliminary plans for Mirik's future. I invite you to peruse it at your leisure."

Tzatia's gaze was unreadable as it flicked to the three figures behind him. "And these are what, your allies? Your fellow Commissioners?"

"These are Aldac Missan and Kemmer A'hane of Mirik. They are my chief officers while I finalize our path to war, your majesty." He turned to An'thor. "And it is my honor to present Warrior An'thoriend Domariigo of the Northlands and Claimiirn. He is my ally in this war, as are his people."

Her lips thinned. "You bring a known exile into my throne room?"

Bren barely hid his relief when An'thor knelt before her, taking up the impending argument. "Your majesty, my return may be unwelcome, but the reasoning is sound. I do not have to be your ally, but I am Lord Commissioner Brentemir's." He looked up and dropped the formal tone. "You think I would let Athrolan go to war alone? As much as you may hate me, I still love this land."

Tzatia's eyes lingered on An'thor for a moment and Bren caught sight of the pale man's gaze. It held a tenderness that was alien to Bren, but he imagined it was that of a father. The queen's face was pale and her eyes fierce, but she drew a breath and rose. Her steps down from the dais were careful. "Well then. We look forward to our future together and the alliance of our joined forces. Lord Commissioner of Mirik, we welcome you, and your people and allies to Athrolan."

Φ

Eras's shifting weight caused her red mare to dance sideways. She assumed the war would require a journey to her former home, but that did not make the duty any easier. Her gaze stopped at Raven. He had come to see her off. "I've commanded the men to follow Hamacad until my return."

Raven had always been the more expressive of the two and she knew he often wondered how much of his affection she returned. She wondered the same.

"I'd rather join you in battle than Hamacad." His voice pitched so only she could hear. His hand covered hers so briefly that she could have imagined it, but for the warmth it left on her glove.

Eras nodded at him and nudged her mare away. "Ride out!" The men broke into a swift trot and streamed onto the road. As she passed through the gate the men were her living cloak, fanned behind.

Φ

The 44th Day of Lineme, 1252

Bren drained the nervous excitement from his body the only way he knew how. The training courts were empty in the evening, the silence punctuated only by his grunts and the shuffling of boots against sawdust. He wondered if Alea wanted to eat supper together, but he could not bring himself to go find her. Darkness wrapped her thoughts and her words since the siege. It was a darkness that even his heart, raised on bloodshed, dared not enter. Even facing it made the bottom drop from his stomach.

It was nearly midnight when he finally lowered his sword and reached for a rag to wipe his face. He froze as he caught sight of the man seated by the door. Bren could only stare.

Arman had changed much since their last visit, and Bren barely recognized him. The Rakos's eyes, fixed on his, glowed yellow. His hair and beard had grown several inches and his skin shone in the torchlight like tarnished gold. "Hello, Lieutenant."

"Actually, it's 'king' now." It wasn't exactly true, but Bren's anger and wariness shoved the boast from his lips without thinking.

"I heard."

"I thought we'd see you sooner." His clipped words were pointed. "You were too busy studying?"

"Somewhat. I leave with a naval fleet for the north soon, and then on to Vielrona."

"More men?" Their tones were equally biting, though the words polite.

"And Rakos." It was the powerful answer to Bren's assertion of king.

It made the latter frown. "And you avoid my sister?"

Arman shrugged. "I saw her arrive." He glanced to the side, but Bren guessed it was as much to hide the confusion on his face as to appear nonchalant.

"The whole city did, you arse!"

Arman's face darkened and his voice lowered into quiet danger. "You never heard what happened to that man in the tavern, did you? I tore his throat out. With my teeth."

It was as blunt a threat as possible. Bren threw his hands up in exasperation. "Whatever this game is that you're playing, stop. Play it with your barmaid whore, your thrice-tupped lass from home. For what I care, play it with your mother, but, Toar, leave my sister be!"

Arman shot to his feet and shoved Bren against the wall. "Bastard!" His voice was a hiss and smoke curled from between his bared teeth. "She spoke to you, but never gave me a word. I guard her. I fight for her. I died for her."

Bren frowned. The smell of burning cloth rose with tendrils of smoke from where Arman's hands gripped his tunic. "For such a perfect guard you were easily swayed into infidelity."

"We never made promises." His face lost its malice and he stalked back to the bench.

"What's going on, Arman?" The argument had clearly run its course. "You're a stranger."

Arman scratched absently at his shoulder. "I don't know. My feelings have changed, but not in the way you might think. I can't make up or down of it. My power changed how I see her. It's as if something crawled inside me and took over. If its nature were the opposite of mine perhaps I could live with it. Instead, it's more like me than anything has ever been. Before all of this I was just a smith who found a strange woman in the desert. I was beneath her. Now I wonder if I'm her equal. I'm so angry all the time. At myself, at Eras, at you. Fates, sometimes I'm angry at her." His face was etched with agony. "Barrackborn, I want her like I've wanted no other woman and I'm so angry she doesn't see me."

Bren just stared. For the second time that day he was lost for words. Finally he scrounged up a piece of history he had read in Mirik. "The Rakos were as old as the Laen."

"Our powers are opposites. Hers are balance, mine are chaos."

"You are everything she is not and she is everything you are not. Arman, you're closer to her equal than anyone. No one, if not you, is worthy to love her." His mouth quirked. "If you stop acting like an arse." He stepped away and turned toward the door. "I'm going to read." He glanced back in the doorway. "You need to talk to her."

"I'm angry."

"You'll regret it if you don't. Besides, so is she."

Φ

The 45th Day of Lineme, 1252

Purposeful knocking drew Alea from the heavy book on her lap. "Yes?"

The steward poked his head in. "Dhoah' Lyne'alea, Lord Daymir wishes to pay you a visit."

Alea laid her book aside with what she hoped was a smile. Her mind was rarely truly present. "Show him in. Thank you, Valadai."

Daymir stepped in on the tail of her words. When she did not rise, he faltered, then bowed. "Good morning, Dhoah' Lyne'alea."

She gestured to the seat across from her. "Good morning. Care to sit?"

He took the place she offered, his pale eyes watching her. "I trust your journey was good?"

"It was uneventful. That is the most we can hope for, during war. To what do I owe the honor?" Despite her agreement to see him, she was impatient and tired of court speech.

He laughed ruefully. "I get your meaning. I was curious about your time in Le'yne." He paused as Giire brought in a tray of tea. When she had gone, he poured Alea a cup. His movements were careful and it was obvious he rarely waited on people himself. "Her Majesty said your return heralded the war."

Alea took the cup wordlessly, stirring in a small lump of sugar. She took a sip and stared at the liquid absently. "I wish Athrolan had *yilj* for the tea. My birth heralded the war, Lord Daymir. The rest is just formality." She sat back, eyes meeting his. "Le'yne was different from what I expected, but served its purpose." She tilted her head at him. "Will you have a part in the campaign?"

He either did not notice, or allowed her easy flip of the conversation. The intelligence in her eyes told him it was the latter. "I studied for Gallantry for a time, but my status as Head of the Royal Treasury prevents me from actually being on the fore lines. I'll have a hand in the planning." His voice was somber. "Shadow showed us we need to prepare for anything."

"Some things we can never anticipate. It's clear that Shadow was just a diversion while Azirik moved from Mirik."

Daymir nodded. "Speaking of Mirik, your brother's declaration came as a surprise. I look forward to reading that document."

Alea's gaze narrowed. "Do you wish Mirik was under Athrolan's flag?"

Daymir flashed her a wry grin. "Athrolan has far too many obligations without dragging a city from the mud. Guiding a new king, commissioner — whatever he calls himself — who has no experience, a bad example, and too good of a heart will be a hard enough task. When I take the throne I do not want to inherit a floundering ally whom we once needed for morale."

Alea allowed the ferocity bubbling in her stomach to sharpen her smile. "It is clear you have not yet read his words. I look forward to your apology when you have."

He stared at her, as if trying to determine how far he had overstepped his welcome. "Perhaps you're right." He sat back, placing his cup on the table. "You said you wished we had something for the tea. Yeel?"

"*Yilj.* It's a spice the Sunamen add to almost everything. I thought it was best with sweet things — tea and fruit and the like. I admit your tea is different, though." The heir's company was too biting to be pleasant, but she decided it was better than sitting alone. "Have you ever had Sunamen food?"

His smile was grateful. "No. I hear the flavors are complex. I enjoy the fruit from Ban. Did you get a chance to meet the Banis ambassador?"

"No, though I got the impression that your alliance with them is tense."

"It's not much of an alliance. They trade in slavery and have become rich in doing so. I know the city-states to their southwest slave-trade with them."

Alea shrugged. "Sunamen did. We only used felons, though. It kept crime incredibly low, actually."

Daymir looked down. "At any rate, we disagree. They are an interesting people and their land is rich. I hope to visit the forest to their west one day — they only have two seasons and the trees grow taller than the mountains, and are so large that other plants grow on their branches and never touch the ground."

Alea laughed. It was a beautiful image, but one out of a child's story. "I think you have been reading fantasies, Lord Daymir." She glanced out the window, at the sun climbing high in the sky. "Would you like to take your midday meal with me? You could tell me more lies about Ban."

He gave her a tiny, joking bow. "Nothing would please me more than to fill your head with nonsense."

Their food arrived shortly and Alea wrinkled her nose as she gathered the meat and bread onto her plate. "Are the Banis as barbaric as you, or do they actually use utensils to eat?"

Daymir shrugged. "I've heard they have so many slaves that they don't even feed themselves."

The dry humor tugged a laugh from her chest finally. "Perhaps I should get a few of my own."

"I was thinking, Dhoah' Lyne'alea, you seemed to enjoy the ball during your first visit. I thought I might suggest Her Majesty hold another one, heralding your return and our future victory against His Majesty King Azirik." He paused, frowning. "What do we call him, now that Bren has reformed the government out from under him?"

"I think Mirik is now two factions — Azirik's military monarchy and Bren's oligarchy." She paused to dip a slice of meat into the heated bowl of gravy and herbs. "I see the sense in holding a ball, but I cannot agree with it. I'll celebrate when I've won."

Daymir frowned. "I thought you would like to have some happiness."

Her eyes flicked up to his. "If I need you to spend hundreds of crown on a single night of excess, I'll let you know." She sat back. "I do like going to a ball, Lord Daymir. I enjoy the music and the food and the conversation. Dancing is wonderful. It's like sparring. Between the steps and conversation I'm too distracted to think about anything more important. This journey, the siege, has been one long, distracting dance." She fixed him with a pointed stare. "Now the ballroom is empty, the music has stopped."

Φ

The 45th Day of Lineme, 1252

Arman crouched on his window ledge, watching the fading light. His lamp remained unlit, and even in the early summer, his room sweltered. The sounds of conversation next door had finally faded an hour ago, but he still seethed. He was past caring that he brooded. He was past caring about most things. Only his anger consumed him. He had been frustrated with Alea before, afraid for her and of her, but never outright angry. Her return only made things worse. Several of the things in his room were broken or burnt from his half-dozen outbursts.

What would she think, seeing you like this?

He snarled at the inner voice. "I don't give a damn what she would think. I know enough of that to fill a lifetime!" His rage rose, like a wave approaching across the ocean. He whirled and began going through his old training exercises. With each block, fire erupted from his forearms and fists, the flesh protected by the scales marching up his skin.

Would she think you pathetic?

He ignored the voice and let fire roar through him. It was not enough to cover himself in flames. It was not enough to singe his rugs with each stamp of his bare feet. The abrupt heat dried the walls of his room, cracking it along invisible faults in the stone. His arms smoldered white-hot. He thought of Alea, the rage and frustration and despair he felt when he saw her. There was another emotion under them all. Something vast and peaceful, but he did not remember its name.

The reddened back of his eyelids flickered with images. It was like reading the Berrin man's mind on the road so many months before, but now the only mind before him was his own. Some pictures he recognized, others made little sense. Memories from Vielrona and the road north scattered among visions of a thin young man ascending the Athrolani throne, the sights of a terrible battle, magma flooding a barricaded city district. Arman drew the power tighter to himself. The cresting wave of power and rage broke over him then. Suddenly he was above a battlefield. Fire covered the ground and chaos crashed in titanic rumbles around him. The ground rushed up to meet him and his body flooded with pain. His chest seized and his consciousness guttered and suddenly there was nothing. His mind was at peace with whatever led him to that end. His body was numb and his vision black.

He dragged himself away from his power, rising back through it until he opened his eyes onto his room, more destroyed than ever. Every textile was burnt, the bed a charred skeleton of former finery.

Do you believe your power now? You believe you are not just Rakos?

He had nothing to say to the voice. The numbness from the vision had been replaced by agonizing tingles. "I've felt that before. I know what that is." He was distantly aware that a dozen emotions stormed through him. His anger was now tinged with poignancy. "I'm still angry, but not enough. I'm her guard and this is my fate. I chose this. And I would choose it again, and I choose it now." He had seen the battle and it was terrible, but his faith was unwavering.

CHAPTER ELEVEN

The 15th Day of Aeme, 1252
The Hartland Forest

ERAS'S SILENCE WAS NOT HER usual stoicism. She pushed the men hard and wondered if it was partly to cover her own nerves. They were well into their third week of riding. The road lay days behind them, abandoned shortly after entering the Hartland. The day before they picked up a dirt track too straight to be a game trail. Occasional stone pillars marked the distance. Whether it was how far they had come or had yet to go, none could tell. The symbols had long been worn away,

Even at midday the sunlight barely filtered through the canopy. The dusky light dappled the twisted trees. The bent rough trunks were terribly tall and so unlike the smooth white trees of Athrolan. Sharp, gray rocks pierced the soil every so often and the track widened and turned to gravel. This area of the forest was familiar. Eras slid her bow into its case and rolled the knots from her shoulders. She drew up her mare when the gravel became paving stones. Two narrow pillars flanked the road. The gray stone was hung with tarnished medallions. The faint breeze clattered the decorations against the moss-covered markers.

"General?" Vinden drew up beside her.

She noted the tension in his back and the narrow line of his mouth. He lacked the skill of a gallant, but not the courage. If he was nervous, the other men would be afraid. "These are Espera's gates. Guards stood here." She nudged her mare forward, but at a walk. "Eyes sharp, man. We'll reach the city just after sundown." The road was overgrown, but had once been wide. The faint rustling of leaves and the crunch of decomposing stone under the iron horseshoes seemed deafening. After an hour, distant grumbling joined the sounds of men and horses. "Vinden, when we reach the river, half the men will make cold camp. You'll bring the others with me into the city."

"Understood, mem."

The grumbling became the roar of falling water. Eras's pace quickened. They emerged onto a riverbank carved from bedrock. Eras raised her hand, but the men had already stopped in awe. Years of water spinning stone against stone carved perfect circles into the bank. Some were the size of a fist, others large enough to swallow man and horse. They stood on the shore of a churning pool. Across the river, water from the mountains cascaded over low cliffs. They were nothing like Athrolan's, but were broad and dark and dotted with hexagonal watch towers. The city itself was small and perched on an island at the foot of the waterfall. A narrow bridge of stairs connected the island to the shore.

She dismounted, allowing the men their gawking for a moment, then barked orders to make camp before jerking her head towards the bridge. The designs carved along the steps were angular and repetitive, as much for decoration as traction. The boots of the half-dozen soldiers following her barely made a sound. Eras did not have to signal for them not to speak. It was evening and any city should have been bustling as it prepared for supper. The buildings were silent. A large tower marked the center of the island and Eras paused before the open doorway.

Vinden placed a foot on one of the stairs, leaning on his knee and Eras surveyed their surroundings. "General, this is wrong. You said there were only a few Asai. I see none."

The lines of Eras's sharp features deepened with concentration. "I've been gone for years. Almost a lifetime. Anything could have happened. The Asai are cloistered enough that we may never had heard of an attack." She nocked an arrow to her bow, fingers curling around the string, ready to draw. "We'll start here." She stepped into the tower, motioning for her men to spread out. The halls were decorated with carvings, but it was austere. Few pieces were solely art. Each blocky design had architectural purpose. Eras knew her men would chalk her expressionless face up to her usual indifferent mask. It was honesty this time. *Espera stopped being home a long time ago.* The young soldier at her back tripped and whispered a curse, then an apology.

She ignored him and eyed the open double doors at the end of the hall. They should have been closed. She crept forward, instinct singing in her ears. *This is wrong. This is all wrong. If they deserted, where is the dust? If they were attacked, where is the struggle?*

She stepped through the doors.

"General, mem." The soldier's hiss was fearful. "You should look at this."

She froze in the doorway, heedless of the young man behind her. The hall took up a whole segment of the six-sided tower. The books that lined the walls were gone, only a few scattered pages left to mold in the moisture. Mist roiled in from the shattered window. The table in the center of the room no longer held maps. Now it held bodies.

Eras did not bother to search for survivors. The chill of the river had kept some rot away, but the mottled cast and sweet smell of the air told her enough.

"General."

She finally turned to the soldier.

He crouched in the hall, peering at an arrow. "This is Berrin."

"It's hard to say when they were attacked. The cold kept them better than usual." She backed out of the hall and shut the doors. *I should bury them.* It would wait until tomorrow. There was little sense in digging graves in the dark. Her two-fingered whistle rebounded off the stone, calling for the others to regroup. She sat on the steps at the tower's entrance to wait for the others.

The soldier shifted nervously from foot to foot, earnest concern lighting his eyes. "I'm sorry, mem. Did you know them?"

She glanced up, wondering briefly if he was as young as he looked. The other men treated her as an expert on the Asai, but distantly, as if she had studied them as a hobby, not been raised in their culture. The boy before her was either too honest or too inexperienced to do the same. "Probably some. Long ago. Not well." She heaved a sigh. "Thank you, though."

The rest of the men arrived from within. Vinden's nodded greeting was grim. "Berrin attack."

She rose. "Agreed. Deserted?"

"Save a few rooms. Looks like someone tidied up—only a few arrows and all the dead stacked." He glanced up at the tower. "This place is eerie enough, the dead only make it worse."

"We'll deal with them in the morning." They were nearing the bridge when footfalls clattered ahead. *Athrolani patrols don't wear hobnails.* They rounded the bend to see crossbows leveled in their direction. Eras raised her hands carefully. "Don't shoot." Her gaze inched over the high-collared coat of the foremost warrior. Other than its gray color, it was identical to the black one Eras herself wore. She reached out, palm up in the Asai gesture for deference. "I'm Nei'phieras liu Aneral, General of Athrolan."

The man in gray frowned. "Daughter of Lenu'phieras?" When Eras nodded, he lowered his bow and placed a hand on hers. "I'm Albi'giran. I know you only by name, but I rode with An'thoriend for a time."

Greetings through, Eras stepped back. "What happened here?"

"It's better told by a fire and after supper. We saw your camp. Might we join you?"

Eras's mouth twitched. "If we can agree to not wave weapons about any more."

Albi'giran's bow was both humorous and genuine. He fell into step with Eras as they returned to the river bank. "You found the tower?"

Her mouth twisted. "Why haven't you buried them yet?"

"We arrived three days ago. We've been scouting, searching for survivors." When Eras looked at him, curious, he shook his head. "None."

The Athrolani guards around the camp sent up whistled warnings, but Eras waved at them. "Hold, they're with me. Lay a fire." She hid a smile at the soldier's grateful sighs. The Asai stayed at the edge of the camp, watching as tents were moved to make room for the fire. Eras's gaze inched over them, curious as to how used to humans she had become. *They are my people, and yet look foreign.* Her features were angular and ashen; those of the Asai were exotic, almost awkward, and gray-brown. Their red hair was long regardless of sex, though it was not immediately clear which were male and female.

As stew was passed about, Albi'giran crouched beside Eras, his bowl balanced on his knee. "This attack — it was due to the war?" His tawny eyes were bright.

Eras glanced over, her surprise mocking. "The Asai are less isolated than I thought."

Albi'giran's smile was humorless. "When we hear stories of the Laen and Rakos, we tend to listen. Our group was a scouting mission to learn more of this war and to protect our secrets."

"What do you mean?" Eras absently watched her men settle into tense conversation with the newcomers.

"We each carry a chest filled with our most precious tomes. Our leaders knew attack would come. They wanted our knowledge to be preserved, if not our people." He scraped his bowl clean then laid it at his feet. "I told you our tale, now tell me yours. You come to ask for help?"

Eras pursed her lips. She was suddenly aware of how expressive she had become while living among the Athrolani. "Her Majesty of Athrolan asked me to see what numbers we could gain."

"And you were sent after half your blood. Do you fight for the gods or the Laen?" Albi'giran's companions glanced over at their captain's words.

"The Laen." Eras forced her hands to stop fidgeting. The Asai read stillness as honesty.

"Ca'nuran, what think you?" Albi'giran's gaze flicked to an Asai woman leaning on a tentpole. Like him, she wore the long coat of command.

"Battle is a cycle. A king too set in his ways, or a land with no one to lead. We rarely involve ourselves and the situation still resolves. Why is this different?"

Eras shifted to see the woman better. "I may have been unclear earlier. You asked if we fight for the Laen. We do. One particular Laen."

Albi'giran's expressionless facade slipped and his brows rose. "I told you, I rode with An'thoriend. I was with him when the Dhoah' Laen was cut down."

"Then you did not ride with him long enough. The true Dhoah' Laen was forgotten in a small city-state. She's trained and returned to us, ready for battle. She has a Rakos guard who has become an Earth Shaker and a brother who is taking over Mirik and allied himself with the Nenev."

The female Asai met Albi'giran's gaze for several moments of silent deliberation. When he nodded, she turned back to Eras. "We'll join you then, when we've laid this city to rest."

Albi'giran frowned. "Will you stay and help us?"

Eras shook her head. "I didn't stay when they were living. I certainly won't for the dead."

Vinden leaned on the tree beside the general, watching as the Asai dispersed into the darkness. "That was it?"

"You expected a conversationalist?" Her mouth twitched. "A great debate? A stirring speech, the inspiration from people united? Really, Vinden, it's like you don't know me at all."

He snorted. "I suppose you are more forthcoming than we realized."

Eras sat back on her heels. "To you I am a stone, to them, a font of expression."

Φ

The 16th Day of Aeme, 1252
The City of Ceir Athrolan

Furtive knocking interrupted Bren as he crouched to bank his fire. He had gotten used to having the evenings to himself at Mirik. He debated pretending he was already asleep.

"I know you're awake—I can hear you messing with the fire." Arman's growl muttered through the door. "Just open up?"

Bren rose with a groan and let the man in. "I suppose I'll have to become accustomed to all-hours-visitors if I'm going to be commissioner." Bren sat on the end of his bed, watching Arman seat himself by the fire. "I was starting to wonder if you were still in the city."

Arman ignored the veiled question. "What do you know of the Rakos?"

Bren shrugged. "Just what I've read, and that's not a lot. Scarce information about you people it seems. They controlled fire, created some sort of monsters." Bren's military training caught the tension around Arman's eyes. "I'm wrong?"

Arman slid from the chair onto the hearth, and rolled up his sleeves. He stirred the fire with his bare hands. The sparks he displaced rolled upwards, across his hands and curled around his forearms. He flicked them away after a moment. He did not meet Bren's eyes.

"You're not burnt." Bren gestured to the yellow, peeling skin on Arman's arms. "Is that what I think?"

Arman stood abruptly and tugged off his shirt. Scales dotted his shoulder blades, wrapping around his biceps and spiraling across his chest. Small ones formed white ridges along his forearms and neck, this skin flaking around them as they grew. The largest, armoring plates were bright gold.

Bren ran a hand through his hair. "When?" He was at a loss. "Toar, what does this mean? You're saying they didn't make the monsters—creatures?" He corrected himself hastily.

"They became them."

"Can Alea do something?"

"She cannot know." The blond man bared his teeth. "This is something out of both our control."

"Then why tell me?" Bren's eyes were taught to see weakness. He picked out the trembling in Arman's hands, the pulse thundering in his throat, but the only weakness in the form before him was in the eyes. "You're going mad." He wished it was only an insult, but the Rakos's eyes were manic.

"I chose this and Alea cannot know." The command held no trace of a question. "I want her to remember me like I was the last time I saw her."

"I won't tell her, not until she asks and I have nothing more to tell her but lies." Arman's first statement caught up to Bren. "What do you mean, you chose this?"

Arman began to pace. "I had to be something greater, so I could help her. I thought of the uncertainty and fear she had when she first learned her power. We are opposite. So I gave myself fearlessly to my Rakos side. I do more than control fire. I create fire. I *am* fire."

"You sound like this is the end. You can't turn back?"

"I saw things in my power—like when I saw that soldier's thoughts on our way from Hero. I saw the future and past. I saw the battle. I felt my death."

Bren suddenly understood. *He needs someone to know. Even if she remembers him whole, he needs someone to know why.* A knock interrupted his next thought.

"Bren?" Alea's voice was soft. "Are you awake?"

Bren's gaze flicked from the door to Arman. The Rakos leapt onto the ledge of the open window. He shook his head, commanding Bren to silence, before jumping into the gardens below. Bren waited a moment then opened the door.

Alea smiled a greeting at him, but her eyes traced the room behind. "I wanted to see you for a moment. I thought I heard talking. Are you alone?"

Bren nodded and shrugged sheepishly. "Just talking to myself. Come in."

She sat in the chair Arman had just vacated and tucked her legs up. "I met Lord Daymir for lunch again. He mentioned a few concerns about your plans for Mirik. I disagree, but many may not."

"What concerns?" Bren knew many took issue with his lack of experience and breeding. Hearing it from a man as powerful as Daymir, however, made his hackles rise.

"How much support you will need from Athrolan. I suggest you meet with him casually. He said he wanted to speak with you and it might ease both your concerns." She shrugged lightly. "Perhaps if you made some plans public, you would gain faith."

He stared at the floor thoughtfully. "Lord Daymir seems intelligent. Perhaps he might have insight for some difficulties." At Alea's pointed look he held up his hands. "Not too much insight, I promise! I can do this without them." He laughed.

She grinned, but he saw it did not reach her eyes. "I just thought I would let you know. I'm headed into the gardens for some air. Care to join me?"

"I should focus on the city. Enjoy the evening, though." Bren took out his captain's log and began turning down his covers.

Alea paused in his doorway. "You haven't heard from Arman, have you?"

"I'm sorry Alea. I wish I had news for you." Bren schooled his features into steadiness before turning. Her eyes were not fixed on his, but on his open window.

Φ

Alea stopped at the room beside her brother's. She had heard voices, conversation, before she knocked at Bren's door. Often she heard someone moving about on the other side of her wall, but there was never any light under the door. When she focused she could feel his location. Sometimes the heat and shimmering power felt only inches away. *And just a moment ago, I felt him in Bren's room. I smelled metal and ash on his chair and heat rolled from his window sill.* Part of her hated Bren for lying, but the rest was still too stunned.

She hurried down the stairs to the garden, not bothering with a cloak. The air was balmy and beautiful, the sky clear. The gentle weather belied the city's dark atmosphere. Clustered in the garden's center were weeping cherry trees, the curtains of their boughs waving in the mild breeze. She found a secluded bench and lay back on it. She kicked off her slippers and let her feet trail in the waving grasses. It took only a mental beckon for her power to rise. Sparks danced across her fingers and palms. She had been practicing with water, but it lacked the excitement of lightning.

She reached out and caught a falling blossom, floating it above her palm as if on the surface of a pool. The silver sparks drifted up from her palm and into the petals. The electricity followed the flower's veins, becoming a miniature lightning storm in the shape of the cherry blossom.

Heat suddenly shuddered through her and she looked up. A figure stood on the path several paces away. Only the silhouette of his shoulder and the golden glow of his eyes were visible.

The lightning in the blossom turned to ice then shattered, littering the ground with jagged crystals that melted after a moment. "Arman?" Her next words stopped him as he turned to go. "You won't talk?"

"There's nothing to say." His low voice lilted familiarly, but there was a new echo of metal.

"You never came to welcome me." Her words were calm, but her heart pounded. She sat up slowly, suddenly afraid she would startle him away. *He's not a wild animal.* She peered closer, wondering at the uncertainty in the thought.

"I didn't realize you were here yet."

She sighed at the feeble excuse. "The fact that my return was heralded from the bell towers aside—I can feel your power across the city, I can feel your pulse. I know you at least sense me, too."

"Is it so hard to think I might not want to see you?" His voice twisted into a snarl. "What did you wish to speak about, anyways?"

Everything. Anything. "What are you doing afterward?"

"After what?"

"The battle. The mending."

The gold orbs of his eyes slivered in a wince and he snorted. "If there is an after."

"I can do this without you, but I'd rather not have to. Why are you bitter? What changed? What made you love another, take her to bed?" She smelled smoke.

He ducked under the bower of the trees. "You could not deign to speak to me while you were in Le'yne, but you snuck about in my thoughts? Can I have nothing to myself?"

Alea jerked back. Her eyes burnt as if he had slapped her. "Perhaps I assumed, Rakos, but I thought friendship meant more than a night's tryst. Fates, we're soul-bound!"

"Our bond was a promise to fight and protect, Alea, not damned marriage vows! I can bed whom I will, without seeking permission!" His sudden use of her name was like a curse.

Alea's hand shook with strange urgency. *Anger.* It had been a long time since she had been this angry. *This is not the Arman I knew.* Her power surged. "You can keep your cheap bar-girl!" A crackling sphere of lightning shot towards him. It collided with a thin wall of flame, handbreadths from his chest. The wall swirled like magma. Alea's power fell, retreating into her arms.

"Think you're the only one who learned tricks?" Arman's dissipated slower, his hair curling as flames licked along the locks. The beds of his nails glowed like coals. Smoke spiraled from between his bared teeth. "You think you really could have stopped that bolt if you wanted? Could you prevent yourself from killing me?" He wheeled and staggered away. "After all, that's what you're good at, Destruction."

CHAPTER TWELVE

The 22nd Day of Aeme, 1252
The Eastern Coast of Athrolan

ARMAN'S STEPS WERE ERRATIC on the dew-dampened grass. He kept his power raging beneath his skin, though it had long since erased the chill of Alea's power. In his mind, he still felt the ice. He paused on the cliff tops, staring down at the dusk-shadowed waves of the ocean. The city was a day behind him. A line of ships dotted the water. *I was supposed to be on one of those. I was supposed to head north.* Instead, he marched east, paralleling their path on the land.

He had left all but his most essential belongings in his room, and the key in the lock. He would not use it again, he was sure. New fire burnt in him, the heat of shame and regret. *She wondered what I'd do afterward.* The cruelty in his words embarrassed him. He could have simply run when she threw power at him, but his anger held the reins to his tongue. It was the only way he knew to drive her away, make it a bit easier to do what he must. *Making amends does nothing, except worsen the hurt when I'm dead. It'd hurt more if we were close.* It might break his heart to drive her away, but he preferred that over causing her deeper grief.

You'll be unrecognizable by the time you regret it enough to change your mind.

He snarled at the voice and quickened his pace. The forest was thick here, and the trees twisted and ugly. His dreams had come more frequently, always the same voice snarling from the monstrous face. It was the voice that taunted him, first with An'thor's words, then with his own. He hated it, but it was a sneering reminder than he was not alone. Each time he sunk into his power the glittering eyes appeared in the back of his mind. The scar over one told him they were Eana's, but he dared not focus on them for too long.

Fear. Fear.

"I'll find you, you bastard. You and the rest of our mad brothers." There were more Rakos in the world. Unrecognizable and forgotten, perhaps, but alive.

Φ

The 23rd Day of Aeme, 1252
The City of Ceir Athrolan

Daymir swirled the berries in the bottom of his liquor glass. The view from his family's manor in the upper tier of the city was one of the best and offered the palace and cemetery beyond. He had been honest to Alea when he said few considered him the queen's heir. The fact remained, however, that he was Tzatia's closest living relative. *And what will I inherit? A bankrupt nation of the dead?* He was rarely given to dour thought, but Bren's recent claim of Mirik's throne had made him think of his own future. He folded himself behind the large desk by the window and pulled over a small collection of parchment.

He was the eldest child of the queen's younger brother. Daymir's sister, Jantia, married young, leaving him in charge of their parents' estate when their father passed. Daymir's head was one of business, and he enjoyed advanced arithmetic and economics while a squire. When he became a gallant, he took a post in the city, governing over the treasury and military coffers, as opposed to commanding men. It was a post that suited him. Now he was glad for the authority and foresight.

The papers before him were the checks and balances of the nation for the last two years. *Since the Berrin began ferreting about on our borders.* Athrolan had benefited from the influx of nobles after Mirik's great exodus — the taxes on wealth increased and the city had padded her pockets, just in time for war. *And war is damned expensive — drains men, resources, money.* The money set aside for such things was long gone and Tzatia had been turning to other savings. Road repairs were two years late and all but the largest unguarded. Daymir helped his aunt pinch and stitch, taxing more and spending less, but it was hard and the cost of protecting their people grew ever higher.

He may have aged, but his interests had not changed since his days as a squire, and his foresight was still clear. "Currow?"

His steward entered with a short bow. "Milord?"

"Can you have thirty-four thousand great-pieces placed aside? Here is the writ authorizing it, and I would like it to be safeguarded in the lower treasury under Authority of the

Treasurer. Today, understood?" His words were quick as he wrote the paper for his steward.

"You're the Treasurer, sir." Currow answered with a frown. "Why not have it under your personal authority?"

"Because this is not for me. It's for our future." Daymir sat back. "Now please, time is wasting." When the man was gone, the heir moved back to his window, watching the clouds thoughtfully. *My aunt is a good woman, but too kind. An alliance with a broken nation? The fostering of a soldier-king? These will only quicken our fall.* With Alea on their side they would win, of that he was confident. *The queen looks only as far as victory, and does not see the hole of bankruptcy that yawns beneath us.* After a moment he checked the time and began to tidy his desk. If he hurried, he could see the Dhoah' Laen just before she called for lunch. With a smile, he grabbed his cloak and headed for the door.

Φ

The 23rd Day of Aeme, 1252

An'thor's stern knocking woke Bren midmorning. He groaned a response and dragged himself to let the man in. "What is it?" He tugged on a shirt and hopelessly tried to order his hair.

"I am sending word to my capital. The queen's address is in less than a month. You should be there."

"I was assuming to be." Bren rinsed sleep from his mouth with the stale water beside his bed. "Everyone else is leaving though. Whatever happened to a united front, with allies and all that? Eras is weeks gone and Arman left a night or two ago."

"He saw you?" An'thor eyes brightened with curiosity.

"I'm as close to her as he'll let himself get." Bren sighed. "So why did you wake me to tell me things I already know?"

"Brentemir, this will be your first public appearance as Lord Commissioner. You need something better than the garb of a Miriken lieutenant. Both for the address and for battle."

"I take it all back." Bren flopped onto the bed. "If being a lord means pompous clothing, I renege."

An'thor snorted. "Valadai will get you squared away, and I'd recommend Master Rulhan for your armor."

Bren rose, composing himself. "All right. Why are you writing home? Are you calling them here? I could use a few troops."

An'thor bated. "Yes, and asking them a favor for your sister." He grinned and ducked out of the door.

Bren looked at his bed longingly, but called for Valadai instead. While he waited, he tugged open the chest at the end of his bed. His Miriken armor lay within. It was boiled leather with bronze mail beneath. It bore as many scars as his own skin. *An'thor's right, though, I need to look the part.* He had been taught to mend armor as well as the next soldier, but this was different. He ran his hands over a few of the deeper dents, feeling unexpected nostalgia. *You saved my life enough times.*

Valadai's arrival pulled Bren from his reverie. "Lord Commissioner."

"Master Valadai. An'thoriend informed me that I will be standing state beside Her Majesty for the address. I need to fit my titles."

The man hid a smile well, but his eyes softened. "I can have your measures taken from any clothes you brought with you. What colors were you thinking?"

Bren dug about in his wardrobe for the set that fitted best. His middle had grown thicker since leaving the army. He paused as Valadai's words sunk in. "Colors?"

"Yes, my lord. You may have noticed the court finery here often has a palate."

"Oh. Well. Mirik's colors then. Vermilion and green. More of the former, though. It's a fierce color. Good for a Military Commissioner, don't you think."

"Certainly. And the style?"

Bren groaned. "Something serviceable. I'm not a peacock. I liked the outfit for the ball during our last visit. But with a Miriken half-cloak, please." He stopped Valadai as the man began to bow himself out. "Might you tell me where to find Master Rulhan? He's a smith."

Valadai's smile broke free from its restraints. "Yes, milord. He is the head of the Smithing Guild, and his smithy makes all the armor for Her Majesty's troops. He's behind the barracks and the stables."

Bren flushed and waved his thanks. He collected his armor with a disparaging sigh and headed across the palace. He followed the smell of burning and metal to the rearmost part of the barracks. The rhythmic noise was close to deafening and he had to shout at a young apprentice for directions. Bren dodged through the smithy toward a Sunamen man twice his breadth. "Are you Master Rulhan?"

The man shoved the metal he was working into the coals and turned, motioning Bren into a side room. His dark skin was stained with ash and his black braids were cinched with copper bands. He wiped a hand on his apron and offered it to Bren. "I'm Master Rulhan. What can I do for you?"

Bren took the hand. "I'm Brentemir Barrackborn."

Rulhan's brows rose and he bowed. "Forgive me, my lord." He grinned as he straightened. "Best be adding those titles on there, though, else some might not take you serious."

Bren flushed and held up his armor. "That's partly why I'm here. I'm told soldier's armor is not seeming of my rank."

Rulhan took the pieces, surveying them with a strict frown on his leathery face. "How have you lived this long?" The question was mild, but the smith winced. "The craftsmanship may have been serviceable once, but it looks like a blind man used this for a chamber pot."

"Given the number of times I had to repair it myself, it's a wonder I'm still here."

"Some god must fancy you."

"I think it's more likely my sister scares the wits from any god."

Rulhan glanced up, eyes unreadable. "She does my people honor."

Bren had forgotten, almost, that the Sunamen had raised Alea. "I'll tell her so."

"At any rate, I'll begin from scratch. The lad will take your measures, but first, tell me of your fighting style and your weapons, so I might design the best piece for you."

Bren's eyes widened. He had always worn whatever was large enough. It was often old and ill fitting. To have armor designed solely for him was a novelty. He grinned and began his explanation, looking over Rulhan's notes and making changes where he saw fit. It took the better part of an hour before he was measured and on his way again. He made a mental note to send Arik and Kemmer to get their own armor to be repaired or replaced. He was headed to his room when

Alea emerged from her own, dressed in a split skirt dress and breeches. Her mood was reserved.

"Good morning." He smiled broadly.

"How have you spent your morning?"

"Busily. I just came from the arms-smith. An'thor made it known that my armor was not fit for me to wear and I had to order new clothes for the address as well. Will you have new things made?"

"Of course." Her eyes sparkled impishly at his ignorance. "My dress is already ordered though." She paused. "I was thinking about having armor made for myself as well. What do you think?"

"I think if I were Azirik I'd piss myself. Where were you off to?"

"I wanted to find an empty training hall. Being still is giving me nerves."

Bren gestured to the rear of the palace. "Those in the palace are often empty. Care for some company?"

She leaned on his doorframe as he changed into old clothing. "I saw Daymir in passing yesterday. He said you trained together for an afternoon?"

"We did. We spoke little, but he seemed more at ease afterward. I hope we can develop a rapport." Bren made a face. "I hope he doesn't think I'm completely incompetent."

She laughed and fell into step beside him as they headed towards the practice courts. "I think he worries about inheriting as much as you. It would serve you well to become friendly." She pushed open the door to the training hall to find it deserted. She surveyed the room while Bren lit the torches. Racks of wooden or dulled practice weapons stood along one wall. The floor was covered in sawdust. "It smells like Vielrona."

Bren began his forms, broadsword humming through the air. His movements were careful and slow, building strength from the control. Every few steps he glanced over at Alea. Power filled his sister's body, black snakes writhing under the pale surface of her skin. She moved her hands in the strikes and blocks of a hand-fighter, but they were careful and slow. Each strike sent lightning crackling across her fists and up her arms, the block smacking with the force of a wave. The patterns her feet traced in the sawdust were edges in ice. Her hair whipped as she turned, water droplets surrounding her as they spun free from her skin.

When she came to a stop Bren applauded. "Toar, Alea, you're amazing." He began to move faster, adding speed to the force of his blade. They moved in mutual silence, pacing around the room like circling predators. The bell tolled close to noon before Alea spoke again.

"I won't hurt you, but stay in that corner, will you?"

Bren turned to see her in the center of the hall. He frowned, but did as she bade, tightening his steps. After a moment even his movements slowed and he simply watched.

"I have an idea about the battle, but it's rough. I was hoping I might have your input."

"I'm not sure what use I'll be."

"Is Arman still ours?"

"What?" His heart faltered at the ferocity in her eyes. "What do you mean?"

"You saw him the other night. I told you I could feel him breathe. You think I couldn't tell he'd been in your room?"

"Alea, I'm sorry—"

"I'm not angry. I saw him, regardless, and I think I understand your reasons. Thank you for trying to protect me. Is he still ours?"

"You saw him."

"I no longer know the man he has become." Her words were clipped from anger or something else Bren could not name.

"Regardless of his words, or yours, he's yours. He always will be, Alea." He frowned. "What is your plan?"

"Watch." She grabbed his hand briefly, just long enough for icy tingling to wash over him, then she let go. "Trust me." She closed her eyes and spread her fingers. He watched her chest heave with slow, deep breaths. With each inhalation the air grew colder. Moisture dripped down the stone walls, pooling in the sawdust. The puddles grew, the water rising. It crept across the floor towards them and Bren mentally repeated Alea's command to trust her. *I hate water.* He ordered his feet to stay still. The water was a pace away from him when it halted, still rising, but moving no closer. It continued to fill the room, roaring, thundering around them, past waist height. Still it did not touch him. *I'm in a bubble of her power.*

Alea was not, however. The water surrounded her, swirling over her head. It crashed against the ceiling and Bren wondered if he should break her concentration, if she would drown. He was about to call her name when her eyes flew open.

The silver light pierced through the water and her voice echoed in his mind. *Imagine this, across an entire battle field. All our allies protected, all our enemies drowning.* The power in her voice pulled terrified nausea to his stomach. *Imagine the battle field covered in the power of the oceans and the other half burning, ignited with Arman's power.* The water retreated slowly, draining the way it had come. The damp sawdust was the only evidence of her colossal display.

Bren reached a shaking hand to his sister as the glow in her eyes faded. He had seen atrocities as a soldier. They had made his stomach tight, at first, even made him sick. Nothing shook him to his bones like she did. "I'll need a bit of time to process that." He sheathed his sword with shaking hands. Seeing the guarded expression on her face, he felt suddenly guilty. She was alienated enough. "I love you, still."

Her smile was brief, and erased by a frown when he sank on to a bench. "Are you all right?"

"We're going to win." He could only manage a whisper, but there was no doubt in his words.

Φ

Alea tilted her face up to the sun. Though Bren had offered to accompany her to the smithy, she declined. He was dear to her, but his energy sometimes only highlighted her loneliness. A squire guided her quickly to the office in the rear of the forge. The door was open and she knocked quietly. "Master Rulhan?"

The broad man glanced up then stared. "Dhoah' Laen?"

She smiled. The sight of his myriad braids and deep, rich eyes made her heart ache unexpectedly. "You're of Sunam?" She used her native language, throat tight around the familiar sounds.

"As are you, I've heard." He followed her lead and fell into the throaty Sunamen tongue. "What might I do for you today?"

"I'm looking for armor. Something light, simple."

He leaned back, broad hands crossing behind his head. "If you care to have a seat, I'd gladly design you something."

She sat, all nervousness erased by his low voice and the punctuating gestures that he had learned as a child. When he asked about her fighting style, she met his eyes. "I'll need something in metal — no boiled leather, and I'll need to move easily."

He sketched a few more lines on his design and slid it across the desk for her to peruse. "May I ask what town you call home?"

"Cehn. I was raised by Ahme'reahn ira Suna, may he be blessed with peace."

Rulhan's lined face softened into weathered wrinkles. "Oh, I am so sorry. I have not been home in many years, but I am lucky that its streets still bustle and my mother and brothers and sisters are as loud and playful as ever. What do you miss the most, besides your family, may they be blessed with peace?"

"The layers." She looked up, noting the perfect understanding in the man's eyes. "I miss the smell of the sand cooking under the sun and the spices blowing up to my window from the market."

"And the way the palm fronds would hiss in the wind, the sand scuttling across the stones like women on their way to do the washing. I told your brother you did us honor."

"Your words are kind, but untrue. I am a poor example of a Sunamen woman." Alea slid the paper back to him. "This looks lovely, thank you." She rose and made for the door, but his voice stopped her.

"How many sandstorms did you live through?"

She smiled. It was a common phrase, noting the speaker's greater age. "Nineteen years' worth."

"You remember them well, then. You remember the rage with which they beat our walls. All those layers you loved, they tore them away until all that was left were our souls, sometimes." He gestured to her. "Dhoah' Lyne'alea, you are a sandstorm beating against the world. You are more Sunamen than anything."

She pressed her brow against the doorframe. "Do you miss it?"

"Every day. Now, let me get to work on your armor, *ahalni*."

Her smile broadened at the Sunamen term that meant both "sandstorm" and "terrible blessing." The mirth felt strange on her sorrow-worn features and she maneuvered her way back across the forge. She took a winding route back to the palace, enjoying the sounds of the city and the warmth.

"Dhoah' Lyne'alea, this is a pleasant surprise!"

Alea shielded her eyes to see Daymir crossing the street. She waved a greeting. "How is your day going, Lord Daymir?"

"Well. Would you care to join me for lunch?"

"Where were you thinking?"

"I was just returning to the manor, and planning on having whatever my household prepared. If you have an idea, by all means, direct me."

Alea paused. *What would he say if I asked to find a street vendor? If I wanted to walk the market?* "Yours is a fine suggestion. I have a brief errand to run, then I'll pay you a visit."

Daymir gave her a true smile then. "I'll await you patiently."

Her errand was as much an excuse as anything. She quickly exchanged her training clothes for a light gown. She glanced in the mirror and frowned. She looked like a noblewoman. *How do I want him to see me?* She never cared which side she showed to Arman. She had been weak and strong and distant in turns, and each new change he took in stride. *Until now.* She ignored the nasty voice in the back of her mind and turned back to her dressing table. Daymir was an ally and she would treat him as such. She unbraided her hair and removed all her jewelry. Another glanced in the mirror before she left told her enough. She was unquestionably Laen.

Daymir's manor was one of the largest in the noble quarter. Centuries of water run-off had stained the white stone gray. The high, iron gate was covered with ivy and led into a small courtyard. She pulled the thin chain beside the gate that no doubt rang a bell somewhere deep inside the house. Moments later a serving man swung the door open for her. "Good morning, Dhoah' Lyne'alea, welcome. I am Master Currow, steward of my lord Daymir's house."

Alea followed him through the large front door. The house was beautiful and she ordered her expression into careful appreciation. The finery of the palace was expected, but the beauty here was surprising in a manor for one family, even a royal one. Daymir himself opened the door and his greeting shook her from her admiration.

"Welcome!" He stepped aside to allow her through. "I'm flattered you took the time to visit me. The meal should be ready shortly. Would you like a tour of the house?"

She could not help but grin at his enthusiasm. "Please, it seems lovely." She followed him through the lower storey. The large dining room led into an intimate parlor and a portrait hall. Everything was rich peacock blue, with copper accents. "Does the rest of your family live here as well?" Alea peered at the portraits of his siblings and parents.

Daymir followed her gaze, hands clasped behind him."Only myself and the household. My sister married several years ago, and my parents are long passed. I manage the estate."

"You seem forever busy. Is there much business being heir and treasurer, or is it the estate that concerns you?"

He led her up the sweeping stairs to the smaller upper floor. "All, truthfully. Much of my time is spent with Her Majesty, advising and discussing matters of government. She listens, though I will not truly be considered heir until she grows ill, I think."

"How is it you became heir?" Bren's new duties had sparked her own curiosity.

"Her only daughter passed as a child. There are only distant cousins after me." He paused to let her admire the potted plants on the broad landing at the top of the stairs before opening a door to his private study. It was off the large master chambers and the other familial rooms were down a short hall. Papers and accounts were neatly stacked on the polished wood desk and a tall bookshelf stood behind. A table was set for a meal for two by the large window and two comfortable chairs were pulled out for them.

Alea took one of the seats, happily noting the steaming pot of tea on the table. "Your house is beautiful, Lord Daymir."

"Thank you, though it is my household to which you give the honor. I'm afraid I'm terrible at ordering such things. In the country, where I am unsupervised, things are in hopeless disarray."

She laughed, thanking him as he poured her tea. "Where are your family's estates?"

"The main family land is to the east, by the mountains. We also had a small manor not far from the Hartland with lovely pasture for sheep. I am afraid it has suffered from the latest raids, though."

"I'm sorry to hear that." The arrival of food interrupted Alea's next words and silence reigned as they ate. "You spoke of sheep, Lord Daymir. What does Athrolan trade in?"

Daymir looked at her curiously. "I never knew a woman who cared for politics if it wasn't necessary."

Alea winced at the assumption. "Athrolan is a land very different from where I was raised—in social customs, food and so forth. It interests me." She pointed at the plate before her. "For instance, this meal's flavor is a variation on a theme. Each part of a Sunamen meal has a distinct flavor." She paused, wrinkling her nose. "Forgive me, I met Master Rulhan today. Seeing a Sunamen face brought my thoughts to family and home."

"It must be wonderful to finally have a family." He looked at her with something that she assumed was intended to be sympathy.

"I'm sorry?" She frowned, glancing up from their food.

"Bren and your mother. Perhaps Azirik negates any stability they offer, but still, after not having a family, it must be nice."

She sat back. "Arman made your same mistake. I did have a family. I had a wonderful, loving foster father, and siblings."

"But they did not consider you such. You always refer the them with 'foster.'" His curiosity was gentle, but nonetheless probing.

"To my ihal I was daughter, to the others I was sister. It was I who add the 'foster,' not they. I do it to remind myself of the great gift they gave me, for which I will be forever grateful."

"It seems I place my boot in my mouth each time we speak." He looked down. "Forgive me, I realize I perhaps do not know you as well as I thought."

She allowed herself a smile, though her eyes were sharp. "How could you? We've barely met." She pushed away her empty plate. "But you are interesting enough for me to be curious to know more."

"In that case, if I may return to the safe subject of food, have you tried our maple syrup?"

"Never even heard its name."

"It's made from the sap of a tree we have here—not the paper birches, but another kind. It's sweet and best with breakfast."

"Perhaps with our next meal I'll try some." She rose as the plates were cleared and gazed out the window. She was aware of Daymir watching her, but did not turn to look. *What must I seem to him, this woman who sends his country to war.* Already his words told her enough of his opinions, despite the apology. "I have yet to visit Athrolan's library, but I was hoping to do some research. Is the collection extensive?"

"Quite. Not what it once was, in Claimiirn, but impressive. What were you hoping to find?"

She raised her chin, running a hand over the window's stone sill. "A way to kill the gods." She allowed herself a mental congratulations as he fell silent.

Finally he cleared his throat. "Your light talk and gentle manners make it easy to forget you embody Destruction."

"Creation as well."

"Right. You healed the Rakos." He looked down, making small folds in his napkin. "Do you mind if I ask you about it?"

She did mind, but knew the questions he would ask were not the most uncomfortable. "What did you wish to know?"

"What was it like? Did you fight the gods for him?"

"Souls go through me to Le'yne. It is a deep place, and guarded by the souls of the Laen. I had to tear them apart to find him, but I did."

Daymir shuddered. "Were you scared?"

She frowned. "I think I must have been. I ignored whatever part of me was scared." She watched as he thought over her words. *Please do not ask me why.*

"I heard he left for the south, to raise more allies?"

"I assume so. I want to investigate the library. Would you care to join me?" The invitation was dishonest, but she feared he would realize why she was fleeing the conversation.

Daymir rose, giving her his hand. "I'm afraid I have business this afternoon. Perhaps another time?" He escorted her to the manor's gates. "I hope you find what you are looking for, Dhoah' Lyne'alea."

She pulled a smile onto her face as he showed her out. Pretending at happiness grew harder each time. She wondered absently if it was the fatigue of pretending that caused some to die so young.

CHAPTER

THIRTEEN

The 28th Day of Aeme, 1252
The City of Ceir Athrolan

THE SUN WAS JUST RISING when Alea startled awake. She curled into the enveloping library chair, an open book forgotten on her lap. Her shoulder and neck ached from the awkward position she had slept in. She frowned. She had dreamt of Arman and of anger, though she wondered if they were one and the same. She straightened with a groan.

"Dhoah' Lyne'alea?"

Daymir sat at a desk by the windows.

Her face flamed and she sat up hastily. "Good morning, Lord Daymir." She smoothed her hair and skirts. "Forgive me, I must have fallen asleep while reading."

He laughed. "I can't blame you. Some books are so dull. I didn't want to disturb you, but seeing as you're awake, how is your research going? Other than dream-worthy of course."

She smiled. "Well. I've learned a few things that might be useful."

When she did not provide more, he fixed her with a curious stare. "Could I help? I know this library well, and I might be able to answer questions you come across." His smile was easy, and she suddenly noticed how few lines it bore. "I want to be useful to you."

"Your help is welcome." She gestured dramatically to the pile of books before her. "I have yet to start these. I'm going to freshen up, but I'll be back in a moment." When she returned, washed and changed, Daymir had laid out parchment and quills neatly. He was already bent over a newer tome and making notes.

"You've gotten farther in a quarter of an hour than I did in five." She sat across from him in a huff of mock anger.

"I also took the liberty of ordering breakfast, as I assumed you had not yet had any."

She leaned forward, eyes narrowed. "Have you ever been filled with cold? I suspect you might be the real Dhoah' Laen."

He grinned. "Yes, you've found me out."

She matched his smile. The expression was still strange, but it was hard not to smile as their quick wits dueled. "We always seem to eat together."

"I believe conversation is more entertaining when stimulated with food. What have you found thus far?"

"Not a lot. I already know how the gods killed Lynelle. I read something that says their being—soul, I suppose—is linked to their power, but it was vague."

"It's a start." Daymir slid writing materials over to her. "And that is better than nothing."

The rest of the morning passed easily, and in relative quiet, save for the arrival of their meals. Alea enjoyed dipping ham and biscuits in the syrup Daymir had mentioned before. They found small details and vague allusions. Nothing was specific, but an idea began to uncurl in the darkness of Alea's mind.

Suddenly Daymir sat back. "Why aren't you attacking them now? Laying aside the lack of knowledge, of course. Not to judge, but wouldn't it be better to destroy the source of Azirik's power first?"

"Yes, if it were that simple. The God's Crown is a conduit to their magic. They could use it as a well to hold their power, thus preventing me from destroying them. Through the Crown I can follow the connection back to them." She looked down. "So unfortunately, for me to protect this world, we must first wage war across it."

Daymir's clear gaze narrowed with humor. "You're terrifying, you know?"

She flushed, embarrassed and oddly flattered. "So I've been told."

He tilted his head at her. "It's a pity you can't sit on a human throne."

The sudden subject change tripped her thoughts. "There's a law against someone like me ruling? You think the Creator and Destroyer is not enough for me? You wish to not take the throne yourself?"

"None. I think you would make a good queen. There are no laws, for there has never been anyone like you. I guess I assumed the Laen would disallow it."

She ran a hand over a tome's cover to hide her sudden anxiety. "Before the war many Laen worked for high-born families, but none took such positions or married into them."

"Until your mother and father." A wary grin crossed Daymir's face. "Given the power that union birthed, perhaps there were more valid reasons."

She laughed. "Perhaps. After being Dhoah' Laen, a queen's duty would be an easy task."

He snorted and turned back to the books before him. They continued in relative concentration occasionally breaking the silence with a humorous comment or puzzled question. It was relaxing, despite the grim nature of their subject.

When Bren arrived just before noon, Daymir rose. "I'm afraid I must abandon you to your work—there are a few treasurer duties I should see to before tomorrow."

"Thank you for all your help." She smiled as he bowed over her hand and disappeared. Alea returned to her seat, staring at her book thoughtfully, though she did not actually read the words.

Bren took Daymir's vacated seat and fixed her with a serious expression. "Sistermine, what's between you and Lord Daymir?"

She looked up, startled. "What do you mean?"

"You've been spending a lot of time together. It makes me wonder at the intentions on either side."

"On either side? Bren I don't see what you're getting at." Her heart faltered and she looked away. She had been enjoying the attention. It may have only been a shadow of Arman's faith in her, but she would take it. She had purposefully been honest about her nature, hoping to avoid the awkward predicament that Bren now mentioned. "Bren, he called me terrifying. I think I'm safe."

He reached over and touched her hand. "Alea, Daymir seems to have grown an interest in you. He's a good man, I think, despite his opinion of me." His grin was lopsided. "But I want you to understand something. He is a shrewd and intelligent thinker. He's circling you, gauging your worth, though perhaps less analytically than that sounds." He sighed. "Alea, unless you mean business with him, I suggest you pull away."

"I resent you telling me what's best. He's an ally, nothing more. He may be circling, but he would be a fool to think he can gain anything. I am the Dhoah' Laen, for goodness sake, not a noble daughter to be used in a power-bargain, or whatever it is you're suggesting."

"Alea, you were raised a noble's daughter and you are very much able to act the part. You have the bloodline. You're incredibly powerful and not the least bit stupid. You're a perfect match for a king raising his country."

She rolled her eyes. "Why don't you marry me then? Fates, Bren, you sound paranoid."

"I know how he thinks. Alea, you're powerful and terrifying, but right now you are incredibly vulnerable. You have suffered heartbreak. Even if no one knows, it was obvious you saw Arman next to never before he left, and your manner about him has been reserved. Lord Daymir will read into that what he will."

"You never brought this up when I was seeing Narier."

"I didn't think your heart was in any danger then. Also, Narier was obviously just enjoying your company, like you were his. I doubt he ever had any intentions beyond spending nights. I just don't want your hurt over Arman to turn into false affection for Daymir. It'll hurt you both in the end." He closed the book before him with a snap. "He was right in one thing—you should leave the books for the evening. Come get some air with me."

Bren found an open hillock with an ocean view. The garden was quiet, the city's bustle only a distant mutter. Alea leaned her head against her brother's shoulder. "I'm angry at him, Bren, and I wonder if I can forgive him, and whether I should. Yet, I miss him."

"What did he say? Do you mind telling me?"

She was quiet for a minute, sifting through the emotions from her encounter with Arman to untangle just the words. She was grateful Bren knew better than to interject. Her voice was calm and incredibly soft. "I asked why he sought company in another woman. He said I had no claim to him, which is true, and our bond was not that of marriage, nor should I treat it as such. I had no right to dig about in his affairs, for they were his alone. We fought, with our power." Her voice wavered. "Bren, I threw my power at him. He blocked it, but I still tried to hurt him. Before he left he asked if I could have stopped myself from killing him if he hadn't blocked." She looked down, picking at her nails. "He said it's what I'm good at." She felt Bren's jaw tighten in anger.

"Alea." He stopped. "I'm sorry. Those words were not deserved."

"Part of me wants to hate him for it, but I can't. I wish I trusted myself enough to name my feelings." She closed her eyes against the burn of tears, but they did not fall. "It seems wrong to save the world without him beside me. That's why I brought him back." She slumped back. "Bren, my heart hurts." The sorrow and understanding on his face only made it worse. "It hurts so badly that I don't know how to breathe sometimes."

"Alea, did you love him?" It was the second time he asked the question, but the depth behind it was totally different.

She did not need to ask to which "him" her brother referred. "I once told Narier no one had seen my soul bared. It's not true, though I didn't realize it. Arman has seen my fear and my despair. My anger, my determination."

"What about happiness?"

"I guess I hoped we would have time for that, too."

Φ

The 35th Day of Aeme, 1252

The scarf over Alea's hair felt both familiar and strange at once as her past warred with her present. The simple dress and plain breeches were less so. She took back halls to the barracks, her steps purposeful. It had been months since the siege, and she was not keen to make a fool of herself, but she was also lonely. The six bed bunk rooms were labeled with surnames and she carefully paced down the rows, reading them. The variety of names told her much about Athrolan's trade history.

A young man stopped at the sight of her. "Miss? May I help you?"

She turned and shot him a smile. "I'm looking for Lieutenant Narier."

"You mean Captain? He got promoted last month. He expecting you?" The narrowed eyes were dark and she saw his guard visibly rise.

"No, not really. We're old friends and I'm finally back in the city. I thought I'd say hello."

He shrugged and pointed further down the hall. "Second to last on the left."

She followed his instructions, pausing outside the half-open door. She could hear the muted sounds of conversation and a deck of cards shuffled between calloused hands. Seeing the names on the doorframe she suddenly realized she did not know his given name. Before her nerves failed her, she knocked quickly. The talk paused and a chair scraped back.

An older man whose face she recognized, but name she did not know answered. "What might I do for you, miss?"

"I'm looking for Captain Narier."

"Hold a moment." He ducked his head into the room. "Narier, girl here to see you." He looked back to Alea. "Your name?"

"Alea."

His eyes inched over her and he stepped back a step. "Of course. Forgive me. Narier, it's the Dhoah' Laen."

Narier suddenly appeared in the door, shoving his friend aside. "Thanks, Jall, I'll take it from here." He did not ask her in, shutting the door instead. The hall was dim without the lantern light from the room. "Hello."

Her words faltered at his uncertainty. "Hello. It's good to see you again."

"And you." He ran a hand through his hair. "Dhoah' Lyne'alea, what're you doing here?"

"I thought we might talk, catch up, have a drink or two tonight."

"You're the Dhoah' Laen."

She frowned. Something cold bloomed in her stomach, but she was not sure why. "I always was."

His smile was sad and faint. "Oh. You don't see it, do you?" He drew a breath. "When we were together, during the siege, you were a young woman, bright and nervous with a big, shining title that didn't quite fit. Now she's grown and I can't even see her because you shine so bright, but if I could see through the glow of how brilliant you've become, I think I'd see that girl is gone. I don't recognize what's taken her place."

Alea stepped back, feeling the frown chase her nervous smile away. "Of course."

He had seen her as Alea, when she thought no one else had. Instead she mistook their indifference for fear and respect. Now she only had the latter two. She swallowed hard and shot him a falsely bright smile. "Of course. I'll see you about then. Good afternoon."

She walked slowly back to her room, trembling hands hidden in her skirts. The sound of her retching echoed against the tile of her privy room. She heaved again and again, wondering if she was sick enough everything she had become would fade, all the monstrous things in her mind would disappear. Perhaps Alea would return if she could rid herself of enough. Stomach empty, she lay on the floor, cheek to the cold flagging. It was impossible. There was nothing left of Alea inside her now, only cold and dark.

CHAPTER FOURTEEN

The 42nd Day of Aeme, 1252
The City of Ceir Athrolan

ALEA'S EYES WERE OPEN, but unseeing. Power filled her, but she did not use it. She reached deep into the earth to touch the massive icy pools within the bedrock. It was a way to center herself when insecurity threatened. Consequently, the exercise had become a daily ritual. Knocking cut through her concentration and her power faltered.

After the third knock, she sighed. "Who is it?"

"Daymir, Dhoah' Lyne'alea."

Darkness retreated from her skin and she smoothed her hair. When she pulled the door open it was with a smile.

Daymir's own smile faded when he met your eyes. "Are you all right? Your voice sounded odd."

She gestured for him to sit. "I was practicing my power."

"Hence the glowing eyes?"

She glanced in the mirror. Power still lit her irises. "Forgive me, I know it's unnerving." Sitting across from him, she changed the subject. "I see you have once again timed your visit to coincide with my midday meal. Shall I call for our food and be done with the pretenses?"

Daymir's smile curled ruefully. "That would be appreciated."

When she had ordered their meals she returned to her seat with a quiet sigh. "Our talks are a welcome diversion from dark thoughts."

"I feel the same. I train with the men, but knowing our skills will be needed soon darkens the fun." He tilted his head at her curiously. "You'll ride to battle again?"

It seemed so obvious she almost wondered if he was joking. "Yes."

"We were incredulous that you went to Shadow. I think only respect kept many from calling it foolish, begging your pardon."

"It was foolish." She was surprised by the embarrassment heating her neck. "I knew little about my power and vulnerability."

Daymir smiled. "I'm glad when you lead us next it'll be with the strength of your peoples' teaching behind you."

She looked down, frowning. Whatever her answer would be, it was stopped as their meals arrived.

Daymir apparently had seen, however, and after a few moments he asked gently, "Why did you frown when I spoke of them?"

"We disagree on several points, one being my power and how I should wield it. I can only hope they see my wisdom and aid me in the battle against the gods."

Daymir tilted his head. "Are you worried you can't do it alone?"

She looked down at her food, chewing thoughtfully. "No, but I went into every battle thus far with allies at my back. I would hope the most dangerous of all would be no different."

"Have you made any more headway with your studies?"

"I believe I have. Your notes about the source of their power helped a great deal." She could feel his senses sharpen each time she mentioned how much power she actually had.

"Yes, I thought that would be useful. Their magic can be destroyed along with their souls—though how you could do such a thing, on such a scale, I would rather not think about."

She smiled. "Understandable. I promise you, though, it will be done." She sat back, allowing their plates to be cleared and replaced with tea.

Daymir stared at her a moment, and she stared back, wondering at the dance of allies, nobles and friends. "I have an offer for you." His voice was lower than usual, and his features serious. "The reason I called on you today, actually."

Alea wondered suddenly if the abrupt tone was due to nerves. She had never seen him nervous. She poured them tea then made herself comfortable, waiting.

When they were both settled, he cleared his throat. "Your brother is acting king—an ally, no less. Your father is a crowned king. This makes you Mirik's princess."

She had not thought of herself as such. In the face of her other roles it seemed trivial. "I suppose, yes." His words hurtled toward the territory Bren warned against.

"Once this war is over, what were your plans?" He twirled his cup in his hands, almost splashing tea onto the burgundy brocade of his tunic.

"I hadn't thought on it. My energy is better spent preparing so there is an after."

Daymir took the gentle, yet pointed rebuke in stride with a smile. "And we will all be glad for it, I'm certain. I had a suggestion for you to think over. I stand to inherit Athrolan. With your political power, and obvious wisdom and level head, we would make a good match. It would be a position of wealth, for your comforts and the challenge of ruling for you mind. And," his voice lowered with well-concealed nerves, "I hope the acceptable companionship of myself."

Alea stared at him for several moments, speechless. "Are you proposing marriage to me?"

Daymir shifted. "I am."

She rose abruptly and went to the window, staring out. She felt his eyes bore into her back. She wished she was alone, so she could pace and worry the way she did on nights she couldn't sleep. Instead she stared unseeing down at the gardens. *Marriage.* Two years ago it had been something she needed to survive. She had been ready to start that life. Daymir posed an equally political and pleasant match, but something had changed. Her mind laughed at the idea now. *I'm not a young girl in need of protection. I am the Destroyer of Gods, the Creator of Worlds.* On the tail of those thoughts came another that she pushed aside. She knew who was the best match for her now. She straightened, still looking out the window. "What do you see when you look at me?"

"Excuse me?"

"What do you see?" She turned, letting only a fraction of the darkness inside her show. "When you sit there, on my couch, staring at me, what do you see?"

"I see our ally, I see Dhoah' Lyne'alea." He frowned.

She looked away. "You are so used to getting your way — not because you were spoiled, for I don't believe you were. You work for everything you have, with your mind and your money that you forgot sometimes other people work harder. You are mighty, Daymir, but my mind is darker than yours and my money far less and this makes me mightier than you. You are so used to getting your way that you only see what you want."

"What am I supposed to see?"

"Your aunt made a stupid mistake."

"Her Majesty is not stupid."

"No, but she is scared, Daymir. So very scared of her kingdom falling to ruin, of her people dying. A worthy fear, to be sure. But fear is dangerous, because it makes us desperate and desperation leads to stupidity." She did not move, save for her lips. Her eyes bored into the reflection of his, but even bounced off glass her expression was terrifying. "She believed me when I told her I would raise Athrolan, when I told her I would save her kingdom from falling. She believed I would even restore the Laen to power. So scared was she that she allowed a monster into her city. And you can't even see it."

His eyes were bright when she finally turned back, and cold slipped into her heart. He was afraid, certainly, for fear of her was an instinct, like fear of a storm.

But some men enjoy the sound of thunder, despite the fear. "Ah. Here I am trying to make you understand my power, hoping you'll stop your pursuit, when really, all I'm doing is making you more curious."

"You can think on it, if you wish. Like I said, after the war."

"Lord Daymir, I appreciate the sentiment, and the kindness with which it is offered. You would make a fine companion. I think, though, your offer shows a misunderstanding." She stepped over to where he sat and leaned forward, placing her hand on his. "I am not lost in this dangerous world. Perhaps I was, when I first arrived, but no longer. You forget I am not a human, and will not sit on a human throne. I cannot bear you heirs. I neither need nor seek political power. After this, all I seek is peace."

Daymir's lips tightened. "Do you seek it in the heart of Arrowlash?" The words were not cruel, but his tone was tense.

She winced. "Arrowlash is my ally and guard. Our relationship is no more than that. It is also none of your concern."

Daymir rose abruptly. "Forgive me for imposing on you, Dhoah' Lyne'alea. Good day." He bowed to her and showed himself out. The click of the door closing broke the tentative surface of Alea's emotions and she dropped her face into her hands. *That very well could have been the last proposal I ever receive. The last chance at the life of a woman.* She curled onto the couch, wrapping her arms around her shoulders and wept. *What chance did I ever really have of marrying and growing old beside a kind man? What wife would Creation and Destruction make?* She mourned that life, but a deeper part mourned the girl she once was.

A gentle knock interrupted her thoughts and when she ignored it a second, more persistent one sounded. "Sistermine, it's me. I saw Lord Daymir leave. His face...did you two argue?"

She collected herself then padded to her door. Bren was turning to leave when she opened it. His gaze ran over her tear-stained cheeks and swept her into a tight embrace. He stepped inside, arms still around her, and nudged the door closed with his foot.

"Toar, what happened?" His arms tightened around her and she felt her tears wet his shirt breast. "Did he hurt you?"

She shook her head quickly, pulling away and drying her eyes. "He asked me to marry him."

Bren's brows shot up and he pulled her onto the couch beside him. "Judging by his face, you declined." He ran a hand through his hair. "Is that tea still hot? I think we could both use a cup."

A tiny, real smile bloomed on her face while he poured her a cup. The world was at war and former Lieutenant Barrackborn's greatest concern was his sister's tears. "He was kind and thoughtful and gave me every reason to agree."

"I wondered if he'd propose and if you'd actually agree. I thought he'd ask after the battle, though." He shook his head.

"He offered to let me think about it until then. I can't imagine that life. Am I wrong? What other offers will I have, Bren? I know I'll never be a mother, but I had hoped to be loved. Am I selfish for wanting it all?"

Bren put down his tea and wrapped an arm around her again. "Alea, where are these thoughts coming from? I didn't know you wanted any of this. You could still have children."

"No, my body is not meant for it. I thought it was a curse, but now I think it is the combination of human and Laen blood."

"What do you mean?" The confusion on his open, angular face was almost comical.

"I don't bleed. Other women bleed with the cycles of the moon, twice a month. I never have." She shrugged. "I made my peace with it a while ago, but I still pictured my old age beside another."

"Oh." Bren sat back. "Why are you suddenly afraid of never?"

She sniffed, steadying her breath. "Perhaps, as a soldier, you made peace with mortality years ago. When my home was attacked I saw death—truly saw it—for the first time. Death surrounded me at Fort Shadow in the infirmary tents. With Arman I reversed it even. Somehow, I never realized that even if the world has an after, some people may not. For them, their world ended with this war." She sighed. "Am I making any sense?"

His soft laugh rumbled through her shoulder. "A bit. Seeing death is one thing. Understanding that it can happen to anyone is another. Understanding it can happen to you? Some people never realize that." He rested his chin on her head. "When did you start thinking this way?"

"It was gradual. Part of it came from Arman and Shadow. Seeing death so inglorious, without the rush and fear of danger. Part of it came from studying in Le'yne. As frustrating as my time there was, I learned a lot from the texts they had. I read about the splitting of the world. It is no wonder why they fear me." She sat up and took a few calming sips of her tea. "I'm sorry. It occurred to me that Lynelle sacrificed herself to split the worlds. It's easier to break than to mend." She was quiet for a moment. "What if I have to do the same to bind them?"

Bren pulled away further to look her full in the face. "You're my only sister and I love you, dammit, and you're not going to die."

She smiled again, broader. "Bren, you're babbling. I love you, too. It's not death that bothers me, mostly. I worry I'll leave things undone. Unsaid."

Bren gripped her hand. "I promise you'll get through this. We all will." He pulled her over and rested her head on his shoulder again.

She let him hold her, her tears drying, the sudden emotions retreating back into her chest. There was another, darker fear that she did not share. She was afraid of herself.

Φ

The 43rd Day of Aeme, 1252
The City of Ceir Athrolan

Alea woke late in the morning, blinking at the bright light streaming in the window. She stretched and the day before rushed to the fore of her memory. She groaned and lay back down. *My focus is waning.* She winced and tossed off her covers. It was late and she should plan for the battles ahead. A soft knock interrupted her perusal of her wardrobe.

Giire smiled as she stepped in at Alea's bidding. "Good morning, Dhoah', I knocked earlier, but you seemed still abed. I brought you some tea and a message from Master Rulhan of the smithy as well." She handed Alea an envelope before pouring a cup of tea.

Alea opened the message hurriedly. "Please inform Master Rulhan he can deliver my armor here. Also, I think a bath would do me good." She paused. "Could you have a note delivered to Lord Daymir?"

Giire curtsied. "Of course. I'll draw up your water." She glanced back at Alea for a moment. "Begging pardon, but you had armor ordered?"

Alea began to undress. "For the battle."

Giire looked down. "You're so mild-mannered, I forget you are a warrior." She stepped into the privy to prepare the bath.

Alea frowned. *Is that what I am?* She wrote a quick note to Daymir then hurried into the bathroom with a happy sigh. *Warrior or not, the luxury of a hot bath will never be lost on me.* As she sank into the water, she thought back to Vielrona. The darkness in her heart then had been a different color, perhaps, but she recognized the signs of the same isolation and depression. *What took me out of that mood, then?*

Giire hummed softly as she worked the tangles from Alea's hair.

Alea suddenly grinned. "Giire, do you often go into the city proper?"

"A few nights, yes. There is dancing and music, not to mention handsome faces." Her hands were gentle.

Alea stepped into the towel that the girl held out, enjoying the rough fabric on her skin. Her mind twisted back to the small purse locked in her desk. "Giire, I have a bit of coin. If I wrote you a list, might you get me a few things?" When she nodded, Alea moved to her desk, drying her hair as she went.

Giire read over the short list Alea handed her a moment later, brows knitting. "Dhoah', why do you want a wig?"

Alea sat on her bed. "Giire, you may have noticed I'm unhappy. It's been a very long time since I laughed and danced and listened to music. I'd like to go out into the city, and I'd like to just be a woman for a night."

Giire's eyes lit up. "I know just the place!"

Φ

The 43rd Day of Aeme, 1252

Tinkling rang through the manor, signaling a message and Daymir pushed away his paperwork. His conversation with Alea the day before left him irritable and in no mood to speak with anyone, even through parchment. Currow brought the envelope up a moment later.

"My lord, Her Majesty wishes to see you before you take supper. And a letter is here from Dhoah' Lyne'alea."

Daymir took the envelope with a frown. "Thank you, Master Currow." He opened it as his steward exited.

> Lord Daymir,
>
> I wanted to apologize for the way our conversation ended. Your offer brought up thoughts and fears that have plagued my mind for some time now, and I cannot face them until after the battle. In another time or place I would be happy to consider marriage and I am honored you thought of me. I hope this will not greatly affect our friendship, for I value it, and would be sad to see it fade.
>
> When, and if, you are ready to speak again, you know where to find me.
>
> Yours,
> Dhoah' Lyne'alea.

He wanted to reply, but his ill humor would help little. He brought Alea's letter to his study and called for his summer cloak. Even as a child, he had met with his aunt in the evenings for private, casual conversations. It was through these, he was certain, that his interest in politics arose. As gentle as she was, his aunt was a smart woman and knew her post well. Daymir waited as he was announced, then stepped into the anteroom. His manor house was larger than the royal suite, but the finery here was unrivaled. The anteroom led into a large receiving room that adjoined a study, beyond which was the queen's sleeping and dressing quarters. They normally took tea in the more intimate study, but this evening, Tzatia waited for him in the receiving room. Here the decorations were the formal colors of Athrolan, as opposed to the queen's favored lavender. She stared out the window. He could not see her face, but her back was stiff.

"Evening, aunt. Shall I order tea, or do you wish to take supper together?"

"Lord Daymir, I am your queen and your should address me as such." Many would have thought the tremble in her voice was anger. Daymir knew better. It was fear.

"What is it?" He ignored her request for formality. "Who has upset you?"

She turned and he saw, regardless of fear, her face was livid. "You, Daymir!" she faltered. He reached to steady her, but she backed away. "You think you can swindle and pinch and I won't notice? You may be Treasurer, but goodness, I am Queen!"

"What are you talking about?" He stepped towards her again.

She slapped him across the face. "A writ to move thirty-six thousand crown to an account accessible only to you? You think I would fall for this again?"

His mouth dropped open, both at her blow and her words. "Fates, Tzatia. You think that was swindling?" His temper rose. "It was for our future! I am not your husband. I inherit this nation and I intend for it not to be bankwasted when I do."

"Not anymore." Her hands shook as she offered an envelope. It was decorated by her royal and personal seal as well as those of several advisors. It was address to him.

Dread filled him. "'Not anymore,' what?" He opened the envelope quickly. It was a formal document stating his attempt to steal from the crown. It stripped him of his titles and power as Treasurer and his right to the throne. "You're jesting." He rubbed a hand across his eyes. "Tzatia, I was thinking of Athrolan. You have seen Mirik fall to the consequences of war. I was trying to aid our kingdom, not better myself! You can stop this now. Revoke it." Alea's words about fear and deseration echoed in his head.

Her mouth set in a determined line. "It's done. I sent it to the scribes. If your actions were only for the kingdom, why did you propose marriage to Dhoah' Lyne'alea? Was that for us as well? You could have destroyed our alliance!"

"She's interesting and intelligent and would make a good ruler. I enjoy her company."

Tzatia turned, running a hand along the back of her settee. "I no longer recognize you as my heir, or Treasurer of the kingdom. You are stripped of your lordship and gallantry, relieved of all estates, excepting those of your father and excused from court and my person."

He realized then that she was serious. "For what little my word is worth, I only ever thought to raise our home." He bowed. "Forgive me for choosing the wrong path by which to do so. Good night, Your Majesty." He showed himself out and moved stiffly down the hall. He contained himself until he once more stood in his manor. As soon as the door shut, he slumped against the wall of the anteroom, a trembling hand over his eyes. Every constant in his world was gone. He drew a breath, then another. This was what he was good at—clearheaded thoughts while the world crumbled. He never thought it would be his world. He swallowed hard, mind racing, and called for Currow.

"How was your visit with Her Majesty, my lord? You did not stay as long as I expected. Would you like me to order your supper?"

Daymir ignored the offer. "Have all my personal effects packed. They are to be shipped home, to the estate. All my accounts and debts are to be paid off—from my personal funds, please. The furniture not owned by the crown will be sold, as will all horses save for my jumper and charger. All but the nuclear household staff is dismissed with compensation though the end of the month."

"My lord?" Currow stared at Daymir, a deep frown on his face.

Daymir looked up. Currow had served the Xain family since Daymir's father had inherited. They knew each other like family.

"Is this about the funds you transferred?"

"I was safeguarding for after the war, so we would not have empty coffers with which to rebuild. She saw it as swindling, like with Parkvenir. She disinherited me and stripped me of all titles."

"Is there anything else I can do for you, my lord?"

"Stop calling me 'lord.' I am no longer one. I am simply Master Daymir."

Currow bowed his head. "I'll set your affairs in order then, Master Daymir."

"Currow?"

"Yes, sir?"

"I would appreciate your utmost discretion and haste."

"Of course, sir."

Daymir watched him go, then hurried up to his study. It was no longer his, truly. He penned a reply to Alea and sent it out. He was halfway through packing the contents of his desk and bookshelves when the second shock wave of the events hit him. He sunk onto the floor beside the trunk of books. He drew off the ring of the royal house and the seal of Treasurer. All that remained was his personal signet ring, alone on his hand. He felt naked.

Φ

The 1st Day of Lumord, 1252
The Feld de Barran

Dense clouds obscured the windswept rocky fields below. The air whipped as Arman passed, curling around him and through him. It tickled. He grinned, though he wondered if it was truly a smile when his body had no more form than smoke. Leaving Athrolan lifted a mass of lead from his gut. He was not sure it if was due to what he left behind or flew toward. Tzatia had asked him to accompany the fleet, but something deeper drove him south. He crossed leagues in minutes, his unsubstantial body wheeling with each gust of clouds and air.

Ahead, the familiar crest of the Orn de Duhtain rose, barely scraping the underbelly of the clouds. He had seen so much, done so much, that even home looked quaint. *Will Vielrona ever be home again? Will any of them know me?* He bent, diving lower as he grew nearer the city. *Besides, if there were ever a place the Rakos hid, it would be in Vielrona.* The arms of the hills below curled about his home. His smile grew as he caught the brilliant glow of firelight. With so many torches, he must be arriving in the midst of a festival.

He banked again, wheeling closer. The smoke smelled of meat and acrid rot. The rubble below still smoldered. Few walls were left standing. *Fates, not this.* His tears and adrenaline sharpened his eyes, and they caught movement on the edge of the destruction. The fields that had once held cows were now a survivors' camp. The bloated carcasses of livestock were piled high. The fact that some bore marks of butchering spoke to the desperation of those left.

Makeshift lean-tos and tattered shelters clumped in vague groups. There were only enough to house eighty, a hundred at most. Grief caused his concentration to stutter and his bones began to reform. He tumbled from the air, muscle and organs writhing back into place as they solidified. He exploded onto the ground, limbs shaking from horror and pain. Rage billowed. "This was my home!" The voice that tore itself from his throat was not one he recognized. The destruction was greater than he ever imagined, greater than anything he saw at Shadow. It was as if the mountains themselves had tried to swallow the city.

He was suddenly aware of the silence behind him. The camp was still, those closest staring at him. They were too exhausted to be curious, and pain had burnt away any awe that might have shone in their eyes. Arman staggered to his feet and turned toward them. They slowly went back about their work, not caring that a man just materialized from the clouds.

A familiar dark figure cleaned ashes from an old well and Arman stepped closer, waving smoke from his eyes. "Kam?"

The man straightened, blinking at him for a moment. Recognition swept the locksmith's features suddenly and he stepped forward. "Arman?"

Arman nodded, not sure what to say, or how to begin. He could scarcely remember what he had looked like when he left Vielrona. They were separated by several paces, a haze of smoke and what seemed like a lifetime. "What happened?"

The darker man sighed wearily. All the characteristic jesting had gone from his face. "Come have a seat and we'll get you what we can for a drink." He brought the Rakos across the campsite to a small tent and gestured to an overturned crate. "Sit."

Arman folded himself onto the crate, clasping his hands to hide his nerves. A woman emerged from the tent, shot a weak smile at Kam and turned to go.

"Cel, look who came back." Kam's voice stopped her. Her hair was lank and her body thin, save for her pregnant stomach.

"Celly?" Arman stood and swept her into his arms. The cold, awkward spell was broken and he embraced Kam, too.

"Arman, I can't believe you're here!" Celly held him at arms' length. "Your last letter was so grim, I wondered if we'd see you again."

"I wondered myself." He gestured at her abdomen with a grin. "I see your marriage has been fruitful."

She smiled and patted herself. "More than halfway there." A shadow flitted across her face. "I expected to raise him on Gratchen Lane, not in a refugee camp."

Arman looked away. He understood unexpected futures, but he had chosen his. Their child never could. "What the fuck happened?"

"The gods." Kam crouched by their meager fire.

"What?"

"The gods struck us down. I don't know how or why, but the very air turned to poison. Great clouds of brown gas covered the streets. It hit the market first, pouring out of the temples. We never stood a chance."

"When? What of the others?"

"Two weeks ago." Kam stared at the fire. "Wes is gone. Veredy, too."

Arman dropped his head in his hands. The panic in his gut returned with a vengeance. "And Ma?"

Kam shuffled over and placed a hand on Arman's shoulder. "I'm so sorry."

Arman moaned. His mother, Veredy, Wes, they were pieces of him. They were the sand that formed the pearl of his soul. He had built his life around their existence. His chest was too tight for him to speak or breathe. He could barely hear Celly's soft words over the roaring in his head.

"We were able to get her out for a proper burial, more than we could do for Wes and Ver. I can bring you to see her, if you wish."

Arman rose with a stiff nod, still too sick to speak. She took his hand gently and led him through the camp. The dead were laid in achingly long lines. Some trenches lay open beside them, but the process was slow and the manpower weak. Celly stopped at one linen-wrapped form. A metal charm hung from the cord binding the shroud. He slid to his knees beside the body, his hand finding the sunburst charm. His fingers traced the metalwork rays, the holes cut in swirls and loops like flames. It was the piece his father made for her. It hung above their door for as long as he could remember. The sharp metal of the edges drew runnels of blood as his hand clenched around it. Part of him, that nasty voice in the back on his mind, had known this would be what he found. The shock still shook him to his bones.

He wrapped his mother's burnt body in his arms, not caring about the smell. His tears finally came, scalding, burning hotter than his skin ever had. He held her long into the night, rocking in the rain. He told her about Alea and Bren. He told her of his conversations with Eras and the journey north. He wept and laughed in turns. His voice hitched as he explained what he was, what he had always been. It was well into the evening when he finally drew back. "I love you. I wish I'd been here. I hope you were proud. I hope you're at peace." He brushed his hand across her covered face. "I'm proud you were my ma." He kissed her brow and stood, making his way shakily back to the tent where Kam waited.

The locksmith crouched by the campfire, glancing up at Arman's approach. "This isn't the homecoming you deserve."

"It's the one part of me expected."

Kam handed him a tin cup of thin soup. "What brought you back?"

"I'm not sure. Her Majesty Tzatia bid me sail north, with the fleet heading off the Berrin, but I had to come here first."

"Tzatia? Fleet?"

It struck Arman then, how different things had become. "The queen of Athrolan."

Kam's expression was closed. "You want to drag what able men survived into war?"

Arman looked down. "No. Your numbers are too small to make a difference against what we face."

"What do you face?" Kam's low voice was disbelieving. "You found a strange woman in the desert. A month later you ride off with her and we barely hear from you. What happened?"

Arman could not find the words. There was too much to explain, too much that he had avoided for so long. "What have you heard from the north?"

"The Dhoah' Laen came. She's fighting the gods and humans joined both sides." Kam shrugged. "It didn't feel like war, until the attack. Everything was so far away."

"Alea's the Dhoah' Laen. We fight those who wish her dead and the world destroyed. Sounds trite when I put it that way."

"I wondered as much, when the news came. You fit with her, you know. Maybe not at first, but the last weeks you were here, we all could see it."

Arman was grateful his friend did not mention who noticed them most of all. He was not yet ready to hear her name again. He watched Kam's gaze inch over the changes before him.

"Dore Jehan said you flew in on the clouds, formed out of the air."

"Fates, you still listen to the Jehans?" The joke seemed to fall flat for a moment, then Kam snorted. His laughter pealed across the campsite, and tears leaked from the new lines around his eyes. Arman joined him, his belly aching with each guffaw. "You know, after all, I think the Jehan's have been right about everything. Just not when we were ready to hear it."

Kam sighed, mirth fading into fatigue again. "So what are you in all of this?"

"You know the Rakos?"

"You're kidding? Fire in the hands and flying?" Kam poked the fire with a stick. "Could have used that."

The accusation was not lost on Arman. "I'm glad you and Celly have each other. What'll you do now that Vielrona..." He could not bring himself to say the words. "Now?"

Kam shrugged. "We were going to move north, settle in a town. We'd need a place for my work and her cooking and for a baby. I'm too scared to think so far ahead."

Arman frowned suddenly. "I know a place you would be welcome, though it's far." The hope in Kam's eyes set a new ache in Arman's chest. "Travel to Ceir Athrolan and take a boat to Mirik. Alea's brother is the Military Commissioner there, acting king right now. He'll give you a good home and work. If you tell him who you are, he'll take care of everything until you get your bearings."

"It's a long way to travel, but I'll tell Celly." He watched Arman glance north. "You're leaving soon?"

Arman's silence was answer enough and Kam raised his hand to stall him. He ducked into the tent, emerging a moment later with a thick envelope. "I was headed to the message hall when the attack came. Fate's would have it that I bore a letter from your mother." He handed it to Arman. "When will we see you again?"

Arman's jaw was tight. "I wish you both the best of luck. You deserve it." He offered his arm, but not an answer. "Take care of each other."

"You, too." Kam gripped his friend's arm too tightly. "You and Lyne'alea."

Arman turned and disappeared into the darkness without another word. He flung himself into the sky, his grief and rage fueling his ascent. He wondered why, when his future was certain, his skin crawled with the pity in Kam's eyes.

CHAPTER FIFTEEN

The 2nd Day of Lumord, 1252
The City of Ceir Athrolan

ALEA STEPPED INTO THE OFFICERS' quarters, suddenly glad for the confidence respect gave her. She wore somber colors, though the seamstresses seemed to sew little else for her. Her knock on the doorframe was purposeful. "Narier, I need to speak with you."

After a moment he emerged, his face tired and his eyes impatient. "Dhoah' Lyne'alea."

"I have a favor to ask of you."

His lips thinned. "Listen—"

"As the Dhoah' Laen I ask a favor of Narier, captain of my ally's military."

His features relaxed and the relief in his eyes hurt more than she expected. "Right. Of course." His words echoed hers from their last meeting and he stepped aside. "Come in."

"I'd still rather it was private."

His laugh was little more than a sharp exhalation. "No one else is here." It was a sparse room, only the trunks and the coverlets showing any homey personalization.

Alea took a seat at the long table before the small hearth. "I'm sorry for bothering you again."

He raised the wick of the lantern and took a seat across from her. "I'm sorry you think that you bother me."

"Narier, please." She looked down at her hands. She wanted to remain as aloof and practical as possible. The conversation was already veering away from her careful plans. "Please be consistent in how you act. I understand sharing the night and I understand distant civility, but I can't waver between the two. I get enough of that from Arman."

"Right." He straightened and rubbed his hands together. "What can I do for you then?"

"I'm leaving Athrolan within the week. I'm headed east. It doesn't matter if I seem male or female, as long as it's not what I actually am."

"How'd you expect to pull that off?"

"I've got the guts. They won't expect it to be me. I need a patrol uniform. An officer's. Do you have a spare?"

"You're too small."

Alea's eyes narrowed. "You're not that much taller than I am, Narier." She faltered. "Why?"

"Why what?"

Her eyes flicked up to his, the layers of darkness and anger and determination peeling back to show the raw confusion and vulnerability. "I wasn't looking for a lifetime, Narier, just company."

"I can't judge what you did in Shadow, Lyne'alea, because I may have done the same were I in your boots. Doesn't mean it feels right. Doesn't mean the dreams I have are good. You ripped the life right out of those people—allies too. You turned the laws of the world upside down for your guard. You might be great and powerful and fucking beautiful. Doesn't mean you're human. Not anymore."

"Thank you for your honesty. I realize you were being kind before, not telling me all the truth. Thank you for that, as well."

He sighed and scrubbed at his face. "Anything else I can do?"

She rose, shaking her head. The black shutters clanged shut over her heart and eyes once more, but she did not trust her voice.

Φ

Alea wondered at Daymir's brisk response requesting her to visit. It made her nervous, but she hoped his bitterness was waning. *Besides he'd be a fool to try to hurt me.* She made her way quickly to the manor and rang the bell at the gate. *Our courtship, if I want to call it that, was barely two months during a tumultuous time. What did he really think my answer would be?* Sunamen courtships lasted years, sometimes even before the betrothal was announced. *Perhaps the Athrolani do things differently.* It was a moment before Currow let her in. His face was lined and looked more tired than before. "You received the message, Dhoah' Lyne'alea?"

She froze in the doorway of the manor, not answering. Portraits and art were gone, and what was left of the furniture had been covered in drapes. Everything personal was gone.

"I believe he left something for you in the study, Dhoah'. I'll be here if you need anything."

Alea ascended the stairs in a rush, thoughts turning, and pushed opened the study door. The empty bookshelves seemed to echo. A single tome and sheet of parchment waited for her on the desk. She unfolded the latter warily.

> *Dhoah' Lyne'alea,*
>
> *I apologize for not receiving you myself, to explain everything, but I have gone home to my father's estate. My forethought for my country was misinterpreted and thus I must leave my titles and power in Ceir Athrolan for another. The events of the past few days have given me much to think on – your decline of my proposal, Her Majesty disinheriting me and my ultimate return to the country.*
>
> *I wish to apologize for my bitterness during our last visit. I expected a refusal due to your feelings for Arrowlash. I could have understood that – what human man truly competes against a Rakos? My pride was wounded when your choice was based on other concerns. The pain of that wound caused my bitterness. I wish I was through with those thoughts but I am just a man and still frustrated that things did not go as I planned.*
>
> *I left you this letter in part to explain myself, but also to tell you my thoughts on your problem with the gods. You mentioned your bond with Arrowlash was a soul bond. If the gods' powers are tied to their souls, perhaps you could make them bleed soulblood. Would their powers lessen? This book contains a section on the gods' various powers – I thought it might help prepare you. It is the only copy in North Athrolan, and my personal one, so I would take it as a kindness if you keep the stains of tea or god-blood from its pages.*
>
> *I am sorry for my poor attempt at humor, and I wish you well. Perhaps we can meet when this is over. I'm*

sorry, once again, for how I acted and my assumption
about our relationship.
    Best wishes, Dhoah',
    Daymir

Alea lowered the letter slowly and ran a hand over the cover of the tome. It was a thin one and the canvas-covered wood was new, as was the parchment. *I forget that being the foster-daughter of an ihal was not nearly as privileged as I thought. Daymir is wealthier than I realized, to pay for a new scribing of a text – one of which there are few copies.* She tucked the tome and letter carefully under her arm before showing herself out. She would respond, but later, when everything was clearer. Instead, she returned to her room, thoughts running amok.

She was so distracted that she tripped over a trunk in the middle of her room. She frowned at it, rubbing her shin. The chest was made of new wood and decorated by the seal of the palace smithy. She paused, taking a breath. *My armor.* The lid rose easily. The breastplate shone muted silver. The metal curved simply, and two tapering lines decorated the front to show her form. It buckled at the shoulders and waist to a backplate. Beside it were matching greaves and rerebraces. The metal was polished, but not to a high sheen, and the soft glow made Alea smile. *He knew what I meant when I said understated.* She laid the pieces on her bed. Underneath the oilcloth in the trunk was a mail hauberk, treated with a wash that made the metal glint blue in the light. The sleeves reached her elbows and the split skirt to just above the knees. It was heavier than she expected, but not too bad.

She drew it out and placed each piece of armor on the stand that in a normal woman's chambers would hold her best dress. Rulhan's work was beautiful. The backplate had simple swirling designs on its surface, ones she recognized from old Sunamen runes. *Sandstorm. Death. Life.* She reached out, eyes spiraling silver and her skin marbled black. Her fingers traced the patterns of the armor, mentally stitching power into each hammer mark. She withdrew after a moment, guilt uncurling at her actions. *This isn't selfish. If I die, the world goes with me.*

Feeling suddenly restless, she rang for Giire. The woman arrived after a moment, a large bag under her arm. She flashed Alea a grin. "Dhoah', I found what you wanted." Her brows rose at the sight of the armor as she entered, but she looked quickly away. She laid her finds on the bed. The wig was dark blond, the curls stitched up around the crown and the lower half left free. Giire had also found a dress more suited to a night in a tavern than Alea's other outfits.

Giire paused as she smoothed the skirts. "Dhoah' Lyne'alea, aren't you worried about going out alone?"

Alea shrugged. "You said yourself that I was a warrior." She turned, already binding her hair up. Her grin was wicked. "Besides, I thought you could come with me."

Giire's eyes widened. "You barely know me."

Alea stammered to a halt. The woman was right. Giire probably knew Alea much better than Alea knew her. She was not even certain whether the other woman liked her at all. "I'm sorry. I forgot what it was like to work behind everything. I don't know you at all." She echoed her thoughts. "I'm not even sure of your opinion of me."

Giire wrinkled her nose. "You're a bit dark-tempered for my tastes, and I have little interest in weapons or war or healing, like yourself."

Alea turned away, taking her hair down. It had been a stupid idea, and her face flushed with embarrassment. "I'm sorry, Giire. I did not mean to offend you." The hand on her hers was firm. She turned about.

Giire's smile was gentle as she held up the wig. "You like dancing, Dhoah' and that is something I can appreciate. Why don't you come with me to my favorite tavern at the end of the week? We can see if there's anything else we have in common."

Φ

The 5th Day of Lumord, 1252

Arman's every muscle was tense. He knew he needed to focus, but his mind spun wildly off topic. *If I'm not careful, I'll slip and fall to my death.* Days had passed since he rested. He had intended stay a night or two in Vielrona, visit his mother, drink with his friends.

He shoved himself deeper into his thoughts, aiming for the narrowed, taunting eyes in the back of his mind. *Eana. I'll find you.* He flung his mind out, spreading his consciousness over the land. Humans were glittering red pinpricks, tiny fireflies scattered on a bleak landscape. He faltered, wondering briefly at the color.

Eana's answer clattered through his musing. *Fear. Find me.*

His response was closer to a snarl than actual speech. *If you stopped the damned riddling maybe I could! It's like you don't even want me to find you.* He threw his power after his mind, pouring himself into the search. A white-gold flame bloomed on the edge of his mind, and another and another. Four brilliant lights dotted the land ahead of him, leagues apart. *No wonder they think we're dead.*

He dove, spinning east toward the Berrin border. The rolling plains of the Felds became hills separated by shallow streams. In the south were the gray waters of Berme's Eye, the lights of Berrinal bobbing with the swells. As a child he had wondered about the floating city, but after living through so many of the legends he read, he was disinterested. Spindly, stilt-rooted trees covered the great mounds punctuating the flooded lowlands. He flew lower, startling a pair of strange birds half his height. They took off, clacking their red beaks in protest.

One hillock burnt in his mind and he wheeled towards it. It was larger than the others, great stones covered with vines and crumbled by prying roots. *This was a temple. One of ours.* He recognized the statues flanking the caved in doorway, the upheld hands. They matched those in Elanal. He skimmed the ground, weaving along the streams until he materialized at the base of the temple. The ground was rocky and marshy in turns and it took a moment to find a suitable place to camp.

He gathered a few pieces of damp wood and flicked fire at them absently. *I'm here. It's your turn to come and get me.* He settled himself onto the ground and pulled his mother's letter from his shirt. The envelope was charred on one corner and stained. The ordered writing on the front was achingly familiar and he swallowed hard before slitting it open.

> *Dearest Arman,*
> *Your letters are a joy and your adventures amazing. I can hear in your words that you're changing. We heard rumors about your allies – the Athrolani for one – and*

*your descriptions are beautiful. I wish I could see
everything with my own eyes.*

*Your latest letter said you never had the chance to
explain certain things. Something about two ancient
bloodlines. The latest news from the north includes a man
of the Rakos. It said his given name is Aud'narman. I
pretended it coincidence, but there were changes in you
even before you left, changes even a mother cannot deny.*

*I hope you found happiness. I hope you found love.
The more your life changes the more I understand you'll
not come home. At least, not as the man who left.
Sometimes I wish it was not so, because you are my baby,
my son. If you found contentment, then I am glad.*

*The enclosed was the ring with which I married
your father. It now belongs to whatever wife you may
find on your journey. Live your life, ride your
adventures, love your woman, but never forget us here,
who love you and who will always keep a lantern lit for
your return, whenever it may come.*

I will love you, always,

Ma

Arman upended the envelope over his palm. The ring
fell into his hand, heavy and glinting in the firelight. Simple
twisted gold held an unpolished sapphire. He slid it onto his
smallest finger before returning the letter to his shirt. It was
as if she had known. *I'll see you soon.* His dour thoughts were
interrupted by a low keening noise. It was too guttural to be
a bird, too metallic to be a dog. His gaze flitted between the
scraggly trees. No motion caught his eyes. He turned to look
at the collapsed temple. *If I were a fallen titanic monster, where*

would I hide? The cry came again. It almost sounded like a word, but so crippled and changed it was unrecognizable.

He scrambled to his feet and began to climb the broken stones. His hardened fingers scraped against the cracks, his scales scoring the stone as he passed. Boulders all but closed the temple's door. Arman rapped on the rocks, letting power fill his skin. "Who's home?"

The call came again, clearer now.

"I've come to find you all. War's not over yet." He squeezed through the opening, blinking rapidly to adjust his eyes to the darkness. "Hello?" The noise came again, a rapid hiss that pierced his ears and echoed off the stone. A figure rocked in the shadows, faint light glimmering off the white scales. The angry yellow eyes glowed orange through the lace of bloodshot vessels.

"Came here before, begging, asking, look what happened. Lookie, lookie, begging, begging. Came here before but nothing to be done, nothing."

"This time we're not alone. What's your name?"

"Aral once and Aral again, but not if you ask, not if you beg. Aral, Aral." Arman saw that the creature's left leg ended in a scaled stump. The lower half was rotting under one of the fallen ceiling blocks.

"Hey Aral. I'm Arman." He unbuckled his cloak and pointed at the handprint scarred across the scales of his chest. "You know what this means? This symbol?"

"Laen."

"That's right. There are a few left, but mine, the one bound to me, she's the Dhoah' Laen. She's real. It's time to come out. Time to fight. It'll be the last time. No one else will call you out of your peace, I promise, but now we need you."

The rocking increased, "Nothing left. Don't beg. Nothing left but fear, fear. No promise, no begging, too much fear, fear."

Dread was a cold lump of lead in Arman's stomach. This was a madman, not a soldier.

Φ

The 7th Day of Lumord, 1252
The City of Ceir Athrolan

Alea twirled around a lantern post at the corner of the street. "Is there a particular tavern you enjoy?"

Giire laughed. "My friend's family owns one." She wore an outfit similar to Alea's, a colorful sarafan over bloused sleeves and frothy petticoats. A broad, stiff band held her hair back from her face. "Her husband is in the army, so she works it to keep her mind busy. It's the Wise Hare, in the slums above the naval yards."

"I've been there." Alea kept pace, her worn boots clacking on the stone. She may not have looked Athrolani, but with the yellow wig, she could pass for Vielronan.

Giire snorted. "I can hardly picture that."

Alea smiled. "I met someone there, I needed the anonymity."

Giire glanced over. "I suppose that's hard to come by. You said you've been dancing before. Not here, surely."

"No. I spent a few months in Vielrona before realizing my power. They have fantastic dances—you don't really need to know the steps, only enjoy yourself and skip a lot. What are they like here?" She followed Giire around a corner and down the narrow walk that edged the top of the tier's wall. The view was striking. The city dropped away on one side, a glittering train of embers.

"Perhaps a bit more organized. Lots of stamping and clapping. Some skipping." She shot Alea a grin. "Tonight they will have bards from other places playing, so there will be some new tunes." She turned right and headed down the narrow, overhung alley that Alea recognized. The Wise Hare squatted at the far end. The bright lanterns were cheery, but showed the filth of the street. The sound of music and singing rattled through the cheap, old glass panes. Giire paused on the steps. "Ready?"

Alea grinned and dashed up the stairs behind her. Warmth and light spilled out as they pressed their way in. The room was low and crowded, music pouring from one corner. Tables were stacked haphazardly along one wall to make room for the dancers. Alea wound back to find free stools for the two of them while Giire made for the bar. The heat and music made Alea's head spin and she grinned. *Everyone needs some chaos from time to time.* Alea watched the feet of the dancers carefully. The steps were repetitive and simple, but fast. Her boots tapped in time, mimicking the moves from her chair.

After a minute Giire returned with Alea's purse. "If you're going to do this, you'll do it proper. I ordered fire ale." She pointed to one of the men who seemed the fastest dancer. "He's one of the scribes from the Scribing Guild. Twice a week he performs dances on one of the stages in the warehouse district. He's quite the mover."

Alea glanced at her sidelong. "You fancy him?"

Giire snorted. "Along with half the slums. The other half fancies Bessel's husband's friend, Sousa. He's a proper Athrolani."

A heavily pregnant woman edged through the crowd, two foaming mugs in hand. She grinned down at Giire as she placed them on their table. "Hey there. Juss said you were here. Who's your friend?"

When Giire stumbled over the question Alea held out her hand. "I'm Veredy. Came up north with family and Giire promised to show me about. My ma knows her da."

Bessel shook the hand with a smile. "Good to have ye then. Let me know if Giire gets too rowdy. I've promised her sister to look after her."

Alea grinned. "Promise." When Bessel had gone Alea took a deep sip of the red liquid, wiping froth from her lip with the back of her hand. "I didn't want you to lie to your friend."

Giire glanced over. "You did that rather well."

"Court antics are all just a series of well-coated lies and vague truths. I did come north with family."

"It must be freeing, to be the Dhoah' Laen and thus no longer an object of court."

"It is a title, just as king or gallant or lady. Titles are no less constraining, regardless of their rank. It simply denotes a new set of rules by which to judge and objectify someone." She finished a good portion of her drink before standing. "Now, show me how to make a fool of myself."

The dancing was fast, as Giire promised, and Alea's muscles ached wonderfully halfway through the tune. *This is what freedom feels like. For tonight, one brief moment, I'm just a person, a woman like every other in this bar.* The dancing circle widened and slowed as the best stepped into the circle to showcase their skills. Alea caught Giire's eye and made her way back to the table. After a minute singers took turns standing and singing a verse of the song, the entire crowd joining in for the chorus. Even Giire took a turn, her voice clear and lilting. It was impressive and Alea found herself humming quietly along. The city was large enough to have a hundred such communities. Everyone seemed to know one another, or know someone who did. It was warming and lonely at once. Alea sat back, running a finger along her mug's rim.

"You don't sing?" Giire slid into her seat, breathless and flushed.

"Never!" Alea waved a hand, as if to dispel the thought from the air between them. Her stomach burnt with the alcohol and her head felt pleasantly padded.

"I suppose the Sunamen don't sing. It seems a terribly expressive recreation for so closeted a people."

Alea raised her brows, surprised at the woman's knowledge. "You know the Sunamen well?"

Giire giggled. "I knew one of their ambassador's guards quite well."

Alea snorted. "Well, the Sunamen sung often. It was one of the few times they were free to express." She shrugged. "Unfortunately I have less than little talent. I can't hear notes well enough to sing. They sound nice when played, but I couldn't tell if someone was off key, or if the tune was unpleasant for others."

"You're note-blind." Giire looked delighted. "I'm sorry, I don't mean to make fun, but it's always encouraging to find great people have weaknesses just like us common folk."

"You do realize nobles are no different than you, except in title?"

Giire made a face. "Rather I think we've got the better deal. Bed whom we wish, work for our coin, and have the freedom to spend it."

Alea nodded. "I think I agree." She caught sight of a cloaked man in a far corner. He could have been watching the singers, but the tingling on her arms told her his eyes rested on her instead. "Giire, where's the privy?"

"Out back. There's a two-person shed."

Alea nodded and ducked out the rear door. She stepped into the shadow behind the rubbish pile and waited. Within a moment the man emerged. To anyone else he would have looked intimidating, or at least dangerous. He was partway to the privy when Alea cleared her throat.

"What are you doing, An'thor?"

He froze and glanced over. "I could ask the same. I think I've more a habit for drinking than you."

"I'm fast catching up." The air was cool, but the burn of drink made it a caress on her warm skin. "Did you follow me?"

"Not on anyone's orders, just my own curiosity."

"You're not here to haul me back to Bren for a scolding?"

An'thor snorted. "Hardly. Besides, I think even he would understand this." He leaned against the rear wall of the Hare. "You're trying to burn back the shadow in your mind with alcohol. Trust me, it won't work. Right now, you think it does, but in an hour, a day, it'll be back and angry at your attempt."

She sighed and slumped onto the stoop. "I know. I've tried it before. It wasn't so much the drinking I wanted, but the dancing, the people." She tried to push back her hair, only to realize she still wore the wig. "How'd you recognize me?"

He snorted. "I'm old enough to trust my instincts. If my skin crawls at the sight of a blond girl in a bar I'm willing to bet there's more than meets the eye. Besides, your brows don't match that color, not even a bit."

She sighed. "You think everyone else noticed?"

"Doubtful. They need the visual to recognize a noble. It's all about symbols with humans. They like tidy boxes with clear labels."

"And you don't?"

"Neither of us fit into any box I've yet encountered." His smile was faint but genuine. "Did you want me to walk you home?"

"I think the Destroyer can protect herself on Ceir Athrolan's streets. I think I'd like to wait a while."

"Maybe I'm the one who wants protecting." He glanced over. "You'll be headed north soon. Do you want me to send word to my people on the border?"

"I'll leave next week, the night after the address. I still hope the Crown is in Claimiirn, but if not, I'd be grateful for their help." She fiddled with one of the wig's curls. "I won't be going as the Dhoah' Laen. It's far too dangerous for people to think I'm on the road, and certainly Azirik has spies enough."

An'thor made a show of examining her. "You'll be going as Miss Sell-Love then?"

Alea glared at him. "I do not look like a whore." Her mock anger melted into a smile. "I'll go as a soldier."

"I'm sure Her Majesty will lend you a uniform or two."

"I'm not telling Her Majesty." She stared at the cobbles. "I said I didn't want many to know. You and one other. Not even Bren, until I'm gone at least."

"Who else? Surely not Arman."

Her expression darkened. "I doubt I'll see him before battle. I had a lover in the army. I'll ask him for the uniforms. He's a captain and not too much taller than I."

"I didn't take you for the lover type. Then again, lovers are like drinking, and lessen the loneliness for a while."

Alea nodded. The warmth of alcohol was curling back, pulling away from her mind. A fragile carapace protected her sanity from the jumble of angry, dark thoughts. Someday, soon, it would crack.

An'thor must have seen something of her thoughts on her face. "Whenever I'm close to breaking, it's because something is coming to an end." He jerked his head at the tavern. "You're about to break, Lyne'alea. Care to tell me why?"

"I've learned about all I need to destroy the gods. It's not like I can practice. The only thing left is finding my Crown."

"Don't forget Her Majesty's address — you get to wear a pretty dress and a serious face once more before you go."

She laughed. "I suppose. Such things seem so unimportant."

"And drinking in a slum tavern doesn't?"

Her eyes flicked to his black ones. "You know these little things matter most of all."

He sank onto the stoop with her and drew a flask from his cloak. "I've drunk too much Athrolani liquor to enjoy it anymore." He tipped it back swiftly before handing it over.

"So what's your plan, with the gods? I assume you've told no one, protecting them from seeing what you're capable of."

She sipped slowly, enjoying the flavor of wood oil and nutmeg. "It's a bit eerie how well you know me."

"Nonsense. I only know myself." His grin bloomed slowly. "So how are you going to save us all and raise the Laen to power?"

Her eyes narrowed. "I'm going to rip the gods' souls from their bodies." An'thor was silent for several moments and she glanced over, handing back the flask. "Should I have protected you, too?"

He swirled the alcohol in his mouth thoughtfully. "No. Not really. I've seen terrible things — not as horrifying as that, perhaps, but to far better people." He rested his head on the wall of the tavern. "The worst part of what you said is knowing what that will do to you."

"That's why I'm here. I'm drinking on the stoop of a tavern in the slums because in a month's time I might be something too twisted and monstrous to do so. I knew becoming the Dhoah' Laen would change me. I knew I wouldn't be exactly human any more. I knew I'd do terrible things, to myself, to Arman. I never bargained for losing my sanity."

"None of us do." His hand was dry and warm on hers.

She laced her fingers with his, tilting her head back to look at the autumn stars. "I'm scared, An'thor."

He followed her gaze, hand tightening around hers. "Me, too."

CHAPTER SIXTEEN

The 11th Day of Lumord, 1252
The City of Ceir Athrolan

BREN STOOD IN THE CENTER of the throne room. It was swept and polished down to the last corner and the walls were hung with great flags of the capital and cities. The wooden panels were slid back so it adjoined the ballroom. It was an hour before the address would begin and he stared at the throne. *How will I help lead Mirik if I can't even face a foreign nation without nerves?* He was already dressed in his finery, a mass of quilted vermilion. *This is a war address and I look like a peacock.* Slippers on stone interrupted his bitter thoughts. Expecting Alea, he turned with a smile. Tzatia regarded him with empathy. "Thinking on your own responsibilities?"

He looked away sheepishly. "Yes, your majesty. I usually need space to think, and with the streets so crowded this seemed the better place."

"Should I leave you to your thoughts?"

"That might be dangerous." He laughed and offered her his arm. "Care to take a circuit with me?"

"Indeed." She took his arm graciously.

"How are you today?" He set off along the pillared wall. It was a poor substitute for pacing, but it would have to do.

"I look forward to today. It feels as if we have been standing still. Perhaps that stillness will break now." She glanced over. "Soldiers are not the only ones to become stir-crazy, Lord Commissioner."

Curiosity nagged at Bren's tongue. "May I be bold?"

Her eyes crinkled. "You're learning court ways well. What makes you wish to be bold?"

"Daymir, your majesty. Alea told me. I'm sorry something so troubling occurred before battle."

Her face clouded and her chin went up. "He made poor choices and I protected us. I know what he said, but I could not take the risk, not when we are at war."

"Hard choices were not named on a whim. Have our other allies arrived?"

"The Banis emperor's offered troops will arrive soon, and your own men will as well I heard."

"Within the week, though I can only bring just under a hundred and thirty. It's something. And General Aneral returned I saw." He paused. "Have you heard from Arman?"

Her mouth thinned again. "Arrowlash ran out on his promise to accompany our fleet to the north. They waited for him for hours at the docks, but he never arrived. I fear the worst from him."

"With due respect, your majesty, I know him well and he is no deserter. If he left there was a fair reason for it."

"I don't speak of desertion, but of madness, Lord Commissioner." She sighed. "You were raised on war, but I was not. As a young woman I thought the most terrifying choice would be whom I married. I chose wrong, in the end, but I was also wrong in thinking that was the worst choice to make."

"And you've learned the most terrifying?"

"Sending our people to war. I love each of them and I send them to their doom."

"Some, yet, will live." They rounded the chamber, close to where they had begun their walk. "If you forget that, war will drive us all mad. A cause keeps us sane."

"I hope you are right. I cannot fathom fighting the gods, but I do not doubt your sister. I need to trust that we can win, and my faith is sorely tattered." She stepped away. "Forgive my dark musings, but thank you for listening." She smiled. "If you ever have concerns of your own, I will return the favor."

He bowed and watched her walk away, his frown reappearing. *I'll have lines deep enough to swallow someone if I'm not careful.* He laughed at himself. *And now I sound like an old maid.* Thinking on the queen's words, he strode to his room, unlacing his tunic as he went.

Φ

The thunder of conversation seeped from the throne room. Behind the lines of nobles were the officers and higher born commoners that could squeeze into the back of the hall with the scribes and clerks. Their retelling would flood the city streets minutes after the queen dismissed the gathering. Bren peered through the door as they waited to be announced. Advisers ringed the throne's dais and the general and commander flanked the throne itself. Instead of state attire, they wore armor and weapons.

Bren grinned, turning to Alea. "I think we made the right choice." After his conversation with the queen, he donned his new armor. He still wore the vermilion shirt and brown breeches, but his bronze-washed mail and breastplate glinted in the torchlight of the anteroom. A vermilion-trimmed forest green cloak was clipped to the backplate and boiled leather pauldrons.

Like him, Alea wore her armor over her dress, the silver and blue skirts the only softness in her out fit. The loose ends of her hair curled in a breeze Bren could not feel. Kemmer and Aldac stood along one wall, fidgeting.

Alea glanced back at them. "Think of it as a battle. It helps, I promise."

Their laughter died as Tzatia rounded the corner with her two chiefs of staff. Her gray and white dress matched the steel of her eyes as she nodded to them. The herald's piercing call stilled the conversation in the hall beyond and Tzatia breezed through the doors on the tail of her titles.

Alea grabbed Bren's hand, squeezing it tightly for a moment. She had her brother, his men, and a room full of allies. She had never felt more alone.

"I'm with you, sistermine."

"Dhoah' Lyne'alea of Le'yne!"

Her power rose, marbling her skin slightly and shadowing her eyes. The chill of the ocean rolled from her shoulders as she moved down the aisle through the crowd. She was distantly aware of Bren and the other Miriken Commissioners entering behind her. The walk seemed to take no time and forever at once.

"My allies, both legendary and human, I thank you for standing beside Athrolan today as we face the growing clouds of war." Tzatia took Alea's hand, and the commissioners' in turn, then turned to face the crowd, hands clasped before her. "My people, I have called you to this assembly to speak of a threat against us all. It is known that Dhoah' Lyne'alea and her guard, Rakos Arrowlash face genocide. The gods and their human army, led by Azirik of Mirik, are their enemies. As allies to the Dhoah' Laen, they are our enemies as well. Mirik's ally, Berr, attacks our borders daily, and this strengthens our resolve against them. In less than a month's time we march to war. I called you here today to listen to your thoughts, your concerns and to answer them." She sat gracefully in the throne, Alea and the others taking seats beside her. "Those who wish may come forward."

Most of the nobles had family in the military and their questions had been answered weeks ago. Those that stepped forward now were city folk, those who were concerned their crops and goods would be siphoned to feed the soldiers of the campaign or if the city would be without protection.

Tzatia heard each concern with patience Alea could only dream about. Finally the queen raised her hands. "Your concerns are valid. Yes, much of your harvests will feed the army, but you will be compensated, as will those of you who have skills of tanning, smithing and the like. Athrolan is my child, my love, and my greatest priority. I will never leave her unguarded. Our army is marching, as are the men of one of our naval flotilla, led by Commander Dorcal. Much of the navy will remain here. They may be unused to land, but they were born on it, and I trust they will do fine." A smattering of laughter broke out and Tzatia smiled briefly. "A battalion will remain as well."

"Your majesty." An older duchess rose and dropped into a curtsey. "What if our troops cannot defeat Lord Azirik?" She stumbled over the title. With Bren usurping Mirik from under his father's reign, titles were unwieldy things. "What if they come for us?"

Alea raised her hand. "Your Majesty, may I answer?" Alea leaned forward when the queen nodded. "This battle is not to defeat Azirik and his men. Not solely. Azirik has something I need to defeat the gods. I will not allow him to win, which is why we have mustered so many allies."

Now a young man stepped forward, the son of a lending house owner, by the expensive outfit he wore. He knelt on the flagging before them. "Your majesty, Dhoah' Lyne'alea, I have a question about those very allies. The Stonefaced and Ageless, they are strong fighters and an obvious choice, but a new government with few soldiers? Is Azirik still not king?"

A stony silence swept the room while Alea searched for a response.

Bren saved her the trouble. "Azirik was king. As his son, I took the responsibility of my small nation from his incompetent hands. There is a law of Mirik, as in some other lands, that a when a monarch puts another person or persons before his nation, then he might be made crownless. I have followed this law."

"What of our other supposed allies, your majesty?" The man continued, acknowledging Bren's answer with a respectful, but dismissive wave. "You bound us to Dhoah' Lyne'alea. She may stand before us, but she stands alone. She claims power, but what of the strength behind her. Where is her Rakos guard? Has he abandoned her and chosen a better side?"

"You'd best speak with respect when addressing milady, boy." The low voice rumbled through the crowd, cutting the man's tirade short. Mutters sprang up as people turned to peer behind them. The doors to the throne room were open, a frightened page holding his hands out, as if to say he could not prevent the intruder. A few paces into the room stood a bright figure. It was not armor that made him gold, for he wore none, but the curls of the flame in his hair and the coal-bed glow between the scales covering his bare arms.

The inside of Alea's cheek bled from her effort to remain silent.

Arman's grace as he approached the throne was nothing less than predatory. "You ask where your allies are? General Aneral returned from the Hartland with two dozen warriors. Lord Commissioner Barrackborn brings a few hundred men. An'thoriend's people number in the hundreds as well. And now, your other concern about milady's guard is put to rest, for here I am. And I did not come alone." He stopped before the young man, his head cocked like a raptor regarding a rat. The moisture in the air from Alea's power evaporated with a hiss in the heat radiating from his Rakos scales. "So unless you have anything else to add: as you were."

The man backed away into the silent crowd. Arman turned back to the dais, nodding to Tzatia and Bren before his gaze flicked to Alea. He took a knee, one fist touching his brow, lips and chest. "Milady, I bring you more Rakos. I hoped to bring men from Vielrona, but the gods saw to it that nothing was left for me to take." His words were quietly sincere, but his voice tight.

Alea's heard plummeted at the mention of Vielrona. "I thank you, Arrowlash."

He rose and moved to stand behind her. He was close enough that she could have taken his hand. The tension was a physical wall between them, connecting and dividing them at once.

Tzatia rose, the crowd following suit with the rumble of feet upon stone. "This assembly is closed. We thank you for your thoughts and trust that we have soothed any concerns. May fates bring us victory and peace." With the closing "So it is said," still echoing from the dome, Tzatia swept from the room, the others following after her.

Bren's breath burst from him in a cascade of nervous laughter. He turned, sobering at the sight of his sister's face. Alea stopped in the open hall that branched to the various wings. "Please, can we talk?"

Arman was already halfway to the stables. He stopped, but did not turn. "I came long enough to say and do what the damned people needed to see. That's all. I will see you at war."

Φ

Narier arrived just after midnight. The room was dark when he shut the door and the hearth was cold. "No one saw me come, promise. I went through the gardens just in case." He edged in, peering from Alea's made bed to the privy door. "You here, Dhoah'?"

She rose from her silent vigil by the curtained window. "Thank you."

Narier tossed her the pack. "Should be everything you need."

The uniform and armor were just the proper amount of worn. She stripped her gown off, the motions devoid of any seduction, and pulled on the captain's clothes. "I'll be out of the gate within the hour."

"I'll stay here until then, in case anyone saw. They'll think you're me."

"You could always don one of my gowns and stay in the library."

"I fear black is as garish on me as vermilion."

She was grateful for the joking reference to their first conversation, even if it was a poor attempt at humor. She fussed with her hair for a moment. "How do captains wear it? I've seen the general wrap her braid around her head."

"Either that or cropped."

She twisted her braid up and about. The second time her shaking hands dropped her hair pins, he took pity on her. His fingers were gentle at the nape of her neck as he pinned the hair into place. "Alea—"

"Don't, Narier. Please." She jerked away as soon as he finished and grabbed the pack.

"I wasn't going to talk you out of it, or be cruel."

"I know." The door clicked softly shut behind her and her boots echoed along the hall. She was not ready for good-byes.

Φ

The 11th Day of Lumord, 1252

The knock was pointedly quiet on Bren's door. He jerked it open, mouth already thin. "Arman. Should have known."

Arman rolled his eyes. "You have time for a drink?"

"Yes, and so does Alea, I'd warrant." He closed the door and pulled a flask from his desk. "Your boorish behavior does not make me like you much, Rakos."

"You don't need to like me."

"Sure would make things nicer, though, wouldn't it?" He poured them both a few finger-widths and screwed the top back on. "What brings you back here?"

"A long story." He looked down at the alcohol, face shadowed.

Bren frowned. In the weeks that had passed, it looked as if he had lived years. "Vielrona?"

"Fell. The gods destroyed it."

"Gods? I thought they only acted through Azirik."

"Their best power is through him, I think. He created that storm on the Iron Sea. I imagine he did the same. This time it was acid clouds and poisonous gas."

"Your family?"

"My Ma's dead, and my friend Wes and the girl I thought I'd marry."

"I'm sorry, Arman." Bren looked away. "I wish there was something I could do."

Arman glanced up. "There is one thing. Nothing large." When Bren nodded, Arman continued. "I've a friend, only one left, really. He's a locksmith and his name is Kam-Rit Eltena. His wife is Celly. By the time you see them they'll have a babe. They need a home and work. I told them to come north and find you. I told them Mirik would be home now."

"I'll do what I can. We'll need craftsmen surely." Bren sat back. "The woman you wanted to marry — how did you leave things?"

"I ran off with a mysterious woman barely a week after proposing marriage. How do you think we left things?"

"Terrible proposals seem to collect around Alea." Bren laughed and poured another drink.

"You botch one recently?"

"No, but Daymir did, before he was disinherited. Asked Alea to be his queen."

Arman choked on his drink. "You're joking."

"I wish I were. He was fuming when he left, which wasn't a bad sight."

"He wanted her power, I assume?"

"I think he enjoyed her company. The power didn't hurt, though. Part of me is surprised she doesn't have more suitors. Perhaps they're too scared of the rumors." Bren hid a smile. "Even Narier no longer visits her."

"Narier, what does he have to do with the price of Banis silk?"

"He told her she was too powerful, too inhuman for him now. He said it gently, but it was still a pointed reminder about how she is viewed."

"He's a coward."

"You're just unhappy he's bedded her."

Arman's eyes widened and he looked up. "He what?"

Bren's expression sobered quickly. "I thought you knew."

"Knew Narier took advantage of her? What kind of brother are you that would allow that?" Arman grimaced. "What kind of guard am I that I didn't notice? The man beheads people for fate's sake!"

Bren rolled his eyes. "Arman, this is war, soldiers kill people. It was during the siege. He was kind and funny and saw her as a woman."

"You should bed him if you like him that much."

"He's not really my preference, I'm more for the darker men." Bren's deadpan grew serious. "Arman, if she doesn't love you, that's the end of it, but you certainly don't make it easy. She doesn't want a guard, she wants a friend. She wants a lover."

"I do see her as a woman."

"You don't treat her as such."

He hung his head. "I know. I'm too damned scared. I'm too much of a coward." He inhaled sharply. "I found more Rakos. Two, at least. Hopefully they'll find more."

Bren leaned forward. The Rakos were something that even most legends did not dare to touch. "What are they like?"

Arman snorted. "I've only met the one and he's mad. He was trapped in a temple in Berr. Chewed off his own leg years ago. Half the words he says are 'fear.'"

Bren's brows rose. "Sounds like quite the army you've got there."

"I know. I'm hoping they'll prove useful."

"What can they do? Besides put anyone off their meal for a day."

Arman laughed, the sound low and rattling. "The Rakos that changed, like they did, like I am, they weren't called Earth Shakers for nothing." He stood abruptly. "Please don't tell Alea I was here."

Bren stood, raking a hand through his hair. "I don't have to. She knew, last time. Asked me flat out if you'd been here while staring at the window where you jumped. Don't bother pretending."

Arman winced. "Was she angry?"

"More at you than me. You've barely seen her long enough, Arman, but she's changed. That mild girl you had bumping along behind you on the road is gone. She's brilliant and terrifying."

Arman paused in the doorway with a smile. "She always was. You just couldn't see it before. I'm headed south again, I've got more Rakos to find."

"You ought to find that fleet before Tzatia beheads you."

"Let her try. I'm sure the navy can manage on their own. I'll be back for battle."

Bren watched him disappear down the hall. When the hall was deserted, he stepped up to Alea's door, knocking. "Alea? It's me." No answer came and he finally turned away. It was fitting, he supposed, after the unity displayed at the address, that their nights were spent in solitude.

CHAPTER

SEVENTEEN

The 12th Day of Lumord, 1252

The City of Ceir Athrolan

BREN HALF EXPECTED ALEA to accompany him to the docks, but his knocking was met with silence. He met Kemmer at the palace gates however, and grinned. The woman's new armor gleamed in the sunlight.

"You look like a general, Kemmer."

She flushed and saluted him, but her grin was wry. "Are you suggesting a promotion?"

Bren snorted and headed towards the docks where Aldac already waited. "I'm barely adjusted to my own new position. We'll talk after the war, eh?"

She fell into step beside him, one hand resting on the head of her axe. "General A'hane does have a fantastic ring to it, Lord Commissioner."

"Insubordinate A'hane has a better one." He flashed the woman a grin. They had made bounds in the weeks working together. Though he joked with her, she was bright and however teasing her suggested promotion was, it warranted some thought. The letters from Mirik were swift and short, as were his responses, but nothing replaced seeing the fruit of his efforts arrive at Athrolan's harbor. He was more than a bit nervous. Aldac stood by the largest naval dock, dressed like Kemmer, though his armor was his own. He saluted Bren, his expression far more serious. "Lord Commissioner. The signal went up half an hour ago. They'll dock within a few minutes."

Chains blocked the naval docks from the others, but a small crowd gathered against them, peering at Bren and his officers. The Miriken would arrive on three of the Athrolani ships, and it had been a long time since Athrolan played host to another army. Another signal flag unfurled from the Naval watch tower in the center of the harbor's entrance. The ships rounded the cliffs and coasted into the shallower blue waters. Bren clenched his jaw against its gaping. They were not Athrolani ships.

The two galleys were long, outfitted with green sails and new hulls. The third ship was larger, almost the size of the Athrolani battle ship. It's prow was narrower, and the men lining the rails were dressed in a familiar bronze and leather armor. Their cloaks and tunics matched the brilliant vermilion of the sails furled along the new wood of the repaired triple masts.

"Kemer, did you know about this?" He tore his eyes away to glance at his first officer.

She shook her head, but her smile was bright. "No, sir. My brother promised a surprise, however. I think he outdid himself."

"I think you have competition for your promotion."

Her laughter drowned in the shouts of the sailors and dock hands as they guided the ships to berth.

Two men stood at the helm of the battleship. The iron hair and weathered face labeled one as Oland, but the other Bren did not know. Arik waved an order to the soldiers as he and his companion disembarking first and striding over to where Bren waited. The soldiers filed out after them, the rumble of armor warming Bren's stomach. Arik paused a few paces away and saluted Bren. His eyes smiled, but his face was serious. "Lord Commissioner Barrackborn."

Bren offered his arm in greeting. "You've done wonders, Arik."

Arik grasped the arm, but raised his chin. "It's Commissioner of the Commons, now." He stepped back and jerked his head at the man standing a pace behind him. "And this is Kole Gallik, Commissioner of Diplomacy and Negotiation."

Something uncurled in Bren's chest at the words. A year ago Mirik was in shambles. A month ago he was acting king of a starved, abandoned city. Now he had a government and army behind him. *Pride.* He took Gallik's arm with a nod. "I look forward to working with you. You've done wonders."

Gallik's grip was firm and his plain face open. "I'm proud to see how far we've come since you arrived."

The final lines of the soldiers disembarked, turning to salute him with a clatter. Bren waved at them, not bothering to contain his impish grin. "Oh, just wait until you see where we're going."

Φ

The 13th Day of Lumord, 1252

The Ruins of Claimiirn

Loneliness was sharpest in the enveloping noise and bustle of
Ceir Athrolan. The rolling expanse of hills and forest edging
the road was different. There were no meetings or calls for
lunch. The noises were hooves on stone and animals
preparing for winter. The leaves chattered in the wind. Alea
realized she had forgotten how to be alone. There was no need
for defenses or verbal sparring. She smiled and it did not feel
strange.

The road east had been maintained until it met the small
canyon through which they had sailed upon their arrival to
Ceir Athrolan. Now, almost at the border, it was barely a
worn line of earth. More often she guided herself based on the
sun, instead of what may have once been road.

The autumn days were bright and crisp, just cool enough
to urge her faster. With nothing to answer to save her own
thoughts and those of her persnickety horse, her days were
long and easy, her nights dark and often wakeful. It was only
after a week that she noticed the first reminder of war.

The trees crowding the narrow road bore marks from
passing wagons and the underbrush was battered by boot
heels. She slowed, muttering an absent reassurance to her
horse. The threads on low hanging branches were green, but
that could mean anything. *The average raider would benefit from
the camouflage of green wagon canvas.* She spent the next hour
on foot, picking out details of the road's previous travelers.
The gravel crunching under her boots was a rosy brown. She
was no tracker, but an army did little to hide their passing and
by the time she emerged on the cliff tops overlooking
Claimiirn, she knew enough to hide. The granite cliffs ringed

the plains in a U that opened to the treeless hill in the northeast.

Athrolan's penchant for cliff-top capitals did not begin with Ceir Athrolan, it seemed. The walls carved from the opposite cliff face were weathered, but the beauty still echoed. The low-slung sun painted the ruins of the former palace pink. The cliff where Alea crouched once sported a fort, only a few walls still standing. She crept to the edge, relying on the setting sun to blind anyone who happened to glance up. Azirik's army camped below. The mass of tents and picket lines impressed her. *And I thought the outguard was an army.* She stopped counting tents at seventy and began estimating by how many fit under her upheld thumb. She was lucky that Azirik was not using the palace ruins for anything other than storage and officers' tents. After a quick noting of guards' locations, she edged back into the protection of the crumbling fort to wait until nightfall. Perhaps it was the approaching winter, but for the first time during her journey, she wished she could light a fire.

Φ

Midnight guard change was marked by a low trumpet and the muttering of picketed horses. Alea rose and stretched her stiff muscles. They no longer ached from the long days of riding, but lying on cold earth did no one any good. After the burning faded, she tied cloth scraps around her horse's hooves and harness metal. It was a tedious process that did nothing to make friends with the intolerant animal, but when she finished they could have walked into the camp itself unheard.

Satisfied that she had done everything she could, Alea headed off along the cliff top, keeping to the tree line where possible. A trumpet marked the death-hour as she came upon the edge of the palace. The trees had dropped away, but she found a wall that still stood tall enough to hide her mount. After a few fumbling minutes she remembered how to tie the reins in a break-away knot and managed to tether the horse to an overgrown bush. The rough map An'thor had drawn was still folded in her pocket, but she had spent enough evenings pouring over it. The layout burnt on the backs of her eyelids. Her boots scuffed on the rough stone, but save for the two guards flanking the old rear gate, she saw no one.

Claimiirn was built at the beginning of Athrolan's might, and her architects were humble. The halls were narrow and the windows small, protecting against attacks. There was none of the hubris shouted from Ceir Athrolan's gleaming dome and arching aqueducts. *Fourth hall on the right. Eight flights of stairs. Second door on the left.* The treasury was an unlikely home for the Crown, but An'thor promised it would be the best to go there first.

No torches lit the stone, but the moon was bright and high in the sky still. At each window, Alea marked its location. *Four hours until dawn.* It would not do to find the Crown, only to be caught as the sun rose. Her impatience almost won out at the fifth stair, but she forced her boot falls into silence and continued down. She realized belatedly that she was tunneling into the depths of the cliff, and the treasury would be beneath even the level of the plains. The air seemed thicker and she felt the weight of the earth above her.

It was not until she paused outside the treasury door that she heard the footsteps. They were quiet, but steady, and approaching from above. She opened her mouth to breathe silently and crept along the wall. Her fingers found the door latch, cords of tendons standing out as she worked to open it soundlessly. The latch clanked as it opened and the footsteps above stilled. She heard a man's cautious sniff. She hoped he suffered autumn allergies, but there were a dozen more sinister thoughts tumbling through her brain. She stepped backward through the door, feeling her way with a groping hand. The darkness within the treasury was absolute, so thick she could taste the black on her tongue. She swung the door almost closed, holding the latch up with a shaking hand. The stone was cold and damp against her ear as she pressed it to the crack between the wall and door. She focused on counting her breaths. She had slowed them to every twelve seconds when the man finally turned and retreated up the stairs.

She turned, latch forgotten as she fumbled with the flint and hand-torch on her belt. The oil-soaked fluff she packed into the tin box shed only a small circle of light, but it was enough to get her bearings. All gold and finery were stripped. The only remaining hangings were torn or faded. The furniture and chests left were either broken or too heavy to easily remove. All were empty. *I'm in the treasury of one of the wealthiest kingdoms ever to rise, and it looks like a tavern's barren pantry.* She checked every corner, each closed drawer, but there was nothing. She briefly dared to raise her power enough to sense the room around her, but the room was as still as before. She snuffed the tinder box and tucked it back into her pocket after a moment. Her fingertips stung from the heated metal, but she missed the comfort of its light and warmth. She crouched by the cracked door for another minute until her eyes were accustomed to the darkness again before slipping out of the treasury and back up the stairs.

Three flights above the level I entered are the royal chambers. If it's in Claimiirn at all, An'thor said it might be kept there. Blood hissed in her ears as her adrenaline surged again. She was happy to be out from under the tangible press of earth. The palace could have been ruined by neglect. The scars of weapons on stone were eroded by wind and rain. The doors that hung crooked had fallen from their hinges. The sharp edges of windows broken by arrows were long since ground flat. The royal chambers were different. The lock was broken on the doors, like the others, but it seemed even time had not ransacked the rooms. Some things were sacred regardless of race or culture. An empty nursery, with all its broken promises was one such sanctity.

The massive wooden beams caved into the center of the room, the catapulted stone that crushed them shattered across the flagging. The bed was broken beneath and a cradle splintered beside it. Alea's heart ached at the sight. Arman had told her the story of this room. Even with the distance of legend, it was heartbreaking. *An'thor lost his son in this room. In that cradle. Beneath that beam.* She shook away the tugging sorrow and turned to the smaller room that served as a study. The bookshelves were mostly empty, their contents stacked on the desk ready for packing. She opened each drawer quietly, fumbling for the latch of any hidden compartments or false bottoms. Next, she pawed through the chests and the wardrobe. Like the treasury, it was empty. *If the Crown's not here then the Ageless brought it back home. Seems I'm headed to Neneviir.* She turned to the door and stopped.

The moon was still up, the cool light spilling across the dusty, scratched flagging. The doorway and the hall beyond were dark, barely distinguishable from one another. A shadow blocked the door. *Was it there when I came in?* Her eyes burnt as she willed them to see better. It could have been the stone moulding of the door. A cloud could have moved across the moon's face. It could have been a thousand things, but her instinct screamed at her to hide. The doorway was only a few paces away and she sunk back against the wall by the study, biting into her knuckles to keep herself silent. She wanted to run, but she had to be certain the Crown was nowhere in the room. *I'm not touching my power without knowing if someone's there. Last thing I need is for them to know I'm not a captain.*

The night was still warm, but the breeze bore winter's teeth. It whistled curiously through the broken windows, nosed around the crushed beams and eddied out to the hall. As it passed through the doorway, it lifted the vermilion edged cloak of the man standing just outside the moonlight.

Her hand tightened into a fist. He was blocking the only door to the stairway. She would kill if she had to, with her bare hands if necessary.

"I know you're in here. Not sure who you are, but I heard you poking about."

She heard the leather of his boot squeak as he made to move. Without another thought she burst from her cover, pelting across the room and to the broad eastern windows. The stone of the sill was cold against her hands. She glanced down long enough to be sure the ground below was deserted before swinging herself over the sill. Her fingers burnt as she hung for a moment. She heard the man rush across the room. With a last look down, she clenched her teeth and dropped.

Φ

The City of Cair Athrolan

Bren pounded on Alea's door. He expected silence for a day, perhaps a night. This was something else entirely. He knocked for what seemed the thousandth time. "Alea, please!"

"Commissioner Barrackborn?"

Bren turned to see Narier jogging down the hall towards him. The soldier seemed to have just come from drills. "I'm busy right now, Narier."

"Trying to find you sister?" He drew up beside Bren and handed him a letter. "She left this for you. When the servants started gossiping that she'd abandoned us, I figured the game was up."

Concern writhed in Bren's chest like a nest of snakes. "Where, by Toar, is she?"

"She's where she needs to be, sir." Narier bowed a good bye and backed down the hall.

Bren did not watch him go. His gaze fell to the thin letter in his hand. He shouldered open his door, hands shaking as he broke the seal and unfolded the parchment.

> *Bren,*
>
> *I'm sorry I'll miss the arrival of your men. I hope you're pleased. I can't wait to hear about it when I see you again.*
>
> *I'm to the east. If I find Le'yne's Crown in Claimiirn there's a chance I'll return before you get this. If not, however, then I've gone to Neneviir. It's the last piece before the battle, and I can't fight Azirik or bind the world without it.*

I hope you understand.
I love you,
Alea

Bren brushed her farewell with a gentle finger before folding the letter into his shirt pocket. Every step farther she took from him, the darker the skies seemed to grow.

Φ

The Ruins of Claimiirn

Blood flooded Alea's mouth as her teeth ground into her lower lip. It was better than screaming at the searing pain in her ankle. She remembered to crouch as she landed to absorb her momentum, but no amount of proper landing made up for uneven ground. She was tempted to make a mad, bumbling run for her horse, but knew the pain clouded her thinking dangerously. The sound of the man descending the stairs drifted through the broken windows of the stairwell. The footfalls paused. She shifted herself as quietly as possible. If he realized she was still there, she would have to run. She gathered her good leg under her carefully and readied herself to spring.

"Don't."

The voice startled her with its nearness. He must have been just paces away. She did not dare to move or respond, but the tone gave her pause.

"I can't see you right now. Keep it that way. If I see you, so will they and I'll have to act." The voice was low and steady, but hummed with energy. "Wait. The moon will set in just under two hours. You'll have enough time to get away before dawn, if no one else finds your horse."

She shifted her weight again, letting her injured leg rest. She felt along her shin and ankle. The bone was straight and unbroken. It was sprained, but she could walk. She breathed a silent sigh and leaned back against the stone. Later she would wonder what he was doing. Later she might question why he let her go. Now there was no time. She had not heard him call for guards, nor had he brought any with him when he followed her upstairs.

"Did you find what you were looking for?"

She could run, she supposed. Even with an injured ankle, she might get to her horse. *If I see you, so will they.* Cold trotted up her back. The ground was damp and the stone behind her hard. The wind that had swirled through the room a minute ago howled through the ruins now. The air smelled sickly, as if something dead had been uncovered when the snow melted. Bren had been like this man, once. She drew a steadying breath. He sat above her, offering her a hand in peace and she was ready to spit in it. *I'm not Arman.* She was tired of paranoia. She was tired of running. "All right."

The silence tightened at her words. "I'll stay with you, if you like, until the moon sets. I can't be sure no one will come, but I'll send them off if they do." There was the sound of fabric against stone and a low sigh. "You must think this a trick or a trap. Let's just say I'm tired, too."

"I didn't say I was tired."

"I hear it in your voice. I recognize that fatigue. You've been fighting a while now, and hard. I'm not saying you're right, but just for tonight, I'd rather talk than kill."

His words were like a journal she had forgotten she wrote. She may never know his name, but in that moment, she knew him better than anyone. "Me, too." She eased herself onto the ground. "Just for tonight." The moon was fat and still golden from summer. The naked hills beyond beckoned it down to bed, not yet lit by the sun. The silence stretched on, broken only by the pounding of her blood and the occasional sigh from above. "What did Azirik say to convince you to fight?"

"My father upheld the gods for as long as I can remember. Fighting for them did not seem like a choice. What about you?"

"What about me?"

"What did they tell you — the queen, the Laen, whoever. Are you Athrolani?"

"No. I'm not really much of anything by birth or raising. Lots of children are like that during war I think. They told me nothing really, nothing I didn't already know. It did not seem like a choice for me either." The ground under her was hard and cold. She had no feeling in her lower legs save for the lancing pain in her ankle whenever she shifted. The sky was a deep blue-green, only a few wispy clouds drifting across. Her breath puffed silently from between her chapped lips. The moon hung low, as if tired from the effort of climbing the dome of the sky. "Why are you doing this?"

"Doing what?"

"Keeping me company while the moon sets." Saying that he was letting her go seemed too dangerous an accusation.

"Perhaps because I finally realized I had a choice all along. I want to make up for all the pain I've caused."

Alea heard her own words from months ago echoing through the broken window. "It is the fault of Mirik, the fault of fate, even the fault of the gods, but it is not yours. No one person is so powerful as that."

The moon slipped happily between the trees, silhouetting their branches. An owl perched on one, feathers ruffled against the cold. It occurred to her suddenly, she had not watched the sky in months.

Finally the plains fell into darkness. The voice above her cracked into use again. "There. The guards should be hard pressed to see you now."

Alea paused, then rose, sensation rushing back into her limbs with agony. She winced and stumbled a few steps before finding her footing. She jogged through the ruins to her horse, heart pounding. She did not dare turn around, but it felt strange to not thank the man.

Φ

The 19th Day of Lumord, 1252

Rocks dotted the bare hills surrounding Claimiirn. Alea's horse picked its way through the mess of stones and scrub grass. Though not mountains in their own right, it was a hard climb. Beyond them, somewhere, was the tundra of the Northlands. Its short summer already passed. The hills all looked alike to Alea, and even with An'thor's carefully penned map, she became turned around twice. They were like the great undulating waves the wind drew in desert sand. *Perhaps long ago some great beast breathed life across this world and these hills are the marks its breath left.*

The clack of hooves on stone was monotonous and wearing on her nerves. Two days of riding and she seemed no closer to meeting the Ageless.

A particularly large hill rose ahead, a tall post erected on its crest. Alea's eyes narrowed. She pulled up, peering through her borrowed spyglass. Each of its four sides bore symbols, like a massive mile marker. She had never seen a mile marker made of iron, or reaching several dozen paces into the sky. She grinned and urged her horse faster.

The door set into the hillside was closed. At first it looked like blackened wood, but as she drew closer, she realized it, too, was iron. Though the hills continued to roll gradually higher, the Ageless seemed to have done even more to hide themselves from the world. Alea riffled through her pack for a moment before drawing out the instructions An'thor carefully detailed to her. A broad circle in the center of the door was polished from countless hands. She laid her hands over the marks, pressing steadily. It receded with a grind. The center was still raised, its edge notched with tally marks. Alea twisted it to the left until it clicked twice, then to the right, listening for five clicks. Lastly she turned it left again for seven. Heavy thuds resounded from within the door as tumblers slid back and gears ground the door upward. *Of course, even their doors wouldn't open normally.* She was beginning to understand An'thor better. *He's like a child with a talented and prideful older sibling.* The door finally thumped to a halt.

A long tunnel burrowed into the mountain, dissolving into darkness. A trough jutted from each wall, and a quick inspection with her fingers told her it was filled with animal fat. She lit it quickly and climbed back into the saddle. The light hissed down the trough, but only made the tunnel seem longer. She nudged her mount inside, her murmurs more to reassure herself than the animal. Several paces inside, the horse's hooves clacked over an iron plate and the door ground closed behind them. *Next time An'thor gives me directions they will not have any tunnels, or narrow halls or dungeon treasuries!*

She steadied her breath and forced herself to recite the poems from her childhood. The tunnel did not curve once, the eerie straightness adding to the illusion that she made no progress. She had worked up to the poems she read in Vielrona when the tunnel ended abruptly. It was another door, but this one was three times the height of a mounted man and equally as broad. The air was noticeably cooler. The circle and tumbler mechanism were the same, though the number of clicks for each direction had changed. Bitter wind squealed through the widening doorway. Beyond were iron gates. The building was unlike anything she had seen, but the pennants and guards dotting the walls told her it was a garrison.

When the door clunked to a halt, she rode through, keeping her shoulders back and head up. *I'm Captain Lenna Grayhill.* Though the brown and gray landscape was stark, the fort ahead was far from deserted. Warriors manned the blood-colored walls, shouting orders and jokes back and forth. Each wore horned helms. Whistled alerts bounced from tower to tower as she approached. No weapons rose to greet her. Either they already expected her, or she was deemed harmless. She hoped it was the former.

At the gate she halted and raised a gloved fist in greeting. "I'm Captain Grayhill from Athrolan." Her shout carried over the wall, loud and sharp in the cold air. "I must speak with your commanding officer."

A smaller door in the gate creaked open and a warrior stepped out. "You come from Domariigo?"

"I do. I trust you received his letter?" She had listened to General Aneral enough to know fewer words were best.

The woman nodded and jerked her head at the fort. "Very well."

The gate rose with a lurch and within moments Alea was dismounting in the courtyard. The building was built in a square, the walls only wide enough to allow a walkway at the top. The only obvious living quarters were a row of rooms along one wall. The rest was open to the elements. What looked like a stable ran along the rearmost wall, steam billowing from the narrow windows cut into the rusted iron. The warriors along the walls watched for a moment before turning back to their work. Alea laughed softly. The horns she thought decorated their helms actually grew from their temples. *Seeing An'thor with his head covered so often made me forget.*

"Athrolani. You're the officer An'thoriend sent?" Everything about the man approaching spoke of the tundra. His furs and leather were thick and battered, as was his snowy skin and ivory ram horns. Like An'thor he wore a tattoo, his of a sword's hilt on his throat and collarbones.

"I am." She offered her arm. "Captain Grayhill. You're the officer here?"

"I'm the one sent to fetch you." He took the arm, his wholly black eyes scanning her face and packs. "Tennic Odrene. We'll take you presently, just loading up the carts." He gestured to the stables. "Come."

The brisk treatment required adjustment after Athrolan's hospitality. Alea expected to stay the evening at the fort before heading further north. As frustrating as traveling was, however, she had missed the constant movement of the road.

She fell into step beside him, leading her horse. "This fort, what's it called?"

"Garrison Kaliim, Captain." He stepped through another mechanized door and gestured to the line of stalls. "Leave your horse here then meet me out back. We don't have time to waste."

Alea hurriedly unbuckled her horse's tack and checked the grain and water before shouldering her pack and heading through the door Tennic indicated. The structure of the fort was odd, and the doors alien, but nothing prepared Alea for the sight before her.

They were under the vaulted ceiling of what seemed like a hall. The stacked chests and freight boxes, however, made it seem closer to a ware house. Two parallel bars of iron set into the ground ran the length of the hall, disappearing through a massive open door at the rear. A great contraption crouched on them. It was twice the height of a tall man and made entirely of iron and brass. Clouds of steam billowed from the short chimney at its front. The small cabin behind the steaming chamber was closed off with thick glass windows. The mechanism churned to life as she approached.

Steam drifted from beneath as well, glowing in the light of the oil lamps along its length. Three iron-bound wood carts of almost equal size were clipped behind the iron machine. The middle one bore a narrow staircase leading inside.

Alea hung back while Tennic held a quiet conversation with one of the several men hurrying around the thing.

A boy sidled up to her while she watched the chaos. "You're Athrolani?"

She nodded, still staring at the contraption. Giant pistons on the wheels hissed suddenly. The fresh, smoky smell and the dim lights seemed unreal. "What is this?"

"A steam engine. It runs on heated water and can pull our heaviest freight without effort. We'll ride in that middle cart there."

"You're coming with us?" She finally looked over at the boy. He was milk-pale and had long white-blond curls. The tattoo of a circlet around his brow was bright and new. His temples bulged out with new growth of horns.

"I'm training under my father's men."

"Tennic is your father?"

"No, Edrodene is." He offered her his arm. "Mel'iend Domariigo." He pointed his thumb at the cart. "Come on, I'll get you settled."

She followed him onto the middle cart, feeling like one of the horses they had loaded on minutes before. Narrow wooden benches were bolted to the floor along the sides. Mel'iend grabbed a bundle from a box by the entrance. "You'll need these. I'll pop out while you change."

Alea glanced down at the bundle, then undressed quickly in her spare privacy. Silk leggings and shirt went under her borrowed uniform. She found a seat on the bench and donned silk gloves under her leather ones. She felt like a sausage about to split its skin and despite the cool air she started to sweat. Heavy steps heralded Tennic's entrance, followed by half a dozen other warriors and Mel'iend. The boy handed her dried meat and a cup of water. The meat had enough pepper to make her sneeze, but she was hungry.

Alea's head was swimming. There were too many new faces and new objects to catalogue in her mind, and with her fabricated name, she struggled to find her place amidst it all.

"Was she terrifying?"

She glanced over as Mel'iend slid onto the seat next to her and brandished a belt riveted to the bench. "Who?"

"The Dhoah' Laen. You must have seen her in the city."

Alea swallowed hard. She had not thought of this. "Only from a distance. She was away in Le'yne for much of the time I was stationed in the city. I saw a good deal of her guard though."

"Mel'iend, leave our guest alone." Tennic's voice cut through the thick air.

"I don't mind." Alea turned back to the boy. "You hear many of the stories living up here?"

"All of them. An'thor writes me letters, and sends news. I heard about the Rakos — do they really turn into monsters?"

Alea was taken aback. She had not heard that version of the story. "I think they create them or something. The Dhoah' Laen's guard, he's fearsome. Fights too fast to see, full of all kinds of anger."

"You fancy him?"

Alea started. "Admire him. You can't fancy the sun." A rumbling growl rose from the engine, and steam rolled past the windows of the cart. Wheels ground on rails and the train lurched into motion. They cleared the hall and emerged onto the tundra. The brown scrub grass was already dotted with frost in the valleys. Her white knuckles relaxed their grip on the bench after a few moments.

"Rest while you can. It's a long trip to the capital." Tennic leaned back against the wall. His eyes closed, but Alea would have bet her last coin that he was wide awake.

Her face pressed to the window as she stared out, listening to their metallic heartbeat thundering across the bleak landscape.

CHAPTER EIGHTEEN

The 20th Day of Lumord, 1252
The Tundra of the Northlands

ALEA JOLTED AWAKE. The Ageless stood and stretched around her. The train still hurtled across the landscape, but now it was dark. She wiped the grubby window with her sleeve and peered out. It was night, though she could not have slept for more than an hour. The moon had yet to rise and the stars spilled across the sky. The undulating landscape could have been Sunam, but the dunes and valleys were snow not sand.

Mel'iend glanced over at her as he rose. "We'll just be a minute. Feel free to stretch your legs, just hold on to something if you're going to walk around." He grinned and followed the others into the cart at the front.

Alea rose, rolling stiffness from her cramped shoulders. The rhythmic motion of the carts on the rails was akin to a ship at sea. *Albeit a very stormy sea.* After a moment of peering out the windows along both sides, Alea sat back down. The Northlands were decidedly plain. The snow was only a few handbreadths deep from what she could see. Despite the thick clothes she was no longer sweating, so the temperature seemed to steadily drop. After a moment Mel'iend appeared from the door to the rear cart. Frost rimmed the fur collar of his jacket and made spires from his eyebrows.

"You went outside?" Alea's heart bounced in excitement.

He nodded. "For a bit at least. You want to come?"

She followed him through the rearmost cart, filled with some of the boxes and chests she had seen in the warehouse. "You use this thing to travel because of the cold?"

"Because of impatience. Cold bothers us little." He held the door open for her at the end. "We've got a few, depending on where we're going and the weather. During the deep snow we can't go very far unless the engine has an icebreak on its bow."

A narrow causeway connected the carts, protected from the worst of the wind and cold by a flexible leather sheath. Alea crossed nervously, staring at the white ground flashing between the slats of the walkway. The other railcarts held canvas-covered boxes and barrels. In the rearmost, Mel'iend showed her how to lace up the face of her hood to cover her nose and mouth.

"Trust me, it hurts when the hairs inside your nose freeze." He grinned at her disgust and shouldered open the door. Instead of a causeway, a narrow balcony hung from the back. Mel'iend gestured her onto the walk. It was achingly cold, but the air was fresh and she took a few deep breaths.

"Thank you for coming out with me. I know you just braved the cold."

His soft, hissing laughter surprised her. "We're born for this weather." His face grew serious. "We should make the capital around dawn. Keep your head down and your eyes open."

A shiver completely unrelated to the cold crawled down her spine. "You're the king's son?"

"Warlord. And yes."

"So you'll inherit?"

"Ah. No. Inheritance works differently with us. The staff does not pass by blood, but to the most worthy warrior. It tends to be a cousin or nephew, but that is circumstance only. Warlord Edrodene's uncle was Warlord before him." He shrugged. "I have no wish to rule, and few skills, so I doubt I'll be chosen."

"You're young yet."

"Seventy-two."

Alea's brows shot up. "You look fifteen."

"That's about the age a human becomes an adult, right?"

"A little bit young, but yes."

"Then the ages are comparable."

"You must at least be a decent fighter for Edrodene to allow you to come with this group."

"He wanted me out of the way." His crooked smile reminded her of Arman's.

"How long until dawn?"

"Five hours. The nights are already growing longer. Less than a month and we'll have no sun at all." He pointed to the frost forming along her hood. "We should get back inside, you'll have ice-burn before long."

When she returned to her seat she leaned back, staring at the snow outside. Mel'iend's suggestion to keep her eyes open threw shadows over her excitement and confidence. The

Ageless seemed a rough race, however, and perhaps it was only the difference in culture that the boy warned her against.

She did not remember falling asleep again, but she woke several hours later. The cool blue of the northern sky heralded dawn. Tennic was rousing the others and barking orders in a guttural tongue. Seeing she was awake, he jerked a thumb at the windows opposite her. "If you want a view, it'll be out those windows. My men must ready for arrival."

Alea crossed the cart and perched on the newly vacated bench to watch. The snow here was deeper, and Alea realized that perhaps it never truly melted. She shuddered. She could never stand to live in a world so cold and dark. The tracks curved north, affording Alea an expansive view of the white tundra. She made out the shape of mountains ahead, pale against the lightening sky. With the cool, thin air, sunrise was swift. There was no gradual bloom of light and color. The sun exploded from the icy horizon, light billowing across the glittering snow. Alea blinked stars from her eyes and looked north.

There were no mountains. The buildings of Neneviir gleamed in the sunlight. At first it seemed as if the walls were made of glass blocks, but as they neared, curving further, she saw it was not glass, but ice. The blocks were as long as she was tall and stacked together with only the cold and snow to bind them. The spires and minarets were supported by delicate iron frameworks. The rust from the beams and pillars bled red across the blocks.

The city was large, predominantly a single building with sprawling wings and several storeys. The western half was still shadowed by its own bulk, and where the light had yet to touch, Alea saw the walls were lit from within by great oil lamps. A row of arched doorways greeted the steam engine as it glided to a halt before the great iron doors to the city.

Every piece of the building before her, the machines used to get there, even the face of the warriors that guarded the door, told her what it took to live in this bitter environment. *This is where An'thor's strength was born.* There was no compromising in this snow-covered land. Compromise brought death. She swiped at her cheeks, half expecting tears. There were none, but her heart ached.

Mel'iend poked his head through the door to the stairs. "Come on."

She stood and quickly gathered her pack. Her bow would only suffer from the weather, but she missed the statement a visible weapon made. The half dozen warriors that had accompanied her flanked the cart's exit. *Honored guest or prisoner?* When it came to politics, she realized they were often similar.

Tennic glanced over at her. "Edrodene will see you within the hour. We're to eat and warm before the audience. Afterward you'll be given accommodations."

"Thank you." She shouldered her pack and allowed them to escort her up the ice-block stairs and through the doors. She had thought the ice would be slippery, but the constant cold maintained the ridges carved on the surface. There was no courtyard, save the line of stables and berths for the engines. She supposed they rarely received visitors who did not also live there. The doors opened into a wide hall. Despite the inherent chill of the ice, it was comfortable. Straw dusted the floor and heavy oil lamps hung from the ceiling. It was militant, but not savage.

They brought her to a large anteroom equipped with an iron-lined fire pit and several chairs made with fur stretched over an iron frame. *No trees means no wood.*

"We'll be a moment." Tennic pointed to the food lain out. "Help yourself." The Ageless huddled in a far corner, rapidly discussing something in their tongue. Tennic barked a harsh rebuke when Mel'iend faltered, clearly wanting to ask Alea more about the warmer parts of the world.

Tired of sitting, she paced around the room absently. There was no artwork or decoration, only serviceable tables with food and drink. She chose a handful of dried fruit. After a moment she looked over at her escorts. Mel'iend's eyes flicked between hers and Tennic. His expression was that of seasickness.

She met his gaze with a frown. His eyes bored into hers, as if willing her to understand. She dared not reach her mind out to his, but the horror on his face churned her stomach. After warring with herself for a minute, she reached her thoughts out to brush his for a moment, looking away as she did so.

Beware.

She pulled away quickly, before he realized what she had done. The conversation stopped abruptly and Tennic cleared his throat. "Captain, the warlord will see you now. Keep it short."

She nodded once and followed him through the larger doors. The hall was closer to a training court than a throne room. The floor was once again covered in straw. A massive iron fire pit sat in a depression in the center. The tiers surrounding it were covered in fur for lounging.

A set of iron stairs stood across the hall. These too were covered in fur, and an older man sat on the second highest. If the other Ageless were weathered, this man was battered. His bull's horns were chipped and scratched, the marks blackened from smoke. Each hip bore one of the strange weapons An'thor wielded. The metal beads in his dry, untidy braids rattled as he cocked his head. "Why are you here?"

She bowed deeply. "Warlord Edro'dene, I come from Athrolan with orders from Her Majesty Tzatia and our ally the Dhoah' Laen."

"Orders? I'm the lord here, not some human queen or Laen girl."

Alea's nerves began to sing. This was nothing like An'thor promised. "Of course. We share an ally, however. Lord Commissioner Barrackborn has allied Mirik with An'thoriend Domariigo."

"So my brother said. He's never been the brightest. Optimism is an unfortunate disease of the Hotlands. He seems to have contracted a rather strong strain."

"He said I would be allowed to look through your great treasury for an artifact the Dhoah' Laen needs. It's nothing valuable to you, and not fine in its craftsmanship."

Metal clanged as Edrodene slammed his gauntleted fist on a bare spot of stair. "Fine? You think we care about finery here? Are you blind, Captain?"

Her stomach sank. "Forgive me, Warlord. Your people are a powerful enigma to us humans."

He snorted. "As for your rank—you think I'd believe they would send a single captain here without other guards or better instructions? They either have too much faith in you or you are not what they think." A flick of his fingers caused

Tennic and the others to draw the strange weapons from the holsters on their belts. A series of metallic clicks rang against the ice walls as their thumbs pulled levers back.

She did not understand how they worked, but she understood a threat when she saw one. She raised her hands slowly. "I come from An'thoriend. I want nothing more than to finish my business here and be on my way."

Edrodene's expression did not flicker and her heart fell. Her thoughts turned to the desolation she had seen upon her arrival. "You're isolated here. It was fine, for a time, but your people are dying, fleeing, and you have no resources. Your machines are all well and good, but you have no one to work them." The growing smile on the warlord's face was grim. "Fates you can't be serious." She sank to her knees and sat back on her heels, hands still raised, but without fear. "You saw what side would give you slaves. You thought the gods and Azirik would help you enslave the world. Your cryptic letter allowed the lie, but I'm not fooled anymore."

"Throw the captain in a cell until I decide what to do with her." Edrodene flicked his hand again before looking away, as if she was no more interesting than the filth under his long, cracked nails.

Her pack was ripped from her shoulder, the force sending her skittering across the floor. She managed to scramble to her feet before two of the men grabbed her by the arms and muscled her through a different door. The stairs down were narrow and twisting. Even with her boots she stumbled often. By the time they emerged into a low hall her shins were bruised and her cheek skinned from the roughly hewn ice wall.

Here the floors and walls were iron, as were the thick bars across the doors of each of the dozen cells. It smelled faintly of decay, even through the cold, and the sickly-sweetness of blood hung in the air. The room at the end of the hall was open. A single oil lamp hung low, illuminating the chair bolted to the floor. She clenched her hands to hide their shaking. She knew an interrogation room when she saw one.

"I don't know what you think to get from me." Her words guttered out when one of the men slammed the side of his fist into her diaphragm. Her breath flew from her lungs and she stumbled sideways. They shoved her into one of the cells unceremoniously and slid the bars shut.

"Whoever you are, the Warlord will find out."

"I'm a captain in Athrolan's army."

The man shrugged before heading back up the stairs with his companion.

Alea watched him go before leaning against the bars. "I'm Lenna Grayhill." Her voice was soft and wheezed over the "h" as she spoke. "I'm an Athrolani captain. I'm Lenna Grayhill." Her words petered out, lips still moving soundlessly as she repeated her false name and rank over and over. Perhaps if she believed it enough, so would they.

It was two hours before anyone appeared, and her stomach was rumbling. Her adrenaline burnt through any food from the past day. This time there were four guards. One she recognized as Mel'iend.

She snarled at him. She had trusted him. A small part of her grinned when he refused to meet her eyes. "You think you'll gain anything from torturing me? I know nothing— General Aneral isn't stupid enough to send a confidant to a strange country, even one we thought to be an ally."

"We don't care about your strategy. We care about why you're here and who you really are." Tennic gestured to Mel'iend. "Read the letter."

Mel'iend cleared his throat. "An'thor, I arrived at dawn on the 31st. Though not the most friendly, the Nenev have been hospitable. I'll begin my search tomorrow. I trust I'll see you soon. Luck and love, Grayhill"

Alea frowned. "You think he'll believe that?"

"Has he seen your handwriting? We can persuade you to write it yourself." Tennic's grin had more teeth than the wind and Alea looked down. "I thought not. Send it out with the next raven." He waited until Mel'iend retreated up the stairs. "Boy has no stomach for learning. It's a shame he's the Warlord's son." His black eyes flicked to Alea. "Now, let's get to learning about you."

The fact that the Ageless used "learning" as a euphemism for torture made her stomach twist tighter. *Should I just reveal my power? Would that stop them?* She had no doubt she could defeat a few guards, but the hundreds of warriors in the city above would be more difficult. *Besides, I'd be hard pressed to escape on horseback.* She grit her teeth as they unlocked her door and dragged her out. She brought her power up, not enough to color her skin or eyes, but enough to envelope her mind. She would feel the pain, but it would be distant. They shoved her into the bolted chair and buckled her arms and legs down. She gathered everything she ever learned, everything that made her Alea, and tucked it behind the walls of darkness.

I am Lenna Grayhill. I'm a captain in Athrolan's army.

The Ageless were not a stupid race, and despite the evidence, were not cruel for the sake of fun. Their abuse consisted of blows and bright lights and superficial wounds. She knew it was to keep her as whole as possible, not to be kind, but she was grateful nonetheless. She felt her lips move, repeating the litany of her identity, but she no longer heard her words. Her thoughts drifted to Reka, and wondered how the woman had fared before her death. Was Azirik cruel? Somehow the only times she pictured him, he was weeping.

Φ

The 25th Day of Lumord, 1252
The Orn de Galin Mountains

It seemed like centuries since Arman had last stood on the slopes of the Orn de Galin. The rocky slopes were stark, hawks circling on the heat waves rising from the outcroppings. Arman drifted upward on his own thermal. A curious bird flew too close, head cocked, eye turned towards the shimmering patch of air. Arman materialized his throat and mouth enough to rattle a warning call at the creature. He did not need distractions now. Below, Aral stretched on a rock, white belly turned to the warm sunlight. His crippled leg was ugly in the light of day, and Arman wondered how much the creature's battered mind would actually help them. The mountain range was quiet, only the low moan of the wind breaking the stillness. He reached out with his mind, as he had before. *Eana, where are you?*

A hideous shriek echoed from the peaks behind him, startling the hawks into flight. *There's a reason nothing lives in these passes.* Arman drifted lower, scanning the tumble of crags and stone. After finding Aral crippled and mad, Arman worried what awaited him with the others. He worried he was glimpsing his own future. A cave opened on a steeper slope below him. Bones littered the outcropping before the entrance. Most were those of animal's, but not all. Arman coasted lower, finally solidifying on the stone before the cave's mouth. At first he thought the creature crouched in the opening was a statue.

It could have been stone, save for the expanding chest. Puffs of smoke rose from the gap in its teeth. It made a low rattling moan, like pebbles shaken from the hillside. It sounded like a death rattle. With the grinding of stone it slowly tilted its head. A hunk of red sinew hung from the claws of its left hand.

Arman still made no move. He did not draw, but his hand stayed resting on the hilt of his knives. The death rattle call sounded again. "Ehnah. Ehnah."

Arman frowned. "Eana? You think I'm Eana?" He lifted his hand from his knife and tapped his chest carefully. "Arman."

The head tilted the other way. "Ahman."

"Probably sounds that way, with my dialect."

Stone ground and the creature's hand rose from its perch and tapped once, twice, on its own armored breast. "Ehnah."

Shock hit Arman's mind as he recognized the golden eyes, the crooked scar. He stepped back, tripping over the bones. Eana's claw tapped rhythmically as he muttered over and over the death rattle of his own name.

Arman raised his hands defensively. "All right, so you're not what I expected. Are any of you sane?"

Aral scrambled down from his perch with the speed of something that had been hunting birds and lizards. He moved like the apes in menagerie caravans, an arm supporting his body when his legs swung forward.

Arman skittered back a few paces. His heel crunched on a skull too large. "You've been eating people, Eana. Is there anything about the Earth Shakers that isn't disgusting?"

Eana made a wholly worse noise that Arman realized belatedly was a laugh. His jaw worked, steaming breath rolling from between his battered teeth. "Not cannibalism."

Arman's brows rose. "So you can speak."

Scales clattered as the creature shrugged. Eana moved to the edge of the outcropping, sharp eyes finding the prone figure of Aral below. "Pathetic."

"You'd be too, if you'd been trapped in your own temple."

Eana's mocking eyes swiveled to look at him pointedly. "Others?"

Arman mimicked the shuddering shrug. "I can sense them, barely. Most shelter in old Laen cities, or temples, like Aral. I'm not sure how many are left—I've found a few dead. Two by their own hands. Claws. The third was poisoned not long ago—perhaps by the gods, same way my city was destroyed. I saw their power, as if it still echoed after they were gone."

"War?"

"The same war we fought centuries ago. Time to finish it." Arman realized each word was a struggle for Eana, the thick tongue and cracked teeth too much for more human speech. As mocking as Eana's eyes were, there was also desperation.

"Help?"

"In the war?" Arman asked.

"Finding. Others."

"Yeah I could use some." Arman looked down. "Thank you, for driving me here. You're a right ass, but it helped. How long have I been hearing your voice, thinking it was my own thoughts?"

"Since I heard yours. Years." He shuffled down the slope.

Arman followed after him, frowning. "You can hear me like I hear you?"

"Started as whispers. Been shouting for months now." He hissed at Aral, the sound of steam on coals. *Get up you bastard. There are others, even if only a few. Don't tell me a missing limb prevents you from flying. I know better.*

The mental tirade startled Arman. "Don't be cruel, Eana. He flew here with me."

"Cruel, cruel," Aral echoed. The creature rose on his good leg, flexing a hand and steadying himself on a crag. At first it looked as if his body rotted, the skin peeling back to muscle and deeper to bone.

Arman backed away as the two dissolved into whirling smoke, spiraling into the clouds and west. *I'll see you at war. Don't be late.*

Don't think we'll miss this. We've waited long enough for you to get your head from your ass.

Φ

The 24th Day of Lumord, 1252

Bren groaned when someone knocked on his door for the fourth time in an hour. "I give up on getting any semblance of work done."

Kemer laughed. "Just ask them to make appointments." Aldac bent over the queen's missives while she and An'thor poured over a strategic map.

"This is war, I doubt Azirik would be so obliging." He heaved himself to his feet.

Eras waited outside, a slight frown curling her copper brows. "Lord Commissioner Barrackborn, I wanted to discuss some plans with your sister, but as I came to call on her, this letter intercepted me." She waved it in the air. "Care to explain what the Dhoah' Laen is doing in Neneviir two weeks before battle?"

Bren looked away. "It's complicated."

An'thor slid from his chair with a rough cough. "I think I'd better explain. Come in, *fetali*."

"This is my room, An'thor, not your parlor."

"I'm your ally and Her Majesty holds a damn fine grudge, so until I have my own, yours will have to do." An'thor leaned on the mantel. "When we met in Mirik, your sister asked a favor of me. She needed to find the Laen's Crown. It was in Claimiirn before she fell, and Lyne'alea suspected it could still be there. I suggested she try Neneviir as well, given the fact that Edrodene ransacked Claimiirn's treasury."

"And you sent her there unguarded?" Eras scoffed.

An'thor rolled his eyes at the general. "Eras, she sent herself. I merely gave her what she needed. May I see that?" An'thor unfolded the letter curiously, skimming it. "She reached the capital."

Bren slumped in his chair. "I still wish you had told me she was leaving."

"And I still agree with her choice not to."

"I'm not Arman, I wouldn't have stopped her. What did she say?"

"Precious little. Says they aren't friendly, but are cooperating. Her handwriting leaves a bit to be desired."

Bren frowned. "What?" He beckoned for the paper. By the time his gaze reached the bottom, his face had twisted into a grimace. "This isn't her handwriting. This isn't her voice. She'd say more, explain more. Complain about the weather."

An'thor grabbed the letter back. His eyes picked out the sharp points on some of the letters, the hard lines at the ends of the sentences. "You're right. This is Mel'iend."

"Who?"

"My nephew. A kind boy, but useless."

"Why would she have him write a letter for her? It can't be that cold."

"She didn't. Something's gone wrong." He tugged the earlier letter from Edrodene from his pocket and scanned it. "'*As always, I weigh the strength of the sides, and the benefits each offers. The choice is clear.*'" He handed it over. "Where does he explicitly name his allies?"

Bren looked it over. "He doesn't. Not once. He could mean anything."

Eras met Bren's eyes. "He's Azirik's. She's been captured. An'thor, take care of this. I'm going to deal with the army. We need to be ready for battle as soon as she returns."

Bren surged to his feet as soon as the general closed the door. "I'm going to get her."

"Like shite you are." An'thor pointed to the stack of papers on Bren's desk. "I understand your sister transcends all else in your mind, but you will lay it aside. You duty is to Mirik now. I'll handle this." When Bren bated, An'thor pushed him firmly back into his seat. "Ready your soldiers. Ready yourself. I know the Nenev, I know the Northlands."

Bren cast a longing look at the door. "All right. But if you fail, I'll gut you."

"If I fail you won't have to." An'thor jogged down the hall to his rooms. Within a minute his packs were ready and he was saddling Theriim. It had been decades since he had last been home. It seemed fitting it would be to make war with his brother.

Φ

The 25th Day of Lumord, 1252
The City of Neneviir

Pain was like water, patient and persistent, worming its way through chinks in the walls until the pressure built up enough to flood. The layers of shadow between her mind and their actions began to crumble.

Her head rocketed back as Tennic's fist rearranged the bones of her nose. Her mind flooded back into her body, her eyes flying open. Her left eyelid was swollen and a stinging on her cheek told her something had split the skin. The fingers of her left hand were black and bent at wrong angles. Nausea hit her stomach like a stone. She heaved, splatters of vomit freezing on the iron floor.

Tennic stepped back, muttering what sounding like a curse in Nenev. "You going to give us anything else?"

"I thought," her voice hitched every few words, "your boots...needed polishing."

The door opened suddenly. Through her bloodshot, good eye Alea recognized Mel'iend. He looked horrified. "Sir, the Warlord wants to see you. Immediately. Something about His Majesty Azirik."

Tennic growled in disgust and gestured sharply to the others. "Put her back. We'll continue this later."

She landed on her knees, the rough iron floor of her cell scratching her skin.

"I'm sorry." The words were low, almost drowned by the muttering of the wind through her barred window.

Alea pushed herself up. Her eye was completely swollen shut now. Mel'iend crouched just outside her cell. "Come to taunt me? Or warn me?" She spit a thick clot of blood from her mouth. "I think I've caught on to the Ageless not being terribly friendly."

He ignored her words. "I had to make sure they were properly gone. You said you came here looking for something. Said it was for the war. We've got plenty of weapons, sure, but I know a fighter and title or not, you're no captain."

Her pride stung at his words. She was never a good actress, but she thought she knew enough of the military to fool an isolated city. "I don't know what you think I am."

He raised his brows pointedly. "Not once did you ask us *who* we thought you were, only *what*. Why are you so convinced we think you're something other than human? And you've got the walk, the stance, the fighter's glare down wonderfully. I almost believe them. That look though," he gestured to her eyes, "that has far too much power and anger for a captain. Whatever you are, you're the damned general."

Her jaw clenched. "You're mad."

"Maybe." He jerked his head at the stairs. "What are you looking for?"

"Allies, that's all. And if you think this sweet innocence will make me talk, you're more stupid than I thought."

"Mad, stupid, you're probably right." The joking act was gone. His black eyes were exhausted and his features broken. "They don't give a shite about me, ma'am. Take me with you and I'll get you out."

Her brows rose. "Help me find what I need and we'll see."

"I'll make the way clear and be back in an hour. Wait here."

"I was planning on waiting in the hall." Her wry smile softened the bitter words. "Go." She shoved herself against the rear wall. Snow had blown in through the barred window, but sitting in a drift was better than being prodded from the door. The blood from her nose dripped down her face, but she was too dazed to stop it. Her vision unfocused as the hot blood melted red canyons through the snow.

Φ

Half an hour had passed when she heard boots on the stairs. She scrambled up. "Mel'iend?"

Tennic appeared before her cell, eyes narrowed. "It seems the Warlord did not actually request our audience. Mel'iend lied." He shoved her cell door open. "What does that coward have planned? He can't possibly think to outsmart us."

"You're right." She raised her hands, backing away. "He's not the bravest. But neither am I. Thought I could stand the questioning. Turns out I'm just too tired of pain. Call me a coward if you wish."

Tennic stepped in, the other warrior following him, weapon leveled at Alea's head. "I think you'll tell us who you are now."

Alea stepped back again, until her back pressed against the hard iron of the rear wall. "The thing is, you don't have to be brave. You just have to be clever." Her power roared through her body. Blackness filled her skin and lightning crawled from her back, burrowing like roots through the iron.

Tennic opened his mouth to scream, but the electricity wormed up both men's boots. Their muscles jerked, bones heating and flesh cooking in a moment. The smell of burning hair and meat flooded the cell as her power bore down. She pushed harder, watching as they fell, still spasming. The life was gone, but she let the lightning puppeteer them across the floor for another minute. The sound of boots pounding on ice broke her concentration and she slumped back against the wall, power curling back into her skin.

"I told you to wait!"

"They got friendly and I wasn't sure you'd get here in time, or at all!"

"Shite." He glanced down at the bodies. "Well. Are they dead?"

"Yes." Alea shoved herself off the wall. "I need my pack. You take care of these two." She slammed her boot into Tennic's face as she passed. The interrogation room still smelled of blood and vomit, and her stomach clenched anew. The table along the back wall held her things, clearly searched. She fumbled with the ties of the pack, one handed when Mel'iend dragged the second body into the room.

"You need help with that?"

"They broke my damned hand."

"Can I see?" He took her hand in his, peering at the bones. "Some of these are just dislocated. Nothing looks crooked. Is there anyone coming?"

Alea ducked her head to peer up the stairs while he continued to examine her fingers. "Nothing yet."

"Good." He grabbed her fingers and tugged them back into place with a swift motion.

A scream ripped from her dry throat and she whirled to glare at him, clutching her hand her to her chest. "Really?"

"You were distracted and that thing would be useless if I didn't." He shrugged. "I've learned things being around too many warriors."

She tried to flex her fingers again. The last two had only been disjointed, but the others were too stiff and painful to move. "Thank you then." She swung her pack over her shoulder. "What about the nose?"

"Can you breathe through it?"

"A bit."

"Then it'll heal all right." He grabbed the weapons from the two dead warriors and headed to the door. "Come on. I'll take you through the rear gate. We'll pass the treasury on our way."

She followed him up the stairs and down a hall. It wound around the Warlord's hall and to the rear of the city before climbing higher. "You only build upwards it seems."

"The ground is too frozen to dig deeply. Our lesser used rooms are higher instead of lower, that's all." He stopped at a large door and began fumbling with the lock. His knobby fingers coaxed it open with his picks after a moment. He shoved the door open and ushered her inside. "I'll stay here to guard. Are you sure it's here?"

She closed her eyes and reached out. The treasury was cold, and the air still. Far in the back, under a rolled carpet and inside a large chest was a leather bag. It buzzed in her mind, a clouded black smudge in her thoughts. "It's here." She navigated through the stacks of books and wardrobes. The chest was thankfully unlocked, but it took her a moment to shove the rug from its top with only one hand. The moment the leather met her hand she shuddered. The Rakos Crown had felt hot and itchy in her hand, but otherwise inert. This was like grasping lightning by the tail. She shoved it inside her shirt, tying the bag's strings to her breastband before weaving her way back to the door. "Got it. Let's go."

He slid the lock back into place, glancing back at her. "You have any plan as to how we're going to leave?"

Alea grinned. "You know how to drive an engine?"

"I have an idea."

"That's more than I do. How do we get there without them seeing us?"

"Luck? They'll be looking for me too, now." Mel'iend broke into a jog. "Can you run?"

"For now." Her adrenaline was wearing thin, but it would carry her home. It had to. She followed after him, not bothering to be quiet. The ice was surprisingly insulating and the sound of their footfalls carried only a short distance. He led her through another series of halls before they emerged behind the line of engine berths. They edged to the engine furthest from the city and ducked to the far side.

Mel'iend handed her his pack and pointed at the engine door. "Hop up into the cabin, I'll grab a few things."

She hoisted herself up into the machine, eying the levers and two things that looked like compasses attached to the wall. A small iron door hid a mound of black rocks and ash.

She heard Mel'iend climb in behind her. "Light her up, I'll manage the speed."

"My powers are ice and water and lightning, not fire!" She said it without thought and winced.

"That's why I brought the torch, ma'am."

She turned to see he did indeed hold a torch from the wall outside. "Sorry."

Either he was more stupid than she thought or he already suspected her true identity. He did not bat an eyelid. "We're escaping from my home and your captors, tension's natural. I'm surprised we haven't had a screaming match yet. Shove this in the coals."

"Right." She poked the mound with the torch gingerly, delighted when they caught. The flames licked high, the coals growing orange. One of the compasses on the wall began to twitch. Mel'iend pumped a lever that must have worked a set of bellows and the coals roared into life. He nudged the door shut with his knee and flicked the latch shut.

"All right. I've seen this before." His tone sounded like he was reassuring himself more than her. After a few moments of tinkering, the engine rumbled and belched a puff of steam from its chimney. "Well if they didn't know, now they do." He depressed a heavy lever on the side and the wheels ground against the rails, lurching into sporadic motion. He depressed it further and the engine lurched again then glided out from under the arched door and onto the tundra. The noise of the engine drowned out any shouts of alarm, but the ping of metal against the sides told her they were most likely under attack.

"Can we go any faster?" She eyed the glass windows. "Metal will hold, but I doubt those will."

"Right. Yes. One minute. I do this too fast and we'll blow cloud-high." They rounded the easy curve in the tracks that led to the city and he grinned. "All right, hold on." He slammed the lever all the way forward. The fire roared and the engine churned before they catapulted forward. The pulse of the wheels on the rails was closer to a rattle and the air screamed over the hard lines of the engine. Mel'iend glanced at her. His eyes were wide with terrified glee. "This is the best day I've had in a while."

She snorted. "My hand is a mess, my ankle is sprained and my nose is broken. Forgive me if I don't share your excitement." Her stomach was beginning to relax, but with the relief came waves of pain she had suppressed during their escape. "They'll probably follow us."

His delight dimmed. "I suppose. It'll take them a bit though. And they'll need at least a cart to carry enough men. We've only got the engine, so we're a bit faster."

"I'll deal with them when they catch up." She sank to the ground, leaning on the hard iron of the cabin walls. "Where are we going? Kaliim?"

Mel'iend made a face. "Yes, let's escape from one Nenev city only to drive right into their garrison. Not your brightest idea."

"I thought we didn't have a choice. The rails only go so many places, I assume." The rumble of the engine buzzed through her skull.

"Well yes, but we could stop before hand. We'd have to travel on foot."

"At least it's warmer there." She heaved a sigh. "How did the Ageless survive in this cold before you developed all these contraptions?"

"You realize Ageless is a slur?" He waved her sheepish apology away. "Doesn't matter. We developed these things precisely because we had to face the cold. Originally we came to the southern border, near Athrolan and Berr, before they were much beyond city-states. We began our work there, gradually moving north when we knew we could. Many think we just thrive in the cold. We do better than most, but the city is heated with generators and radiant heat. We're not tough as all that." He shot her a smile.

"I'm tired of cold, to be honest. I would have liked it more, perhaps, had I not experienced it in a jail cell."

"You grew up in the desert, didn't you?"

She turned to look at him. "How long have you known?"

"I told you, I knew you weren't a captain. I know about General Aneral from An'thor. There is only one other woman who I imagine has that much power and anger in her eyes."

She looked away, a frown growing on her features. "Do you think they knew, too?"

"I doubt it. It pays to be nobody. I've learned to observe much better, since no one takes the time to talk to me mostly."

"Why did they disregard you so much?"

"I spent a lot of time with my uncle when I was younger, and some of his philosophies influenced me too much. Up until a few years ago we corresponded regularly. He and my father don't exactly see on level."

"Have they always been that way?" An'thor seemed a kind, if wounded man. It was no small leap to assume Edrodene might have been the reason. "Why did he trust him at all?"

"Hope, I think. My father was the younger of the two, and the general of the army before the former Warlord died. An'thor was an ambassador in Claimiirn with his wife. Edrodene wanted to invade, and An'thor tried to prevent it." Mel'iend's expression was tight and his eyes narrowed.

Alea winced. "I've heard the aftermath of that story. Never the cause. His son died in that battle, didn't he?"

Mel'iend nodded. "I think that's why An'thor took such an interest in me. His son and I were born around the same time, though I was too young to remember him properly. His name was Elostrii."

"That's a pretty name."

"It's the word for Mother's Breath — the great blue clouds we see at night." He glanced out the window. "If you'd like, I can manage this for a while. You probably need to sleep. Who knows what'll await us further down the rails."

She nodded, hearing that the topic was clearly over. "Wake me if you need to." She curled into the corner. The iron was hard, but warm, and it felt like days since she last slept. Counting back, she realized her last true night's sleep had been over a week ago while traveling to Claimiirn. She shoved her pack into a more comfortable shape and settled in. "Mel'iend?"

"Yeah?"

"Thank you for helping me."

His soft laugh was almost silent against the churning engines. "No, ma'am, thank you."

Φ

Screaming metal jolted Alea awake. She braced herself against the side of the engine. "Fates, that is one way to wake a woman up."

Mel'iend's expression did not lighten. "Ma'am we're almost at Garrison Kaliim. How are we going to make it out of there?"

She winced. "Honestly, I didn't think that far ahead." She hauled herself up to peer through the fogged windows. The fort crouched darkly against the gray backdrop of the southern tundra. "There must be a hundred warriors there."

"Maybe closer to 50. My father is calling everyone home for war."

"Still too many for just us." She closed her eyes. "Too much heat will cause an explosion?"

"Yeah, why?" He caught sight of the power rising in her hands and blanched. "Ma'am, they won't survive a steam engine exploding, but neither will we."

"Only if we're in it." Her lip curled and she grabbed his hand. "We'll open the door. When I tell you to, jump."

"Ma'am—"

"I didn't bring us this far to burn to death." Alea flung the rear door open. The wheels screamed on the rails and she braced herself on the side. "Maximum speed, Mel'iend."

"Right." He unlocked the thin bar that prevented the engine from exceeding safe speeds and slid the lever all the way up. "Full steam ahead."

The engine growled, the fire roaring behind the thick metal of the furnace door. *I may not have fire, but I have water.* She drew the ice, the cold, from the fire. The acrid smell of creosote and fire filled the tiny compartment. The fort jolted closer in the tiny window. Tiny figures waved a welcome, then a more frantic gesture to slow, to stop. "Almost." The massive double doors reared before them. "Now!" Alea launched herself at Mel'iend, her arms locking behind his back as she propelled them through the steam engine's door. They hit the frozen ground, ribs cracking. Alea's shoulder ground into its socket, but her left arm still gripped the boy.

Air rushed past them, sucked into the fort by the fire's hunger. Blackness erupted in Alea's mind and she surrounded them with her power. She could barely focus through the pain. Instead of cool air, icy water enveloped them. She blinked against the sting of salt to find Mel'iend had been stunned by the fall. Her broken hand fumbled over his face and she pinched his nose shut, covering his mouth with her palm. She held her power in place, barely, as the explosion spread over them. The water began to boil at the edges as a second explosion rocked them. Her lungs burnt for air. Finally, the fire retreated to what was left of the fort.

She pulled her power back and the water splashed to the ground. What had been frozen earth was now charred, churned mud. Her skin stung from salt and the heat roiling from the burning fort. She dropped Mel'iend and began slapping his face. "Wake up, you silly boy." Her voice croaked over her aching throat.

It was another moment before he opened his eyes, gasping. "What happened?"

"We jumped, you fainted." She stumbled to her feet and started towards the hills behind the flaming fort. "We need to get out of here." When the Nenev boy did not follow her, she turned back.

He stared at the fort. The flames etched the contours of his face in yellow and black, adding lines he had not earned yet. "Where am I supposed to go?"

"Come with us. An'thor will surely help you."

He shrugged. "He's a solitary man. And what if he does? I'm no good at the sword. Or farming. Or mathematics."

"You're young. But you won't survive by standing in the mud waiting for your father's men to arrive."

"Right." He shrugged deeper into his cloak, though he seemed not to need the warmth, and fell into step behind her.

Alea noticed the rider after two silent, cold hours of walking. After another hour they were within shouting distance of one another.

Mel'iend glanced up from glaring at his boots. "He'll be on us in another minute. This is why I wanted us to take the tunnel."

"Along with anyone who might have survived the explosion? I think not. Besides, whoever they are, they come from Athrolan."

"Or Claimiirn."

Her lips thinned. She wanted to avoid that possibility, though it was far more likely than the option she voiced. "One rider does not worry me, Mel'iend."

Her words were cut off as An'thor's gray charger crested the hill before them at a lope. The warrior drew the horse up and raised a hand. "I wondered if I'd make it in time. Seems I worried for nothing."

Alea jogged the last few paces between them. Her laugh was weak. "Not for nothing. There were a few harrowing minutes."

An'thor dismounted, glancing between her and Mel'iend. "And were you successful?"

"I was." She nodded at Mel'iend. "I have your nephew to thank for that."

An'thor's expression hardened. "About that." He drew the revolver at his hip with a flick. "You're not coming back with us."

"An'thor, don't be ridiculous, he helped me."

Mel'iend raised his shaking hands. "Please. I'm with you." His uncle's only response was to pull the hammer back. "I'm not going back to them, An'thor."

"Pick a direction, I don't care which as long as it's not ours—and start walking. Don't stop until nothing looks familiar."

He backed up several paces then turned and began to walk. When he finally disappeared into the whipping wind, his hands were still raised.

"An'thor, he said he wasn't going back."

"He might have if Neneviir was closer." An'thor returned his gun to his belt and turned to adjust his saddle.

"He could freeze to death!"

"He could return to Edrodene and be ripped to pieces. Worse, he could return and become something I no longer recognize. Given my druthers I'd rather he die in the snow."

"That's not really your choice to make, An'thor."

"Today it was." He whirled. "This world, here in this fucking nightmare of snow and gunpowder, isn't yours. It might be mine, and it's certainly his, but it's not yours and you have no place telling me what choices to make." His voice was an angry rumble and his black eyes narrowed. "And like you have a right to judge me. In a few weeks you'll be deciding the future of every person on this damned world!"

"You think they want me to let them die? Fall to chaos?" Her thoughts jumbled under the black wave in her mind. Her body hurt and her nausea returned. Whatever nerve she hit was unexpected and clearly affecting his level head. This was not an argument she had expected, and not one she was willing to have with An'thor.

"That's not what I'm talking about and you know it! You think Arman's happy with you playing martyr while he becomes a monster?" An'thor's face was twisted. In fear or anger or hatred, she was not sure.

She crossed the distance between them in two strides and gripped him by the collar. "Do you know what happens to a person's mind when they break a law of nature? It doesn't snap, that'd be too easy to fix." Lightning chattered over her shoulders and through her hair. "Something crawls in and makes its home in their thoughts. You looked in my eyes months ago and said you knew what I was afraid of. You can't tell a monster just by looking, An'thor, and the only thing that frightens me is the one I've become!"

An'thor's expression broke with her last word and he cautiously raised his hands. "You're right."

Her remaining thoughts howled in the space her words left. Her power drained from her body. "An'thor."

He placed his palms on her shoulders. When she did not spring away he wrapped his arms around her. "I know."

"I didn't mean to yell."

"Me neither."

"That anger wasn't at you."

"Well I pray we live long enough for Arman to hear it all, and everything left you haven't said." He patted her hair. "My anger wasn't at you either."

"I know. I'm sorry about your son."

His arms tightened, but he said nothing. She felt him swallow hard, and knew he probably did not trust his voice just yet. "Can we go home now, please?"

He pulled away, eyes more tired than ever. "I've got something to take care of first, someone I need to see. Take Theriim, I'll find another mount. It's more important that you make it back."

She climbed wearily into Theriim's saddle. "Stay safe."

He tapped his fist against his brow, lips, and chest. "Luck and love go with you."

The smile that flitted across her face was as haggard as the mountains. "I'll see you for battle."

THE SHAKING IN THE EARTH

CHAPTER NINETEEN

The 37th Day of Lumord, 1252
The Ruins of Claimiirn

AN'THOR FROZE WHEN THE KING'S eye found him. "Ah, hello milord king."

Azirik's brow quirked. "I thought you were the best in the world."

"Depends on who you ask, I suppose. I thought you were all abed."

Azirik's snorted laughter was not soothing. "You should try sleeping with a vice around your head."

An'thor eyes flicked to the Crown. He had heard the king was mad, heard his devotion had turned to insanity. An'thor knew better: Azirik was sane as any war-time king. Bloody times were not meant for sane men. The Crown glimmered from within the embrace of bruised and angry flesh. Now An'thor wondered if the rumors had been true.

"Would you sit?"

An'thor gaze narrowed. The king should be calling the guard. Azirik's expression was not one of vindication, but of loneliness. The Ageless took the chair by the door. He did not want someone to enter behind him, but he needed an escape route. "Why haven't you killed her yet? That should give you power, enough to attempt it." He gestured to the king's brow.

Azirik snorted again. "Why do you use your sword when you could end any fight with a squeeze of your finger?"

An'thor sat back at that. He had always assumed he knew the king far better than the king knew him. He had forgotten that over forty-five years he'd allowed a lot of little facts to penetrate their conversations. After all, lies were best taken with a dusting of truth. "What do you mean?"

"You have a revolver, a mighty weapon, and yet you have fired it how many times? Four?"

"Six." An'thor rubbed his hand down his scimitar's scabbard. "My blade is the best sword I could have found in Neneviir."

"It's pig iron folded over a dozen times to keep it from shattering. The best your people bothered to make, but still shite."

"And I'd still prefer it. I detest what my people did. I detest what they stand for. The revolver exemplifies both."

Azirik met his gaze. "And likewise, I prefer my own mind. It may be out-classed, it may be weak and twisted to prevent it breaking, but it is my own. This thing is my revolver."

"You aren't afraid they'll strike you down for that admittance?"

"They would lose the power I have over my men, and the connection to my allies. Besides, for a great cause, you would use your revolver. For a great cause, I would use the Crown."

An'thor stared at the man. Something in the king's gaze seared with its intensity. There was nothing he had left to lose, and that made him powerful. There were moves left on the gameboard, still, and An'thor was suddenly certain Azirik still had enough autonomy to sweep his enemy clear.

Φ

The 1st Day of Valemord, 1252
The City of Ceir Athrolan

Bren's mug shattered on the flagging. "Toar, Alea, what happened to you?"

Alea grinned weakly. The benefit of sneaking out of the palace was she had no fanfare to contend with on her return. "The Nenev have an odd way of saying hello."

He shook his head. "You should have brought guards."

"So they could be interrogated? I think not. Could you call your maid in? I'd love a healer. And perhaps something to drink. And food that isn't dried beyond all recognition."

Bren laughed and raised the flask still in his hand. "I'll have to call for new mugs, but you can have some of my wraith." He handed it over, peering at her face. "Did they break your nose?"

"Yes, but Mel'iend said as long as I could still breath through it, it would heal straight. I could barely see out my left eye for half the journey back though." She heaved a sigh. It was a relief to see his face after the ordeal of the last weeks. After a hard sip from the flask she glanced up. "I'm sorry I didn't tell you."

"I'm sorry, too. You were right not to. I might not be as bad as Arman, but I still wouldn't have understood. Did An'thor come with you?"

"He had to take care of something first. He'll be here before long though." She absently picked at the scabs on her left knuckles. "What did he say?"

"The same as before. I told him it was useless lying to you about his visits."

"What happened at Vielrona?"

"Azirik. Well, Azirik wielding the gods' power. I think it was something like the storm on the Iron Sea."

"His friends, his mother?"

"He said Kam was all right. Asked me to give him and his wife and child a home in Mirik. His mother's dead, same with his friend Wes and a woman called Veredy."

Alea groaned. It felt wrong that Veredy had already been dead when Alea had borrowed her name for a night of drinking. "I can't even imagine what he must be thinking."

"I imagine he must feel much like you did a year ago." Bren eyes were sad and gentle. "I'm sorry he hasn't seen you."

"It's funny, he saw me as the Dhoah' Laen when I was as far from that role as could be. Now, when that is all I am, he sees me as a woman. But part of me wonders if we'll ever see on level. Will we always be in this dance? Me leaving when he's arriving?" She shook her head.

He frowned. "What happened in the Northlands? You left angry and cold and lost. You come back almost as changed as when you returned from Le'yne."

She looked down. "I thought I learned to control my power by learning there was no difference between it and myself. Trouble was I didn't know who I was anymore. When you understand something, you can control it. I had to learn who I was, but even more I had to accept it. I can't spend whatever is left of my life terrified of what I am."

He slid from his seat and wrapped his arms around her unceremoniously. "I love you. Whatever you are, whether you accept it or not, I love you." He pulled away and met her eyes. "When do we leave?"

"As soon as General Aneral says the army is ready."

"It's been ready for the past two days. Waiting on you."

"I thought no one knew I was gone."

"They didn't. I told them you were meditating on battle. You haven't been the most sociable the past months, so it wasn't odd that no one had seen you."

Alea glared at him. "I suppose you're right."

Bren rose at Valadai's knock and relayed Alea's requests. "And if you could inform General Aneral that we'd like to speak with her at her earliest convenience."

Alea laughed. "I'm glad I had the forethought to bathe before coming to see you."

Eras arrived before both the food and the healer. Her brows shot up at Alea's appearance. "I learned you went to Neneviir. What happened to your face? Did you slip on the ice?"

"Yes, and they caught me with their fists." Alea grinned. "I had something I needed to get, and An'thoriend's brother was kind enough to relinquish it to me."

Eras's eyes darkened. "I wondered if An'thor was wrong in assuming they would be our allies."

"Edrodene explained that his brother seems to have caught the terrible human disease of optimism."

"He was always an ass." Eras pointed to the chair across from Alea. "Brentemir, may I?" When he nodded, she sat, leaning her elbows on her knees. "What is your plan, Dhoah'?"

"Battle. Within the week. How quickly can you mobilize the men?"

"They can be ready at dawn the day after tomorrow." She glanced at Bren. "And your men, are they ready to march?"

"They arrived a few days after Alea left." He glanced at his sister. "You should have seen it—I've never been more proud. And the Asai arrived shortly afterward." His grin faded and he drew a long breath. "It's been a while since I went into battle, and this one feels different."

Eras glanced up. "You, too?"

Alea glanced between the two. She did not know what they felt, but she agreed everything about this battle tasted differently. *There is certainty in me. Acceptance.* The shadow had not lifted from her spirit, but its blanketing darkness had changed.

Eras looked at her hands, clasped before her. "Dhoah' we're putting a lot of faith in you. This is just the beginning of your battle, but it is the greatest of Athrolan. You made a promise to Her Majesty, and to our people, that Athrolan will not fall. Are you still holding to that promise?"

Alea wondered briefly what Daymir might have said. *I am not so mighty as to keep a city from falling.* She did not look away from the general's gray eyes. "Athrolan will always stand."

Φ

The 3rd Day of Valemord, 1252
The Eastern Forest of Athrolan

Alea noticed the men on the second day of the march. There
were five. She began the journey among Indred's men, but
after the first day another group of soldiers formed around
her. Narier was among them, but she recognized two others.
One was a former guard at Daymir's manor and the other she
had tended during the siege. None ever spoke to her, but they
were clearly a silent rotating guard. She discovered why on
their third night after making camp.

The nightmares from Cehn were now speckled with her
days trapped in Neneviir. Between them, she woke, bedroll
tangled and drenched in sweat. She tumbled off her cot, the
images fading slowly from the backs of her eyelids. "Damn."

"Dhoah', you all right?"

Alea turned at the soft voice outside her tent. She rose
and peered through the flap. A man stood just outside. She
recognized him as one of the men she tended during the siege.
"I'm fine, what are you doing?"

"Just keeping an eye out, Dhoah', nothing more."

"You don't have to do that, there are plenty of eyes out
tonight."

"Just the same, I'm here." His smile was wary, but
genuine.

Her head still pounded and her limbs buzzed. "You were
out here before?"

"No, Dhoah', Kal had last night and Narier the one
before."

She frowned. She was tired and sorely needed sleep. The
thought that these men had taken up her guard without
question was uncomfortable. *The fact that I can defend myself*

aside, this is ridiculous. She was about to tell the man so, when she caught sight of his face. "You guarded Daymir's house."

"Yes. It's Gord, Dhoah'."

"Thank you, then. Good night." She ducked back into the tent and crawled into her bedroll. Her body ached, but her mind was whirling.

Φ

The 5th Day of Valemord, 1252

Alea shrugged deeper into her cloak and wound her way through the tents until she found the campfire. Narier was alone at the fire, peering into the crackling heat with a vague frown.

"Care for some tea?" Alea held up a tin from her pack and her tin mug.

Narier shrugged. "Might as well." He settled the kettle in the coals and pointed at the fading bruise lingering around her eye. "I see your journey was eventful."

"Rather. I got what I needed, though. Thank you for your help. Then and now."

He grinned. "Gord told me you caught him. Said he thought you were angry at first."

"At first I was. I'm capable of defending myself."

"We all know it, Alea. But you're tired and worn and everyone can see it. You deserve to rest safely."

Her thanks were interrupted by the arrival of a younger man with thick curls. He froze, staring at the woman by his fire. "Fates."

She grinned and patted the ground beside her. "Come on. I won't hurt you. If you insist on guarding me, the least I can do is share my tea."

The man edged over and carefully sat. "Right. Thank you, Dhoah'."

"I don't recognize you." She held out her arm. "What should I call you?"

"I'm Kal Smytheson. I was friends with your guard for a time. Sousa, too."

Alea's response was interrupted by the arrival of the other three.

"And I told her, that's exactly what your sister thought!"

The men crowed with laughter and Kal glanced uneasily at Alea. "Sousa, knock it! We've got company." He looked over apologetically. "Forgive them, Dhoah' they didn't know. They just returned from getting a bottle from the trail army."

Gord flushed, seeing Alea and stammered to a halt. "I'm sorry, Dhoah', I didn't see you."

She waved his apology away. Her time in Vielrona had not been ill spent, and she remembered most of Wes's and Kam's wicked humor. "Nonsense. I'll tell you the one about the Berrin scout and the crow if you share a thumb of that wraith."

Narier snorted into his tea at the expressions on their faces. "I doubt you're what they expected, Alea."

Alea shrugged and smiled at the three still standing. "Come and sit. You with the dark hair must be Sousa, and Gord I know." She held her arm out to the third man. She recognized his face, but could not place where from. "How do I know you?"

"I'm Henack, Dhoah', and you healed me during the siege."

"You were the first man I cared for there. You had an arrow in your thigh."

He smiled. "Yes. You promised it would not rot." He patted the healed limb. "Now I believe it works better than the other."

She laughed and sidled over. "Sit down so I don't have to hurt my neck talking to you. Would you like some tea before it chills?"

Φ

The 7th Day of Valemord, 1252
The City of Ceir Athrolan

Tzatia's mind was as restless as her body was tense. Her forefathers faced onslaughts, not the least of which brought Claimiirn to her knees. They handled them with might and grace and no small amount of retaliation. *And I have proven myself weak and fearful these past months.* Even at her busiest, her thoughts would turn abruptly to Daymir. With distance, she realized that disinheriting the man might have been brash. The queen was nothing, if not stubborn, however.

She scarcely could sit through her corset lacing without pacing. Now she sat in her parlor listening to the details of the army that would crush her city. The corporal across from her looked as grim as she imagined herself. "Tell me when."

"A couple of hours, maybe."

"And you are from the siege at Ceir Felden?"

"I am. It broke several days ago. They left in the dark, and the weather was such we saw nothing but their campfires. They left them burning, to fool us. We didn't know they'd gone until morning."

"And you're certain they are coming here?"

"I got here scarcely before them."

"Thank you for your dedication, Corporal. Go to your barracks, eat and rest."

She was silent for a full minute before she turned to the steward. "Valadai, sound the alarm. Athrolan is under attack." The guards flanking the door snapped to attention as she swept through the door of the throne room. "Leave me!"

She approached the throne when the guards had left. She knelt before it, lacing her shaking hands on her skirts. She knew it was impossible, but she thought she could already hear the enemy hooves. She had not prayed in years, not since the war on the gods began. She missed the comfort it had given her. Now she just thought on her father. "Though I've fallen many a time, I rose on my own. I tried to carry the land as you and grandfather, but I'm faltering now. She promised to keep our crown from shattering, and I pray she succeeds, for I no longer can."

The door behind her creaked and she whirled, ready to reprimand the guards for interrupting her. The words stalled in her mouth at the sight of the figures in the doorway.

At first, Tzatia thought they were some noble women coming to shelter from the battle to come, but a tingle threaded its way up her spine. She rose, head tilting curiously. They wore gray dresses and their hair ranged from black to cloudy gray. The woman at their fore stepped closer. Her eyes, like the others', were dull silver. "Lady queen, we come to offer our protecting."

Tzatia frowned. "Who are you?"

"Your people fight for my daughter, we'll fight for you."

Tzatia's legs gave way, but the woman caught her elbows. "You're the Laen."

The woman nodded. "I'm Elle. These are my sisters, those that would come."

Tzatia collected herself and straightened. "What do you need?"

Elle grinned, and the wolfish gleam in her eyes was suddenly Alea's. "Show us to your ramparts."

Φ

The 6th Day of Valemord, 1252
The Athrolani Camp at Claimiirn

Alea stood on the cliff tops, watching the Miriken below. Anxious thoughts urged the soldier's boots faster. A journey that should have taken over a week had taken only six days. She was among the first to arrive and for the next two hours the army trickled into camp. The sound of hammering tent poles and barked orders faded from her mind as she stared at their enemy. Their arrival had not gone unnoticed and she took dark pleasure in watching the hurried squires and knights sending word. *You'd better be afraid, Azirik. I'll be the death of you.*

"Alea, the general is calling us together." Bren's voice arched over the tents. After a last look at the camp below, she turned and followed him to the officers' camp.

The officers crowded into Eras's tent. The press of armor and road sweat was cloying but familiar. A captain unrolled a map of the plains and cliffs. "We've got an idea of the terrain and their locations. Azirik appears to have most if not all of his troops—roughly two thousand two hundred. Most are cavalry."

"And the Berrin are down there as well, but they're camped behind the ruins." Alea pointed to the place where she had seen the Berrin forces."

"Are there caves in these rocks?" Bren pointed to their path down to what would be a battle field within a day.

Eras shook her head. "That rock is hard. If there are any they are infrequent and small."

"It's difficult to say what Azirik will do," Alea said. "It's safe to assume he will not engage in direct combat, but he will use the gods' power to attack. I cannot say whether he will attack me or the men."

Vinden glanced at her and another man shifted angrily. "Dhoah', is there danger the soldiers should be warned of?"

Alea barely kept the impatience from her face. She was ready to face Azirik now, and the plans were only muddling her thoughts. "I thought soldiers knew battle was dangerous."

"Dhoah'," The general's warning was low but pointed.

"The men will be protected." She only partially listened to the rest of the plans. They would undoubtedly change as Azirik and the Berrin responded. The army was divided into three, Bren leading the various allied troops of Banis, Asai and Miriken, Eras and Raven leading the others. As orders were given the men filed out until only Bren and Alea remained with the colonels, commander and Eras.

The general turned to Alea. "Where will you be?"

"I need a clear view, above the fray."

"The old Claimiirni battlements should do nicely. I'll dispatch a detail of guards for you as well."

"With respect, general, I already seem to have acquired some guards. Perhaps you might consider them."

"I'll look into it. Is there anything else we need to know?"

"Tomorrow, before the charge, I need to see the men. All of them." She glanced up at Eras. "I'll lay protections over them, shielding them from what I'll do. Once my power rises they'll need to be still." She looked over at Bren. "You remember the training court?"

Her brother shuddered. "I wish I didn't. It gave me nightmares, you know."

Eras's stoic expression tightened. "Perhaps you could enlighten us, Lord Commissioner?"

"I need you to pass this through to every man under your command. When you give the signal everyone is to drop to the ground. If you are mounted, get off. You will want to run, to scream, but stay down, no matter what you see."

One of the colonels frowned. "That's it, drop our weapon and take a knee?"

"Only an idiot would drop their weapon," Raven interjected.

Eras ignored them. "Drop and hold and pray to whatever still listens that we live?"

Alea cleared her throat. "I'm still listening, general. Your men will be fine."

"And the signal?" Raven's frown was deep enough to swallow his eyes. "Will we hear it?"

Bren grinned and looked at his sister. "It's her name, and I promise you'll hear it."

Φ

Bren joined Alea and her guards that night. His reception was better than Alea's had been while on the road, but perhaps it was due to the mound of smoked meat and wraith he brought to share. The meat sizzled over the fire as Bren warmed it. He glanced over at Narier. "The Miriken have a tradition before battle — singing and dancing and drinking. I brought my flute. Would you mind a few songs?"

Narier grinned. "It's not like they don't know we're here. Let's make them think we don't give a damn about tomorrow."

Sousa let out his characteristic crowing.

They took turns eating and suggesting songs. After a few, Narier joined Bren's playing with his low, scratching voice. There were drinking songs and war ballads. "Alea, you know any Sunamen war songs?"

"I know many, though they're not Sunamen. I refuse to sing them — I'll send you running to Azirik for protection if I raise my voice." Finally Bren's insistence won out and she began clapping against her leg. "It's Athrolani, so if you know other verses I beg you join in." She hummed a few lines for Bren to copy the notes, though her lack of tune made for a rocky start.

> *"Well, this is war and I'll probably die*
> *Yes this is the end it seems*
> *But, eh, won't you tell me if I'm wrong*
> *Please tell me what we'll be?"*

Narier laughed. "It's an echo song. One of my favorites. We sing back and forth.

> *"Hey, it's Spring in the thick dark wood*
> *But no wife you'll find for thee*

> *Oh, it's Summer on the cobbled streets*
> *But no babe she'll carry for thee."*

Alea whooped, and Sousa joined her next verse,

> *"Death's a bastard by three and a right boor at*
> *that*
> *And we'll never be his, you'll see,*
> *But this is war and we'll probably die*
> *So let's drink to our bitter end."*

The lines came faster, the singer alternating with each one. Henack rose and pulled Alea to her feet, spinning around the fire as they shouted the words back and forth.

> *"You'll have a limp and a scar down your face."*
> *"Well, you'll be fat if battle don't take you!"*
> *"I'll stand tall with my men and sing with the*
> *horn."*
> *I'll be grizzled and old before Toar takes me!"*
> *"I'll become king or maybe a duke,*
> *I'll be rich and more handsome you'll see!"*

Alea fell back laughing breathlessly. "Dancing is better than singing by far. What other steps might you know?" Across the camp came the sound of others singing, a fiddle and horn joining the raised voices.

"Reka taught me one of the Border dances for victory in battle." When Alea urged Bren, he handed his flute to Kal and began to stomp gracelessly around the flames. After a moment the pattern emerged and Alea joined him. They whirled, the others rising as well, Kal abusing Bren's flute to their steps.

Φ

The music pierced through Arman's mind as he and the other Rakos edged along the outskirts of the camp. The myriad songs and dances combined oddly, but the desperation and joy were not lost on him. He had almost reached the cliff tops when he caught sight of Alea. She was spinning around with Bren, a strange series of steps that looked more like combat than actual dancing. He crept closer before realizing what he had done.

The woman before him was not the Alea he remembered. Eras's hard words about his expectations echoed through his mind. *No, she's not what I expected, but she's everything I could want.* His steps brought him closer still, until he stood in the trees just outside the ring of firelight. Her power pulsed over him, her off-tune singing drawing a smile onto his face. He warred with himself, watching her dancing and feeling the firelight between them. It was likely the last night he would live through and he knew exactly where he wanted to be.

There were three lights that burnt in the heart. The first was the bright, violent flash of passion. The second was a slow steady burn—the approach of spring, knocking ice from the streams and frost from the grass. It was freedom.

The third was brighter than the sun. It boiled through his body, burning everything else away until a single thought remained. *Surrender.* He swallowed hard and stepped into the firelight.

Φ

Alea's breath came in gasps of laughter. The campfire roared higher, shedding light onto the man standing a few paces away. Alea's steps slowed and her breath faltered. Kal's music stopped. The man across the campsite was different. His blonde hair was longer and his tanned skin dusted with strange metallic scales. She would recognize him anywhere, not from the color of his hair or the set of his wiry shoulders, but by the crackling heat of power crashing against her mind. *Of course he'd be here. At the end of all of this.* She felt Bren's eyes fixed on them, but he did not speak.

Arman took a step closer, more like a wary animal than a man. He cautiously extended his hand, the low hum of a tune drifting from his throat. Bren pulled his flute from Kal's loose grip and echoed the notes softly. He played again, faster, the notes dissolving into the liquid of music. Arman's hand still reached between them.

It fit that they would meet at the end of this journey, in the firelight before the glare of battle. She thrust every thought from her mind, every bitter word, and grabbed his hand. The stillness broke and they whirled, the steps coming faster now, more assured as Bren's tune wailed through the night. She danced for victory without hearing the music, pouring her heart into the steps with her Rakos guard. The tears on her cheeks were salty and warm and she was not sure if the sobs racking her body were of laughter or weeping. Her boots and his beat into the still soft ground, and she hoped their steps would shake the very earth under the gods' feet.

CHAPTER TWENTY

The 8th Day of Valemord, 1252
The Athrolani Camp at Claimiirn

THE FIRES WERE BANKED and the remaining music quiet. Alea nestled the kettle further into the fire. She glanced up to see Arman disappearing into the forest. "Arman?" He froze at the sound of her voice and she could see his jaw working. "I understand if you're angry, but could we talk?"

"Resolution before death?"

"As grim minded as you are, you were never a fatalist."

He drew a breath then followed her inside her tent. When she sat on the edge of her cot he took a seat on the chest across from her. His body was that of a man, not the boy who followed her to war a year earlier.

"I can't understand your anger."

He looked down. "A lot of things have changed since we last spoke. Civilly, I mean."

"We both deserve honesty. I haven't always given you that, or known what to say."

"Then I will be honest as well," he offered.

"After this battle the true war starts for me. I fight the gods. I will do terrible things, things that I've damned the gods for. I'd rather not go alone."

"I've learned what this war will do to me, and it's changed my face and my body and my thoughts. What has it done to you?" His eyes were narrowed and glowing in the darkness. "I've asked a dozen people, and none of them, not even Bren, know what you'll do. They have assumptions and the echoes of promises you've made, but you haven't told a single one."

"They won't understand, Arman. I don't blame them, really. Battle has to be a dichotomy. Wars can't be muddled or they'd never be won. I'm letting them believe I'm good, that I'm some benevolent creature come to save the world. And I will save it, but not the way they want me to."

"What are you doing, then? Raising the Laen to power? Creating new gods for them to worship?"

"I'm not making anyone worship the Laen. I'd never make anyone worship them—I barely tolerate them." The vehemence in her voice surprised them both. "No, I think humans have had enough of worshiping. It's time to turn our eyes outward."

His eyes widened. "You can't."

"Arman, it's the only thing left. All the power bound up in the Laen and the gods and even the Rakos, it needs to go back. We're strangling the world just with our existence. I'm not raising the Laen to power. I'm destroying them, too." The confession ripped itself from her heart, leaving her gasping for air to fill its place.

"Then whatever you need from me, I'll give it." His eyes shone with the bravery it took to care for her and the strength needed to leave his world behind.

"You said this has changed you. I'm sorry for that."

"It's all right. Truly." He looked at his hands. "My place has always been here and this creature has always been me. I realized something, too." His pause was not for effect or out of pain. He finally met her eyes. In that moment everything they had feared was bared between them. "Alea, this battle will kill me."

She reached across the distance between them. "Your power lies in sacrifice."

He shook his head. "No. It lies in surrender."

"Then can you trust me? Tomorrow I need there to be no barriers left between our power. Whatever anger you feel, whatever resentment, needs to be set aside. You've begged me to let you into my thoughts. Now it's my turn to ask you to do the same."

"Of course."

"No, Arman. I tried to talk to you while I was in Le'yne. My thoughts just slid right off yours. I could see everything, hear everything in your world. I even screamed for you to hear me, but I was like a ghost."

"You saw everything? Shite. I thought you were angry with me. I thought if I found someone else it would stop hurting. In the end kissing her moved me about as much as a dry history book. She was angry and frightened—she should have been. She thought I chose her because she had dark hair and pale eyes. Truthfully, you're so far above anything I could not really see the resemblance."

"You can't fancy the sun." She laughed softly and waved away his questioning gaze. "I thought I asked you to take me off that pedestal."

"Did I mention I'd been drinking?"

"From my experience that had little to do with it." Her laughter joined his, low and warm in the confines of the tent. "I'm sorry I was distant."

"I'm sorry I was an ass."

"I'm sorry I never let you in."

"I'm sorry I never gave you a reason to." He glanced outside. "It's late and we'll have a damned early morning. I'll let you rest."

She touched his wrist as he went to rise. "Please. When we were on the road you were always there. Just for tonight." He faltered and she edged over on the cot, patting the vacated space.

Finally he toed off his boots, nudging them to sit beside hers. He slid under the coverlet with her, one arm propped behind his head. "I missed you."

She rested their clasped hands on his chest. "And I you." Her eyes slid closed, the lines of worry relaxing for the first time in months. "Good night, Arman."

"Good night, Alea."

Φ

The 9th Day of Valemord, 1252

Alea woke once, shortly before dawn. The body beside her was incredibly warm. She blinked as the face before her came into focus. Arman's features were drastically different. Scales spiraled over his brow and cheeks, larger in the center of his forehead and the bridge of his nose. They were white-gold. The unaffected skin was tanned as always, but with a metallic undertone.

This war is making monsters of us both. Difference is, yours is beautiful. She closed her eyes and nestled closer. There were only a few hours of peace left.

When she woke again it was dawn. Arman was gone and the bed cold. The camp began to bustle outside, the clatter of metal pans and armor sounding through the campsites. She rose quickly and dressed before turning to the chest of armor. A dirty, battered envelope sat atop it.

She did not need the plain script to tell her it was from Arman.

> *Alea,*
>
> *There are so many things I wanted to tell you, to share with you, but never had the words. Now, when I have them, I realize that you probably already know.*
>
> *I know what I said in the gardens in Athrolan, but our bond is the closest to vows, our friendship the closest to marriage as I suspect I'll ever come, or ever want to. This ring was the one my father gave to my mother. It doesn't belong to anyone, if not to you.*
>
> *With everything I have and am,*
>
> *-A*

Alea tipped the envelope over her hand. The gold gleamed dully in the early minutes before sunrise. She tucked the letter away and slid the ring onto her middle finger. Each motion seemed a ritual as she donned her armor. Each added weight was a manifestation of what rested on her shoulders. She was braiding the top half of her hair back when someone rapped on her tent pole.

"Yes?" She turned about, wrapping a leather tie around the end of her plait.

Bren stepped in. He watched her silently for a moment before gesturing to the breast and back plate she had yet to put on. "Would you like help?"

She nodded and allowed him to buckle the metal at each shoulder and about her ribs.

"I saw Arman this morning." Bren's words were soft. "I'm glad he came to see you."

"I am too." She reached for the box that held the two Crowns when Bren grabbed her hand. He examined the ring, his gaze thoughtful. "It's what Arman's father gave his mother," she explained.

"You know what this means to him? What you wearing it means?"

"I know." She shifted. "Bren, I—"

He drew her into a sudden, hard embrace. Their armor clunked as his arms tightened around her. "You can say it later." He drew away. "We should be going, the men are gathering for you to see them."

"I'll be along." She watched him go before sliding the Crown onto her head. It was cold, and sent slivers of tingling pain through her skull as if she had drunk something incredibly cold too quickly. She ducked from the tent and wound through the tents to the cliff tops. The assembled army was quiet, and she could hear the shouts and commotion of their enemy below. The sunlight moved slowly across the fields, inching down the cliffs. Alea moved down the line of men, her steps quick and sure. She reached the first row. She grinned at Narier. Her hand brushed his and she moved down the line, touching hands, faces, shoulders, bleeding cold into their armor and skin. It took the better part of an hour before she was through. Finished, she returned to their front.

"What I gave you allows me to find you and protect you when I must. It will not save your lives against every sword blow, but it will help in the end." She tried not to think of all the faces that would not smile the next day. "You have my deepest gratitude for standing with me today." She fumbled with what to say. There were no words that did not sound trite, or like a battle ballad. Finally she raised her fist to her brow, her lips, her breast, then threw it into the air. "Luck and love go with you."

Her salute broke the stillness and the men mounted up or drew weapons. The forces moved forth, where the slope down to the fields was more gradual.

Narier appeared, followed by Kal and her other appointed guards. "We'll go scout the battlements. We'll be ready when you are, Dhoah'"

"Thank you Narier." She was moving to follow when she caught sight of the approaching figures. Arman's stride was purposeful, the four creatures loping beside him something out of stories. He stopped a pace away from her. "You have something of mine."

She tugged the Rakos Crown free and placed it gently on his brow, brushing his cheek with her thumb as she drew away. Scales exploded across his skin at the contact. His pupils were blown and flames erupted through his hair. She grinned at him. "You look brilliant, Arman."

His teeth bared in an answering smile. "And you're magnificent."

She squeezed his hand and stepped away. "On my signal, Earth Shaker." She jogged up to the fort. The sound of horses and armor and orders faded as she entered the ruins. She saw the place she had camped weeks before, and found the winding stairs up to what was left of a watch tower. She passed Sousa and Henack on her way, returning their wan smiles. The battlements were broad and high, the granite warming to pink in the sun. She looked down at where Arman waited on the cliffs with the other Rakos. Catching his eye, she grinned wolfishly. *Is it bad that I wish I could see their faces when we let our powers loose?*

His laugh rumbled through her mind. *Ready when you are, milady.*

She watched the army move into place, horses wheeling and weapons gleaming. Below, Arman shrieked and leapt into the air. Power rose into her body, faster than before, pouring through the conduit of her Crown. Black fog erupted from her palms and the battle began.

The connections to her power were multiplied, as if what was once a river now roared as a delta. Every nerve seared with cold. The fields below were vast, covered in waving gold grasses. *It will be a pity to stain it red.* Her thoughts were absent and drifting. Everything was both muffled and magnified through the lens of her power. *Azirik, come on.* The sound of rending metal cut through the air and a mass of bloody-red power bloomed from the ruins of the palace. It expanded, blotting out the rising sun and the scant white clouds high above. The air stained crimson and grew thick and cloying. *Vielrona was destroyed by burning clouds.* The clouds pulsed, with each contraction they spit out sheets of glistening, oily rain.

The crawling wrongness centered around a brilliant spark of copper in her mind's eye. Her fingers twisted, fumbling due to her injured left hand. With a snarl she ripped the bandages and splints away and began again. Her black fog writhed, weaving itself into ropes and bindings of a net. With a flick of her wrists, she flung it over the spark. Azirik's attention swiveled toward her as she tightened her hold. The familiar reek of rot and sickness wafted towards her. *Where have I smelled that?* In her mind she saw the bright blue of Azirik's eyes, bloodshot and stained with jaundice.

Φ

The general drew up, ignoring the stinging in her ribs. This was not the time for distractions. Her piercing whistle rang against armor. Those with halberds rushed to the fore, planting the butts of their weapons as another charge approached. The pain hit her, driving breath from her lungs. She cursed and pulled back, shouting for the colonel of the North Regiment. "Hamacad!"

The man finally crashed through the tangle of weapons and horses, wiping blood from his sword. "General?" His gaze fell to the blood drenching her side. "Shite!" He grabbed her reins and pulled her horse away.

"Enough!" Eras spat blood with her words. "You're acting general now. Leave me!" She slapped his horse's rump with the back of her gauntleted hand. He glanced at her before rushing away to regroup her men. Her dismount was closer to a stumble. Her vision blurred and she ripped her helm off. The Asai rarely thought about their own deaths. It was a given, not something to be fought, and the Asai part of her knew it well. The human part of her mind raged against the relief in her limbs, and the sticky gore covering her tabard. Each breath sputtered through the blood in her throat. She dropped her bow and drew her knife before throwing herself into a knot of Miriken.

Φ

Bren whirled his horse about, twisting his blade in a circle above his head. "Regroup!" The rain splattered thickly against his new armor, the vapor rancid. He drove his men against the wall of Berrin again. He thanked the general silently for sending his charges against men he had never known. The enemy outmatched them by easily a thousand. He signaled for the men to press out, driving the wave of Berrin towards the general's men. It took Bren several sword-swings to realize they were not the only ones protected by power. From the corners of his eyes he caught sight of the glittering coat of red deflecting all but the most direct blows. "Toar!" He blinked sweat from his eyes and whirled into the fray.

Berrin archers found purchase on the cliffs and rained bolts from above. Though distracting at first, the steaming rain did its work, the noxious smell choking air from faltering lungs and burning through exposed skin. Bren caught Hamacad's eye and they signaled to fall back. The sight before them was bitter. More than half their number littered the fields. The Berrin and Miriken did not pursue them, retreating for the moment to gather their own forces.

Bren grinned. Whatever the cost, they had dented their enemy's number. He trotted over to the commander and colonels. "We took a third perhaps," he noted, drawing up beside them.

"We're being crushed," Colonel Currow spat.

Raven glanced around. "The general?"

Hamacad shook his head. "Fallen. I'm acting now."

Raven snarled and fixed Bren with a glare. "Where's your damned sister? She made a promise to us!"

Bren grabbed the man's tabard. "She promised we would win, she did not promise there wouldn't be a cost!" He thrust the man away and spun his horse. "Those shields Azirik laid are powerful. We'd be drinking to victory already if not for them. Blame that if you must." The thunder of hooves behind them interrupted his next words. "Toar!"

Raven wheeled, blinking against the burning red clouds. "To me!" The men rallied, preparing for whatever new attack approached. A rider dashed past them, then another and a third. Dozens of gray chargers bearing pale, horned warriors.

A crack rang through the battle and gun smoke joined the acrid gas. An'thor broke from the group, slowing as he passed Bren. His teeth were bared in a vicious grin. "You just going to stand there or join in the fun?"

Bren whooped and kicked his mount after them. Raven led his men about the flank again, mirroring Hamacad's infantry in a second charge. Bren's riders streamed after the Ageless warriors. The chaos and smell and noise filled Bren's head, strangling any thought beyond staying alive. His new armor already bore marks, earning the dings and dents he would value and love like those that had marred his own armor. His broadsword looped with the momentum of his charging horse. The mount came to a shuddering halt, pole arm embedded in the muscles of its chest. The squealing animal thudded to the ground, thrashing. Bren's left thigh was pinned under its heavy girth. Bren checked for imminent descending blades, then kicked his right foot from the stirrup, planting it on the seat of the saddle for leverage. He groaned, his leg already beginning to tingle as the weight pinched his nerves. "Dammit!" He shoved again, harder, flexing his trapped limb in an effort to free it. Suddenly two hard arms gripped his chest.

"Help, you damned oaf!" Arman hissed. Bren pushed a third time, wriggling free. He lurched to his feet. Arman backed into the fog. Scales covered his entire body, white and gold and green. Bren staggered, his leg still regaining its feeling. His view of the Rakos was blocked by the bulk of An'thor's borrowed horse.

An'thor grabbed Bren's arm. "Up you get, Barrackborn."

Bren swung himself into the saddle behind An'thor. When he looked for Arman again there was only swirling white smoke.

"You can swing that sword if you want, but if you take my arm with it I'm kicking you from the saddle faster than my blood will cover you."

Bren laughed and held up his sword, shouting to form a phalanx of riders. They punched through the Berrin forces, scattering them to the sides then wheeling to pursue. The Ageless had helped in number, certainly, but what men still stood were marred with blood and Bren could see Miriken scaling the cliff face beneath Alea.

Seeing a rider-less horse, Bren pounded his fist on An'thor shoulder and pointed. He slipped off the gray charger and jogged towards the lighter Athrolani mount whose reins were tangled in a mess of weapons and bodies. He was up in moments, tugging the animal about. All order had gone from the battlefield. Pockets of fighting made it seem as if the ground between the cliffs seethed. Bren rounded as many of his men as he could before leading them towards a dense group of Azirik's men. *Please let there be no familiar faces here.*

Φ

Alea felt Azirik's hold falter. *Azirik, stop!*

You think this is me? You think I have the strength to wield this anymore? You want to destroy the gods? Then come and get me.

She felt the ferocity in his snarl. *Careful what you ask. You should be terrified. The past year cauterized any mercy I could have felt.* Cold bloomed in her abdomen, spinning up her spine and down her limbs. Her focus turned to the sparks of white flames dotting the clouds. *Arman, are they ready?* She felt the brush of power on her mind as he opened his thoughts to her.

We lost Erek, but the rest of us hold strong. What do you need from me?

I need you to mirror what I do, with your fire.

How?

You are connected to the earth and the sun as I am to the ocean and the air. Her voice was gentle.

Alea tested the threads to each of her allies and held them fast with one mental hand. With the other, she drew power from the aquifers deep in the earth. She pulled from the ocean to the north. The power exploded through the Crown. Cold from every ocean in the world answered her gentle beckon. She wove her power into each wave. *This might hurt.*

I've died before, Alea. It can't be much worse. Now!

At Arman's shout, Alea gripped her power. The ground trembled beneath her boots. Her thoughts coalesced into a single word, bursting into Bren's mind, the commanders', the colonels'. *Now.* With a last great tug, she ripped herself open. There was no difference between Alea and Destruction.

Φ

Arman whirled through the clouds, a white spiral of smoke worming through the poisonous brown. He sank through the conduit ringing his brow and into the power beneath. He felt the billowing chill of Alea's breathing, but now he could not distinguish between her breath and his, between the thunder of her heartbeat and his own pulse. He had been wrong. The pain ignited every nerve. He curled in on himself, hands clenched in fists, arms wrapped around his head.

The pain exploded every thought from his mind and his body solidified. He plummeted towards the ground. A grating moan began deep inside his chest, turning into a keening cry that dragged itself from his lips as his power snapped open. His skin burst into flames, a burning ray of light piercing upwards through the clouds from the body of each Rakos. *Sun. Earth.*

His clothes turned to ash, metal dripping from the heat of his body. The flesh between his scales glowed brilliant yellow, like magma in the heart of the earth. He glanced down as he fell. He had seen this before, seen the ground rushing to meet him, seen the body of an Earth Shaker replace his own.

Arman, the fire!

His power punched through the clouds again, light igniting the poisonous air as he channeled the power of the sun. Below, the earth growled. He closed his eyes. *Surrender.*

CHAPTER
TWENTY-ONE

The 9th Day of Valemord, 1252
The City of Ceir Athrolan

ELLE CROUCHED BEHIND WHAT was left of the palace's southeast tower. It had been decades since the Laen used their powers in battle. Even then, most who fought, died. But she, who had run for months to find a place to hide her daughter, knew more about deception and bloodshed. Her hands shook and she brought them to her brow. Hooves tore the fields to pieces and the shining white walls of the city were cracked and blackened from Berrin war machines.

Tzatia had taken up a post in the kitchens with the household staff and noble women who would not fight. The eastern wing of the palace was crushed under catapult ballast and the walls threatened to fall. If the walls gave, it would be over.

A young boy dashed from cover to cover, finally sliding down beside her. He offered a water skin in the hand he still had. "Milady Laen, here." His voice cracked from puberty and smoke.

"Thank you." She smiled and took a few sips before handing it back. It was the third time he had brought her water and food. "What are you called?"

"Bren, milady."

She winced at the snap and whistle of another missile being loosed. The air screamed before its passage moments before it crashed into the wall beside her. The stone shuddered. "Excuse me?"

"Vanabren Westing, milady. They call me Bren." His eyes somehow still sparked through fatigue and wariness.

"It's a good name," she offered. "My son's short-name is Bren." She watched the wall with the men below, wondering if it would hold. "That cannot take another hit."

The boy glanced at her. "Athrolan cannot fall, you know. The Dhoah' Laen promised us."

Her heart chafed at the innocence in the words. "I hope not, Bren." She stepped from behind the tower, arrows slicing the air around her. Her body trembled from fear and exhaustion. Power flowed from her hands, holding the stones. Deep moaning filled the air. The sound went on and she realized it came from the north. Wind whipped the ocean's surface, whirling the water into the air. The water continued to rise. The sound deafened her and stinging droplets shot across the waves, collected more and more and racing over the cliffs and hills as if drawn by a great storm. The scent of ocean and salt and time drifted in its wake. *Lyne'alea.* Elle straightened and raised her hands. "Bren, give the others a message!" Her voice arched against the buffeting wind.

"We're balance and all things end. Age them. Fray the ropes. Rust their weapons."

The message was passed along the chain of Laen on the ramparts. Pale hands rose, gray hair whipping back. The Berrin did not notice until their catapults no longer shot. The swords rusted from the hilts. Horse leathers dried and cracked.

The battle did not end with the Berrin driven into the hills amidst Athrolani war cries, though the legends would tell it so. The attackers eased back, staring at the sky that still swirled with rain. Their ruined weapons littered the hills and the machines crumbled where they stood. Those who still could disappeared back into the trees. Elle turned as Vanabren emerged from behind the remnants of the tower. His hand shielded his eyes from the smoke and dust in the wet air.

"Your queen shelters in the palace, in the kitchens. Tell her Athrolan is saved."

"Shall I tell her you'll see her when you've rested?"

Elle shook her head and relayed the rest of her message for the queen. She straightened and closed her eyes. They had saved their power for so long, waiting for battle. Now, it was finally over.

Vanabren scrambled down the shattered tower and into the palace. Walls were toppled, rooms destroyed and the royal suites were nothing more than memory. He found his way to the barred doors of the kitchen after three tries. The guards let him through and he slowed, peering through the dark to find the queen. She perched on a barrel of smoked meat, holding quiet conversation with one of the other women.

Her gaze turned to him as he knelt. "What is it?"

"I bring a message from the Laen, your majesty."

"Has the city fallen?"

He dared to look up at her. "Athrolan stands."

Tzatia stared, almost in disbelief. Finally she rose and smoothed her skirts. "Thank you." She turned and issued orders, sending guards and nobles and servants rushing through the palace. Seeing that he had not moved, she glanced back at Vanabren. "Was there something else?"

"Yes, your majesty. Lady Elle, with the black in her hair, told me something else. She said Lyne'alea will win."

Φ

The Ruins of Claimiirn

The blow of Alea's mind against Bren's sent him reeling. Pebbles dislodged and skittered down the cliff faces, larger rocks tumbled after. "Alea!" His voice was joined by that of the commander and the colonels. Officers took it up, her names bounding across the battlefield. The ground heaved, cracking as geysers burst through the stone.

Bren urged his horse alongside An'thor's. "Get out of here! She protected us, not you!" His warning came too late as black water exploding from the screaming earth. He grabbed An'thor's cloak and dragged the man from his horse. The scent of salt filled the air. The fields flooded in minutes and still the water came. Moaning rose in the south and the clouds above burst into flames. The ground shuddered again and gouts of thick magma roared through the dirt. The screams of opposing elements meeting each other drowned out those of the men caught between. Bren shielded his eyes against the battering forces, looking up as water solidified the lava coating his shield of power.

The destruction seemed to last forever, the roaring outside the shell of rock fading slowly. The silence replacing it was far worse. After a moment Bren glanced over at An'thor. Bren had pulled the warrior under the protection just in time. An'thor shook, his eyes wide. His face paled further and he retched.

Bren looked away. What his sister had done was terrible, but he had killed Laen, and nothing twisted the gut worse. He pushed himself to his feet and tested the shell. It was like black glass, shot through with flecks of red and green and blue. After a few solid blows it cracked then shattered.

Bren stumbled free and stopped. He stared at the battlefield before him, heedless of the blood drawn by the razor edges of the glass shell. "An'thor."

"I know."

Corpses were strewn everywhere, those in the lowlands charred to ash and skeletons. Piles of blackened bones marked fallen horses. Water dripped from the higher plain, salty runnels of seawater waving their way back into the earth. The bodies it left were pale and bloated. Flies already gathered. Dotting the fields were other shells along what had been the boundary of the two elements. Others rose from crouches, their armor and uniforms dry and unburnt. There was nothing left of the Berrin or the enemy Miriken that he could see, save a few hundred troops what managed to escape the carnage by climbing into the ruins.

Azirik. Alea's mind-voice howled through Bren's thoughts, devoid of emotion or haste.

"Right." He looked around for a mount, only to wish he had not. The only horses near enough were swollen bodies or blackened grizzle. He staggered across the field to the stairway winding up to the palace. Adrenaline raged in his limbs, but it faded quickly. Hard, cold hands caught him the third time his boots slipped on the granite stairs.

The creature that crouched on the landing before him was not his sister. Her features echoed in the face, but the resemblance ended there. Her hair writhed like black snakes, rivulets of water trickling from her solid black eyes. Shadows filled her skin. "Almost there."

He pulled himself up and followed her silent steps. The journey ended at Claimiirn's great hall. A pair of guards flanked the door, blades drawn. Bren's laugh was closer to a hoarse bark. "Everyone's dead. Forget it."

"Lieutenant Barrackborn, sir?" The younger guard stepped forward, peering closer.

Bren wiped blood and sweat from his eyes. "Captain Sorier?"

"Don't you remember? You made me lieutenant before you left." He frowned, glancing from Bren to the figure beside him. "Is this where you were going?"

"It appears both our roads led here, eh?" Bren swallowed hard, hands tightening on the hilt of his broadsword. He had recognized enough faces under his blows for a dozen lifetimes. "I've about had it with killing for today. Please don't try to stop us."

Sorier glanced at the other guard, a man Bren did not know. "We're not here to stop you, Barrackborn. We're here to escort you."

Bren glanced between them, then over at Alea's sparking eyes. Her hand was ice freezing around his own. "What?"

"Come in and he'll explain. Hurry, though, he's got little time left." Sorier led them into the hall. Unlit torches lined the walls. Trees grew through the cracked flagging and vines draped the pillars. Several tents stood along the rear wall. Azirik slumped in the center of the hall, body still wreathed in bubbling red-brown light. Bren stopped a few paces away, distantly aware of Alea beside him. Azirik's eyes were narrowed in pain and disbelief and a hundred other things that stampeded through Bren's own mind. His hands shook. "Do I have to fight you?"

Azirik jerked his head. The bruised, rotting flesh around the Crown pulsed and blood-laced fluid seeped over the copper. "No. Not anymore." His eyes flicked to Alea. "Hello, again."

Φ

Power thundered through Alea's head, almost drowning the words. *Again?* She took in the mess of Crown and skin and bone on his brow and heard the rattling cough of his voice. The smell of decay met her nose. "It was you. You talked to me while I waited for the moon to set."

Bren turned to look at her, by his expression clearly wondering whether she had lost her wits.

Azirik's body racked with a strangled gasp. After a moment she realized it was a laugh. "Yes. You didn't know?"

"How could I have?"

"I recognized you immediately. If I saw you, so would the gods, and neither of us were ready for that." He hauled himself up until he sat on the flagging. "You think I could see you now?"

Alea shuddered and her power rolled back into her skin, writhing into the Crown on her head and disappearing. She would never look entirely human, but she was recognizable. She tilted her head at him. "You let me go."

"I spent these last months putting everything in place. An'thor was the last piece. I had close to a hundred Ageless just waiting for my word." He swallowed hard. "Tell me what you'll do. Will you raise the Laen to their rightful place?"

She shook her head. Her cheeks were damp and salty. "Is that why you did this? You thought you could reverse everything that ever harmed the Laen? Oh, fates, no." She stepped forward cautiously, ignoring Bren's murmured warning. "No. The gods weren't wrong. Everything has an end. Every reign will fall. Some in fire and some in death and some simply ease away like an old dog in the night. They weren't right, either, though. They are not what comes next." She was a pace away.

"Is it your people? You and your Rakos?"

She knelt beside him and reached out tentatively. She had never felt more vulnerable. This madman gave his last months for her victory. He tore his people, his allies, his masters apart from within and all for her. "No, something new. I don't know exactly, but I know it's coming. It is mighty and different, and beautiful."

"Can't be more beautiful than you." He took her hand. "Take it. Please."

"You won't live though it."

"I know. The world you're saving has no place for people like you and me. We're killers. We are not meant for peace. We might walk in it a while, but never will we fit." He squeezed her hand. "Go on. I'll hold them back for the second it takes, but I can't do it forever."

Alea did not look away, but raised her voice. "Bren. If you wanted to say goodbye, now's the time."

Bren crouched beside her. "I don't know what to say."

"All of my apologies seem too small. You took over Mirik?"

"I'm her Military Commissioner now."

Azirik's sobbing laugh shook his body again. "You were never cut out for being a king."

"Neither were you." Bren's grin was awkward and faint, but Azirik returned it after a moment.

"Are you ready?" Alea met his eyes. She watched him frown as he recognized their color, and the set of her face. He nodded. She rested her hands on either side of his face. "Thank you." Before he could respond, her fingers dug into the twisted, burnt flesh and wrapped around the Crown. Her skin bubbled against the surface of the metal. She clenched her teeth and pulled. The metal popped free with a sickening crack, and she fell back, pieces of skull and blood still clinging to the metal. Azirik slumped onto the stone, blood and power pooling from his head.

Bren staggered back, heaving up everything he had eaten that morning. "Is he gone?"

"Yes." She glanced over at him. "Are you all right?"

His body shook. "That was my king. My commander. Everything I ever knew for almost thirty years."

"I'm sorry."

He glanced up. "It wasn't your fault. It was never your fault." He edged back to Azirik's body, closing the bloodshot eyes.

Alea reached out and gripped his hand. "It wasn't his, either, in the end."

Φ

Bren blinked against the bright rays of sunset as he emerged from the hall. Smoke still drifted low over the burnt and bloody fields. Long graves carved the earth. Infirmary tents lined the base of the cliffs below the Athrolani camp.

Alea glanced over at him. "I've got to get this to my pack. You'll be all right?"

He nodded and sank down onto the stairs. "In a minute."

Sorier crouched beside him, watching Alea go. "She's terrifying."

"She's my sister."

The lieutenant frowned. "What?"

"Azirik's second child." Bren heaved a sigh. "Thank you for seeing sense when he did."

"I saw sense when you did, you know. War turns your guts, for sure, but killing the Laen? That was something else entirely." He paused a moment. "We're prisoners of war, now, I assume."

Bren shook his head. "No. I'm tired of violence and war, Sorier. Take your men, take all the men, and leave. Give it a few months then come home. I'll have Mirik ready for you then."

"We heard there was new ruling there. You took her crown?"

"No. She's an oligarchy now. I'm Lord Commissioner of the Military, acting king until the war is done." He laughed humorlessly. "I guess that's now."

"Sir, there are prisoners, down in the Berrin camp. A patrol taken several months ago. They'll need tending." He stood. "I guess I'll see you in Mirik."

Bren's eyes were too tired to make his smile look sincere. "See you at home." He listened as the man's bootfalls faded into the low din of battle's aftermath. Finally he pulled himself to his feet and tottered down the cliffs and across the field.

A gallant paused as he jogged past him. "Lord Commissioner, good to see you. Thought you fell."

Bren glanced over at the Berrin camp. "There are prisoners in their camp."

"We found them, sir, already bringing them in."

Bren nodded and went to the infirmary tents. They were surrounded by cots and blankets for the hundred of wounded who did not fit in the tents themselves. Healers walked down the rows, checking breaths and wounds. More than once they murmured a few words and closed unseeing eyes. Bren had seen enough battles to be familiar with the screams and moans, but this was different. He led some of these men. He caught sight of a familiar figure as he turned towards the cliffs. Reka lay under a blanket, her skin pale and her braids dirty.

Bren hurried over and crouched beside her. "Reka."

She turned towards his voice. Her eyes were a bloody mess of angry sockets, thin slashes running through them and across her cheeks. A cut sliced through the wing of the butterfly tattoo on her nose. "Bren?"

"How are you doing?"

"I've been better, sir. I fared better than many of the men, if my ears serve me."

Something in his chest twisted. She would live by her ears and hands now. "I've got to see to my men, but I'll be back." He squeezed her hand briefly then headed back up to the officers' tents. He paused at the general's and rapped on the tent pole. "It's Brentemir."

"Come in." The commander's voice was quiet. Bren ducked in. Raven sat at the camp table, head in his hands. Several officers and Asai ranged about him, all equally stoic.

"Commander, sir, I—"

"We'll work till dusk, bringing the wounded and bodies in. We have wagons for the dead. The honored ones at least, to bring them home. The rest we bury here. Fates willing someday we can erect a monument." Raven turned to Vinden. "Keep the men moving until we've finished this."

Bren swallowed. "I'll help." He glanced at Narier. "Where is Alea?"

"Resting, I think."

A soldier burst through the tent flap. "Colonel Hamacad, sir, we found the general."

Raven's face paled and he stood, interrupting Hamacad's order. "Bring her here. Lay her in state." After a moment he cleared his throat. "We've little daylight left. Let's use it while we can."

Bren helped the soldiers in their morbid duty, hauling the bodies of soldiers he never knew. Each was laid to rest beside its companions. The pallor of death fell the same over each, whether human or Asai or Nenev. The evening wound on, gray and cold. Bren staggered to their campsite late. Alea's tent was deserted, the three Crowns perched in their box on her desk. He hung his cloak on his tent pole and ducked inside.

The lit lantern hung from the ridgepole and Kemmer sat on his trunk in the corner. "Lord Commissioner, I just came from the infirmary." She looked down. "Aldac died. He was doing all right for a while, but I think years in the city weakened us. I was with him, when it happened. He said he was honored to have served you, even for such a short time, made me promise to do well by you. He didn't need to, I already would have." It was the most Bren had ever heard the woman say at once. She jerked her head to the east. "You kill him?"

Bren shrugged. "The Crown was part of him. He couldn't survive the removal of it." He sat on his cot. "You're promoted now."

"General?" Her laugh was a hoarse cough.

"Captain of the Guard." He grinned wearily. "But drop the Lord Commissioner bit when we're alone. I need friends now, more than anything else."

"I'll try, sir." She raked a hand through her tangled hair. "What now?"

"Home. It's time to rebuild."

Φ

Alea left the general's tent. It was close to midnight and her body was exhausted. Her mind refused to rest. The battle was only half done for her. What remained would be infinitely harder. The air around her hummed. She repacked her armor in its chest before changing into clean clothes. Her hand froze at the box on her desk. The Rakos Crown glimmered with the others. "Arman?"

She reached out, feeling for the brilliant white-gold spark of his life. There was only darkness. She snapped the box shut and tucked it into her pack.

By the time Bren stopped to check on her, the tent was deserted and she had disappeared into the forest.

Φ

The 11th Day of Valemord, 1252
The City of Ceir Athrolan

Winter sunlight pierced the naked, white branches of the trees. A journey that took the army almost a week, Alea made in just two days. Now she drew up at the tree line. The formerly pristine slope down to the city was churned and scarred. War machines crouched between the tree trunks. Alea's eyes narrowed. The ropes were frayed, the wood rotted. Rust enveloped what metal remained. But for the raw wounds in the stone walls of the city, she could have looked on a battle centuries old.

A hole punched through the false sun of the palace's dome. The walls were breached in three places that she could see. The city was quiet, smoke rising from both cook fires and smashed lanterns. Alea's heart twisted at the sight. *Athrolan was pillaged while her warriors protected me.* Something more tugged at her mind. There was an undertone to the smell of the sea, to the chill of the winter morning. *Laen.* She nudged her horse into a trot and towards the battered gates.

They had yet to open for the morning, though she would be surprised if they did not remain closed for days.

"Halt!"

She shielded her eyes and peered up at the ramparts. "I'm Dhoah' Lyne'alea." A low conversation ensued atop the wall before the gate finally opened. Alea dismounted and tugged her horse into the city.

A woman stood in the center of the rubble-strewn city street. Her clothes were covered with burn holes and stone dust settled on her shoulders and graying hair. "Lyne'alea."

Alea stopped to survey her mother. "Elle." She nodded to the city. "What happened?"

"Athrolan fought your battle, so we fought hers."

"We won."

"Yes. I know. So did we." Elle shifted her weight. "You should rest. We can leave for Mirik in the morning."

Alea shook her head. "I can rest on the ship. The world has waited long enough. I have waited long enough."

"What will you do?" Elle tilted her head.

Alea reached out a tentative hand. "Something terrible. Something necessary." When her mother took her hand, Alea squeezed it. She did not care that her grip twisted bones and ground Arman's ring into her knuckle. With the brief moment of contact, Alea saw the gravity of what she was about to do. "I'm so sorry."

Elle frowned, her face paling. "I don't understand."

"You don't need to. Just be with me. For now." Alea suddenly wished they had the time to be mother and daughter.

Elle looked down. "If you will not wait, then we can at least get this over with." She sent a whistle arcing over the city and palace walls. The other Laen appeared, as tattered as she. Some bore bruises and wounds of more direct battle.

"Together, we can bring you home." She laced her fingers with her daughter's, others coming to take Alea's hand or brush her shoulder.

"Don't waste your power," Alea protested, but her voice was soft. Silver fog writhed around their bodies, threaded between feet and curling across shoulders.

Elle smiled. "Really, Lyne'alea. What do we have to save it for? It may be terrible, I might not understand, but you will not be alone."

Φ

The Isle of Le'yne

Le'yne had changed little. The sky still crackled with its ceaseless energy, and the grasses still waved in the distracted breeze. Alea blinked and turned. She stood on the steps of the great hall. The Laen ranged about her, more exhausted than ever. The rumble of their arrival rippled through the village below and she saw lantern light bloom in the windows of those who had not made the journey to Athrolan.

Alea pushed open the door to the hall. Her feet would not cross the threshold. *How can I turn my back on them with a promise of a victory when they will never see it?* "Elle?"

"I'm here."

"Tell Mera to pack her books. The most important, the best, the rarest. Where I'm going, you can't follow."

"I'll tell her. And I'll see you when you've won."

Alea met her mother's eyes. There was defiance behind the older woman's lie, a strength Alea recognized. She drew a steadying breath and stepped into the hall. The door at the end was still propped open and the stairs unchanged. She did not stumble in the darkness, her feet forgotten as she descended into the bowels of the earth. She refused to think beyond her next action, refused to listen to the screaming in her mind.

She emerged into the cavern, her boots whispering on the stone as she approached the swollen globe of wounded souls. She knelt, opening the box and laying the Crowns on the ground before her. She stripped her clothes off, raking her fingers through the snarls of her hair until it hung loosely around her. She gripped the Crowns against her naked stomach, relishing the sting of metal against her cool flesh.

First I fight the gods. Then I bind the world. The actions seemed so simple when put into words. She wondered what would be left of her. The Laen would not be there to return whatever it was to Athrolan. Bren would never know what happened to her, down in the darkness of Le'yne and the blackness of her soul.

She clenched her teeth and stepped into the souls. The screaming grew louder and the darkness closer. She gripped the gods' Crown, sinking through the connect to their world. It was akin to the dizziness when she left her body to resurrect Arman. Whistling filled her ears. A beach appeared quite suddenly around her. The air was almost balmy and the rough sand beneath her feet ground as she stepped back. Most of the island was overrun with jungle. Behind her the ocean was flat calm, not a single wave lapped at the strand, even when an eddy of wind caught Alea's hair. She had the distinct feeling that the entire landmass had turned to look at her. She shook it away and moved up the overgrown path before her.

Her journey was quiet and uninterrupted. Her thoughts turned inward. *What steps have I taken to bring me to these? What path did I choose to bring me to this?* Though her hands were unadorned and her body bare, she felt the warm squeeze of the ring on the middle finger of her physical hand. *What friends have I lost to save the world?* At any moment the gods might rain fury upon her, her blood might be drained to stitch the world together.

The trees fell away and a castle rose before her. It was built from the same brown stone that made up the island itself. The wooden gate was barely taller than she, and the double doors carved only with the stylized mountain sprouting a twisting column of smoke that was the gods' symbol. She pushed the doors open carefully and her heartbeat rose to a thunder. Torches lined the brown stone, guttering in the stillness. The hall she followed ended in an arched doorway to a spiral staircase that led up into the dark heights of the castle. The similarity to the stairs she had just descended in Le'yne was not lost on her. She lifted her chin and began the ascent.

The castle's rooftop was large and open. The plants had taken over, tangling across the stone. Some vines and leaves were held back, a path carved through the vegetation to the open, sunken hall in the center of the rooftop. Chipped, worn pillars held the dome protecting it from whatever weather no longer battered the island. The floor of the hall stepped down into the center, where the gods' symbol rested. Scorch marks marred the copper inlay of their symbol. The pieces of what once had been fine chairs were scattered across the stairs. Only one stood, whole, at the bottom, facing the marred symbol. A man sat, waiting for her. There were others, standing in the shadows, seated on the stairs across from her. She caught herself counting the bloody sparks in her mind. *A dozen, two hundred, it does not matter.* Everything that had brought her there thundered to life in her mind. The months of running, the lives that were lost and changed and the rage that fueled her every step.

"Desmondu!" The ground trembled and plaster rattled from the ceiling at her voice.

The gods turned to stare at her. Desmondu rose. His hair was pale copper and hung in loose curls to his shoulders. A brown robe covered his crimson tunic. His piercing amber eyes narrowed. "You are alone."

Alea smiled. "You've been without us for far too long if you think that matters." She stepped carefully down into the hall, her bare feet hissing on the warm stone. "You know why I'm here. It can't have escaped your notice that the world is unraveling. It's my duty to sew it together. The power that makes your world, your magic, will change."

"It will end."

She laughed, but it was not the sound of mirth. "Nothing ends."

"You will destroy us."

"If you fight me, yes. I just thought you might like a warning."

"You will fall, torn apart, burnt until nothing is left but a mark on the ground. We will fight you until there is nothing left of you to bleed dry." His words rattled like husks on the ground. The other gods rose, converging on his throne. Their eyes were wary, afraid, exhausted.

Alea picked out her brother's oft-invoked god of death, Toar, and his consort, the goddess of the desert mirage Ikate. There were others that she recognized from the temples of her childhood, or from stories. "Very well." She beckoned. The gesture was gentle, almost tender.

Desmondu's laughter faded as copper mist emerged from the floor. It rose slowly, picking up speed as Alea's body filled with blackness. Her irises bled silver until her face shone in the light emanating from orbs brighter than any sun. The mist thickened as she pulled the energy of the gods' realm from the world.

Bolts of bubbling bloody brown exploded against her skin. She ignored the burning. Desmondu shrieked in fury and rushed her. His fist, encased in power, descended on her skull. Something uncurled in the depths of Alea's soulblood, where her heart lay in her physical body. It was gold and scorching in its anger, and familiar as her own power, but it was not her. It raced to the surface, bursting from her skin in an explosion of white fire. She heard nothing through the ringing aftermath in her ears, but the message was unmistakable. *I'll protect you. Do what you must.*

She dragged power from the earth, swallowing it with her own, forcing it into the Crown waiting, clutched with the others in Le'yne. All that was left was their souls. The only thing binding their power to the world were tentative tendrils curled around everything that kept them alive. Tears, held captive in the corners of her eyes, froze. Her fingers sprouted lightning. It writhed, branching myriad times and rooting itself in the chest of each god in turn. Electricity burrowed into their pulsing copper centers and she pulled. Their souls tasted of blood.

Φ

The blast leveled most of the castle. Alea was cocooned in a ball of writhing souls. She was beyond consciousness, beyond enlightenment, beyond death. She was an unborn child, fragile and infinite in its possibilities. Her hands were claws as she ripped the souls apart. Her fingers dripped soulblood as she tore into the barriers between the pieces of the world. She flung the humans' souls into the void, followed by the gods, the Rakos, the Laen. Silver soulblood splattered her face with each violent gesture.

There were three darknesses that grew in the mind. The first was brief and flashing in its anger. But it was small. It was sand in the face of the wind, dust in the face of the rain, noticed only in its absence. The second was slow. It loomed on the edge, muttering and glaring. It was not acknowledged. It could be ignored. Still, it swirled around thoughts, biting them with bitter, savage teeth.

The third was a great law that could not be broken. It was a shadow that fell on a mountain side. It simply waited. It was the night at the edge of the firelight, patient and calm. It was peace. *There are no monsters.*

Only three Crowns hovered in her mind's eye, burning white-gold, stinging bloody-copper and sparking silver-black. She grew or they shrunk, spinning into her palm. She clenched her hand around them absently, as if they were insects. There was stillness. Then the world trembled, shuddering within the fist of Alea's power.

The void around her changed. Images flashed before her, thousands of people, thousands of lives, each imprinted on her mind. Her heartbeat raced, faltered, paused. Her mind was blank consciousness without feeling or judgment. Silence reigned for a second, for an eternity. Waves lapped at Alea's skin, nudging her against a rocky shore.

CHAPTER
TWENTY-TWO

The 14th Day of Glasmord, 1252
The City of Mirik

BREN GROANED AS HE LIFTED the heavy lintel into place
above the doorway. He shrugged deeper into the wool of his
cloak. The air off the ocean was bitterly cold. It took days to
lay the honored dead to rest in Athrolan. He arrived in Mirik
a week before and began work as soon as his boots hit the
cobbles. He pounded a fist against the heavy wood. In a few
weeks it would overlook the entrance to someone's home.
Now it's just a pain in my arse. In the glorious absence of war,
Mirik's new military traded swords for hammers. Bren had
forgotten how much blisters burnt. It was close to evening
now and the lintel was all that was left of his day's work.

He hammered the last of the wooden pegs home, face
knotted in concentration. The tool fell from his hands when
the scream started. It was not a human scream, he realized,
even as he rushed into the street. It was as if the air itself cried
out. Lights flickered across the city below and the

watchtowers blazed into life. The sea was choppy, like a cup of water, shaken. Great waves surged over the new stone breakwater. Thunderheads thickened from horizon to horizon.

The scream faded to a guttering sound, like pebbles bouncing down a slope. The ocean parted in the east, as if an invisible bowl pressed to its surface. The water roiled and black fog burst from the air above the depression. The sound of rending flesh was followed by a concussive wave of air that knocked him to the ground.

He wondered, briefly if this was the end. As abruptly as it began, everything stopped. Bren pulled himself to his feet. A soft breeze eddied about him, tugging as his cloak. Two islands stood where the ocean had been disturbed, within a long-boat's journey from the cliffs. Faint outlines of buildings dotted the new islands. He found that he was shaking. He took off at a run. He finally stopped in the open air of the harbor, peering up at the sky. He almost expected the stars to have changed.

Others had followed him, the entire city spilling into the streets. "Sir, what is it?" Arik paused, panting, beside Bren. "The air."

He lifted his nose. It was as if he had never smelled fresh air before, and now the soft, crisp breeze came from off the sea. "I know." He thrust his fist into the air, letting out a wild shout. Around him, windows were thrown open, sailors climbed into rigging and guards tossed their helms into the air. They shouted with him, screaming joy across the ocean. Bren fell to his knees. "It's over. She did it."

Kemer wove through the crowd, her frown a stark contrast against the exaltation around her. "Sir!" She slid to a halt beside him. Her eyes glittered with tears that matched his, the ones they were trained to never shed. "Sir, my cousin found your sister." She took his hand. "They just pulled her body from the water."

Φ

The 17th Day of Vurgmord, 1252

Bren leaned his brow against the cool, un-hewn stone of the temple. It was the only such building left standing. The past three mornings he found himself within its enveloping darkness. What he felt could not be called grief. He could not pray, for there were no gods, and he could not talk to Alea. She lay in the palace, barely breathing. After a month of watching her lifeless form, he stopped visiting. Now, instead, he sat in a forgotten temple and talked to her. The black stone seemed to listen.

He turned at the rapping on the stone. "Yes?"

"We were told to ask you about work and housing." The man was roughly Bren's age, though his skin and hair were far darker. A woman stood a pace behind him, smiling tiredly as she murmured to the baby in her arms. "I was told Mirik welcomed refugees. Might you know where to find Brentemir Barrackborn?"

"You already have." Bren held out his hand. "I'm Commissioner Barrackborn. Where was your home?"

"Vielrona."

Sorrow settled around Bren again. "Ah. You're Arman's friend. You're welcome here. Find the stone building on the corner. Talk to Commissioner Oland. He'll set you with a proper house." Bren called through the door as the man turned away. "Did you hear of him?"

"I heard he gave himself for his lady. Good day, sir." The dark man's words were tense and pained.

Bren felt suddenly guilty he did not mourn Arman as deeply. He turned back to the altar. His previous offerings of flowers wilted in the cold. Midwinter was only a week away. His eyes pinched closed at the soft cough behind him. This was his only privacy in the day, and it was precious.

"Am I interrupting?"

Bren's eyes widened. The slight woman was silhouetted by the faint morning sun. He rose to his feet, unable to turn away, even blink. His words stammered from him. "I thought—"

"So did I," Alea answered. Her smile was faint, almost shy. She glanced at the temple. "I heard you, you know."

His own smile eased across his features. He caught her up in his arms, lifting her off the ground. Her arms were hard around his neck and her body thin. "I missed you. I love you."

"And I, you. The city looks wonderful." Her voice faltered. "Bren, the islands, were those my doing?"

"Yes." He pulled away. "It was weeks after the battle and I had begun to wonder."

"Weeks?" She shook her head. "I fought the gods for a long time, then."

Bren squeezed her hand. "It was terrifying here, during the joining. I thought the world had ended."

"It did. At least, the world we knew." She seemed to stare at the flowers, but her focus was far distant. "I was in a dark, strange place, beyond time and sense. I remember it like a dreamer remembers the true world during sleep." She glanced up at the words Bren had carved above the altar during his first visit. "Why did you dedicate a temple to me?"

"When you joined the world, after the terror, there was joy. I can't explain the relief and happiness. It's my experience that people need something to believe in. The hole you left by killing the gods needed to be filled. I felt it fitting you be the one to fill it."

Alea pulled a bag from her belt. She handed it to him. "Did you look in this while I was sleeping?"

"No. I don't think anyone did. Most were too scared." The bag was heavier than it should have been. He untied the strings and peered inside. The crown was a hard, dark metal. He recognized the black glass embedded around the edge. "You made this?"

"That's the Crown for this world. Whole. It is not for me, just as this temple is not mine. It is for whomever comes afterward." The expression flitting about the corners of her eyes was both grieving and relieved.

"Afterward. The battles are over Alea. Life can start."

"I can't stay here, Bren." She looked down. "I'm leaving today. I'll go to the mainland, maybe south. I'm not sure, but I need to see this world a bit. I need the earth under my toes and the sun on my hair for a while."

He wanted to yell at her to stay, beg her to stand with him when he made Kemmer his wife. He wanted to weep until she promised to never leave again. Instead, he sighed. "I'll walk you to the harbor." He took her hand and allowed her to lead him into the sunlight.

Φ

The 21st Day of Vurgmord, 1252
The City of Ceir Athrolan

Alea rode higher into the hills. Her horse's hooves scrabbled on the frozen earth. The clearing opened before her, barren and black. The trees were scarred by fire. She dismounted, and as soon as her boots thudded onto the baked earth, she knew this was where Arman discovered his power. She ran her fingers along a tree trunk, scraping ash from the wood. She pitched her tent facing south, overlooking the Felds beyond. She laid her bedroll carefully, every movement collected, as if a sudden motion would shake the tears from her clenched heart.

The fire she lit was small, and she did not bother to set any soup to boil. She crouched beside the flames, exhausted. She would not rest, though. She had rested enough for a lifetime. The clatter of dry leaves across the hard ground seemed almost like foot falls, almost like speech.

She found herself replying. "I wish we'd said more, that night. I wish I could have been there for you. I'm here now." She lay against the ground, frozen dirt scraping her cheek.

The nervous snorting of her horse woke her. She pushed herself up, blinking to clear her vision. It was dark, the fire nothing more than burning coals. The woods were silent. The horse paced around its picket, eyes rolling. A familiar sensation tickled the back of her mind, but she could not place it. She rose to a crouch, stirring the coals into flame. It was then that she saw the eyes.

They were low, like those of a wolf, and burning yellow. She reached for her bow behind her and nocked an arrow without taking her eyes from the predator. She raised it, breathing like Arman taught her all those months ago. She would never be able to say whether it was the color of the eyes or the heat in them as they met hers that gave her pause, but she relaxed her hold, tilting her head as she peered back. The campfire burst to life between them, casting the trees into bright contract with the dark woods.

Gold scales plated wiry shoulders, and a great bony crest parted the yellow hair down the crown of his head. A clawed hand worked in the dirt, clenching over and over. The scales over his heart fluttered with each beat, flashing the silver of a handprint scar. "Sun."

"No." Her knees gave out and she sat back on her bedroll. "Not this. You thought you'd die. You thought you would fall to your death." She reached out a shaking hand. This was worse than death.

"Sun." The word crackled from his chest again and again.

Even if she had pressed her hands to her ears it would not have blocked the sound. His eyes held none of the familiarity that made him Arman. She moved to touch him but he skittered back. "It's Alea." She inched closer, her words low and careful. "And you're Arman. We met in Vielrona, where the moss turned the rooftops green."

He did not move, but let her creep closer.

"You taught me to shoot and fight and drink there. We stood together in Athrolan's throne room and allied ourselves with her queen, your voice and mine." Her hand stopped beside his and she spread her fingers on the cold ground. The longest one brushed his. The scales there dimmed, retreating to the first knuckle. The skin left behind was pale under its tan, but unmistakably his. The darkness faded as dawn approached.

"We rode north together, just you and me and the white sky in winter," she murmured to him. Her fingers slid over his hand, the scales rough and warm against her cool skin. The scales rolled back up to his forearm.

"I'm Alea and you are Arman. I broke the laws of the world to bring you back when you died. It wasn't so you could protect me. I just couldn't imagine saving a world without you in it." Her arms slid up his and over his shoulders until their noses were just inches apart. Her words were barely more than breath. "I am Alea and you are Arman. We danced on the cliff tops at Claimiirn and all of our enemies trembled at the sound."

His skin was sickly-pale and his hair and beard were overgrown. Angry scars peppered his back. His eyes burnt into hers. The eerie glow faded from his body then, and he was suddenly human. He shoved himself away from her. He scrabbled in the dead leaves, vomiting up stone dust and dried blood. He collapsed on the ground and shuddered. "I need sun."

"The sun will be up soon." He shied from her touch when she reached to help him up. She followed his unsteady gait out onto the outcropping overlooking the dark fields. The sky was gray. He pressed himself to the cold stone, face tilted toward the dawn.

Alea sat a few paces away, watching his chest rise with each breath. His color returned with the day. The faint warmth of the winter sun eased over muscles and skin, chasing madness and darkness from his face. It was afternoon when he finally opened his eyes. They blinked once, twice then swiveled to look at her. "Alea."

She jerked her head in a nod. "I'll make us something to eat." She rose with a soft groan. Her muscles were cramped from sitting still for so long. She scraped snow into a pot absently, every thought on the man sunning himself on the rock behind her. The water had been boiling for several minutes, Alea staring unseeing, when Arman finally approached. He crouched by the fire, heedless of his naked body.

Alea's gaze flicked to him. "Your things are there." She pointed at the tattered pack beside hers.

"I think I want to wash. There's a stream down the hill." He gathered the packet of noodles and meat and pressed it into her hand. "Water's boiled."

She took it and set about preparing the soup. When the soup was set she gathered more wood and unrolled the second bedroll. He recognized her, but more than that she did not know. The world that created them was gone and she was not sure where to turn. The tent was broader and the soup bubbling eagerly by the time he returned. He settled himself by the fire, near enough to touch without crowding her. They ate in silence, sniffing in the cold weather and shivering when a breeze was too insistent.

"That's some faith you had to bring my things."

She laughed softly. "You know far more about faith than I." She poked at the coals to avoid looking at him. "The little piece of you that's in me, it protected me. I knew if it was alive so were you."

He frowned at the flames as if they had given him some great insult. "I thought I was going to die."

"Madness is a kind of death." Her gaze inched from the fire to his boots and up his body to his face. His eyes held understanding.

"I'm sorry we didn't talk of little things that night before the battle."

She drew her glove off and slid her hand to rest on her knee where he could see it. "You think this is such a little thing?" He stared at it, expression unreadable. *Soul bared. Completely.* She swallowed hard and barreled on. "When we were running, every night we slept in different places. We changed horses, changed plans. We even changed our names when we had to. Even my own idea of self changed. And you were there. I was broken and lost with no family in a world I did not know, and when I closed my eyes to sleep, you were there." She slid her hand across the leaves, closer, like she had done the night before. "You are my one permanence."

"And you have been mine, Alea. It's not about finding someone who changes your world, or who molds you into a better person. It's about finding someone that fits with the shape in which you built yourself. You fit. Each step of the way, even when it hurt to see you because what you were told me what I was becoming. We've changed, incredibly, but we've only grown together. You fit." He took her hand and a smile bloomed.

Φ

It took Arman several heart-pounding moments to remember where he was when he awoke. Alea's hand was tangled in his and he extracted it carefully before climbing from his bed roll. Their bodies were too exhausted and their minds too raw for anything more intimate than conversation. He tidied the camp and set water on to boil before slipping out into the forest to hunt. He was dressing the second squirrel when he saw the riders. There were less than a dozen and they rode easily up the hill. He marked the Athrolani uniform and wondered if they were searching for Alea.

His boots were silent as he returned, mind whirling. He did not want to go back to Athrolan. He did not want to see Tzatia and hear the story of war retold myriad times. He glanced at Alea while he packed. *Does she want that life?*

"Is that tea?" Alea sat up, rubbing sleep from her face. Her hair was a tangled mess and one lock sported a twisted dead stick.

He handed her a mug, debating how to ask. Giving her a ring was easy when he thought he would die. Asking her to run into the wilderness was something else entirely. "An Athrolani patrol is on its way up. They'll be here in about twenty minutes." He schooled any emotion from his features. He wanted an honest answer.

"We could live in Athrolan or Mirik. Bren wanted me to stay."

"And live like a noble? Is that what you want?"

"Is there another option? We're war heroes."

Arman kept his eyes fixed on the fire. "If you could go anywhere in the world, where would you choose?"

Her silence was agony to his ears. Somewhere, below, a horse's hoof rang off stone.

"There was that clearing in the Hartland where we stayed our second night after leaving Vielrona. I'd go there. I'd live away from people and memories of what I've been and done. I fear that I owe Bren, owe Athrolan to settle with them."

"When those riders crest this hill your choice will be made for you. I'd miss the open air, but if I had to, I'd live the rest of my life without ever seeing the sky again."

Alea stared at her hands. "What would you do?"

"I can build and we both can hunt. A cabin and a garden would take just a year to build. Winter in the Hartland would be mild." He glanced up and their eyes met. Somewhere, deep inside her chest he felt a gate open in the battered wall erected around her heart. With a smile, he stepped inside.

Φ

An'thor shrugged deeper into his cloak and called for a dismount. The day was steely and cold. The clearing was empty, frozen grasses crunching underfoot. He eyed the tracks. The remains of a fire smoked through the hasty coating of frozen earth. There were marks of a tent and the smell of meat and tea. The tracks of Alea's single horse were evident. There were faint scuff marks from her boots and deeper ones from a larger set. He turned slowly, looking at the marks of two people crouching by a fire. His frown deepened.

"Should we go after them, sir? Her Majesty wanted her back in the city."

An'thor went to stand beside Metters on the outcropping. A horse was just visible on the road, bearing two riders south. He watched them a moment. Finally, he heaved a sigh and pulled himself into the saddle. "There's hot food and good stories back home. Let them have their peace."

END OF REFORGED

ACKNOWLEDGEMENTS

Thank you to Angie Frazier, who first suggested splitting the first half of Reforged into two books. If I hadn't I would never have explored the world more fully and found the path to which this story was leading. Your continued support and guidance – as well as your success – was a wonderful inspiration.

Thank you, also, to Ben Donahue, whose incredible talent lent this series its beautiful covers. Your vision and colaboration has helped bring my characters to life.

Thank you to Dr. Greggory Knouff for teaching the fantastic course "Modern U.S. Military History." Your enthusiasm and wealth of political and military knowledge was invaluable

Thank you, also, to the wonderful people who put together National Novel Writing Month and the programers who developed Scrivener and Krita.

As always, thank you to my irreplaceable friends, co-workers, and family.

SNEAK PEEK AT THE NEXT
INSTALLMENT OF BLOOD OF TITANS

BLOOD OF TITANS:
RESTORED I

MADNESS
AND
GODS

from internationally bestselling author
V. S. HOLMES

CHAPTER ONE

The 27th Day of the Month of Rainfall, 1272
The Forest of the Hartland

Arman stood in the doorway. The bed was made as usual and the desk tidy. The clothes chest was shut and a pair of breeches hung on a hook. *It's all wrong.* The same way his gut had known what Alea was, he knew his son's room was more than empty. *Deserted.*

They had kept the truth of their identities, their bloodlines, from him. They hoped he would be live the life they never could. One of peace. Of anonymity. *Perhaps it was a mistake.* Arman was surprised at his reaction to his son's leaving. He would have thought Alea would panic and he would comfort her. Keplan may not have told them what happened, but Arman would see it was something horrifying.

He stepped into the room hesitantly, as if unwilling to have the last person to cross the threshold be someone other than his son. It was only upon entering that he saw the folded parchment on the pillow. He touched the ragged edge before tucking it into his pocket. He retreated to the main room and set water to boil. Soft footfalls sounded behind him as he took the kettle from the fire and poured two mugs of tea.

"Has he come back?" The circles under Alea's eyes spoke to how well she had slept.

He jerked his chin at the tea cup waiting on the table before her. "I don't think he will for a long time."

"How can you think that?" Her voice rasped from tears and fatigue.

Arman heaved a sigh and sat. "Alea, when I left home I packed my bag, made my bed, swept my floors. Trust me when I say I know what running looks like." Saying it broke his fear, replacing it with a strange mixture of confusion and understanding. "I found a note."

Neither spoke or looked at the letter until the tea leaves had slowed their spinning around the bottoms of the two mugs. Arman opened it carefully, smoothing the tidy crease down the center before drawing a breath.

> "'Ma, Da,
>
> 'I cannot imagine what my leaving might do to you, but I hope you understand. Something happened to me. Not an injury or illness, but something deeper than that. I saw things that no one knows, that I shouldn't know, that I've never seen. I do not know why or how, but I know I cannot stay here. Perhaps I am mad, in which case I am saving you from seeing me succumb.
>
> 'I will be more scared if I am sane.
>
> 'I hope you do not mind that I took one of Da's drawings, the one of Ma holding me from years ago. I hope you understand I need answers, ones I cannot find here. I love you both.'"

"Mad? How can he think that?"

"Alea, we denied him the truth. You did to him exactly what your mother did to you."

"I was trying to protect my child!"

"So was she!" Arman's hand shook again, but now it was not panic.

Alea pointed at the backside of the paper. "He wrote more."

Arman turned the letter over. 'Da, I found the letter from the man called An'thor. I cannot fathom why he would need to see me, but I know why you kept it secret. I know you and Ma hid things, things greater than just a letter. I do not understand, but I forgive you.'"

"Letter? What letter?" Alea shifted nervously, refusing to look Arman in the eye.

He was tired of secrets, tired of protecting. *Look where it brought us.* "Tzatia is ill. Dying, probably. She's named whatever child you have. You promised Athrolan's crown would be safe, and I guess she interpreted it differently. An'thor did not say it in so many words, but the meaning was obvious. Keplan may not know what we were, but he damned well knows they want him in the capital." Arman rose, dropping the letter to the table, driving home their son's leaving.

Alea trembled, eyes frantic. "Arman, what have we done?"

Her words paused him as he tugged on his cloak. "I protected you both. You blinded him." The words he threw over his shoulder were more biting that the draft that blew past him. "You better thank fates he forgives you." He slammed out the door. "I'm not sure I could."

Look for the rest of Reforged from Amphibian Press, wherever fine books are sold

READ MORE OF THE REFORGED WORLD IN "THE TEMPEST" IN THIS DARK FANTASY ANTHOLOGY:

The taste of the ocean was the same salt as Nubon's blood. The waves beat in the pulse at her wrist, her throat, her thighs. Battered wood bit into her clenched hand. *Thirteen years and three days. I've heard the sounds of this sea for thirteen years and three days.* She absently wondered if the sounds of the womb she heard before were the same, an echo of this, much larger, water.

"It's almost dawn."

Nubon glanced at the man beside her. His sprawled stance lacked its usual playfulness. "Are you excited, *urhun?*" She had uttered the Berrin title for teacher a thousand times more than that for "father," and it held the same tenderness.

"No. Not today." His voice was as wave-beaten as the city bobbing at the horizon.

She heard Berinnal's streets from here, smelled the tar and kelp that kept the city afloat. The ships bearing the seven other potentials for the throne were visible, dark blots appearing occasionally through the morning fog. Nubon mentally ticked off her list. *Tua from the east. Buen from the south-east. Lebon from the south....* She continued, the words familiar in her mind, a touchstone she worried when her mind stormed. The snap of the junk's rigging dragged her eyes to the mast. The plain, dusky-orchid flag rose, the color of a warning sky. *And Nubon, from the north-east.*

A skiff slapped into the water. She followed Urhun down the ladder. This would be the last time they took to the sea together, at least, with her as his pupil. He pushed off from the ship, allowing her to simply be the passenger for the first time since they departed Berinnal a year ago.

"I think I'll miss this." She watched the knots of wrinkles in his beige face soften.

"I know I will." He paused in his rowing and looked at her as if her features were a map he needed to memorize. "Nubon Northeast. Remember everything."

"You taught me all I needed, I'm sure. I'll remember, I promise."

"You'll have to." Something darker shadowed the sadness in his voice. They could not speak about the week to come, the trials that would decide which of the eight scions could bear the weight of the Warlord's title.

Nubon forced herself to sit straight. Her tarred wooden armor was suddenly cloying. They were close enough to hear the smack of the others' oars. Close enough to see their faces were as apprehensive as hers. By the end of the day they would be enemies. Nubon looked to the city, glimmering like the inside of a shell in the sunrise. She wondered, for the first time in thirteen years and three days, what happened to the scions who failed.

Read the rest of Nubon's story in *Out of the Darkness* or at vsholmes.com/tempest

ABOUT THE AUTHOR

V. S. Holmes is an international bestselling author. They created the BLOOD OF TITANS series and the NEL BENTLY BOOKS. *Smoke and Rain*, the award-winning first book in their fantasy quartet, became an international bestseller in 2018. *Travelers* is also included in the Peregrine Moon Lander mission as part of the Writers on the Moon Time Capsule. In addition, they write game content for Stone Blade Entertainment.

As a disabled and non-binary human, they work as an advocate and educator for representation in SFF worlds. When not writing, they work as a contract archaeologist throughout the northeastern U.S. They live with their spouse, a fellow archaeologist, their dog Rory, and own too many books.

www.vsholmes.com